ASSEMBLING THE WINGPEOPLE

Nicky Bond

Take-Away-Tea Books

Nicky Bond/Take-Away-Tea Books
https://nickybondramblings.blogspot.com

Book Layout © 2016 BookDesignTemplates.com
Cover Design/Portal – Design and Illustration

Assembling the Wingpeople/ Nicky Bond. -- 1st ed.
ISBN 978-0-9956574-3-4

For Delilah and Sullivan

CONTENTS

Day one of the reunion

Later, the paramedics would comment on the timing. Responding to a medical emergency was challenge enough. Additional obstacles were not necessary. This evening they had battled traffic, double-parking, and the curiosity of strangers. In the small town in which they operated, the presence of all three was unusual. Each of them had noticed it. Once they were finished and waiting for their next call, that was. At the time of the actual emergency, they had simply got on with the job.

Half an hour earlier, the scene had been calm. The summer sun had begun to dip as children paddled in the tide. Parents supervised from a seated distance whilst older couples strolled by, smug that they'd reached an age where they bore no responsibility for the youngsters in the water. The gung-ho spirit of the British holidaymaker, battling the cruel elements time and time again, was finally being rewarded. There were no waterproof jackets or umbrellas to be seen. No one sat behind rain-splattered windows searching for a hint of blue amidst a grey sky. Cardigans and coats packed just in case, remained in suitcases stowed in Airbnbs along the seafront. A carefree air had settled. Over the sounds of splashing water and gleeful shrieks of paddlers, snippets of conversations could be heard.

'*Another ten minutes? Sure, why not kids. We're on our holidays! One more pint? Might as well make the most of the view. Shall we watch the sun go down?'*

Light-hearted conversations floated freely on the breeze. The mood was decidedly relaxed.

The bandstand by the sea stood proudly amid the early evening tableau. Not the open-sided wrought iron version akin to a horseless carousel. Instead, this was an enclosed space; a small performance area used by choirs, poets, and the occasional rock band. It was said that Led Zeppelin had played there in the eighties, although the details were sketchy to anyone who purported to have been there. Its seafront location meant it had borne decades of crashing waves and was no stranger to a damaging flood. A few refurbishments and upgrades later, it was a landmark known to all. It looked outwards to sea and inwards to town, as bars, restaurants, and hotels gazed back.

With no obvious warning, the bandstand - that had been closed of door and proofed of sound - opened. An interval. A slightly sweaty, middle-aged audience spilled from their musical evening of culture, and milled around on the surrounding pavement. Overdressed for the promenade, they made small talk, sipping room-temperature wine from plastic glasses. From a side door, the performing musicians emerged for their own breather. For them it was a quick vape or swig of water that gave them the energy for round two. A slowly-forming crowd was now blocking this section of the prom. Not that it should matter. Not on an evening as tranquil as this.

'Thank you, folks. If you could move to one side it would be a big help, thank you. That's it, Madam, thanks

for moving. Let us through please. Thank you, Sir. That's it. Quick as you can. That's the way.'

The interval was nearly over. The quartet's cellist had kicked off her sandals and was enjoying the sand between her toes. Her viola-playing colleague had ambled towards the water, being careful to jump back before the wave soaked his shoes. Some members of the audience - the ones happy to stretch and bend - clambered over the low wall separating the beach from the pavement and used it as a makeshift seat. A few minutes of Vitamin D were not a bad thing. Not after being cooped up for the past hour.

'Stand back everybody. Sir, please. Put your phone away. Stand back. Make space. Can you hear me? Can you hear me? I'm Elin. What's your name? We're going to help you. Don't worry about a thing. Can you tell me your name?'

As the musicians enjoyed the sensory thrills of the beach, they were oblivious to much around them. And as crowded as the promenade was, those identifying as *holidaymaker* tended to let the rest of the world pass by unnoticed. Their immediate focus was taken with their glass of wine, box of chips, or their small child enjoying the water. Spotting a situation unfold around them, even when someone might be in distress, was unlikely to happen. It would take flashing lights or an alarm to force people to notice something beyond the end of their nose.

The five-minute bell rang. The quartet gathered their bags and water bottles, and moved back towards the bandstand. In the distance a siren could be heard.

'Can you tell me if you're on any medication? Can you hear me? What's your name? We're going to help you. Have you taken anything we need to know about?'

Ten minutes later and the situation had escalated. The incident was no longer unnoticed. Along with the concert-goers, holidaymakers from the beach bars had joined the crowd. One particularly nosy man had sent his son to weave through the huddle to see if he could get closer. He received loud tuts from those nearby who were nevertheless interested in any information the boy might glean. Meanwhile the ambulance was hampered in its access to the beach. It had parked as near as it could, on the opposite side of the road. One of the paramedics was doing her best to beat a path through the bystanders, as a worried woman rushed alongside her, showing her where to go. The faces of the onlookers wore the correct expressions. Concern, support, a willingness to be as helpful as possible. It was always the way. It didn't stop their morbid curiosity, though. The glare of the low sun bouncing off a multitude of smart phones was especially galling.

'We're going to move you now. We're rolling you onto the stretcher, don't worry, we're going to help you. Can you hear me? One, two, three... there we are. We'll be at the hospital in no time. Are you together? Are you family? Can you tell me what happened?'

Inside the bandstand, most of the audience had not

returned. The seated musicians awaited the start of the second half, wondering what was holding them up. This particular evening was filled with popular concert pieces that a certain generation enjoyed. TV themes, film scores, and the odd bit of real classical music; the kind that would be recognised from adverts. The first piece of the second half was Camille Saint-Saëns' *Dance Macabre*. The *Jonathan Creek* theme tune seemed an odd choice for a summer evening's concert. From the vantage point of the waiting musicians, there was nothing macabre about the evening. Nothing at all.

PART ONE

CHAPTER ONE

Six months before the reunion

That was one bold seagull. Perched on the window ledge sporadically tapping the glass with its bill. Its pitch was the exact tone to cause maximum irritation. Did it want food? Attention? The freedom to annoy at will? Tilda wasn't sure, nor keen enough on giant flying creatures with no sense of boundaries, to find out. What would summer be like? Nothing like a Hitchcock film, she hoped. Or that Christmas movie. The one with the bird woman, from *Casualty*? *No thanks not for me*. Wildlife was fine as long as it kept its distance. It was about mutual respect. Her mind wandered to the *Dirty Dancing* line about having demarcated dance spaces. She couldn't remember it off the top of her head. She knew the word *demarcated* wasn't used but it was something like that. A bit sexier probably. She hoped she hadn't unknowingly moved into a habitat where all living things danced together in a shared space.

Tilda waited for the kettle to boil. The tapping continued. She tried to distract herself with something funny, something upbeat, but nothing came to mind. That was the problem with emerging from a mid-life crisis. There was so much mental effort involved, all frivolous thought was stopped dead in its tracks. It had definitely been a mid-life crisis. That much was clear. She could own it, marvelling at the unprecedented courage she had found, just when it mattered most. Her sudden departure from the dull life she had been living, caused carnage. Short term carnage, at least. There had been a few chaotic months at the start. Months that were now a blur. Half-remembered phone calls would occasionally resurface. Angry paragraphs from the past would leave her trash bin and re-enter her head. It was hard to embark on a big life change when there was emotional fallout to handle. And then there were the tearful conversations. Conversations, it seemed, that were not fully covered in the note she had left on the fireplace. A recent text uploaded to her consciousness, just in case she had been in danger of forgetting.

FFS. There's water pissing from the kitchen ceiling. Who was the plumber you called that time? I've been in work all day and I can't be doing with this now. Was it Dave? Doug? Get back to me. ASAP.

The kettle continued to boil, the seagull continued to tap. It was not her fault he had a leak and it was not her fault he'd paid no attention to their preferred tradespeople over the years. None of it was her fault. It just felt like it was.

The clock on the wall said it was gone five. Her old house would be empty for another half hour at least. She mentally scanned the scene. The mantlepiece, the corner where the TV hid the stain, her armchair. Did anyone sit in her chair these days? Did Mike mix things up and sit somewhere different each evening? Did he have friends over? What did Mike, alone, even look like?

The guilt was rising to unacceptable levels so Tilda

stopped. No good could come of it. She had learnt that over time. She opened the cutlery drawer and counted the spoons. Then the knives. Then the forks. She picked up the tea towel and wiped the teaspoons in the drainer. When the kettle boiled, she poured the water, and watched the teabag bob to the top of the mug. By then she felt better. She could handle her feelings again.

It had been a difficult time for everyone. Once the dust settled, and her soon-to-be ex-husband's calls calmed down, a new rhythm emerged. Tilda did just what she had planned all those years before. Before she made the choice to play it safe. After leaving the note, she got into her campervan and drove to the nearest bit of coast. Then she began to travel.

Tilda's new rhythm sounded different from the one before. It rose and it fell. It contained the intensity of pizzicato alongside the indulgence of lingering notes. She listened for a while, letting it carry her without participation. Then, when she felt able, she quietly hummed the bars she recognised. If she caught herself, she'd stop, surprised at her ability to adapt. It was an inevitable process. As time passed, she adapted again. By the end of her adventure, she sung loudly every day. Belting out the guttural sounds that came from her core as she embraced the freedom of accepting her new situation.

Looking back, from the safety of the present, she was convinced she had made the right decision. It was easy to say now it was over. There had been some moments, when she had felt truly overwhelmed by the irresponsibility of it all. But looking back, she was proud of herself. To leave a loveless marriage was one thing. To leave and simultaneously embark on the gap year she'd never had, was downright hilarious. Tilda accepted the ludicrous nature of the past couple of years. Travelling around the coast, spending a chunk of the money from her dad's house sale, being off-grid for weeks at a time. There had been moments when she thought she were going mad. It's possible she did once or twice. The long winter of the first year provided a truly hands on understanding of cabin fever. And when she became mildly and undramatically run down with a summer cold, it hammered home how isolated she had allowed herself to become. The fear of dying alone was strong, coupled with the fact that no one knew exactly where she was. She had envisaged her rotting corpse being eaten by stray dogs on more than one occasion. After that, she made a better effort at keeping in touch with friends. Her only friend. One-time colleague, now-time pal. She messaged every couple of weeks. It meant there was someone to point the police towards the vague geographic direction if all contact stopped. *Yep*, Tilda mused. *There had been some dark times.*

Not that it mattered now. When she thought back to how stifled and clenched her previous life had been, she thanked the universe with all her being, that she'd found the strength to break away and start again. And now here she was. Starting again. Again. Her campervan adventure had come to an end. A second winter had shown Tilda that she wanted more from life than to sleep in a hat and gloves for months. There were only so many times you could travel the perimeter of the country. She had done it once in full, and then cherry-picked her favourite parts. Now she'd picked the ultimate cherry and stopped. It had never occurred to her that Wales would be her location of choice, but it turned out it was. She had spent long enough doing her research, after all.

She was now into the second month of a six-month lease. Renting. At her age. It went against everything her old financial acumen advised. But these days, her gut instinct was all over the place. Her gut instinct, had it allowed itself to be pinned down, would have said, 'Do what you like. Rent, buy, squat - I don't care. Life's too short to worry.' A one-bedroom rented apartment on the Aberystwyth seafront was evidence Tilda was doing what she liked. For now. She'd had long-term plans before. It was time to try something else.

The tea had brewed so she fished out the bag. She hadn't discarded all aspects of her personality, just the parts holding her back. And life-long habits were hard to shift. Her post-work cup of tea was engrained. Of course, *work* was a tenuous term these days. The phrase implied paid employment. She had none. The local temp agencies had assured her they'd be in touch if they had something. Her savings were dwindling, especially after paying six-months rent up front – the price to pay for no backlog of pay slips - but she wasn't worried. Old Tilda would be having kittens. New Tilda was taking it in her stride. More or less.

She sat in the armchair by the window and sipped her tea. The tiny flat was not so tiny compared with the campervan. Rubbing shampoo into her hair without her elbows banging the shower walls, was the height of luxury. And then there was the sea view. She didn't need more than that. She had walked away from a house filled with possessions and she didn't miss any of them. The few items she had packed, fitted into one box and were memories of the past. The khaki coat now hanging in her wardrobe. The old photo of a young man, displayed in the frame on the mantlepiece. The leather notebook that same man had given her for her 21st birthday. It sat next to her bed. Every night she meticulously recorded the aspects of the day she wanted to remember. These scant belongings were clues to a previous life, but there was nothing to indicate a present. Nothing to show Tilda was living in the now. Her travelling transition period was over. It was time to plant roots. It was time to become.

Tilda finished her tea. She knew all this, of course, but hesitated at doing anything. One day she'd pluck up the courage to say hello to someone on the prom. She'd find a friend, she'd make a plan, she'd do something with her day other than walk, read, and think. One day, she was sure, a new life would fall into place. For now, she was still mustering courage.

She knew the problem. In the great upheaval of her recent life, her imagination had taken a battering. She struggled to picture a happy future. It was beyond her. Right now, her energy was spent living moment to moment. A satisfying cup of tea here, and an enjoyable morning walk there. All the fantasies about her wider existence were frozen inside. One day she would work out how to thaw them. One day she'd feel comfortable with herself. That hadn't happened yet. She was still counting cutlery whenever she dwelt on the pain she had caused.

As she thought about courage, her mind went back

to her friend. The woman from the office with whom she had never broken contact and who would never compromise her own happiness for a second. Tilda picked up her phone and typed.

It's been too long. Can we timetable a massive natter at some point? Hope you're as splendid as always.
Tilda x.

She hoped she hadn't come across as desperate. She didn't think she was. Not yet.

Later, sitting in bed, Tilda would open her journal. Listing the day's events for which she was grateful had become an exercise in creative thinking. She considered what she might find to note down later.

1. *No rain.*
2. *No calls/messages from Mike.*
3. *Library books returned on time.*

When written in black and white, the highlights of her day were bleak. The absence of bad, rather than the presence of good. They could hardly be described as personal achievements or moments of joy. Tilda sighed. She rinsed her mug, dried it, and then returned it to the shelf by the sink. No good could come from dwelling on the negative. She would thaw at some point. For now, she had a new library book to start. There was no hurry with planting roots just yet. Not when she could procrastinate a little longer.

CHAPTER TWO

Friday afternoon should be bottled, thought Bea. *It should be bottled and prescribed on the NHS.* She buzzed herself out through Reception and let the door slam behind her. *No matter how utterly shagged a person feels midweek*, she continued to muse, *they can't help but be perked up to frig by the sniff of the weekend.* She strode across the car park and beeped open her car. *Friday afternoon is nature's antidepressant. It's a weekly dose of Prozac from the universe. It's...*

Bea's quasi-pharmaceutical train of thought could have carried on for some time, but she had made it to her car. Seconds later she executed a perfect reversing arc, and was ready to forget local council bureaucracy for as long as she could. The afternoon was chilly but she opened her window to feel the wind in her back-combed hair. The experience lasted less than a minute before she got cold and pressed it shut. She wasn't a masochist. Not since that one time with that one guy. She settled for cranking up the radio instead.

'*So, Debs, it's almost time to kick in the doors of the weekend and sound the klaxon. Anything you want to tell the listeners before we do?*'

'*Have a great weekend, everyone. How's that?*'

'*I was hoping for more enthusiasm Debbie. How about a WOOOHOOOO?*'

'*Wooohooo, Dave. Shall I do the travel now?*'

'*One more thing. Did you know the boss told me I'd been late five times this week? He said, 'You know what that means?' And I said, 'It means it must be Friday!' Ha ha ha ha. What do you say, Debs? D'ya like that one?*'

'*Sure Dave. Very funny. Now I've reports coming in from the M60 to say there's been a breakdown near Cheadle...*'

Drive Time Dave, the irrepressible veteran of local radio, was happy. Debbie With The Travel, less so. But Bea didn't care. Work and all its craziness could be forgotten for forty-eight hours. With the end of the financial year on the horizon, it meant, in laywoman's terms, that deadlines were looming and shit was getting real. It amused Bea to frame her working day as if she were a Mancunian Gal Gadot, having to Wonder-Woman her way out of every situation. At her age she should really reference Linda Carter, but Bea had felt deeply encouraged by the feminist leanings of the more recent superhero incarnation. She had jumped right on board with the kids. Gal was her gal! She channelled her regularly as she replied to frantic email chains, schmoozed council officials, and jollied along the entire office so that they were at their most productive as well as their most amenable. Bea metaphorically crossed her wrists and fought off every challenge. Now it was Friday and she'd saved the day for another week. It was time to enjoy herself.

As if reading her mind and emphasising the point with a sledgehammer, Drive Time Dave played The Cure's *Friday I'm in Love*. The intro of which caused Bea to scream aloud before belting out lyric after lyric. The years spent memorising song words from her fortnightly *Smash Hits*, had never once proven to be a waste of time.

Bea drove through the communal gates and parked up. Almost six months on and she was still getting used to this luxury. Her promotion last year not only provided a boost to her finances but had forced her to consider her newfound management status. Could she still queue for the 368 with the high school students and pensioners now she was responsible for an office staff of twelve? Of course she could. But the thought of being reckless was appealing. There were also the aches in her knees when she stood at the bus stop for too long. There wasn't much internal debate beyond that.

She treated herself to her first vehicle since a childhood pushbike. It was a car that patronising types might call *a runaround*, but she wasn't bothered. Unremarkably black in colour, she'd stamped her mark on the inside as soon as she'd been handed the keys. A yellow throw covered the back seat, and two zebra print cushions were artfully arranged on top. On the left-hand side of the dashboard was a plastic bunch of orange gerberas - the excessive Blu Tac that secured them, was strategically stuck below the line of sight of anyone peering in from outside.

Despite its fabulous interior, the car didn't get out much. Apart from work and Asda, it stayed in its space outside the flat. That didn't matter. Bea had wheels. Bea was a car-owner. Bea was growing up. Her friends had taken the piss, of course. Her first car at fifty-two. Had she finally accepted she was an adult? Was she settling down and admitting middle-age at last? She had taken their jokes in good humour, long after they had stopped being funny. She would feel perpetually youthful as long as her friends hung *Mum's Taxi* signs from their own vehicles. Bea could take their teasing and brush it off. She loved her car. The three decades of being a free-spirited public transport user had been happily forgotten as soon as she experienced her first bad weather commute. Any residual longings for the open-air of the bus stop washed away with the driving rain that pelted the windows. She couldn't believe she'd stuck it out so long.

Her phone pinged as she turned off the engine. A message from Mal. Bea struggled for a moment. Mal? Mal?...Mal! She'd been so used to her latest online-flirt's pseudonym of usedbutgoodcondition54 she had momentarily forgotten his real identity. An identity he had revealed in their last conversation, when they agreed to take it off the flirt 'n' wank app, and move to the next level. Mal was the guy she had agreed to meet later. She really needed to get his name right.

She opened his message.

Hey you. Just wanted to check you were still on for later. It'll be great to meet you in the flesh. Our recent chats have been a lot of fun. Looking forward to it. M.

Bea smiled. He wasn't wrong. Their recent chats had been fun. The suggestion of a beer, to see if their app-based chemistry would survive out of captivity, had been his. Bea hadn't felt the need for anything more than the masturbatory support his messages could provide. But then again, it was Friday night. She'd had no plans up to yesterday, and it was a shame to waste freshly-shaved legs. So, as she'd eloquently articulated to herself at the time, why the frig not? His photos were neither showy nor insecure. He was a couple of years older but seemed to be wearing well. His choice of casual jeans and rugged jumper made him appear he could handle himself, were he to be snowed-in during a bleak Canadian winter. All good signs. She had no idea where she'd got the Canadian winter imagery from, especially as he was seventeen kilometres away from her, whenever they chatted. Salford Quays was no Canadian wilderness. It was, Bea decided, much better than that. It was a place that someone she might feel like sleeping with, happened to be. Far handier than North America. Far easier to get a taxi late on.

Bea typed a message. Her finger darted from letter to letter, as fast as it was inaccurate. She slowed down, corrected the typos, and read back.

Mal! Lovely to hear from you. Yes, still on for 8. Will see you very soon. Bea.

It wouldn't do to be too keen. Signing off with a X or any form of affectionate emoji was out. And despite their online fun and games, a row of aubergines felt a little presumptuous. That didn't mean she wasn't open to whatever the evening might bring. If Mal turned out to be as arousing in real life as his typed messages could be, then Bea would happily go with the flow.

With that admin done, she got out of the car and grabbed her bag from the passenger side, strategically ignoring the empty crisp packets from the foot well. They would keep. As she walked towards the building she was spotted by an elderly woman on all fours, perched on a first-floor balcony.

'Happy Friday, dear. Are you coming round for a glass of wine later?'

Bea looked up.

'Kit, darling, what are you doing? Open air yoga? Is that a good idea with your osteoporosis?'

'Jamie got me kneepads for my birthday. The fool thinks I still have my garden. I'm breaking them in while I have another bash at the thyme. Anyway, leave my bones out of it. I've eaten two yoghurts today. Wine?'

'Sorry Kit, I can't. I'm meeting someone. How about tomorrow?'

'Is this a new man or one of your arrangements?'

Bea knew Kit enjoyed living vicariously through the comings and goings of her social life. She proffered mock disapproval occasionally but never stopped her from sharing the details at a later date.

'It's a potential new one. It might just be a drink, or it might be mad passionate love-making. Who's to say at this stage? Can I drop off the basics before I go out?'

'Of course, dear. I'll add them to the pile.'

Bea wasn't stupid. She hadn't remained STI-free and physically unharmed as a sexually active woman in her fifties, without taking precautions. One of those precautions involved giving Kit a print out of all the information she had about the hook-up in question. This was usually his name, age, photo, and the location of the meeting. Sometimes, and purely for Kit's amusement, she would add a screenshot of a snippet of conversation. Only if it was entertaining, nothing too personal. Kit didn't get out as much as she once did, so Bea liked to liven things up for her when she could. Besides, she needed to keep her on board. Between the holding of a potential criminal's details, and the, '*Are You OK?*' message she would dutifully send a couple of hours into the evening, Kit was essential. Bea owed her big time. She shouted up to her neighbour with a suggestion.

'How's tomorrow night for that wine, instead. Shall I pencil you in? You can always cancel if you pull the window cleaner, or the Asda delivery guy seduces you amongst the groceries. I won't be offended.'

Kit laughed and waved a dismissive hand towards Bea. She took a moment to get to her feet before confirming that a glass of wine the following evening would be marvellous. Bea waved back, and fobbed herself into the building.

A couple of hours later and she was ready to head out again. A shower, better underwear, and - as a last-minute thought with one foot out of the door - a change of sheets, she was good to go. If usedbutgood-condition54 was as self-deprecating, funny, and interested in Bea as he seemed online, then there was every chance clean sheets were a good idea. Bea booked a cab and grinned to herself. It never got old, this feeling. The tingle of nerves and excitement, the thrill of what might happen if the chemistry was real. This was the best feeling in the world. Who needed commitment and companionship if they were at the expense of actual goosebumps?

Bea and her goosebumps got into the cab. When the driver asked, 'Where to?' she managed to control her impulse of replying, 'Possibility and adventure, if you don't mind.'

It was what she was thinking, though.

CHAPTER THREE

The York traffic was terrible and Stewart was irritated. There were no lane closures, no accidents, and no sign of any road works. It was just unfathomably busier. He watched the meter tick over from the backseat and tried to suppress his annoyance. It wasn't the money he objected to. Nor was it the waste of his time, which he was more than happy to fritter away. The irritation was because something wasn't going his way. That was the source of his frustration. The universe was against him and he couldn't do anything about it. This was not a feeling he was used to, nor one he liked. To top it off, the taxi driver was a chatterer. The worst kind of taxi driver, in Stewart's opinion. The worst kind of person, full stop.

'Doing anything nice?'

'What?'

'Doing anything nice today?'

'Work.'

'Ah. The late shift. Will it be an early hours job?'

'I'm sorry?'

'Your work. A late one? Coming home when the rest of us are snoring?'

'Hardly. I aim to be no longer than a couple of hours.'

The driver had no immediate response for this. Clearly Stewart was an enigma. His casual clothes, straggly beard, and odd arrival time had fallen into a specific mental category. He was giving off the visual cues of a casual shift worker, but his responses, along with his general disdain for others, were confusing.

Stewart would have been relieved to see the driver give up his attempts at small talk, had he been paying attention. He didn't notice details anymore. He was no longer a details kind of guy. The fact he once was, felt as alien to him as his previous workaholic regime now seemed. In the last couple of years, everything had changed. Definitely for the better. He was sure of that. Life was great now.

It had been several weeks since he had last been to work. This was a longer gap than he'd intended but it was how things had worked out. He had stayed in the villa a week longer than he'd originally told them. Then when he got back, he'd become immersed in the Six Nations tournament. Live sport, cold beers, and no one nagging him to be anywhere he didn't want to be. There wasn't a person in the office who would care one way or the other. He had no need to apologise. Every single one of them would have been glad of the break from him. It was all going to be fine.

He continued to ply himself with platitudes as he tapped in the security code next to the *Grady and Son Solicitors* sign and made his way up the stairs. It didn't stop the butterflies. Like the heavy traffic, the nerves were also unexpected and unexplained. Except that wasn't true. They arrived whenever he approached the building. Every single time.

The hum of productivity hit him as he walked through the doors. The staff were occupied. On phones, at desks, typing into keyboards. He assumed they managed *not* to sink into party mode whenever he was away, but it was still good to see no one taking the piss. Everything was as it should be. That's when

Rosie walked out of the office. He gulped. She was holding an open file, as she walked towards the copier. It wasn't too late for him to leave. No one who actually mattered had seen him so far. He froze for a second. His legs didn't want to make the decision for him. And then it was too late. She looked up, did a double take, then shot metaphorical laser beams at him.

'Do my eyes deceive me? Am I having a vision? Alert the Pope, I'm witnessing a miracle.'

There was no hint of friendly sarcasm. Rosie's tone was distinctly dry.

'Morning Rosie. I thought I'd check in and see where we're up to. Sorry I'm late, the traffic was a nightmare.'

'I imagine that's because it's slap bang in the middle of school pick-up time.' She moved closer to him, to be discreet against the backdrop of colleagues and so her angry seethe would be less detectable. 'Morning, my arse, Stewart. It's half past three on a Friday afternoon. This place will be deserted in a couple of hours. Do you really think you're going to be of any use now?'

Stewart blinked a couple of times. He knew it wasn't the crack of dawn but he'd had no clue it was Friday. Where had the week gone?

'I should have let you know what was happening. I didn't realise...'

Rosie motioned for Stewart to come into her office, as if she were a Headteacher having a reproachful word with a wayward student. In the open plan area in which they stood, people had started to notice something might be going on. She had no problem sharing what little she thought of him, but Stewart knew Rosie valued loyalty over having a visible row in front of others. She wasn't going to bollock him in public. Small mercies.

He followed behind. His automatic swagger wasn't going to help matters. He tried to tame it as he walked. It was complicated because the swagger was only there to mask how much he didn't want to deal with Rosie's tongue lashing. He ended up with a mix between a hobble and a leg drag. His best attempt at maintaining dignity and appearing calm.

Stewart resented the school boy and Headteacher comparison even if it were an accurate representation of their current power dynamic. Not least because this was *his* school. He was the Head. Rosie wasn't even the Deputy. Yet here they were, with a truly confused management structure, and with the metaphorical Headteacher about to be disciplined by someone several ranks below them. What would that be? A supply teacher? A parent helper? A Governor? Stewart's train of thought had come to a natural end once he realised he had no idea of the details. But the musing distracted him from Rosie for thirty seconds more. She closed the door behind him.

'Stewart, I think we should talk.'

'Ah, the old *I think we should talk* routine. Are you dumping me Rosie? Is this it?' Stewart's attempt at humour did not land. Yet despite the clear absence of romantic inclination from either side, the image of an old married couple held together by rows and grievances, was hard to shake.

'Do I *need* to dump you Stewart? You aren't here enough for that to make a difference. What I want is some idea of your plans. Buggering off for weeks on end without telling me is NOT on. I have to deal with the clients that get left in the lurch. It looks bad. It looks unprofessional. It makes ME look bad, and I am *not* bad. I'm holding this together by the skin of my teeth. What I need to know is am I wasting my time? Does it even matter to you anymore?'

Stewart shifted on the spot. She had a point but he didn't have the answers to her questions. He didn't know anything. His mind had been a fog for so long. Since the moment everything changed, two years ago. That was the first time Rosie had had a massive go at him. She thought she'd overstepped the mark. What neither of them had known back then, was that this would be a regular occurrence. He reminded her now.

'You told me to make changes. You told me to take time off and have a break. That's what I've been doing. You must see things are better here than they were. My father's gone and I've stopped barking orders and being a carbon copy of him. You've got to admit I'm better than I was. This *firm* is better than it was. We must be able to agree on that?'

Against his will, memories surfaced. Conversations in the same office, decades before. His father, always in a suit and tie, resting both hands on the desk as he leaned over and bellowed.

'If you think that's good enough you're more stupid than you look. How dare you represent this firm - this name - so shoddily. That should have been an easy win. Not the meal you made of it. Get out of my sight. I can't even look at you.'

A standard dressing down. One of many variations on a theme. As a young solicitor, he had assumed it was part of the job. It wasn't as if he were singled out.

It was simply something to brush off. Later, when the firm became his own, his attempts at discipline were futile. He didn't care enough. He could definitely match his father's bad temper, but struggled to use it as a motivating tool. It finally dawned on him that his father had never motivated him once. He had simply taught him to feel fear and hatred. And for some reason he had consented.

Back in the present, his question to Rosie remained unanswered. *This firm is better than it was. Surely we can agree on that?*

She had taken her time. Now she looked straight at him, causing his discomfort levels to rise further. No one gave him eye contact. He didn't surround himself by people who got that close. Some holiday friends, the odd romance lasting a couple of dates at the most, and then the staff. No one faced him head on and called him out. No one except Rosie. He watched her take her time, choosing her words carefully. She wasn't one to sugar coat sentiment but she was usually polite. She would be finding the right way of saying something negative without resorting to insults. He felt sick.

'You ask me if this firm is better than it was? Well, I just don't know. When your father retired, it was like a breath of fresh air swept through the place. We felt huge relief. Then you took over and started copying his ways. But - and I say this with gratitude, Stewart - you didn't have it in you to be as awful as he was. You just didn't. Sorry, but he *was* awful, wasn't he?'

He blinked an assent. She was right, but he still felt guilty. Better to keep it inside and then drink away the feelings later. Rosie took the blink for consent. She continued.

'So this was still a good place to work, even if you were grumpy all the time. We coped with you. We managed. But then he died. And all that terrible stuff came out...'

'Steady on. He wasn't a paedo or anything.'

'No. But he *was* abusive. Mentally, psychologically, however you want to describe it. That still doesn't stop the fact that he was your Dad and he died. But the stuff about your brother? You were broken. I didn't know how to help but I could see you were crying out for someone to guide you. So I told you to take a break.'

'I hadn't forgotten.' Stewart winced at the vague memories he had of that night. There had been tears, and most inexplicably of all, a hug. Stewart hadn't hugged anyone in decades, but there he was, sobbing into Rosie's middle like a toddler with grazed knees. He'd struggled to think of it ever since. It was far too raw. Their unspoken agreement of never mentioning it again had been upheld by both. But in that moment of rare vulnerability, Stewart had listened to Rosie. He had taken the first leave of absence of his career. Suddenly he'd had time to process the events of the previous months. He had been able to prioritise his life and focus on dealing with the unexpected turmoil that had been unleashed by the wholly expected death of his father. He could get fit, eat healthily, and unpack the pain he'd bottled up since his youth.

That had been the plan. Of course, the reality turned out nothing like that. He went on holiday. Then he went on another. Then he went on a third. Rather than eating well and processing his life, he escaped from one hedonistic adventure to another. The south of France, Mauritius, Las Vegas - each place had been different enough from the last to provide a momentary lift before reverting to monotony. He'd wiled away two years that way. Popping into the office from time to time, the odd week here, the odd day there. The months continued to pass.

Rosie had given him space for as long as she could. She had let him unleash everything he had suppressed for years. Her tolerance couldn't last forever though, and it didn't. He was surprised she had left him alone for this long. He saw the difference when it came. Eighteen months of acting up to a role she had never formally been given, switching from one potentially wrong call to the next, and her nerves were fraught. That's what she had said, anyway. She'd had enough. She went from being an understanding and supportive assistant, to the hard-hearted whip cracker she was to-day. It hadn't made a great deal of difference. He felt empty regardless of how Rosie treated him.

She cleared her throat and began her lecture.

'I think the time has come for you to *stop* taking a break. You have options. You can be in control of what happens next. Something needs to change though. You can't go on like this.'

He remained blank. His voice was even.

'What do you expect me to do exactly?'

Rosie responded immediately.

'Come back to work. Or sell up. Or work part time on set days. Or officially retire and hire a replacement. It's completely your choice. We just need clarity.'

Stewart felt his head nodding. On the outside he was showing Rosie he had listened and that she had made a good point. On the inside he was concentrating on standing upright, playing the game, and not causing any more alarm. He didn't begrudge her giving him this speech. He had to keep her onside for as long as he needed the business to tick over. One thing was certain. It wasn't just Rosie and the staff that needed clarity. He could do with some of it too. Clarity would be very welcome. He hoped some clarity would arrive soon.

Stewart booked an Uber. He filled the five-minute wait by hiding in the gents, and then was back outside making his latest escape. All within thirty minutes of arriving at work.

CHAPTER FOUR

Five months before the reunion

It was a dilemma. One over which Tilda had been torn since moving in. Was this the best thing to have ever happened or the start of a slow bloat towards morbid obesity? The thought was never far away. On the way to her temp job, on her walk back a few hours later, or on milder evenings when she opened the living room window that overlooked the prom. It had caused all sorts of mental gymnastics and internal wrangling. The issue? Six doors away from Tilda's apartment was a chip shop. A salt-and-vinegar-toting, wooden-fork-providing, traditional seaside chippy. The smell was mouth-watering. The temptation, constant. Combined with the nasal umami of the ozone and the constant caws of the gulls, it evoked deep sense memories of happy childhood holidays. Walking past as a grown adult, however, was torture.

In the early days, when she hadn't worked out the location of the big Tesco, she had given in. Three times in her first week. It was an outbreak of spots that caused her to rethink her new diet. It hadn't helped that the chip shop in question provided the best chips she had ever tasted. The spots had been worth it.

Now, a few months into her lease and with a full working knowledge of where to buy vegetables, she was determined to stay strong. The daily cravings had to be controlled. Tilda had searched for a solution and eventually found a compromise. Convincing herself that a monthly chip shop meal was acceptable, she had circled a designated Chip Shop Night on each page of her calendar for the rest of the year. Even if she didn't renew her lease, even in the non-likely event she ran back to Mike saying she had made a mistake, she was going to eat chip shop chips, one night a month, for the rest of her life.

Tilda left work and began the downhill walk to the apartment. She felt a shiver of happiness. Tomorrow was the night. Four weeks of anticipation at its peak. It had been all she could think about as she had walked to the University that morning. She'd felt a glow as she had inputted data and shredded files. The other temps - every one of them half her age or younger - were un- aware of the red circle on Tilda's calendar. They were busy with their own plans for the weekend. Plans that involved people and places, food and alcohol, sex and drugs. Plans that involved sharing laughter and - later, for some - each other. Tilda was happy for them. She felt no jealousy. She had Chip Shop Night. That was much more fun at her age, not to mention something exciting for her journal.

Twenty minutes later, she was curled up in her chair with her post-work cup of tea. The sky outside featured a new blue. One she hadn't seen before. Not a warm day but a bright one. It felt satisfying to be in one place. To see the colours change in the same bit of horizon. While she was travelling, her appreciation of the seasons had intensified, and her attention to the detail around her was sharp. A lifetime ago, someone special had told her to stop and look. The man whose photo was framed on her mantelpiece. He had recited a long-dead essayist with words she had taken as a personal mission. '*Though we travel the world over to find the beautiful, we must carry it with us or we find it not.'*

Emerson. That was the essayist. Her memory whirred into action, providing Tilda with the name she used to recall immediately. It wasn't a bad mantra. She was forever grateful for everything she'd shared with the man on her mantlepiece. He'd been instrumental in her decision to leave Mike, even though she'd only managed it twenty years after his departure from her life. She listened to his advice - of carrying the beauty with her - in her own time, but it had happened. Eventually. She carried everything with her; the sunsets, the sounds, and the peace. They were all inside. All part of her. Perhaps soon, she would find the strength within to appreciate the seagull that was transfixed by her window. Right now, the constant tapping was not beautiful in the slightest.

The sky changed and the evening drew in. After watching the world pass by, Tilda ran a bath. She put her library book on the loo seat and pulled out clean pyjamas from the pile. Old Tilda would have had the washing hung up and folded the second it was dry. New Tilda smiled to herself. The buses were running and the world was turning. Civilisation had not ended because she had a three-day old pile of laundry to fold. With a towel to hand and a fresh cup of tea on the side, she grabbed her book and lowered herself into the bubbles.

Her last library trip had highlighted how much she had read since she had come here. Her favoured genre of *thriller* had been exhausted since her move. Everything she had liked the look of, she'd had on loan already. Clearly a higher power was nudging her to move away from the tiny section she favoured, and explore the rest of the shelves. The upshot was that she got flustered. At her last visit, she found herself walking away with a self-help book. This had come as a surprise. When she got home, she felt like she'd been duped by a pushy salesperson, except that salesperson was her own head, forcing her to try something new. And now here she was, a couple of chapters into a book of which she had no interest. She couldn't even remember the name of it without looking, but here in the bath, with nothing else to do, she persevered. It was about living your best life, finding the strength within, and other positive epithets that were amusing her as she read. She was too old to be seduced by hashtag buzzwords. She had no interest in being up-lifted and influenced by the Instagram generation. They were too cool for Tilda. She was happy to stay in her analogue lane.

There was just one part of the book that had stuck with her. A passage she had read a few nights before from a chapter entitled *Wingmen*. Upon reading it, Tilda had felt a surge of irritation. Gendered language annoyed her more, the older she got. She'd had to swallow the impulse to disregard the argument, and read on. *Wingmen*, according to the self-appointed, self-help guru, *are the team of supporters that each of us curate. They're the cheerleaders that egg on a person to reach their potential. They're the friends that can be called day or night, when a shoulder to cry on is essential. They're the people to phone when one is rushed to hospital and needs a toothbrush and change of underwear.* According to the book, *each of us need a minimum of six wingmen. We need six phone numbers that can be called in an emergency. We need a team of six around us. All of us. All the time.*

Tilda had laughed it off when she read it, but that section had stuck with her. It reminded her of the time, years earlier, when Mike set up the *Friends and Family* discount on their landline. He had worked out the numbers they phoned the most and typed them in to get the saving. It had come as no surprise. There were his parents, his sister, his best mate, his boss, and Tilda's Dad. She had found it faintly depressing back then. Now it was even worse. All those numbers were dead to her - quite literally in the case of her Dad. Her extended gap year was over. She was no longer in the madness of a transition phase, escaping her life. She was living her life. It was happening right now. And all she could think was that the only person she thought of as a friend, had struggled to find time for a catch up. A few texts with her old workmate over the past month and that was it. The gendered language wasn't really the issue. Tilda had no wingmen or wingwomen. She had no wingpeople of any description. She could drown in this bath and no one would know. In the campervan it had been temporary. Now this was her life forever.

It would be a waste of time, but she did it anyway. She messaged her friend again. The suds on her fingers blurred the screen but she managed to type a few lines.

It's been ages! Let's catch up. I'm in the bath reading a terrible book. I imagine you're out having sexy fun with multiple men. Or women. How can I forget your epic threesome tale by the shredder? I thought Si and Alex would explode. Anyway, I'm rambling. Ring me. Any time. I miss you. Tilda x

She pressed send before she could change her mind. The office banter had been mortifying on regular occasions, but now she wasn't there, she missed the gossip. And the friendship. She missed that more than anything. She hoped she would ring back.

Tilda put down her phone. She considered returning to her book but decided against it. It would make her brood and she needed no help with that. Where could she find some wingpeople? She was too old to make new friends. It was just the way it was.

She lay back in the water, wallowing for the last few moments. Wingpeople or no wingpeople, she still had one thing going for her. Tomorrow night was Chip Shop Night. Nothing could take that away. Nothing and no one would spoil her date with a chippy tea. With that thought, Tilda felt a momentary release from the ache that had begun to settle. She was glad. She didn't want to have to get out of the bath and count cutlery right now.

Just as Tilda began to salivate, her daydream was interrupted. The phone rang. She hurriedly dried a hand and scrabbled to answer the call. When she saw who it was, her mood was instantly lifted.

'Bea! Long time, no speak!'

CHAPTER FIVE

Stewart had tried to make an effort. Over the last month, he had been to the office most days. Some days. At least two days a week, anyway. He wasn't good with the early starts, but if he made it before lunch, he knew no one would comment. It was a slow process to get back up to speed. As far as the staff, and the outside world were concerned, he was still not over his bereavement. Nor was he above using that as a reason for his lack of commitment to the firm.

At the thought of his father, the usual memories surfaced. A hotchpotch of barked instructions and commentary. *Make the firm proud... don't be a disappointment like your brother... you have a responsibility to the family name... a half-wit child could have won that case... if you think that's good enough, you're more stupid than you look.* These memories were never welcome. They provided neither comfort nor nostalgia. Instead, the dull ache of badly-mended broken bones. Stewart may have survived his childhood physically unharmed but the mental scars could be just as painful.

Still, he continued to use grief as the explanation for his lack of effort. That he viewed the death of his father as an essential upgrade for the human race, didn't need to be shared. Not as long as it could be the reason for his laissez faire attitude. Besides, he had a system. Whenever he arrived, whatever time it was, he would make sure he was coatless and bagless as he walked through the door. He would stash them in the cleaning cupboard, or if that were being used, in the staff toilet. Then, when he walked into the office -

hours after the 8am arrival of the rest of the staff - he'd look like he had been there for ages. Sometimes he made sure he was carrying a pen, as if he were in the middle of a task, rather than fudging his late arrival to look less unprofessional to his unofficial second in command. He would see Rosie in the distance and busy himself with a sentence or two of small talk with a junior member of staff. The confused employee would panic that the temperamental and volatile boss was talking to them, so would nod and commit to the conversation, even when Stewart was making no sense. He didn't care. It was all for Rosie. So that she'd think he had been in the vicinity for ages. So that she would think he was deeply involved in the details of an on-going case. So that she wouldn't give him any more grief.

There was a quick rap on the door before it opened. He lifted his head from the desk. The woman with whom he was involved in a daily battle of wits, stood in front of him. It was as if she were telepathic.

'Rosie.'

'I've got the notes from the meeting yesterday. Do you want them now?'

Stewart nodded. His wordless reply masked the fact that he had no idea what notes, what meeting or what case this was about. Rosie continued.

'And the Cooper-Jones man has been on the phone.'

'The who?'

'The Cooper-Jones man. The buyer for your Dad's house?'

'What did he want?'

'They've emailed some replacement forms. You

haven't returned the Fittings and Contents? Said you'd had it weeks.'

'Christ, he needs to back the fuck off.'

'Well I'll be honest, Stewart, I won't pass that on directly, but if you fill them out as soon as you can, I'll get the papers over to his team and he can *back the fuck off* with his completed forms. How's that?'

'Fine.'

'Last thing. There's a pile of cheques to double-sign. I've done them, so if you could too, I can get them posted.

'Right.' He took the cheques from her.

'And fill in the Contents forms as soon as you can. I looked all over your office when they told me, and I've no idea what happened to the first lot.'

Stewart stifled his irritation. He knew where the forms were. They were sitting amidst a toppling pile of official correspondence on the desk in his study. He hadn't found the stomach to face that sort of thing yet. It was simply easier to ignore it. Besides, he hadn't worked out what he wanted to keep from the house.

Stewart paused, and processed the lie his own brain had just repeated. *He hadn't worked out what he wanted to keep from the house.* It was exactly the sort of thing that people in his position might say. Except it wasn't true. That was what he might tell other people but there was no point lying to himself. He knew the truth. Everything from his childhood home had been sorted months ago. He had taken his own belongings when he moved out as a young man and left nothing in the big house on the hill. There'd been nothing of sentimental value left except a medium sized cardboard box.

It had been found by the house clearers in the weeks after William Grady's death. Stewart had felt no hesitation at getting the house emptied as soon as he could. He was motivated back then. He wanted to move on and close forever that particular chapter. The cardboard box had been underwhelming to anyone not in the know, but for Stewart it was the only item of value in the place. It contained a bundle of love letters, a few photos, and some mementoes of his brother. There were also paintings and sketches, indicating the artist he'd had the potential to become. Stewart had looked through it once, passed on a couple of items to the writer of the love letters, and then stashed it at the back of a cupboard in his apartment.

That was it. The big house was cleared. Gutted might be more accurate. The furniture, the art, the extensive library? Gone. He had felt a subversive pleasure in getting rid of the treasures his father had curated over a lifetime.

Don't touch my books with your filthy hands. Do you know how much that costs? Go to your room before I thrash you!

The man would have been livid at the desecration of his prized possessions. *Good.* The lack of love shown by William towards his children throughout their lives had been returned tenfold in the lack of interest Stewart had shown in sourcing new homes for his belongings. Homes that included a large skip, a few charities, and his neighbours. The art had been sold to collectors. And the personal items - awards, papers, the scrapbook of news clippings that mentioned *Grady and Son* in the legal press - been ceremoniously and cathartically burnt, just weeks after William

Grady's demise. That was the last time Stewart had felt anything positive. He was relieved he could draw a line and become his own man.

Best laid plans and all that. It was never going to be so easy. Here he was, a couple of years down the line. His head was on the desk, he was urging the remaining minutes of the working day to pass, and he was exhausted from pretending everything was rosy to Rosie, and her incessant disappointment. It was all so tiring. He thought things would be better once he was free of the past. Instead he felt untethered and dangerous. He didn't know where he was heading and it frightened him.

Stewart watched his assistant leave the room and stride back through the office. One thing was clear. The firm ran more smoothly without him. As long as Rosie was there, he was never going to stop being a spare part. She was just so damn capable. That was what made it all the more galling. He needed her. He needed her to keep things going. There were plenty of times he wished he could have told her to *fuck off*. When even her presence made him feel inadequate. She had an uncanny knack of bringing to the surface the full range of insecurity he felt about himself. This could be done by handing him a file, or passing him a phone message on a sticky note. Rosie didn't need words.

He glanced at the meeting notes she had left on the desk. Before she had started nagging about the forms. It was basic stuff. It could have been dealt with by the most junior of legal staff. But instead he was being humoured and patronised by the woman that had started her career as a sixteen-year old in need of a Saturday job. Well she could back the fuck off too. It was his firm now. What was once *Grady and Sons*, was now simply *Grady*. Or *Son*? Which role was he meant to be? He didn't know. Nor did he care enough to work it out.

There was half an hour left before the official end of business. Stewart didn't care about that either. He needed a drink and knew it would set a better example if he left the building for that. *See,* he told himself. *I can be responsible when I try.* He signed the cheques, grabbed his coat and bag, and left his office. Stopping outside Rosie's door, it was clear she wasn't there. She would be being organised and competent somewhere else. He swallowed down the annoyance about those exceptionally useful qualities in the woman to whom he regularly left the running of his business. He didn't mean to be personally critical. It was because he fell far short of her that he struggled to be kind. He knew that. He knew that she knew that too. That was the kicker.

Stewart left the cheques on her desk. Her perpetually *neat* desk. No lidless pens or scrunched up balls of half-typed documents lying around. Just the one piece of paper perpendicularly placed in the centre. It was always that way. Whatever she was working on was left out, and nothing else. He almost smiled. The sight was reassuring. He might be in freefall, but Rosie was the anchor. Her and her spotless desk. She was the same as always. She hadn't changed when the rest of his world had. That thought was comforting, and he felt a small bubble of relief. He put down the cheques and turned to leave. That was when he spotted it. The paper on the desk. The task with which she was currently dealing. It was a printout of a job specification. *Office Manager. York area. Salary upon inquiry.* Rosie was job hunting. Stewart's bubble of relief burst into nothing.

CHAPTER SIX

Tilda stretched for the towel and dried her phone screen. In her eagerness to answer the call and put her friend on loudspeaker, she had managed to spread bubbles everywhere.

'Tilda, darling! Sorry for being the worst friend in the world. Life, as they say, has most definitely got in the way. Are you busy? Can you chat?'

'Other than getting out of this bath before I resemble an old prune, I've nowhere else to be. What about you?'

'I'm all yours, darling. How's life in the wilderness?'

Tilda laughed. Already she felt better.

'It's wild, Bea. Barren. Post-apocalyptic.'

The sarcasm was lost on her friend, whose instant concern made Tilda audibly snort.

'Don't worry, I'm in a busy town. Students everywhere. I just happen to have a sweeping seafront and cliffs nearby.'

'But isn't it lonely? Don't you miss us in the office?'

Tilda smiled to herself. Loneliness was not solved from working in an office with colleagues who mostly ignored her.

'I'm as lonely as I was when I worked with you. I just don't have to put on a front at home anymore. It's better. Honestly.'

'And how is the lovely Mike? Still at the begging and pleading stage?'

'I get an occasional late night, sweary text, when he's had a drink. Then an apologetic one the next day. But we're mostly down to basic formalities. He's polite now, which makes me feel worse. It's not his fault I stopped loving him.' Tilda paused for a moment. It was worse than that. The truth made her squeeze her hands into fists as she muttered, 'Or that I don't think I ever did.'

Bea ignored her change of volume.

'Either way, it's as much his responsibility as yours. He took you for granted for too long. You broke free from feeling nothing so now you can feel *everything*.'

'Hmm.' Tilda was non-committal. Feeling *everything* was some distance away. 'He's been quiet for a while. Long may it last.'

She relaxed her fists and felt the blood return to her hands. She had never felt the urge to do anything worse to herself, but she understood the impulse. The need to distract from one pain source by providing another. With the unbearable feelings nipped in the bud, she changed the subject.

'How about you? What shenanigans have you been up to? Or are you going to surprise me and tell me you've taken a late-in-life vow of celibacy and re-thought all your previous behaviour?' Tilda smiled as she conjured up the image of Bea taking holy orders. No convent would stand a chance.

'You may scoff, Tilda, but I am a changed woman. I have discovered the joys of... wait for it...'

'Oh God, I can't begin to imagine how this sentence is going to end. BDSM? Men who wear nappies and suck giant dummies? Does it involve one of those black rubber masks with the mouth zip?'

'...no, not a gimp mask, although I'm very happy that the years of sitting opposite me provided you with at least a basic education regarding fetish. But no, none of the above. I have discovered, at the grand old age of fifty-two, the joys of... *monogamy.*'

'Yeah, right. As IF!' Tilda was having none of it. 'What's it really?'

'I'm being serious. Honestly. I've met a man.'

'You've met lots of men.'

'Agreed. But this one - and I know I sound stupid saying this but it's true - this one's different.'

'Are you really not winding me up? This shouldn't be a big deal, but it's enormous. It's huge. Who is he? What's his deal? What's he done to you?'

'Tilda, my lovely, you don't want to ask questions like that unless you want to hear the unspeakable *filth* he's done to me over the last month. Trust me.'

'I really do trust you on that one. Spare me.' Tilda knew Bea had no filter or sense of embarrassment when it came to sharing details. That wasn't what she was interested in. It was more basic than that. 'Who is he? Where did you meet? And why him? I want to know everything.' She paused for a second before making herself clear. 'Within reason.'

Bea took a breath, presumably to build the dramatic tension. Tilda didn't need the suspense ramped up any further. She was intrigued enough as it was.

'His name is Mal. He's a couple of years older than me, and he's quite possibly the loveliest man in the whole world.'

Tilda struggled to make sense of it. The Bea she had left in Stockport was not a one-man woman. She loved *people*, plural. It had once occurred to Tilda that by refusing to compromise on her life choices, Bea demonstrated great love for herself. And because of the self-assurance that provided, she had the strength to be there for others when they were in need. She had been a brilliant friend to Tilda when she had needed a stronger person to guide her through her meltdown. Bea had understood that *no* relationship was better than a mediocre one. Tilda had benefited from her far worldlier friend's perspective. If Bea was happy and single, Tilda could be too. That's why Bea's news was so unexpected. Tilda wasn't sure how she felt about it.

'How did you meet?'

'On an app, of course. How does anyone meet each other these days?'

Tilda was relieved the question was rhetorical.

'And who is he? What's his background?'

'His background? Are we in a period drama? Will I bring shame on my family if I marry beneath me? I've no idea about his background.'

'OK, where's he from? What does he do?'

'He does me, mostly.'

'Bea! You're being deliberately annoying.'

'Oh, all right. He lives by the Quays...'

'Ooh, fancy!'

'...I know! He's something to do with marketing, based in Media City. I don't know the details except he's always busy and always taking work calls. I swear to God, his PA can't piss without phoning him. I make him turn off his ringer in bed. But his actual day to day job hasn't come up much. Not that it matters to me. All work's dull, isn't it.'

'And are you... I can't believe I'm even asking this... are you *seeing* each other? Is he... a *boyfriend*?'

Bea laughed down the phone.

'We're just having fun. *Regular* fun.'

'Exclusive fun?'

'Yeah. That's how it seems.'

'Since when?'

'When did we meet?'

'No, how long have you been having exclusive fun? You know, as opposed to the non-exclusive kind? I'm trying to work out how serious this is.'

Tilda was still deciding whether this was good news or not. If she asked lots of questions, it would delay having to reach a conclusion.

'I've no idea.' Bea sounded amused by the specific technicalities she was being made to recall. 'I suppose it's been about... three months since anyone else.'

'Bea! That's HUGE.' Tilda sat upright. Memories of her relaxing bath shattered by the monumental news her friend was sharing.

'Darling, I'm worried about your blood pressure. Do some deep breathing, for the love God.'

Tilda realised that her mate knew this was a big deal, but she needed someone else to confirm that. It didn't bother Tilda. She was happy to be trusted. She could and would ask the questions that matter.

'Not wanting to be superficial in any way, but what does he look like?'

'Ah, now we come down to it. I knew your *beauty comes from within* attitude was just an act. You want to know if he's hot? I hear you. Let me think.'

Tilda laughed. She wasn't shallow. Simply curious.

'I reckon he's a cross between Daniel Craig and an older Matt Damon. Kind of.'

Tilda was sceptical.

'Oh right. So, he's a regular Hollywood action man? Sounds like the classic Mancunian bloke. Athletic, sexy men on every street corner just waiting for the chance to save the world. It's a shame I left.'

'You sarky cow.' Bea laughed at herself, as well as Tilda's ridicule. 'Oh I don't know. He does look a bit like that. He's got fair hair, with a bit of grey around the temples. You know how it works. Men get to be distinguished, but women are full-on hag? Well, he's definitely distinguished. And he's got pecs, darling. Honestly. They're rock-hard, not man-booby at all. And his thighs, my God, he could crack nuts with them. And his...'

'Enough! I've got it. He's a Greek God and statues should be erected all over the North.'

'Talking of erections, let me tell you, I've never seen such a...'

'BEA. MY FINGERS ARE IN MY EARS AND I'M LA LA LAAAING UNTIL YOU STOP.'

Bea's laugh rose above the din as Tilda blushed. It was always the way with Bea. She was embarrassing, provocative, and forever highlighting how innocent Tilda was in comparison. But despite that, the mortification was familiar. It was silly. She felt carefree and wanted to throw her head back and laugh. Tilda acknowledged the levity, chose to contain herself on this particular occasion, but held onto the comfort of the conversation as long as she could, before changing the subject. Practicalities had to be dealt with.

'I need to go in a minute. The water's getting cold. What other news have you got? How's work?'

'Work, schmerk. Nothing more to say. It's much

less fun without you.'

'How's the promotion going?'

'You mean the promotion you'd have been a shoo-in for, if you hadn't left me being the last grown-up standing?'

Tilda giggled.

'Yeah, that one. Sorry. I didn't mean to force you into responsibility.'

'I never realised how dull Tan Tight's role was. I thought she was boring because *she* was boring. Now I think it was the job. She might have been loads of fun outside work.'

'Unlikely.'

'Yeah, fair enough. The best thing was being able to move Si and Alex. They're in Pay Roll now. We all felt it was best.'

'Even Si and Alex?'

'Especially Si and Alex. They panicked when I took over because I knew all their skives. I had that much dirt on them - all the times they were hammered in work, or remember when no one owned up to pissing in the potted palm? I knew it was Si, and they knew I knew it was Si. When I suggested a move, they jumped at it.'

'I wouldn't know anyone there now. It doesn't seem that long ago, but it is.'

'It is. Are you still OK for money? You know you only need to say the word and you're back in. If it came to that.'

'Money's fine as long as I'm cautious. It'll be better when the house is sold. I'm temping now and I don't spend much. I appreciate your offer though.'

'No problem. I know it'd be a last resort.'

'Yeah.' Tilda looked at her fingertips. She had passed the wrinkled prune stage a while ago and knew it was time to call it a day. Still she paused. She didn't want the light-hearted atmosphere to be punctured by the silence that would fall as soon as she hung up the phone. But she had to deal with it. She had to face it.

'Bea, I need to go. I'm shivering. Can we do this again some time? I need regular updates about the Man-God that is Mal.'

'Don't you worry about that. I'll keep you updated on ALL aspects. Especially the filth.' Bea cackled to herself. 'Now, what are your plans this weekend? Got anything fun on the cards in your new town?'

Tilda was about to open her mouth to reply, but paused. She was comfortable with Bea knowing her social life paled into insignificance when compared to her own. She knew Bea wasn't expecting her to announce a hot date or boozy party. Even so, she considered making up something a little less pathetic. She could have said she was going to the cinema. She could have said there was an exhibition at the University. She could have said she planned an evening walk along the sea before stopping for tapas and a glass of wine at the Spanish place on Pier Street. None of that would be true, though, and Tilda didn't like lying. She could have said all sorts of things but she told the truth.'

'Tomorrow night is the best night of the month, Bea. Tomorrow night is Chip Shop Night. I've been counting the days since last month's Chip Shop Night and I cannot wait.'

Bea seemed momentarily lost for words. That

didn't stop Tilda hearing *pity*. She laughed it off as they said their goodbyes and she wrapped herself in her towel. She put it out of her mind as she pulled on her PJs in the bedroom. She tuned it out as she poured herself a glass of wine and sat back in the chair by the window. She did not need pity. She needed to keep busy. She needed to enjoy her chips tomorrow night, and she needed to keep getting up every morning and putting one foot in front of the other.

Tilda finished her wine and washed the glass. She straightened the sofa cushions, wiped down the work-top, and turned out the living room light. Tomorrow was a new day. Who knows what could happen?

CHAPTER SEVEN

The forced positivity from the previous evening ran through her head as she looked for her purse. Buoyed up from her bath time gossip, or still enjoying the spring weather? Tilda wasn't sure but the cause didn't matter. Only the feelings did.

Last night she may have felt a stab of pity after Bea's call but today Tilda was feeling almost content. She knew it wasn't contentment for real. Not when it was food-related. That's not how things worked. Just because Chip Shop Night had arrived, it was hardly the basis for inner peace. Contentment for real could only come when *all* aspects of her life provided a sense of fulfilment and purpose. She was a couple of light years away from that. She doubted she'd *ever* felt wholly positive about all parts of her life at the same time. Did anyone? Maybe smug people were smug for a reason. Perhaps when you're truly happy it's so rare that you have to bang on about it to those less fortunate. She didn't know anyone like that. Not in real life. Surely everyone was clinging on and making do, just like she was. Tonight, however, her monthly treat had arrived. She was doing slightly better than clinging on and making do. Just for this evening.

She locked the door, walked down the communal stairs, and out onto the street. Hitting the prom, she made her way to the back of the chip shop queue, snaking out of the door. She waited in line as her mind wandered. The thought occurred to her that 'monthly treat' could be a sarcastic euphemism for her period. She smiled, knowing Bea would have enjoyed her joke.

If she still worked opposite her, she would have shared that during a lunch break.

The queue shuffled forward. She ordered her meal. Her mind continued to wander. Was Bea smug in her new-found happiness? Tilda wondered with genuine interest. She was truly pleased for her friend and her whirlwind relationship. It was just unnerving to hear Bea sound so different. But if that's what made her happy then...

'Salt and vinegar?'

'Sorry?'

'Salt and vinegar. On your fish and chips?'

'Oh. Yes. Thank you.'

Tilda focused her attention on paying and then left the shop. Time to find the perfect outdoor spot.

She wasn't the only one making the most of the evening. The recent clock change, when spring had sprung forward, had prompted a flurry of activity along the sea front. All the nearby benches facing the water were taken. Dog walkers taking a break, elderly couples sitting in contented silence, joggers using the seat to stretch out their leg muscles. She kept walking. She'd find a seat somewhere. A few months ago, when she had moved in, the prom had been deserted once evening arrived. She wondered how busy it would get in the summer.

Tilda kept walking. Just before she reached the end of the promenade and the start of the cliff, she spotted an empty bench. She plonked herself in the middle of it and let the smell of her favourite food fill her senses. Faux contentment was better than nothing. She might not have all the pieces of her life sorted, but she had chips and they smelt delicious.

Tilda had only eaten a couple of forkfuls when her phone buzzed. She looked at the screen then regretted it instantly. An email from Mike. Her stomach jerked as her guilt level rose. Why did she react this way when it took two to neglect a marriage? She scanned the email quickly. She needed to get back to faking happiness and eating her meal.

The solicitor has been on. She needs something called a Property Information Form. I've done as much as I can but you'll have to do the rest. It's not fair everything is on me. We can't all bugger off and expect the house to get sold. Email it back when you've done it.

Tilda's appetite that had been on high alert all day, took a dip. The weather hadn't changed but the air had cooled. She pronged a couple more chips with the fork and swallowed them down but she wasn't in the mood. She tried again with some fish, but it was no use. Her al fresco evening meal was done.

She dragged herself and the chip box back to the apartment. Maybe she would be hungry later. As she unlocked the door, her seagull stalker flew to its usual spot on the window sill, as if paying witness to the change in her mood. She had made it inside and was boiling the kettle when the tapping started.

Tilda looked at her calendar, hanging on the wall of her kitchen. Another four weeks to go. Another four weeks until she had something exciting planned.

CHAPTER EIGHT

Alone in bed, Bea arched her back and stretched her limbs. Her body ached but it was the good kind of ache. The kind that came from sharing it with someone else.

'I couldn't find your champagne glasses. We'll have to make do with these.' Mal's knee nudged the door open. He was carrying a wine glass in each hand whilst wearing a robe that could only have belonged to Bea Charleston. Fuchsia and black leopard print on a satin blend. It was loosely tied around his waist but, she was relieved to note, far too small to provide full coverage. She accepted her curves as a healthy part of her but it still wouldn't do to see her robe swamp the rugged torso of her lover. Crazy animal prints on her man were fine, but him being skinnier was not on.

'Bless you for thinking I'm mature enough to have champagne glasses. It's official. You can stay.'

Mal grinned as he placed her drink on the side.

'Why thank you. I had assumed you were a woman of great experience and class. Was I wrong?'

'Darling, I have never *once* used mugs for wine. Never ever, in all my days.'

Bea smiled, wondering if any recent wine mugs were hiding under the bed as Mal climbed back into it. He half propped himself on the pillows, as his other half became a head rest for Bea. She nestled against him, inhaling his chest, as she forced him to fish her hair out of his mouth. She loved how he smelt.

'Hang on, let me arrange you. Your hair's all over the place. I still don't know how you cope with it.' He smoothed down her mane and got more comfortable. When he was in a better position, he used his free arm to pick up his glass, then held it out in front of him.

'To you, Bea. I'm so glad we met. I only wish it'd been years ago.'

Bea picked up her own glass, after less than elegantly using her lack of core muscles to achieve a sitting position.

'Right back atcha, darling. But if it had been years ago, I'd have panicked and run a mile. I think I needed to be old enough to handle something as fabulous as this.'

They sipped their drinks. A moment passed. Wine glasses were placed back onto bedside tables and a comfortable snuggling position resumed. Bea settled against Mal's chest as he continued to stroke her hair with his free hand. Eventually he broke the silence.

'What would have made you run away in the past? Someone like me? Being in a relationship, or something else? Tell me everything. I want to know what makes you tick.'

This was one of the surprises of having a boyfriend. She had forgotten how much time was spent talking. It wasn't unwelcome. Just different. Her conversational skills centred around small talk, dirty talk, and overblown drunken hyperbolic talk, that was happily forgotten the next time you bumped into the person in question. That's what she understood. That's what she had been happy with. But now? Now it was different. Mal liked talking. And Mal liked talking about real things. About her childhood, about her teenage years, about her *day*. No one asked her about her day. It was quite a change. Even more surprising to Bea at this mid-stage of her life, was that she found she quite liked it.

This question wasn't about her day though. It was deeper than that. It was about what had taken her so long to be open to the possibility of a relationship. That was the crux of the issue. She didn't have any ready answers either. She gave it a few second's thought before attempting a satisfactory reply.

'There are no deep-seated issues, don't worry. I just value my independence, so I've never wanted that taken from me. That's probably what's at the root of my commitment avoidance.'

'Fair enough. Sounds reasonable.'

Bea carried on mulling his question over. She didn't feel like she had explained herself adequately, so had another attempt.

'You see, sometimes, when I had multiple dates with someone who seemed nice enough, it was only a matter of time before they suggested doing something that I didn't want to do.'

'Ah, I see. You mean in bed?'

'Oh no, darling. I mean like ice skating. Or woodland walks. Or one young man, who was perfectly charming in many ways, thought I would like nothing better than spend my Sunday afternoons watching him play five-a-side football. Can you imagine? It, and he, were not for me.'

Mal answered with a straight face.

'Here's my solemn vow to you. I promise I will never make you watch me play five-a-side football. Ever. How's that? Also, it's fair to say my ice-skating days are over. I'm probably a bit old for mastering new skills now. Woodland walks might be quite pleasant though. A gentle stroll through nature? Are you still against them? It could be something to try.'

Bea didn't care about woodland walks one way or the other. It was just the kind of couples shit she had avoided like the plague.

'I may or may not revise my opinion about woodland walks. I shall weigh up all the evidence before I make a decision. You'll be the first to know.'

'That's good enough for me.' Mal manoeuvred himself to access his drink, as Bea snuggled back into her pillow.

Her face was still hot from earlier. It was either the post-shag glow or her hot flushes had come back. She couldn't necessarily tell the difference. Not now she was having regular sex again. HRT had been a revelation when she'd finally got her hands on it, but it could only do so much. And whilst her libido had greatly benefitted from the help, everything else was less clear. It was no fun trying to second guess herself and function as glamorously as normal, whilst battling wits with her ever-changing hormones, and – and this was the really unwelcome guest at the party – the anxiety. Bea realised she had never truly understood anxiety until now. Who knew it was more than a few nervy butterflies before a stressful event? Not her. Her mother's generation had a lot to answer for, keeping this to themselves. She'd had no clue until it hit her. There had been some days when the uncontrollable worry had been debilitating. That it had mostly faded with her patch-based pharmaceutical help, had come as a huge relief.

She sat up and held her glass to her forehead. It might cool her down. It might not. Either way, she had to do something in the face of having no control.

'I'm glad we met too, Mal. It's a whole new world but I'm loving every minute.'

Bea meant it. Mal and his intoxicating smell had come along and given her the reassurance she needed. He made her feel good about herself when everything else was in flux. Her sweaty forehead and rosy cheeks were grateful for his presence.

'It's an absolute pleasure, Bea. There's nowhere I'd rather be and no one I'd rather be with. Now, while I remember, I've had an idea for your birthday. I want to spoil you. Will you check your diary at some point and see when you're free?'

Bea's heart soared. Someone wanted to spoil her. This year's birthday would be with someone she had known the month before. Everything was changing and she was thrilled. She didn't mean to be smug, but if that's what she was, she wasn't going to apologise.

CHAPTER NINE

Stewart slumped on the sofa. His right hand scrolled through the emails that spammed his inbox. His left, loosely held the stem of an empty wine glass. At just after seven o'clock on this Friday evening, he was alone and a bottle of red down. He had eaten a take-away meal from tinfoil boxes, watched the News, and was now contemplating a boxset to fill the coming hours. His only other dilemma was what to drink next.

Ten minutes later he was nursing a tumbler, filled with the warming arms of a single malt. His eyes were on the TV, scanning the series available. Mindlessly scrolling once more. Only a beep from his phone jarred him back to full consciousness. Rosie.

Being emotionally cushioned by alcohol, he was able to open her message without too much worry. It was the weekend. Her power over him was dormant until Monday.

Stewart. This is your first friendly reminder. FILL OUT THE HOUSE FORMS. You've had them for over 24 hours. The sooner you do them, the sooner I can get things moving. There's no reason this has to drag on. No chain and eager buyers so it's all down to you. I shall be providing friendly reminders on a daily basis until I have them in my possession. Enjoy your Friday night.

Fuck off Rosie, he thought. *The office is closed.*
A full day had passed, but seeing the job advert on her desk still jolted. If she were leaving, she had no

business involving herself in his evening.

He was convinced he was right but that fact made little difference in the end. Against his will, he found himself moving. He continued to curse her as he took his drink to the study and found the original forms in the pile on the desk. Chunnering under his breath, he leaned back in the chair and scanned his eyes over the first page. *Bloody Rosie. You can't control me. I'm not your employee.*

The first page was standard. It asked for the names and addresses of the parties concerned. He knew those without looking them up. As he carried on his one-sided argument with the spirit of Rosie that lived in his head, he found himself reach for his document pen. Then he was pulling the office chair towards the desk and then he was making a start. All against his will. *Damn you, Rosie.*

There were a couple of clues that this particular set of forms would not be the ones delivered into Rosie's hands on Monday. The overenthusiastic placing down of his glass on the table gave the first hint. A splash of whisky landed on his father's postcode, obscuring the last two letters. His hasty wipe and the ensuing smudge didn't give off a good impression. That alone hadn't stopped him. He had kept going, right up until he spelt *Yorkshire* incorrectly. Being the second word of the county he had resided in his entire life, this came as a something of a surprise. But he drew a neat line through the extra squiggle and initialled the change. It looked clumsy and along with the whisky smudge, didn't show him in the best light. But he'd seen much worse over the years, so kept going.

One page down, seven to go. Legal documents

might be gobbledygook to some but he had lived and breathed them for decades. He would have this boxed off in no time.

Another swig of booze, and onto Page Two. He looked down the list of basic fixtures and fittings. A tick was required to indicate whether each feature was included or excluded in the sale price. It was bog standard stuff. Stewart got his pen ready, keen to tick everything off and get back to scrolling Netflix.

The reality was not so simple. The first item listed caused him to pause. *Was there an immersion heater at the property?* How the hell would he know? Was that the same as the boiler? The abiding memory of his youth was that it was cold. Was there *no* boiler? Had it been heated by fires alone? He looked down the rest of the list. Was there roof insulation? Where were the carpets? What was the location of fitted units and light fittings? Whether he had suppressed the memories, or it was simply too long ago to recall, Stewart had no clue about any of it.

The rolling irritation he felt towards Rosie was overtaken by the realisation that he was going to have to put some effort into getting this done. This was not how he wanted his evening to pan out.

Stewart's anger came as a delayed reaction. It took time for it to push through the insulation of alcohol. Or maybe inebriation obstructed his view of the bigger picture. Either way, as the seconds passed and reality dawned, the anger fought through. From Rosie and the house sale, to the years he wasted doing everything his father demanded. The result of his death was that Stewart didn't know who he was or who he had ever been. His motivation to function had died along with his father. He had no idea what to do, how to act, or why he should bother in the first place.

He drained his glass and slammed it down, full of impotent fury. He breathed fire in a flame-resistant world. His rage held no power. It changed nothing and did nothing. He found himself standing at the desk, the forms becoming shreds in his fists. From his gut he roared aloud, to himself and to no one, all at once.

Moments later, when he became aware of himself again, Stewart flopped back into the chair. His outburst was over. He sat limply, catching his breath, before making the decision that had been inevitable since waking that morning. He picked up his coat and went to the pub.

CHAPTER TEN

Four months before the reunion

It was well into Saturday morning before Bea stirred from the face-down, starfish position in which she had slept. Her refusal to process anything immediately, meant the facts of her situation had to emerge in their own time.

There was pounding. Like a painful heartbeat, its thud-ache kept a constant rhythm. Upon tentative exploration, the slightest twitch caused all nerve endings to reach an unbearable cacophony. The message was clear. Movement was to be avoided. With that knowledge, came the second unwelcome sensation. Thirst. Like scorched desert earth, all moisture had evaporated. It had been there last night, but had left under mysterious circumstances. There was no handy oasis to provide refreshment. There was nothing at hand to irrigate and soothe. It was impossible to thrive under these conditions. An inhospitable environment for life.

That's what Bea's body was. Inhospitable for life. It has shut down for survival. An automatic response to the excessive abuse it had suffered in the hours before. In her semi-conscious state, she knew she felt awful but couldn't fathom why. That would come later. The post-match analysis should be saved for when she had mustered the strength to open her eyes. That wasn't happening any time soon. Her conscious mind was struggling. It was too much. She drifted in and out of awareness.

In her delirium, she imagined a team of lecturers inside her brain, leading students through a lesson in how not to misuse alcohol. *These are the clinical effects of trying to drown in gin. This is a textbook case of an emotional anaesthetic. Don't forget to make notes!* Her throat attempted to swallow but it was a struggle. The throb in her head intensified as her efforts went into the most basic of reflexive skills. This was not going to be the start of her day so she sank back into sleep. She would try again later.

Later turned out to be lunch time. Bea's head was still pounding but she managed to open her eyes. Not only that, but she made it out of bed and into her kitchen. It was a slow process but she got there. A pint of water, two soluble paracetamol, and a mug of tea were all placed on a tray. She carried it back to bed with enough shakes of her hands to spill both drinks, and then got back under the covers. She wasn't ready to do more than that. Not yet.

It had been a while since she had felt like this. Not even last week after her birthday had she felt so rough. Bea was no stranger to an epic hangover but this one was bad. She could still taste the blood orange gin in the back of her throat where its acidity had settled. It was a handy reminder of her main drink of choice last night. She should have made herself sick before falling asleep, but that ship had sailed. Doing it now would make her feel worse. She had to ride this out. Besides, she could handle the physical effects of the evening. She was used to the morning-after routine of a good night out. There was tea, stodgy food, and hours spent in pyjamas catching up with her TV planner. The day after a big night out was restorative, cosy, and part of the fun. Just not this time.

The physical aches and pains weren't the real issue. There was a new sensation that had come to play. Like a stranger standing too close, Bea felt unsettled by it. She knew it had a name. She had heard others talk of it, but it always missed her out. It knew she wasn't meant for it. Except today, here it was. Like the stranger too close, it was creeping up on her, and she didn't like it. She now understood what others had talked about. The universal hangover symptom of... The Fear.

The Fear was thriving most within her lack of memory. Her stomach lurched when she tried to piece together what had happened. Had she made a show of herself in front of her team? That wasn't really on these days. Not now she was in charge. They had gone for post-work drinks and she'd had a couple, but her plan was to move on after that. Did she move on? Yes! The other bar, but who with? Had there been flirting? Had she tried to kiss someone? God, she hoped not. Not now she was being the best girlfriend in the world and doing commitment. Had she had a row with anyone? Were there apologies to make today? Had she got too heated in a political debate or kicked off at someone for their causal sexism? That wouldn't usually bother her but something had gone on. She could tell. Something bad had happened. Her whole body told her so. The Fear was real.

She must have been conscious when she got into bed. She had woken up in an old T-shirt, with her clothes on the floor. The black and silver makeup on

the cotton pads in the bin told her she'd had the foresight to cleanse. That was good news. Not only for her
middle-aged skin that needed its nightly application of
moisture, but that there had been no burly taxi driver
or newly-found acquaintance to help her into bed.
Small mercies. She'd also had the presence of mind to
charge her phone, the last thing she did before turning
out the light. That routine was in-built too. More relief.
Except now she had to look at her phone. That's where
the clues to her evening would be found. She had to
summon the courage to look at the evidence and piece
it together. Her acidic throat and lurchy-stomach
joined forces to remind her that they were still there
and she wasn't out of the woods just yet.

Bea picked up her phone. Her finger hovered for a
second as she braced herself. *Rip off that plaster,
Charleston. Do it.* One deep breath later and she tapped
her photos. Scrolling fast initially, and with one eye
closed, she took it all in. It seemed all right. Maybe it
was safe to slow down and give the pictures a proper
look. Her finger continued to scroll. Nothing too
damning it seemed. A few selfies in the first bar by
work. A couple in the second place with... whatsher-
name from the sandwich shop. The memory of
bumping into the woman that made Bea's regular tuna
salad roll, came back to her. The picture of them both
grinning to the camera reassured Bea that Whatsher-
name had been as hammered as she was. The photo
was timestamped 21.09. Fair enough. That wasn't the
issue that was bugging her then. She kept scrolling.
There was a shaky shot by the taxi rank, and then
some of Kit's place. She had been to Kit's apartment?
That was new information. She had no recollection of

that. The photos were mostly accidental. A blurred section of coffee table here, then a bright flash against a window there. Nothing had been deliberately posed for but it was unmistakably her neighbour's living room. The first photo had been taken at 22.46 and the last at 00.28. What had that been about?

Bea leaned back against her pillows and breathed deeply. She would message Kit and apologise if she had been too drunk. It wasn't usually a problem. Kit barely slept and was happy for a nightcap whenever Bea was free. They had put the world to rights many a time, losing track of the clock and having 'just one more' until the bottle was empty. That'd be where the orange taste had come from. Kit stuck to gin but liked to experiment with flavours. Bea resolved to buy her a bottle of something suitably random as soon as she felt able to go into town. That could be a plan for later. She breathed again and reckoned she could be up and dressed within the next two hours. There was no point rushing. She had loads of time.

With that settled, Bea absentmindedly opened her notes. She kept a rolling shopping list stored there. Nothing too specific, but a list of things she needed the next time she went near the shops. She automatically opened the note that was titled BUY ME, and added *interesting gin* to a list whose recent additions included *daffodil leather jacket from Zara* and *milk*. She closed the list. It was done in an instant but something caught her eye. As she was about to close the app, she spotted another note. Underneath BUY ME there was a new instruction. READ ME. A fragment of a memory from the previous night bobbed around Bea's head as she did as she was told. It seemed Drunk Bea was bossy. Bossy, in full CAPS LOCK, and riddled with typos.

WHATEVR YOU DO, GIVE HIM SSPACE HE NEEDS TIME. DO NOT CROWD HIM. LET HIM SORT TIT OUT AND GET BACK TO YOU. HE WIL CALL WHEN HE CAN. THIS IS BIG DEAL AND EVEN THOUGH YOU DON'T FEEL IS REALLY, IT DOESNT' MEAN IT NOT .LET HIM COME BAK WHEN READY. IT ISNT HIS FAULT ABOUT POPPY. ITS' BAD TIMING. HE NEEDS DO WHAT HE NEEDS DO. COUNT THE PLACES! COUNT THE PLACES!!!!!!

Bea groaned loudly. Most of it made sense. Not the urging to count the places. That meant nothing. But everything else flooded back. Poppy. Of course. The call had come through yesterday afternoon. She had answered it in her office, wondering what lovely, sexy things Mal was going to whisper from his work phone. As soon as she heard him speak, she knew something was wrong. *I need a bit of time*. Those were the words he used. *I need a bit of time*. He was full of apologies, of course. It couldn't be helped, but he would make it up to her as soon as he could. She believed him. Or at least, she believed that he meant it. The fact that she was struggling with his need for time away in the first place was the issue that was bugging her. It must be why she had made it her mission to get as drunk as she could, in the shortest amount of time possible. Bloody Poppy. And whilst she'd had no firm plans with Mal this weekend, she knew they'd have seen each other at some point. They always did. He'd find a few minutes to call, and then arrange to come around. Her place, never his. That was how they did things. She assumed that would be the case this weekend too, but then he called and told her about Poppy. Bloody Poppy.

Mal's voice had shaken when he told her. It had surprised her that it affected him that much. It was to be expected really. She knew that. After all, Poppy had died. Bea didn't want to diminish the power of grief, and she knew that lots of people felt differently than she did on the matter, but she was still surprised that Mal had asked for space. Poppy was a dog. Just a dog. She had managed to avoid uttering that line on the phone, but it was how she felt. She wasn't an animal person. The fact it now seemed that she was seeing someone who was, had been jarring. His dog has died, and that meant he needed space away from the person he was seeing. It didn't make sense. She could have been there to make everything better, to support him in his time of sadness. Instead, he had realised she was not the person to do that. He clearly recognised a non-dog person when he saw them. He didn't want to be around Bea and her lack of empathy, so he preferred to shut himself off from her, and wallow alone in his empty house.

That was the scenario Bea was forcing herself to imagine. That was the ideal situation she was telling herself. The real truth was less incomprehensible. She just didn't like it. Even when the first of her suspicions had arisen, Bea had chosen to push them away. She had ignored her gut for weeks. After last night's bomb-shell, she no longer had that luxury.

Poppy, the family dog, had died. Mal's kids were

devastated. He and his wife were focusing on spending time together as a family. A family that, apart from Dad's punishing work schedule that kept him away quite a bit, was as happy as it had ever been. Poppy the dog had died and the family were spending quality time together, making sure all other distractions were minimal.

The main distraction, the one that took up all of Mal's spare time, sank back into her bed and pulled the pillow over her head. It seemed Bea wasn't ready to get up after all.

CHAPTER ELEVEN

Without the hint of a fuzzy head in sight, Tilda had risen from a good night's sleep. The temping job was into its fifth week. Easy work, if not a little dull. Not that she minded, of course. Dull was fine. And five weeks of paid employment had shifted Tilda's perspective. Obviously there was the financial relief. The fact that she could leave her savings alone, eased the worry that never left. But that wasn't the only change her work schedule provided. What had become clear, from the first week of the university admin placement, was that she had begun to look forward to the weekend again.

Now her extended holiday was over and she had re-joined the human race, she could mentally share in the collective apathy of the last office hour of a Friday. She could experience the communal high that leaving work for the weekend automatically brought. The five day countdown was real. And it wasn't just the Friday feeling either. A lazy Saturday morning with only the radio for company, was a thrill. The past week had seen Tilda spend hours a day shredding files that had long since been digitised. Her back had ached from hours of standing, so seeing the clock reach 5pm on the previous afternoon had been welcome. And now it was Saturday morning. Her plan had been to lie in bed as long as she could. She wanted to luxuriate in the lack of need to be somewhere for a specific time. Work was done and she wanted to relax.

The reality turned out a little differently. Tilda woke naturally at 6.45am without the aid of her alarm.

She lay there, attempting to drift off again, but the gulls and waves had other ideas. They were relentless. By the time her seagull stalker began his window-tapping shift, she gave up. By half past eight she found herself strolling along the front with the dog-walkers and joggers, and everyone else that had been forced out of bed before they were ready. It wasn't a bad thing really. It wouldn't do her aches and pains any harm to walk them out in the fresh air. But it reinforced her powerlessness and lack of control over her own life. Nothing new there.

The morning weather was pleasant. Nowhere near the stifling heat of summer but a long way from the windswept bluster of winter. Tilda's hoody remained wrapped around her waist the entire time. She felt hopeful that this weekend would be a good one.

'Morning Alun. All right?'

A man over the road was shouting to the dog-walker ahead of her. His dog was on an extendable lead and had sniffed its way towards Tilda as she had followed them both.

'Good Bryn, thanks. Hold on. I'll come to you.'

The man retracted the lead and organised his dog as he waited to cross the road. By the time Tilda passed their position, both men were in full chat mode on the other side. Locals. Part of the community. That was what Tilda wanted. It was what she had missed during her transient months. One day, someone might call *her* from across the road. It didn't matter that she had yet to make friends with anyone. It was still early days. She was hopeful.

As she reached the end of the prom and turned around to retrace her route, Tilda made a mental *To*

Do list. Once upon a time, micro-managing the day was her way of survival. Now she simply wanted to make the most of her weekend. And the first thing would be to wash her bed linen. Strictly speaking that should be classed as a chore, but with the weather being so amenable for sheet drying, it would be a crime to miss out. And everyone knew that fresh bedding was the best thing in the world. That was job number one. No brainer.

As she fantasised about her washing line, Tilda passed one of the bars that faced the sea. It had a name she assumed was Welsh and she wasn't comfortable attempting to pronounce. She didn't want to cause any offence. A man, probably a student, was unstacking chairs and arranging them around outdoor tables. It looked like somewhere she would have once enjoyed. Small but modern. Large glass windows but dimly lit inside. If she ever made a friend, she would suggest a drink in that bar.

Tilda's mind turned to food. She didn't need to go shopping as she had stocked up in the week. But the thought of her uber-sensible haddock and veg didn't appeal as much as it had when she'd bought it. That would do tomorrow. Today she wanted something frivolous. Something befitting the weekend. Tilda quickened her pace as she made her plan. She'd go to the little Tesco on her way back.

Ten minutes later, Tilda had a basket in hand and was working her way around the aisles. Now that her campervan days were over, old pleasures had returned. Pleasures like cooking. She had tried to cook on the road as often as she could. She hadn't wanted to pile on the pounds with daily Ginsters just because her kitchen circumstances were reduced. It took a bit of creative thinking, but the tiny gas hob and microwave had been adequate. It was true that there had been more ready meals along the way than she'd have liked. Some days the four-minute wait for the *ding* was more than enough to deal with. But then there were other evenings. Times when she'd made the effort to make chilli from scratch. Stirring the pan of seasoned mince until it was cooked through, meant the gratification was truly delayed. The best kind of gratification in her opinion. But even though she'd kept up her standards during her travels, the knowledge that she now had a real kitchen meant that food had taken up much more importance. Tilda had vowed she would never again refer to *beans on toast as* an evening meal. Breakfast or lunch, yes. But not for tea. Not anymore.

Her reminiscences had taken her down each aisle and through all the items on her mental list. Now she had arrived at the till where a man she recognised was scanning her shopping. His name was Iwan. She knew that because someone had said, *'Hey Iwan'* when she had been there before. He also wore a name tag to confirm this, although Tilda felt proud that she hadn't needed to see that to remember.

Tilda assumed Iwan was a student, in the same way she assumed the man outside the bar had been too. In a University town the odds were in her favour. Out of nowhere, a flash of a memory from her own student days filled her brain. Freya, Jonathan and Dhanesh, in fancy dress, getting thrown out of a pub. Had it been Jen's twenty-first? Was Tilda there or had she been told about it later? It was too vague to pin down. A million years in the past; a lifetime ago.

With no gang of mates to corroborate or refute her flashback, her attention returned to the Tesco till. Maybe Iwan could be one of her wingpeople. She was still concerned about her lack of backup in a personal emergency. Iwan and his shelf-stacking skills might be called upon to save the day.

'Are you all right for bags?'

Tilda's daydream was interrupted by the not-unexpected question from the guy she was currently facing.

'No, I need one, thanks.' She cursed herself for not having the foresight to include a *bag for life* on her spur of the moment walk.

'Do you need any help packing?'

'No thanks, I'm fine.'

Iwan scanned each item. Barely moving as he passed the deli items over the red light, he did the courtesy of throwing her a glance as he scanned the wine. It took a millisecond to see that yes, she was over eighteen and no, he would not be contravening any laws by selling her alcohol. He gazed away once more.

'Twelve pounds, thirty-two.'

Tilda rooted in her purse for the twenty she knew was in one of the slots. Finding it, she smoothed it out and passed it to an increasingly bored looking Iwan.

'Seven, sixty-eight change.'

She took the money and picked up the bag.

'Thanks, bye.'

'Bye.'

Tilda walked back along the seafront towards her apartment. Cheeses, garlic prawns and bread, all washed down with a glass of white wine. It was something to look forward to, along with the clean sheets, and the usual Saturday night TV. There were definite challenges about moving to a new town alone, but she was getting there. And now, after her chat with Iwan, she had spoken to another human being that day. *Good for Iwan and his banter. Good for Iwan being the only person to say hello to me today.* She couldn't remember if he actually had said hello, but it didn't matter. *Good for Iwan for giving me a bit of human interaction and companionship for two and a half minutes. Good for Iwan and good for me.*

CHAPTER TWELVE

Stewart's lack of commitment towards the working week meant Saturday mornings were as dull as any other. Even with yesterday's news, he felt nothing. Was he as dead inside as he'd always presumed? There must be *some* effect on him? He wasn't sure whether he should expect a positive or negative slant to his mood, but he thought there'd be *something*. Anything. Instead it was the usual. His old drinking buddies of apathy and indifference. He was numb.

The previous day had seen the exchange of contracts of his father's house. The big house on the hill was no longer his problem. The home of his childhood was sold. The Cooper-Jones', whoever the hell they were, could move in and make all the cold, detached memories they liked. As much as his head told him this was a significant step, his heart and gut were yet to climb onboard.

Rosie was excited though. Her constant weeks of nagging were the only reason the sale had happened. Her phone call last night held all the glory of victory and triumph against the odds.

'*Stewart. Are you sitting down?*'

'*No.*'

'*Sit down.*'

'*Rosie, I'm getting a drink.*'

'*Do it.*'

Stewart had sighed, pretended he was moving when he wasn't, and then lied.

'*Right. I'm sitting down. Go on.*'

'*It went through.*'

'*What did?*'

'*The house. The sale. It went through. In record time, too. The money's in your bank. It's done. Can you believe it? It's all done for you.*'

Stewart had heard the excitement in her voice. She was thrilled for him. The phrase '*It's all done for you*' held a double meaning, of course. That over-long chapter of his life could be put to bed. It was finished and closure could begin. That was one way of looking at it. Alternatively, she could have meant, *I have done it all for you.* The unspoken afterthought to that was, *you lazy sod.* She might have meant it either way, but he took the latter interpretation. She *had* done it all for him. That was true. It was also true that Rosie thought he was a *completely* lazy sod. No question about it. He sighed and accepted the criticism he assumed she was sending his way. It would be more than deserved if Rosie thought so.

He had tried his best to convey appreciation, but it was beyond him. She was happy that her house-selling project had reached a successful climax. He was glad for her, knowing that it mattered to her Completer-Finisher personality. He just couldn't care less. He tried but struggled to find the words.

'*That's good news Rosie. Thanks for letting me know. I'm glad it went through for you. Was there anything else?*'

He knew it wasn't enough when he said it. He knew *he* wasn't enough. He never stopped getting it wrong. She sighed audibly before replying.

'*No, Stewart. There was nothing else. I thought the news was enough for a call all on its own. Have a good weekend.*'

She hung up before he could reply. His response had been inadequate - he got that - but he didn't know what else to do. She wanted him to be ecstatic that a part of his life that had been closed off long ago, was now over to everyone else. It was official rather than seemingly so. She wanted him to emote, to be moved... to feel. She was wasting her time. He hadn't *felt* for as long as he could remember.

There was also, of course, the unspoken business of her job search. He hadn't forgotten the wave of nausea when he'd seen the circled ad on her desk. When he had given it some proper thought, he had wondered whether she'd left it there deliberately. Was she trying to piss him off, or kick start a salary renegotiation? He had pretended he hadn't seen it. He would wait for her to bring it up. There would be a request for a meeting somewhere down the line which would result in him asking her to stay. He could picture it now.

'Stewart, I've scheduled a meeting for us. You're free tomorrow at two, so we'll do it then, yes?'

'What's it for?'

'I'll email you the agenda. That way we'll have both have a record that it's been sent.'

She would turn up with a list of demands, all of which he would pretend to dismiss until ultimately conceding to every single one. He had planned ahead, to be prepared when the time came. He wouldn't be caught off guard and could appear in control throughout the process.

In the end, it hadn't happened. Not so far, anyway. Rosie had not called a meeting, she had not asked for more money, and she had done nothing other than her usual high standard of work. He was starting to think he had imagined the ad. Or perhaps she had found it for a colleague. Maybe she was being helpful for a friend. Maybe one day in the future he'd summon up the courage to ask.

The rest of the day continued to be unremarkable, up until an hour before Stewart decided to call it a night. He had spent the evening in the pub, pretending to watch highlights of a football match he didn't care about. He still felt nothing from the house sale but found himself thinking about it nonetheless. Somewhere along the walk back to his apartment, his business brain kicked in. He should check his bank balance. If there had been a problem with the money transfer, it should be sorted straight away. His walk home continued with a bit more purpose.

Twenty minutes later, he was inside, pouring a malt and logging on to his account. The balance was as it should be. A huge amount of money to have in one place, even for someone as financially secure as he was. Money had never been an issue for him. He'd grown up having everything he'd ever needed, in terms of financial support and belongings. An unloving primary caregiver, however, had really dimmed the shine from any toy, or in later years, computer, car, or career he had asked for. At the time he hadn't known any better. By the time he did, the damage was done.

The laptop screen illuminated the room as his bank account provided a flare amidst the darkness. Stewart marvelled at the size of the sum. A little less than the asking price but a life-changing amount nonetheless. It was far too much money to have in one place. His pension man should really be involved. He tapped a note into his phone. *Email Richard*. He might get around to doing that this week. If he could muster the energy.

Stewart leaned back on the office chair and drained his glass. His mind was struggling to focus. He tried to think about ISAs and investment plans but found his mind wandering towards less practical thoughts. All that money for a house. Bricks, mortar, and emptiness. Nothing more. He had paid a visit a few weeks ago, to fill in Rosie's forms. It hadn't changed. It was still freezing. He'd kept his coat on the entire time. And no matter how many lights switches he flipped, the house could not shake its air of gloom. He felt nothing. Just a tightness inside, where his emotional response should have been.

Stewart felt his eyes prickle. He pushed back the chair and returned to the whisky bottle. A refill later and he was back. The money was still lit up on the screen. A huge amount superficially yet very little in reality. No price could be put on his memories. His mind flashed back to his visit.

It has been the central staircase that did it. He had numbly got on with his form-filling task, through each room of the ground floor. Dispassionately opening cupboards and counting sockets. It had taken no time and he hoped the upper floors would be as simple. But then he climbed the stairs. *Second from the bottom, left hand side*. He had a split-second's warning as his subconscious threw him a bone. The creak was instantly recognisable. He was thrown into a slew of memories. Of creeping downstairs, leading his little brother to the silent steps. Of making it as far as the bottom before being spotted. Of feeling the exhilaration of the post-bedtime adventure and the lessons learnt for the next one. *Second stair from the bottom, left hand side*, he would dictate later, as his brother dutifully noted the pitfall.

Thirty years later, Stewart, may have successfully remembered the staircase route, but he felt punched in the gut. It all came back. The playroom where they'd shared their adventures, the water fights in the garden, the hushed giggles of the Grady boys as they ran around the hallways. All in the past. All dead. He'd sunk to the floor on the top step and sobbed. For his brother and for himself, all while continuing to believe he felt nothing.

Stewart swigged his drink to steady himself, knowing the uninvited memories were here for the night. He had carried unspoken grief for John longer than John had been alive. No one had known the truth. The secret of his brother's final moments had been kept for decades. Until the day his father died. And then he met Tilda. His brother's girlfriend. The woman he had known would appear one day. She had found him at the exact moment he needed to talk. And he *had* talked. He told her everything. Long suppressed feelings, childhood memories, he had shared it all. And when she returned home, there had been emails. He had sent her John's coat to keep as a memento. He had told her he'd like to keep in touch and remember John with her – or as she knew him, Grady. He had meant it too. He fully intended to be a good person. He would reply to her emails and share a friendship with her.

Stewart's glass was empty but so was the bottle. He reflected on how his good intentions had petered out.

He checked his emails. His last message to Tilda Willoughby had been eighteen months ago. It was a brief reply to something she had sent him. He didn't need anyone to tell him that wasn't good enough. He should have been better. There had been many times in his life that Stewart had behaved badly, especially towards women, but Tilda was different. She wasn't a casual fuck, or a holiday fling. She had been special to John, which automatically meant she was special to Stewart. He just had no idea how to convey that to another human being.

Perhaps if he hadn't finished the bottle, Stewart's evening would have ended with him turning off the laptop and drinking himself to sleep. Instead he went a different way. Out of nowhere, Rosie's words echoed around his head.

'Come back to work. Or sell up. Or work part time on set days. Or officially retire. It's completely your choice. We just need some clarity.'

An idea popped into his head. He knew what he should do. From out of nowhere, his thoughts were unobscured and blur-free. He didn't stop to question his plan, but instead opened a new email message. He wanted to do right by his brother. He wanted to feel something.

Dear Tilda,
I think I need to see you...

Stewart typed quickly until he got everything off his chest. He let it all come out. It was therapeutic. He was *doing* something instead of numbly opting out.

Once it was written, he didn't bother to read it back. He would only chicken out. He pressed *send* before he could change his mind. Then he staggered over to the settee, collapsing in a heap and falling asleep within minutes. A sleep that was a little easier to reach what with the slight lifting of an emotional weight.

The lifting of an emotional weight and the copious amounts of alcohol. That too.

CHAPTER THIRTEEN

Her headache had eased. That was the one upside to which Bea was clinging. The unrelenting sensation of a boot-wearing sadist repeatedly kicking her temples, had finally gone. One day on and all that was left was a slight fuzziness, as well as an inexplicable urge to cry. Earlier, she'd found herself blubbing at an episode of *Columbo.* It hadn't been sad but she'd welled up and let herself go with it. The Fear was strong and, it seemed, multi-faceted. Emotional breakdowns were part of its power. All she could do was wait for its end.

She remembered the ease with which she could bounce back in her younger days. A good breakfast, a hot shower and she'd be as good as new. At the first suggestion of another drink, she would have been ready to hit the town. These days, the recovery period was essential rather than desirable, and lasted much longer.

Despite that, the previous day hadn't been a total write-off. She had managed to make it to the shops. Unwashed, wearing a hoody and old yoga pants, she had shuffled along to the Bargain Booze and bought the replacement gin for Kit, as well as picking up some suitably stodgy comfort food for herself. Today, as she was less delicate all round, she had managed to make it to the shower. Hangover or no hangover, anxiety or no anxiety, she was on the mend. Things were getting back to normal. Except of course they weren't. Things were not normal. Not anymore.

Mal was married. Mal had kids. Mal was spending time with his family as they mourned a dead dog. Bea's headache had eased but her head still throbbed.

As Columbo and his mac did their thing over back-to-back Sunday episodes, Bea lay on the sofa and read through the messages he had sent. He hadn't cut off all contact. Just the face-to-face kind. He had messaged her repeatedly over the last twenty-four hours. He wanted to make sure she understood his situation.

It's been over for a long time. Dead. We're in a sort of limbo because of the children. We don't communicate unless it's about them. If they've done their homework, what date is sports day, who's giving them a lift to football, that kind of thing. I didn't realise how stifling it was until I met you. You have shown me there's more to life than basic functioning. I want to live again. I want to feel happiness again. I know you're the one to help me. Please know I meant every word I said to you. You're the only person who's ever made me feel this way.

She scrolled down. Her replies had been polite. Kind but brief. He took their brevity for anger and had responded with a view to winning her over.

I promise I never meant to lead you on. It happened so fast and took me by surprise. I was only looking for a distraction and some fun. Something to make everything less grim. I had no idea I was going to fall for you. Please give me time. I want to sort things out and do everything right.

Bea wasn't stupid. She had suspected Mal wasn't being entirely honest about his home life for a while.

Mainly because he changed the subject every time she asked about it. It didn't take Columbo to sniff out the clues. Along with the lack of flexibility over which days he could meet, and the request to only call him at work, it was all fairly obvious. At least it was now. Back then, she had preferred to give him the benefit of the doubt. Repeatedly.

She thought back to her birthday. He had spent the whole day with her, both of them living out a *Pretty Woman* shopping spree fantasy that had filled hours.

'*You look stunning. But how about a calmer colour? Something sophisticated. Ah, sorry, it's the office, I need to get this.*'

His phone had rung constantly. She had smiled and pretended it was fine. Well, it *was* a work day. There was nothing wrong with colleagues needing his input now and then. At the time she had been more irritated by his animal print ban - the clothes were for her birthday, not his - but even so, his constant work calls had become annoying. But they hadn't been work calls. She knew that now.

Columbo looked hard at his suspect and waited. He knew he was guilty and so did the viewers. The opening scenes had been full of the grisly murder and there was no doubt who was responsible. Bea tuned out Peter Falk and thought back to her first date with Mal. She had probably suspected it then. Deep down. Had it been a TV movie, the viewers would have watched Mal leave the bar and return to his wife whilst Bea floated home full of lust and denial. She *must* have known, somewhere inside. None of that mattered now. Even with her gut instinct telling her he might be in a relationship, it hadn't been enough to stop her arranging a second date. It hadn't been enough to put her off. He wasn't a monster, just flawed and fallible like everyone else. Besides, she was in the same predicament. She had only been looking for fun too. She hadn't been in the market for anything more serious. No one was as surprised as she was, when it became the soppy fuzz it was now. Damn Poppy and her unexpected death. They could have carried on pretending everything was fine, if it hadn't been for that... bitch.

Her phone pinged.

Just returning your missed call. Everything OK? I'm free to chat if you want. Or message again. Tilda x

Bea smiled. Not just at the contact from her friend, but at the way she signed instant messages like they were letters. *Good old Tilda. Never change.* Bea was glad of the distraction and returned her call. Hearing her calming tones down the line made her feel better, although she found herself explaining her fragile state as soon as the opening pleasantries were over.

'Darling, I'm hungover and hormonal in Heald Green. It's bleak.'

'Poor you. What did you do last night?'

'Not last night. Friday! This weekend has been a struggle.'

'Blimey, Friday? Were you out with work?'

Bea cast her mind back to the fog of two days ago.

'I'm a changed person these days. I still go out for Friday drinks, but scarper after two.'

'Really? What about your FOMO?'

'Partying with the kids isn't as much fun now Tan Tights isn't there to unite against. Now they're united against me. I'm happy to let them crack on without me.'

Bea thought back to her predecessor, whose frumpy shade of hosiery had provided her with a nickname that had stuck. Poor Susan. Doing her job had given Bea a whole new appreciation of her former boss.

'You know what they call me?'

'You've got a nickname?'

'I overheard Jeff when they didn't know I'd come in early. He said, 'Better get that sorted before *Queen Bea* sees it.'

'Queen Bea?'

'Yeah! Queen Bea. Can you imagine? I glowed for the rest of the day.' Bea beamed. She'd felt a genuine thrill to hear it.

Tilda laughed down the phone.

'It's definitely more empowering than Tan Tights was for Susan.'

'Exactly. And I *am* a queen. I should make them kneel when they want something signing.'

'Who did you end up with on Friday? The gang?'

Back in their office days, Tilda would lap up stories of Bea's long-term female friends. Some mates from school and some from the early work years. A bunch of pals that had been through everything together. Bea soon realised Tilda didn't have any female friendships of her own. It was around that time she had made a concerted effort to befriend Timid Tilda, and show her the ways of the world.

'To be honest, it's been ages since I've seen them. Lou's IVF finally worked so she's up to her eyes in nappies. Twins at 48! Last time I saw her, she looked knackered. And the rest of them are all mad busy with kids and teenagers and husbands. Or wives in Emma's case. Some of us manage coffee or lunch now and then but nights out are rare. The last one was Nat's divorce party.'

'Wow. That's changed. You were inseparable.'

'Yeah.' Bea stopped talking. Her friends were still her friends. She knew that. But being asked how they were doing was jarring. She didn't know. Months would pass before someone would try to coordinate a date to suit everyone's hectic lifestyle. It was always a logistical challenge. The days of weekly drinks were long gone. Now she was left with horrific hangovers, the menopause and the arrival of The Fear. Getting older was less fun than she had planned it to be. Why had no one warned her?

Before she got too reflective, Tilda dragged her back to their conversation.

'And how's the lovely Mal? Still perfect?'

Bea paused. She trusted Tilda, and knew she would try to be supportive, no matter what. But she also knew that there was no way she could share that Mal was married without hearing suppressed disapproval in her friend's voice. It was best to keep that detail to herself. At least until a time she could explain things properly. She changed the subject. Not unlike the way Mal would have done when Bea asked him about his living arrangements.

'He's great, yeah. We're good. But forget about him for now. I was ringing for another reason.'

'OK. Sounds ominous.'

'No, it's a good thing. I've had an idea. An absolute belter.'

It hadn't taken Bea long to outline her plan. The thought had come to her during the previous day's horizontal slump. Happily, it appeared, Tilda was open to the idea. When Bea finally hung up, she couldn't stop grinning. All it had taken was a phone call, but she felt way less mixed up inside. She had been reminded of who she was, what she wanted, and what she was doing next. And what she was doing next, it appeared, was to plan out her epic idea now that Tilda was onboard. She could spend the next few hours doing that, whilst her subconscious processed what she thought about Mal.

What *did* she think about Mal? She had no idea. Except, of course she did. She missed him. She was struggling to work herself up into the outrage she knew a woman in her position was supposed to feel. Mal was in an unhappy marriage and he wanted out. She was supposed to feel used. She was supposed to feel anger at his lies. Except he hadn't lied. He had evaded having to do that. His relationship with his wife sounded terminal. It couldn't be easy living in an unhappy home, having to fake positivity in front of children. Bea had never felt a fraction for anyone the way she felt about Mal, even when his opinions were at odds with her own. He had made her want more. He had made her want commitment. That fact alone, made him seem worth the hassle.

That was enough thinking for the day. Between her

friends she never saw, the angst of her frustrated love, and the lingering remnants of Friday's excess, Bea could have spent the final hours of the weekend in a slump. Instead, she made a cup of tea - forgetting for the twentieth time that she had moved her kettle in her recent kitchen rejig. Then she curled up with her laptop, opened a Word Doc. and typed *Bea and Tilda's Exciting Plan*. This was exactly what she needed right now. Poppy the Dog, and all who mourned her, could have as much space as they wanted.

CHAPTER FOURTEEN

Three months before the reunion

From the safety of the station platform, with the knowledge she was leaving town for the night, Tilda opened her emails and scanned the one that made her stomach ache.

> *Dear Tilda,*
> I think I need to see you. No, it's more than that. I HAVE to see you. I've got lots of decisions to make, and I need your help. If John were alive, he'd be involved with all this. I'd be splitting the burden with him. But he isn't. So I'm not. When are you free? Things are going to shit up here. I don't trust the people I've always relied on. Everybody leaves me but I can still trust you. When are you available? Everything is a mess. I can come to you. Or you could come here. I don't mind. I wish I could talk to John. I need you to help me. Can we meet? Anytime. Whenever you're free. As soon as you can.
> *Stewart*

She had no cutlery that she could count. The cringe of awkwardness that began to rise had to be kept at bay. She stood with her bag at her feet as her mind scanned for an alternative.

A month's a long time in pest control.

Tilda sighed with relief. The line popped into her head from nowhere. It had once been said by the Chief Exec, with a straight face and zero inclination for comedy. Uttered at a meeting years ago, in reference to a problem whose origin had long been forgotten. *A month's a long time in pest control.* It had become a punchline in the office for months afterwards.

'The photocopier's out of toner?'

'A month's a long time in pest control.'

'How many weeks till the end of the financial year?'

'A month's a long time in pest control.'

'They didn't have cheese and ham so I got you plain cheese.'

'A month's a long time in pest control.'

Tilda inhaled and repeated the line to herself. Her feelings about the email were back in their box. A month *was* a long time in pest control but her wobble was contained once more.

The previous month had either flown by or dragged depending on Tilda's mood. Until Bea's grand plan, life had continued with its gentle monotony. But the last few weeks had been different. She'd had something new to think about. Alongside the walks and the books, Tilda had scoured Trip Advisor. She had looked at train timetables. She had restocked her toiletries bag. It wouldn't have been everyone's choice for a fun Saturday afternoon but she had enjoyed the task of filling mini plastic bottles with shampoo and shower gel, all ready to pack. With a new event on her calendar, the month had felt unpredictable and exciting. That was, apart from those moments when she opened her inbox. Her inbox containing Stewart's email. When she remembered that, time seemed to crawl.

Now she was standing at the station, she marvelled at the speed Bea had put the details together. Bea and Tilda's Adventure hadn't taken long to organise at all.

According to the online map, Birmingham was the most central, rail-connected place for them to have a night on the town. The day after their phone call, Tilda had checked her calendar and sent Bea a couple of weekend dates that would be best for her. It went without saying that all weekend dates were best for her. She also knew Bea would know that, but she had appreciated the pretence. The only notes on Tilda's calendar had been the following month's Chip Shop Night, and the probable date of her next period. *Rock and roll, Tilda. You social animal, you.*

Bea had replied immediately. It was sorted. Tilda received a forwarded hotel confirmation, along with screenshots and links to cheap train tickets. Since then, there had been regular contact. Tilda's phone would buzz at all hours, with a restaurant review or a bar that Bea insisted they must try. She appeared to be on a mission and Tilda was glad of it. She wondered what Mal was doing while all this was going on but knew better than to ask. This was what Bea enjoyed - alleviating work boredom with a fun side-project. It was her detective work that had been the catalyst for Tilda's meeting with Stewart Grady. The meeting where she had learnt the truth about his brother. The meeting that had kick-started her mid-life gap year and had led her to embark on this brand-new life she was incubating.

Tilda swallowed down the lump in her throat. This was meant to be a weekend of fun. Bea and Tilda's Birmingham Adventure was here! Hurrah. She blinked away memories, and focused on the announcement screen. The arrival of the 1130 train to Birmingham

New Street was delayed by fourteen minutes. They were sorry for any inconvenience. She found a bench on the platform.

It wasn't only Bea's planning that had taken Tilda back in time. Stewart's email was another blast from the past that had to be dealt with soon. It had arrived a month ago. Still current; still active. It couldn't be filed because she hadn't decided what to do with it.

She had opened it with trepidation. She always did with his emails. Stewart was a virtual stranger, yet someone with a remarkable physical resemblance to Grady - the man in the frame on her mantlepiece. It wasn't his fault, but it unsettled her. She remembered their only meeting as a numb blur. The pain had hit later. What had been clear, however, was their mutual desire to keep in touch. They were the only people in the world that knew Grady, and so that meant they needed each other.

But real-life kicked in. The emails became briefer before drying up completely. There had been no contact for months. It was sad but understandable. Beyond Grady, they had nothing in common. Looking back, Tilda had not felt comfortable around Stewart. His emptiness scared her. He might have looked like Grady, but that was where the similarity ended. When their short-lived email relationship drifted away, she was relieved. Yet eighteen months later and it was all back on. Stewart wanted to meet. There had been no ambiguity to his rambling sentiments. He had made his feelings blatantly clear and been aggressive as hell in the process.

She looked at her phone again. It was still there. It would be there until she decided what to do. Her stomach lurched. She swallowed and breathed. *A month's a long time in pest control. A month's a long time in pest control.*

The arrival of the train signalled that the fourteen minute delay was over. Tilda made her way to the platform's edge. The journey would provide plenty of time to work out what she should do. Staring at scenery as she sped through the countryside might provide some clarity. It might also give her a headache. She would arrive for her first night out in two years feeling angstridden and depressed. She couldn't spend all that time brooding. It wouldn't be healthy. Yet to ignore Stewart for much longer was making her feel bad. She needed a solution.

Tilda settled on a compromise. She pulled out her headphones and chose an album she had downloaded to her phone. It was an acoustic set by Bob Dylan. Grady had introduced her to his music when she was a student and it had been the soundtrack to her post-Mike life. As she wedged her case in the rack and took her seat by the window, she felt a little happier with things. She wasn't dismissing the problem of Stewart completely. Listening to his brother's favourite music was recognition that he existed and she would work out what to do soon enough.

The train left Aberystwyth and she was on her way. The lyrics to *Like a Rolling Stone* seemed particularly pertinent but Tilda tuned them out. The melodies were what she clung to, what anchored her. Tilda the stone, rolled along, onwards and upwards towards Bea. Towards her first night out in forever.

CHAPTER FIFTEEN

All they had done was choose a seat. It was the vision of Tilda hoisting herself up on the barstool that had done it. Bea had been in uncontrollable giggles ever since. She watched Tilda make several attempts before being fully seated. Then she had promptly collapsed in her own hysterical fit too. Bea had offered her a hand but that had only intensified their laughter. All the while, they could see the bartender watching from afar. His patience was verging on passive-aggressive as he waited for them to calm down before taking their order. Once his back was turned, Bea commented with her loudest whisper.

'Bless him, he's too young to have to deal with us. Two middle-aged women on an afternoon piss-up? He needs danger money. He needs PPE.'

Tilda nodded in agreement, taking seriously the very real hazard the young man could be in if they sat at the bar all day.

In the half-hour since they had met at New Street, they had checked into their hotel, dumped their bags, and were now hitting the hotel bar like they were characters in *Sex and the City*. Bea needed no help to recognise who was Charlotte and who was Samantha.

'Is this really the first time you've been in a bar since you left Manchester? I couldn't tell if you were joking before.' Bea had been thinking about this since they arrived.

'Yes. At least, the first time I've been to a bar like this. An *evening* one. When I was travelling, I sat in a few campsite beer-gardens when the weather was warm. And there's an open-air place on the prom near the flat. I had a cup of tea there once.'

'There will be no tea today. It's cocktails and shots for the rest of the night!' Bea raised her fist in the air to emphasise her point. At that moment the bartender arrived.

'Two Cosmopolitans, ladies?'

'That's us, thanks. Tilda, you will love it. I know you weren't keen but think of me as your constant horizon broadener. You can get wine for the next round.'

The man placed both glasses on the table. Bea took a sip of her drink and punched the air.

'Yes! That's perfect. Tilds, get it down your neck. Our adventure has begun.'

The bartender, despite having to move suddenly, managed to sidestep Bea's emphatic gesture and picked up his tray unscathed. An embarrassed looking Tilda offered apologies as the young man forced a smile and went back to the bar. His expression was professional but his silence was telling. *You're old enough to know better. I've got two more hours of my shift and I don't need to be dealing with Mums on the piss.*

Bea had been concerned that Tilda might have changed since she had last seen her. She had worried that their chemistry might have disappeared without the safety net of the office. Instead, the opposite seemed true. Tilda was exactly the same. A little bit older in the face, perhaps, but her personality was identical. She was still the best listener. She was still generous with her time. She still made Bea feel a mix of protective and proud. Tilda was living life on her own terms which Bea found deeply impressive Her renewed respect and friendship allowed her to open up and share more of the Mal-details. It was easier than over the phone and even easier with alcohol. Everything was the same. Tilda was just as she always was and Bea felt comfortable sharing the truth about her current situation.

She had taken it well. There had been an initial wide-eyed expression at the mention of the wife and kids but she had known to calm it as Bea talked. She had questions though.

'And you didn't know he was married before?'

'Not for sure.'

'But you suspected?'

'Not really. It was less black and white than that. I just didn't think about it.'

'Bea.' Tilda's tone implied she smelt bullshit. 'What do you mean?'

Bea sighed.

'I mean, I don't usually care about the marital status of the men I sleep with.' That sounded bad when she said it aloud. Tilda's eyes narrowed as she struggled not to frown at her. *Go on Tilds, keep with me. I need you onside. I need you to understand.* Bea attempted to rephrase her feelings. She wasn't expressing herself well.

'It's not that I don't care but it's never an issue. If I'm only having the odd date here and a bit of online flirting there, then the guy's marital status doesn't come up. And if it does, it's a turn off. The men that are upfront about wanting a bit on the side behind the wife's back, count themselves out by sharing that with me. I can't speak for anyone else, but that's just how I roll. The guys *I* have fun with, don't mention it. They could be single or married, but I never find out.'

'But what about Mal?'

'With Mal, it didn't come up because it was all online at first. As far as I was concerned, usedbut-goodcondition54 was a man who could type eloquently and get me off with the right choice of words. Anything else was irrelevant.'

'But you decided to meet him.'

'I know. It took a while. And only at his suggestion. I wasn't really that bothered. The online connection was enough for me.'

'But he suggested it?'

'Yeah, I get your point. *He* knew he was married even if I didn't. I'm not saying he's a saint. Obviously, I'm not saying that. But he's never lied to a direct question and by the time I knew for sure, well, I was too involved to tell him to piss off. Not that I wanted to. When you get to my age, every person has flaws. Everyone's got baggage. It would be weird if they hadn't.'

Bea was starting to feel like she needed to defend her man. She didn't want that. His smile, the way he made her feel, the look in his eyes when they locked with hers, all spoke for itself. It was hard to convey that to someone else without having him there to prove it.

Perhaps Tilda sensed she needed to be positive. Bea heard her friend audibly switch tones by asking about their first date. She felt her face flush as she recounted the moment it all changed.

'Oh darling, it was like a film. I walked into the bar, looking around for the man from the photos. Although I'll be honest, I was fully expecting them to be ten years out of date. And fifty-four can mean anything can't it. It could be Matt LeBlanc or Michael Gove. But then I saw him and he saw me at the exact same time. We looked at each other and knew.'

'Your eyes met across a crowded room? For real?'

'For. Real. I swear I could feel sparks. It was instant. And it didn't matter what online shenanigans we'd got up to before that. It was suddenly sweet and beautiful. It took ages before we went to bed. Once it was real, we wanted to do things properly.'

Bea smiled to herself as she remembered Kit. She had said the same thing to her neighbour, in a bonding moment over a Sunday gin. She had explained she was taking things slowly and doing them properly for once. '*Hardly*', the elderly woman had replied. '*These walls are paper thin. There's nothing slow or proper about your antics*'. Bea had laughed and promised she'd get her some earplugs. Kit's reply of, '*Don't worry, dear, I'm only jealous. Your sex life's better than Corrie,*' had sealed the deal on what Bea had known for the last few years. She had the best next-door neighbour in the world. Fact.

'He sounds too good to be true.' Tilda snapped Bea out of her day dream and back to reality. She heard the renewed cynicism in Tilda's tone but was grateful her friend was trying her best to hide it and not banish her for bad behaviour.

'He is and he isn't. I feel like I've met my match. For the first time, I want more. *He* makes me want more. It's intoxicating, and I'll be honest Tilds, horny as hell. I think I understand why people stick together for more than five minutes.'

'But?'

'Yeah, there's a *but*. He is, as his profile name told me, used. He's taken. At least legally and technically, if not emotionally any more. I believe him when he says it's over. I don't think he's lying about that but it's messy.'

'And his kids?'

'It seems way too harsh to describe *them* as messy. It's not their fault that Mummy and Daddy aren't friends anymore.'

'And that Daddy has a friend who wants to be their new Mummy?'

Tilda's cocktail had loosened her tongue. She burst out laughing.

'God, I'm sorry Bea. I'm only teasing. It's just that I can't really imagine you playing the step-mum role. Can you?'

'Fuck no! Tilda, it's a nightmare. That's not my plan at all. I'm an awful influence on young people. They are only safe around me when they're old enough to drink alcohol and find their way home in a taxi. I can't handle responsibility. Can you imagine?'

'Not really, no. But then a few months ago I couldn't imagine you being loved up like this. Does he talk about them with you? Do you want to meet them or is that really weird?'

'We're nowhere near that point, darling. They're a part of Mal that I don't know. A part of a home life that's still in place until it's not. I think it would be weird to hear about them.' Bea paused for a second's consideration before carrying on. Tilda might as well hear everything now she was here. She took a breath and continued. 'I *did* find myself following them around Asda a few weeks ago. You know, after school. Standard stalker behaviour.'

Tilda blinked a couple of times.

'Course you did, Bea. It's the most natural thing in the world. Get petrol, pick up bread, stalk random kids.' Tilda shook her head and laughed as she did. 'Blimey, did he know?'

Bea groaned at the memory. It wasn't her finest hour. She had still been reeling from the unexpected changes that Poppy the Dog's death had heralded into her life. She wasn't thinking straight.

'He messaged to say he was doing the school run, then nipping to Asda, and did I want him to give me a call that evening. It was when things were odd and he was having some space. Except he kept messaging me. It was only physical space he needed because he'd promised his wife he would be home more.'

'So what happened?'

'I went to Asda. I knew the branch. I timed it so I was in the car park when he'd be picking them up from school. Then I waited for half an hour till I saw his car.'

'Was this a work day?'

'It seemed I had a *meeting*'. Bea made the obligatory inverted commas gesture with her fingers.

'Oh Bea.'

'I know. I'm ridiculous. I watched him get out of the car and open the back doors. A boy and a girl jumped out.'

'How old are they?'

'Both primary school age. Old enough to not need hand holding or picking up. Maybe eight and ten, or seven and nine.'

'He's quite old to have kids that young, isn't he? Did they struggle to get pregnant or did they just leave it late? Or is his wife much younger? Does she work?'

Bea smiled at Tilda's pressing enquiries.

'I have no idea.'

'You haven't asked?'

'No. None of my business. His homelife is nothing to do with me. That's the stuff he needs to handle for himself. The dog dying was really bad timing. He'd been planning on moving out before it happened. Now it's not the right time.'

Bea stopped talking. She felt her eyes sting with emotion. This was karma for having responsibility-free fun for far too long. Happiness came with a price. It was only fair but that didn't mean she liked paying it.

'Right, let's change the subject. What is it the kids say? I'm harshing our buzz? Let's talk about you. How the frig are you, Tilda Willoughby? I do like your name change, by the way. How's reverting to your old name working out?'

Tilda laughed, presumably as glad of the lightened mood as Bea. She considered her reply.

'I like it. It's still strange at times. Part of me feels like I'm rewriting history by changing it back. But then another part of me feels this was a way to find the courage to start again. If I'd stayed being Tilda Rudd, it might have been easier to go back home when things were tough. I feel like me, if that makes sense.'

'It does. You look like you, too.'

Bea smiled as she spoke but felt a pang of jealousy. *She* only felt like herself when she was HRTed up and sometimes not even then. It would take more than a name change to turn back time. She fiddled with the stem of her glass as she pulled herself back to the task of grilling Tilda.

'Are you happy? I worry about you, alone in the middle of nowhere.'

Tilda laughed.

'Come and visit me. You'll see it's a proper town. I've got the National Library of Wales up the road. It's not some rural, off-grid, back-water, don't worry.'

'I'd love to come and visit. I want to see where you've landed. Let's work out a date before we go home tomorrow. I'd be well up for that.'

'Yes, let's do it. I'd love a visitor.'

Tilda's face changed. A cloud had descended. Bea waited for her to share what had bothered her. She hoped it wasn't the thought of a visit from Bea. She hadn't been lying when she said she'd love to visit. She was intrigued by her friend's new life.

Tilda sipped her drink then found the words.

'I had a random email recently. Do you remember Stewart?'

Bea knocked back her drink, shook her head, and ordered two more shots from the bartender, all with a couple of gestures and a smile. She was determined to win his approval, as well as keep Tilda relaxed.

'Who's Stewart again?'

'The guy I met in York. The one you booked the appointment with, thinking it might be Grady.'

'Right. I'd forgotten his name. What does he want?'

Tilda found her phone and opened the message. She passed it to Bea just as their drinks arrived. Tilda paused as the man placed both glasses in front of them and returned to the bar.

'I've not heard from him for months. We barely know each other really. It's a little bit... I don't know...'

Bea read the message and answered for her.

'Intense? Batshit crazy? Needy as fuck?' She handed the phone back to Tilda.

'I'm not sure what to do yet. I don't want to ignore him.'

'You definitely could. You don't owe him anything.'

'No. But I feel a sense of...' Tilda paused to find the right words, '...a sense of solidarity with him. We have an emotional link. I don't want to ignore his pain but I'm just not sure I can do much about it. I told him I'd be in touch once I knew my work schedule but that was only to buy some thinking time.'

'So will you go and see him or meet him somewhere neutral? I'm not sure how safe it is to go alone, Tilds. He sounds a bit full on. A bit unhinged?'

'I don't think that's the case. At least, it wasn't last time I saw him. He was just sad and broken. Although so was I, let's be honest. I don't think he means any harm. But it's been stressing me out. I'm going to have to answer soon but I'm not sure what to do.'

Bea was aware she had pins and needles in her legs. It turned out, the bar stools had not been the most comfortable way to spend a couple of hours, no matter how much of a Kim Cattrall vibe she'd exuded while she'd been there. Wiggling both ankles to force the blood to return to her feet, she caught the bartender's attention for the final time, requesting the bill.

'Let's think about it tonight. We've got all evening to come up with a solution. We'll finish these then move to the next place to work out our mutual game-plans. Your dodgy email and my Mal issues. It'll make sense once we're really pissed.'

Bea jumped off the stool, whilst Tilda took a more nonchalant, clambering approach. Minutes later they were heading out of the door to continue their night of adventure. There were always solutions once you chose to look for them. They just needed to be found.

CHAPTER SIXTEEN

The meeting with Richard the Pension Man, had been over for hours. The brochures and leaflets regarding suggested investments were still scattered across the dining table. A table that had yet to play host to any dining event despite being in place for decades.

Over time, Stewart's apartment had morphed into a place for working from home, drinking from home, and sleeping. The few cosy touches it contained were down to Rosie. She was responsible for all the positive events in Stewart's adult life. These now ranged from the sale of his father's house and running the firm in his absence, to choosing a tasteful wallpaper print for his bedroom's feature wall. If she ever wanted to branch out as an interior designer for a certain type of man, she would have a great side business. When he moved in, she had found an artistic map of Viking York to hang in the living room as well as a set of burnt orange cushions to add a splash of colour against the stark lines of the walls. As the Office Manager for a legal firm, it would be fair to say her job description was fluid.

This particular Saturday night, Stewart's mind was distracted. He couldn't settle and had spent the past few hours wasting time on his iPad. He jumped from thinking about his financial future to checking out the current prices of flights to Dubai. The image of Rosie with steam coming out of her ears made him stop and divert his thoughts back to the earlier meeting. Now was not the time to abscond again. Besides, he had plans to make. There was a sense of purpose in the air.

All his for the taking. Richard had outlined a variety of investment plans and he was keen to give them some thought. So far, however, flight prices were winning the battle for his attention.

The distractions needed to stop. Now that he had some half-formed ideas for the future, he should give them his full concentration. It's not that he was overly cautious. He was considered a risk-taker when it came to money. The trick was to avoid focusing on daily market fluctuation. That would only cause panic. It was far better to leave the worrying to someone else. Richard could have the sleepless nights instead, which was the role for which Stewart was paying him. So it wasn't the unsteady stock market that was causing him the current distractions. It was something else.

A Facebook message popped up on the screen. Stewart scanned the contents quickly.

Great to hear from you, Stewart. You look well. It's been ages! Thanks for the offer of a drink but I had a baby seven months ago, so my Saturday nights are a little different now! Take care xxx

Stewart grimaced. This was the third *thanks but no thanks* message in the past half hour. He double-checked who it was from, not that it mattered. The women from his past seemed determined to stay there. That included Tilda. Not that Tilda was a *woman* woman. That wasn't what was bothering him. It was simpler than that. Her promise of a reply had been a lie. He needed to talk to her and she had fobbed him off. And now, as he attempted to distract himself with the potential of casual sex with any old flame he could find, he was being fobbed off again. No one wanted to come and play. He really had lost his touch.

Resigned to another weekend alone, Stewart got a glass and filled it. As he passed the mirror, he caught his reflection. Despite what he had just been told via Facebook, he did *not* look well. Perhaps it was better that he didn't meet in person these days. The charm that used to win him cases and girlfriends had run out. He peered at himself. The beard from his last holiday was still in place but compared to his once neat goatee, it gave his dishevelled appearance a vagrant air. His skin was blotchy with dark circles under his eyes. He was *old*. The thought crossed his mind that if he were to be cast in a film, he would only be considered for the role of *bad guy*. There was nothing *leading man* about the way he looked these days. Nothing at all.

He returned to his iPad on the sofa. It was probably a good thing that no one was free. The effort it would have taken to look presentable, would have invariably meant he would have stood them up. Better that they stay in with their husbands and babies and enjoy their lucky escape. He was not someone to be around anymore. *Run for the hills, women. Stay away from the terrible man.*

Still, he couldn't shake the thought. If he tidied himself up on the outside, could it prompt a positive upturn on the inside? Maybe. He pondered the thought for a moment before dismissing it out of hand. It was going to take more than a hot shave and some skin balm to drag him up from the depths. He needed a project. He needed purpose. Not with the firm, of course. That would always be linked with his father.

He needed something of his own. Something to get him up and out in the mornings. It was just unfortunate how little energy he had for anything requiring effort. If this was how it was going to be for the next forty years, then he wasn't sure he was game. *No thanks. Stop the bus, I want to get off.*

Back on the sofa, his search for comfort ended as he had always known it would. He logged on to the site that he turned to in emergencies. It didn't make him feel good. Well, only for a short time. It was always afterwards he felt emptier than usual. He typed in the box.

Anyone online? I'm all alone and bored shitless. Want to cheer me up?

Within seconds he had a response. WetandWild was ready to chat. She - he always forced himself to assume it was a *she* - was equally bored and keen to connect. What were the odds! Mostly, it seemed, she wanted to chat about what he was wearing and how hard he was.

Stewart typed carefully. He wasn't hard at all and the description of his grey joggers was best kept to himself, but this was better than nothing. It was better than drinking alone. It was better than *being* alone. Stewart typed the desired responses that WetandWild seemed to want. He imagined she was doing the same in return. It's what the website expected of them both. They played their roles, said the right things, and faked the appropriate responses. If he had stopped to think about it, he would have known deep down, that neither WetandWild nor himself had received sexual satisfaction or emotional comfort from the encounter. But still. It was better than being alone.

CHAPTER SEVENTEEN

The door swung shut in Tilda's face as Bea made an overly enthusiastic entrance ahead.

'Sorry darling. Are you OK?'

'Don't mind me. It's only my face.' Tilda rolled her eyes at the potential broken nose and concussion that could have cut short their evening. 'Let's get a seat and decide what we want.'

'We want shots.'

'*Do* we though?'

Tilda followed Bea as she moved seamlessly from potential injury, to striding purposefully towards the bar. Settling in direct eyeline of a member of staff who, like his counterpart in the previous establishment, was unlikely to be paid enough to deal with drunk, middle-aged women, Bea slapped the bar with both palms and gave him her biggest smile. Tilda did her best to loiter casually in the background as her friend took charge. Not that it mattered. Everyone was distracted by Bea.

'We want shots!'

'OK. Anything in particular?'

'What do you have?'

'We have all of them. What do you want?'

'All of them, of course!'

'Anything specific to start?'

'I'm easy. Just line them up. Is there a dentist's chair?'

'There's not. I can bring over some Sambuca if you want to find a seat?'

'Perfect. Let's go, Tilds.'

'Right behind you.' She made to follow Bea's lead before turning back to the man.

'Two beers and a couple of glasses of tap water too, if that's OK.'

Tilda needed to eat soon if this was the way the evening was going. Yet even with misgivings about her lack of lined stomach, she was calmer. Putting the world to rights with a friend; drinks and banter. She used to be good at this, during the odd time she'd had the chance to socialise. Not everything from her old life had been bad. Christmas parties and work events had been more fun than she'd realised at the time. Looking back, she could see she'd taken her mediocre social life for granted. She missed it.

Tilda followed Bea as she weaved through the standing drinkers before making it to a seat by the window. She was happy to be led. Bea was calling the shots - quite literally - and she was a willing side kick.

Meanwhile, Bea continued her train of thought – the one she had started en route from the last bar. The train of thought that she had kept coming back to all evening. Mal, his marital status, and his children.

'The thing is...' she pontificated, as if sharing great truths about the human condition despite having a tendency to slur, '...I was never really into that Athena poster. You know? The topless hunk and the baby? I couldn't fully relax knowing that such a beautiful man would put me second to a baby. Who would want to compete with a child?'

Tilda left it a few seconds before she pointed out the obvious.

'But he has kids. You *would* be competing if you

were a legitimate couple.' She didn't want to nag but it wasn't something Bea could ignore.

Bea's face fell. This can't have been the first time she'd considered the kids would come first, could it? She was in serious denial and Tilda didn't know what to say next.

The potentially awkward silence was interrupted by the arrival of the man from the bar.

'Two sambucas, two beers, and two waters. Do you want to start a tab?'

Bea visibly activated her game face, declined the offer and paid with her card as Tilda sipped her beer. She tried to stop worrying. Bea was always in control. She just needed to talk it out.

Her thoughts were interrupted as Bea threw back her Sambuca and screamed.

'Your turn Willoughby! Down. In. One.'

Tilda held her breath and did as she was told. It was bad. She managed to suppress the urge to make a noise, but grimaced with the taste of it. The next one, she decided, would be discreetly absorbed into the carpet.

With the sticky shot glasses moved aside, Tilda tried to steer Bea back to the topic in hand, whilst cleansing her palate with water.

'So, the kids. What's the specific problem? Because I'm sensing there is one. Has something happened or are you not keen in general?'

Bea considered her question with slightly glazed eyes. This clearly wasn't sitting well with her.

'The problem is, as marvellous as I'm sure they are, it would be a hell of a lot easier if they didn't exist.'

'But they do. They exist.'

'But if they didn't, I'd be able to have unwavering attention all the time. I'd feel interesting and special and valuable again. It's what I've come to expect after waiting so long to even consider a commitment that lasts longer than thirty-six hours.'

'But they still exist.' Tilda felt the repetition was necessary. Bea needed to grasp the whole picture. If Mal was to be fully in her life one day, the kids would take precedence.

'Yes. They do. And right now, they are mourning the death of Poppy. All together. Bloody Poppy.'

'Poppy?'

'The dog.'

'I see.'

'Somewhere along the way, without me realising, it took a turn I wasn't planning. Looking at my phone every ten seconds, wishing a bloke with two bigger priorities than me would message the slightest bit of communication. I'd settle for the *thumbs up* emoji right now.'

'Oh Bea.'

'Exactly. I've turned into a twat.'

Despite her protestations, there were three more shots. Tilda sipped one and faked two before gently suggesting food. She also made Bea drink her water. She had no intention of going back early because her friend had vomited in an alley.

Bea ignored the idea of eating whilst her stream of consciousness continued to flow. It occurred to Tilda that whilst Bea may be surrounded by far more people than she was, the isolation was just as real. She tuned back into what Bea was saying by asking a question about the last thing she heard.

'What was that about a shit show?'

Bea rewound her monologue to the comment she had made a moment ago.

'You know. The usual *other woman* madness. I got drunk. Searched his Instagram and scrolled back through five years of happy family photos. The wife even looks like a thinner version of me. And isn't it terrible that I hate her?'

'Bea, you don't hate anybody.'

'I never used to. But I can't stand her. I think she's pathetic to be cheated on by a guy that should be with me. Isn't that a fucked-up mess? She's blameless but the control she has over him drives me mad.'

'Do you think he'll leave her?'

'He said he will.'

'But do you think he will *really*?'

There was a pause. Clearly this wasn't the first time Bea had entertained this question. She sighed.

'I have no idea. But if he doesn't, he's a complete shit for leading me on.'

'Maybe he's a complete shit anyway?'

'Hmm. There are times in the night when I can't sleep and my mind is racing, when I would be in full agreement. Then I drop off, wake up and somehow have the strength for another day of waiting for his call. I'm not great at the waiting.'

'This can't be what you want?'

'Right now it isn't. But then he'll do something lovely. Like really sincerely tell me he needs time, and I find myself agreeing. Maybe it will be all right in the end. Maybe every great relationship goes through this sort of stuff at the start.'

'Maybe.'

'This must be what people mean when they say they're stressed?'

'You say that like you've never experienced stress before.'

'I haven't. Not like this.'

'Are you serious?'

'I've been in stressful *situations*. But that's different. They're over quickly. A late period, having to sack someone... that kind of thing. They make a funny story for the next time you see your mates in the pub. But now, none of my mates go to the pub. Now I don't have anyone to share my stories with, so they stay with me and weigh me down.'

'Is Mal a funny story?'

Bea swigged her beer. A moment's pause to find the right words.

'He was at the start. Now, because I've not talked about him to anyone, he's taken over. He's become a serious story.'

'Is that a good thing?'

'Not sure. Yes.' Bea shrugged. 'Probably.'

Tilda sipped her drink. Bea mirrored the action. They sat for a moment before Bea broke the silence.

'Let's stop talking about this. Christ, darling, we've got deep. The night is young. Time for drunken navel-gazing later. The good news is I've come round to your way of thinking. I can confirm I am now ravenous. Let's go and eat.'

Bea was putting on a brave face. Tilda could see that. A brave face that kept her only seeing the good in

Mal. Maybe Mal was Bea's soul mate. Maybe they would live an eventual happy life together. Maybe he wasn't the two-timing arrogant user that he appeared to be. Maybe.

CHAPTER EIGHTEEN

The much-lauded restaurant whose Instagram Bea had followed the moment she made the booking, had been an excellent choice. They were experiencing foodie heaven.

As instructed by their server, Bea opened her mouth and ate the Yoghurt Chat Bomb whole.

'Christ, that's good. You have to try one. It's like a coriander explosion in your mouth. I'm going in again.'

Tilda watched as Bea took another, proceeding to have the same beatific reaction to her mouthful of starter as she had experienced thirty seconds before. Looking around at the other diners, relishing the chilled atmosphere of the restaurant, she could feel the smile on her face. It reached the full corners of her mouth and had done since they met at the station. It wasn't just one thing. It was the whole package. One cool bar after another, and now they were sitting in a fairy-lit restaurant eating Indian street food. Who was she? A Nineties It-Girl? Even though the weekend had been well-planned, it still felt spontaneous. It still felt reckless. The good kind of reckless, though. The kind that came with living in the moment and having fun. Tilda wasn't only a functioning member of society once more, but an interesting one at that.

A waiter bounded over with their selected dishes. Five metal tins were placed between them as Tilda's mouth started to water. This was as far away from her campervan culinary attempts as she could get. She speared a piece of Gunpowder Chicken on her fork as Bea topped up their glasses.

As their afternoon had worn on, it slowly dawned on Tilda that Bea had been as anxious about today as she had. She had repeatedly said how little Tilda had changed, in a tone suggesting relief. They had fallen back into their friendship with ease and Tilda was glad. It was reassuring to see she had not lost the ability to have fun, even if she were a little rusty.

Bea continued to make squeals and groans with every new mouthful as Tilda laughed at her theatrics. Yet beneath the sense of relief and reassurance, there was something unsettling. Something that had been obvious the second they were reunited in the station. *She* might not have changed, but Bea Charleston had. It wasn't just her relationship status, either. It was far more dramatic than that.

'Try a bit of the lamb, Tilds. It's orgasmic.'

'Orgasmic you say? I'll be sure to get right on it.' Tilda smiled as she scooped up some curry with a piece of puri. It was delicious. She licked her fingers and tried to push her concerns away. Time to change the subject.

'Thanks for letting me unload about Stewart. It's been bothering me for weeks. A problem shared is a problem halved and all that. My shoulders feel lighter. Or my head. Something like that.'

'Do you know, that's my least favourite saying. *A problem shared is a problem halved.* It's not halved for the person getting another problem.'

Tilda laughed.

'I apologise for giving you another problem. Or half a problem.'

'That's all right. I apologise for giving you the problem of Mal. A thousand apologies for that one.'

'S'ok. He sounds nice. It's just the married bit.'

'I know.'

Tilda felt the level of inebriation meant she could finally ask the question she'd been mulling over for past few hours.

'Bea?'

'Yes, darling?' Bea took a mouthful of paneer with a facial expression that indicated it was as good as the lamb.

Tilda breathed deeply then went for it.

'What's with the hair?'

'The hair?'

'Yes. Your hair. It looks lovely. All sleek and shiny. It's just that in the two decades we worked together, I never saw you with anything other than backcombed, multi-highlighted, crazily big hair. Usually accompanied with some sort of clashing print on your clothes. But here you are looking stunning, but with sleek, shiny, straight hair that I do not believe has ever seen the hint of a backcombing brush. What's going on? Have you been on a makeover show?'

Bea swallowed her food and shook her head, her smile indicating she wasn't offended by Tilda's questioning for a second. Now that she'd said it out loud, however, it felt like she'd gone too far.

'Sorry, Bea. You look amazing. And you're wearing clothes that I would *love* to wear. If I had the money and confidence and style, and all that.'

The slim-cut jeans and fitted shirt were definitely stylish. Tilda didn't want to sound critical in any way. She just didn't understand where all the patterns and colour had gone.

Bea shook her head as she considered her answer.

'I don't know, Tilds. I think it's been a gradual change. Since I hit fifty I've been struggling to do my usual hair. You think the menopause is just the end of periods, but Christ it's bigger than that. It's like being twelve all over again. My hormones were exploding all over the show and my hair was getting thinner. I think the calmer style was because of that.'

'It looks great, Bea. I wasn't saying it didn't.'

'I know, I know.' She was quick to reassure her. 'It's easier to sort every morning, I'll say that much.'

Tilda still felt the need to back-track.

'You haven't really changed, Bea. Not deep down.'

'You mean apart from the hair, the clothes, and the boyfriend?'

Tilda nodded with mock solemnity.

'Yes. Apart from all that.'

The awkward moment over, Bea raised her glass.

'To getting older, and more stupid, and more reckless, and happier, and more brilliant, and everything else we're going to be, when we work out how to achieve it.'

Tilda picked up her glass in response.

'To all the things you just said, Bea. To all that.'

They clinked glasses and drank their wine. The moment was interrupted by the buzz of Tilda's phone. She unlocked the screen and saw the notification.

'Do you need to answer that, darling. Go right ahead, I'm ploughing on with the food.'

'No, it's fine. It'll only be spam. Everyone I know for real is sitting opposite me.'

'Oh darling. We need to get you more friends.'

Tilda opened the email, poised to swipe away a

marketing mailout. When she saw the sender, her face gave away her surprise.

'Oh wow. It's my other friend.'

'I have a rival?' Bea teased.

'Freya. We lived together a hundred years ago. Don't worry, she's been in Australia for ages. She can't cramp your style.'

'Tilda Willoughby, I have never heard of her. How are there still big gaps of your past I know nothing about?'

Tilda smiled but was preoccupied by the message from out of the blue.

'We send a newsy email every couple of years so I guess it's that time again.'

'What's she like? Are you very similar?'

Tilda laughed. Bea was wide off the mark.

'Absolutely not. She's much more like you than me. Or at least, the single you. Not the loved up, getting-her-head-around-step-kids version. Although, she has kids herself. These days she's probably *exactly* like the loved up, soon-to-be-step-mum you.'

Bea groaned and held her head in her hands.

'I *cannot* be a step-mum. Not when I see them as my natural competition. What have I become? Quick! Distract me from the massive mess I'm in and tell me about Freya. Is she fun? Would I like her? What did you get up to together?'

'Let me read out her message. That'll distract you and give you the answers you need.'

Bea agreed that was a plan. Tilda drank some wine to clear her throat and opened the email.

'Hey Tilds, you utter legend! How's it hanging in BLIGHTY? I can call it that now it's been fifteen years since I left. I can officially start to sound like a monarchy-loving, afternoon-tea-on-the-lawn-eating, ex-pat. Blighty is what I am allowed to call the old country. Handle it, Willoughby...'

'Fuck. I love her.'

'Yeah,' Tilda replied. 'And you're the only two people that call me *Tilds*. Clearly there's a telepathic connection.'

'She sounds phenomenal. Keep going.'

Tilda looked back at her screen. Whenever she read anything that Freya sent, she felt exhausted and invigorated, all at once.

'...I have heaps of news to tell you. Well, obviously I do. It's been months and months (probz years tbh) since I've been in touch. So I need to fill you in on all things Freya. But here's the thing. I'm not going to do it here. I'm not going to tell you all about my comings and goings in this email. 'Why not Freya?' you ask. 'Why not, you beautiful person, you lovely lady that occasionally still gets ID'd when she buys grog? Why not, you utterly gorge hottie?' (I KNOW that's exactly what you'll be saying! Hahaha.) Well let me tell you, I've got a big surprise...'

'Oh wow,' Tilda said for the second time in five minutes. She'd read ahead and saw what was coming. She reread it aloud for the benefit of Bea.

'...Well let me tell you, I've got a big surprise. This

summer (that's your summer, not my summer) I'm getting on a plane and returning to Blighty! Yes, Blighty. The old country, the motherland, the place of village greens, of apple crumble, of disastrous referendums, and Christmas pantos. I'll be there. I'm coming back. I'm visiting you all!'

Bea took it in.
'Is she visiting or moving back for good?'
'Not sure, hang on. She's nearly done.'

'...So clear your diary for August. I'll be over for three weeks in total, but most of that will be with my parents. BORING. I have to do the dutiful daughter thing and let the kids see where I grew up. Brace yourself Chester! After that, I'll need some excitement thrown in. I don't want to regret this whole thing. So here's my plan. And when I say 'my plan' what I really mean is 'your plan.' You are the details woman. You can make this happen. This will be your baby, I am merely full of good ideas for you...'

'Here we go,' Tilda sighed. She could smell the stitch up a mile off.

'...Let's have a reunion, but not just you and me. We'll definitely do that, for sure, but let's get the rest of the gang involved too. I'm still in touch with most of them, but I don't have time to do the rounds while I'm over. Let's box it off in one weekend. The geography team, for one night only! You, me, Jonathan, Dhanesh, Sam, Jen, even Kenny if he isn't incarcerated for perviness.

Let's have a big old Liverpool Geographers Class of '99 knees up. What do you say?'

Tilda paused. She could imagine the last part before she read it.

'...If I pass on the contact details I have for everyone, what do you think about organising something? It can be wherever you're based now - I've lost track of where you ended up but we can make everyone else travel to you. It just needs a nice restaurant, a bar, and some nearby accommodation. What do you think? I know you love a plan. I reckon this is right up your street. Go on, Tilds. You KNOW you want to.'

Tilda put her phone on the table and ate a forkful of lamb curry. Bea looked at her, waiting for a response.

'What are you going to do? You've gone all quiet on me.'

Tilda took a moment to think, filling it with the consumption of more food before she answered. The feeling of lightness had left her.

'I think,' Tilda said slowly, 'that it would be great to see Freya again. I think that catching up with her in the summer would be something fun to look forward to.'

'But?' Bea knew it was there.

'Yeah, but. I guess I don't feel I'm in the best place mentally, or emotionally, to reawaken long dead friendships with people that are now strangers, and arrange accommodation and catering, and all the other things that would be needed. I'm trying to settle into a new place. I still haven't got a dentist. I'm currently experiencing my first night out in two years, and now I'm supposed to organise a college reunion that would include some people that live in *London*. It's too much.'

Tilda topped up her wine glass and took a long swig. It already felt stressful and all she had done was read out the idea. Goodness knows how she would feel in August when this mad plan was supposed to be formulated into a fabulous event. She drank more wine. Then there was the added problem of needy Stewart and his email.

'Everyone wants a piece of me, Bea. I'm either a travelling recluse or a beacon for multiple people who want to meet up. I have no idea what I'm going to do.'

Bea was listening, eating, and thinking all at once. With a fragment of puri she wiped the last remnants of butter chicken from the bowl. Then she dipped her fork into the paneer. She left Tilda in her silence for a few minutes as she swallowed the food and drank some wine. Then she spoke.

'Tilds, I've got an idea.'

At the sound of Bea's alarm, Tilda got out of bed. She used the room's mini kettle to make them both a cup of tea and then showered, dressed, and packed her bag. Bea, on the other hand, switched off her phone and hid her head under the pillow. By the time she managed to open her eyes and take a Paracetamol, she had less than an hour until her train left. There ensued a panicked frenzy as shoes, clothes, and makeup removing pads were thrown into her suitcase. All the while, Tilda sipped her second cup of tea and smiled. The memory of the previous night's fun was fresh and she felt a glow inside from the experience. The fact that Bea's crazed disorganisation was amusing only added to her lighter mood.

They made it to New Street with only moments to spare. Bea flung her arms around Tilda and urged her to think about her suggestion. Tilda promised she would, then suddenly she was gone. A figure dashing into the distance, her coat billowing behind her like a parachute as she rushed to the platform. Tilda was alone once again. The laughter and buzz of constant conversation was over. This was Tilda's normal. She was fine. Yet the warmth of the previous twenty-four hours seemed to make the return to solitude that bit cooler.

She had thirty minutes to kill until she needed to find her own platform. Around her were shops, bars, and cafés. She wished she were the kind of person that could walk confidently into a bar on their own. She wished she could politely ask for the wine list and then expertly assess which of the grape varieties would be a good choice. She wished she were able to pull off the appearance of a successful independent traveller; a successful independent *anyone*. Someone with the confidence to drink alone as they waited for their connection, needing no one to keep her company. *Yeah right*. As if she were going to do that. She might be used to solitude but drinking alone in public was beyond her. Besides, she had the start of a slight head-ache. Even if she *were* comfortable with striding through the doors of a pub unaccompanied, it wasn't going to happen this morning.

Pushing her bar fantasies out of her mind, Tilda headed for a nearby coffee shop. She bought a large tea and returned to the concourse with her lidded cup. Standing alone in a crowd was more manageable. More *Tilda*.

Her thoughts were interrupted by the tannoy.

'Now arriving on platform five is the twelve twenty-four train to Aberystwyth. Passengers for the twelve twenty-four to Aberystwyth should make their way to platform five now.'

This time around her train was on time. Tilda found platform five and lugged her bag into the carriage. She was the first there so had time to wedge it overhead without having to jostle in the aisles with her fellow passengers. Squeezing herself into the window seat, she settled in. The return journey was definitely less exciting than the incoming one. She was going... home? No, that wasn't right. Aberystwyth wasn't home. Not yet. If it were, she'd do what everyone else did and call it *Aber*. She wasn't comfortable with that.

It didn't sit right. It was simply where she was living. Where her things were. It was scenic and she was happy with her decision, but it wasn't home. Home didn't exist anymore.

A lump rose in Tilda's throat. *Damn. Not again.* She banished visions of her long-gone Dad in their old lounge. With his woolly cardigans and indulgent smile, she forced herself to think of something else. Anything else. She didn't fancy spending the entire journey fighting back tears.

Tilda wasn't stupid. She recognised this was a symptom of the comedown of having had a brilliant time. She had been building up to the previous day for weeks. Now it was over, emotion was to be expected. Besides, the slight throb in her temples was gaining momentum. It was still too mild to class as a hangover but she felt more delicate than usual. *Of course* she was on the verge of tears. It would have been odd if she were not.

The train pulled away. Tilda breathed deeply and sank into her seat. It was early days in the journey but for now she was surrounded by empty seats. No one next to her nor in her direct line of vision. She was thankful. Tilda forced away the lump in her throat by pinching the top of her nose. A practical decision. She didn't want to cry here. She wanted to think. She wanted to think about Bea's suggestion.

It wasn't long before the urban bustle of the Midlands became the open space of the countryside. Tilda watched the fields blur as she formulated her thoughts. *It seems everyone wants a piece of me, Bea.* That's how she'd worded it last night. She'd been making a stab at humour but the sentiment was bang on. Everyone wanted her to do something. To *be* something. Their expectation on her energy made Tilda shrink. She wanted to curl into a ball. She wanted to delete her email account. She wanted everyone to leave her alone. It had been Bea who had talked her down from the particular anxiety ledge she'd found herself on.

'*What's the problem exactly? Break it down. What is it specifically that's stressing you out?*'

'*I don't know. It feels overwhelming.*'

'*Do you want to see Freya?*'

'*Yes, of course. If she's over here then it'd be terrible to miss her.*'

'*OK. And do you want to see the rest of your student pals again?*'

Tilda had to give this question some thought.

'*I suppose so. I've lost touch with them but I liked them when I knew them. Except Kenny. If this was some-one else's reunion, I'd be happy to turn up and see how they were getting on.*'

'*Right. Good. Now what about Stewart? Do you want to see him again?*'

Tilda had groaned.

'*I feel like I should.*'

'*There's no such thing as 'should'. It's 'Do you want to?' and 'Will you?'*'

Tilda had appreciated Bea's clarity. It was what she missed from her old life.

'*I feel as if we have unfinished business. I should meet him. I know you said I can't say 'should', but that's how I feel. I don't want to, but I don't want not to, either. I can't ignore that he reached out. I just think it'll be the most intense meeting ever. The logistics of it worry me. Where would it be? What will I do if it's really awkward and I want to make a run for it? I've no one to back me up when it ends up being weird. The best-case scenario is I'll find it really sad.'*

'He sounds a right nightmare.'

'I've no idea. It's not ideal, though, is it?'

'No, but you haven't heard my plan. One last question. Now sleep on it if you need to, but be honest. Do you want this reunion as a bit of a project? You like admin, Tilds. Is this not one big exciting admin job to keep you busy over the weeks?'

Tilda had replied immediately and with feeling.

'Absolutely not. Freya doesn't know how much has changed. I do love organising but only someone's birthday collection or ordering new office supplies. Simple stuff. Nothing big. I'm already overwhelmed trying to start a new life. It's like I used up all my energy leaving Mike and now I'm empty. I'm a hermit most of the time. Well a hermit that likes a walk most evenings. But the thought of trying to plan a brilliant event for loads of people? Well, I just can't. It's too big. I wouldn't know where to start. It's not me. Not anymore. At least, not right now.'

Bea had listened as Tilda worked herself up into a panic about some old friends she used to know. She let her get it out of her system before she intervened.

'OK, hear me out. This is my suggestion. Give me the email addresses you have for Freya, the geography people, and Stewart. Yes, him too. Then tell me which weekend you want for the reunion. And that will be the end of your involvement and worry.'

Tilda had laughed. Then she saw Bea was serious.

'What would you do? And more importantly, why would you do it?'

Bea had been crystal clear once again.

'It's simple. I'm dealing with a married lover that isn't free to be with me the way I would like. I can either drink myself silly every night or I can busy myself in a project. You and your predicament have provided such a project.'

'But...?' Tilda had questions.

'So, effectively, I will be your PA. If you were a busy exec and Freya had sent you the same email, you'd have palmed it off onto your right-hand woman, wouldn't you? That's what this will be like. I'm your right-hand woman!'

'But what would a geography reunion have to do with Stewart? I wasn't at Uni with him. I wasn't even at Uni with his brother We just met then.'

Bea had been ready with her answer.

'I get that Stewart's the round peg in the square hole. But think of it. If you invite him – or get me to invite him – to the same weekend as everyone else, it kills loads of birds with one stone. You fulfil the obligation you feel to him. You aren't on your own and can have backup if need be. You can avoid any hugely emotional outbursts if there's a crowd of you, and – and this is the genius bit – I will be there. I will come too. Mostly it'll be in the PA and party planner role but I'll also have your back.'

'You'd do that?'

'I would. Plus, I need to keep busy while Mal sorts his life out and realises he can't do without me for a moment longer. You'd be helping me out as much as I would for you.'

'Where would it be?'

Bea had considered the options.

'I reckon your place is best. Your town, at least. You said there's lots going on there? I assume that means

places to socialise. It's the seaside so there's bound to be hotels.'

'But how will you know where they are?'

Bea had sighed.

'We've got this thing called the Internet, Tilds. It's great. You can read all about the world from your own home. Even Wales. It's modern and everything. Trust me.'

Tilda had laughed but there hadn't been much else said. The conversation had moved on as Tilda pushed away the panic that Freya's email had caused.

She didn't feel like she'd slept on it. She had drifted off the previous night, full of wine. There had been no sense that her subconscious was sorting out the problem below decks. Back when she didn't know any better, she thought that writing a nightly diary gave her subconscious closure and kept bad dreams at bay. She wasn't sure she believed that any more. It was when she was young and naïve. These days, her journal was for cherry picking the day's highlights. One thing was clear. The anxiety from Freya's email would not be making the list.

The journey continued. Through Shrewsbury, past Welshpool, on to Machynlleth, and finally pulling into Aberystwyth. The train slowed into the dead end of the station as passengers made moves to disembark. Tilda waited for the people around her to retrieve their bags. She watched them stand, stretch their legs, and lumber down the carriage towards the doors. Only then did she copy them. With her case in her hand and her handbag dangling from her shoulder, she stepped onto the platform, down the slope, and onto the road.

She passed the Wetherspoons she had never entered, and crossed the taxi rank she had never used, as she made the short walk to her apartment.

Maybe in Birmingham, she *could* have pretended she was a power-dressed executive that drank daytime wine as her PA organised her diary. Maybe she could have pulled off that role if she'd given Bea permission to go ahead with her plan. Maybe she could give off the impression she were confident and accomplished if she had someone in her corner, assisting her social life. Tilda walked on, trying to find reasons not to let Bea enact her suggestion. There were probably loads. She was just struggling to think of them.

By the time she had her key in the lock and the smell of chips in her nose, she knew what she was going to do. There was only one answer. She gave her tapping seagull stalker a hard stare and let herself into the building. She needed to text Bea and give her the green light. She would do it now, before she changed her mind.

CHAPTER TWENTY

Two months before the reunion

Stewart cursed himself for the mistake. This had never happened when he was chained to the office. Back then, he had never once considered what was going on in his apartment when he wasn't there. Now that his working hours were more sporadic and he was away on holiday far less, this was the second time he'd made the miscalculation.

The first time it happened, he was caught off guard. He hadn't known what was happening. When he heard the front door open, he had panicked. Leaping out of bed, he'd grabbed the nearest heavy object he could see, and hid behind the bedroom door. In hindsight, attacking his cleaner with an ironing board could have been misinterpreted as a politically motivated move. Was this an aggressive way of suggesting she might want to increase her hours and take on his ironing? The fact she had been wearing earphones and had not realised his panic made him feel a little less mortified whenever the memory resurfaced.

Today there had been no fear when he heard the door. He knew immediately what was happening. This time he simply kicked himself for making the same mistake twice and swore under his breath. He should have gone into the office. It felt wrong to be in the apartment when someone else was cleaning it. That he saw it a sign of personal strength that he was embarrassed, was an upside. He was not so entitled that he was comfortable lying in bed whilst a virtual stranger vacuumed his crumbs and moved his empty mugs to the sink. It showed him in a good light that this made him feel awkward. He was the victim here, after all.

Once he had given himself a silent three cheers for being heroic, there was the other matter to deal with. The general inconvenience that the presence of the woman provided. It was hard to make toast when the kitchen floor had just been mopped. It was impossible to go for his morning dump when the minute he was done, she might try to clean the recently abused toilet. With her in the apartment, it was difficult to relax.

Stewart sighed and sat up. He retrieved the jeans from the bedroom floor and picked the cleanest T-shirt from the chair. Now he couldn't shower and it wasn't his fault. It was hers. The cleaner. Whatever her name was. With an effort that felt Herculean, he attempted to conform to the social niceties he knew were expected. He edged around the doorframe and into her line of vision.

'Morning. Hi. Hello?'

The woman looked up. She didn't do a great job of hiding her annoyance at the presence of the home-owner. It dawned on him that his mistake probably impacted her day too. He wondered what would be different had he been at work. Was most of her time spent having a snoop? Did she vacuum naked? Maybe she drank his vodka and replaced it with water. His mind wandered but her reply made him focus.

'You here all morning?'

She was direct. Stewart got flustered.

'Erm, probably. I mean, if that's all right. I work from home sometimes, you know, just sometimes.

When I get the chance. I won't be... I mean, I'm not going to be... Is that OK?'

She stared blankly and then nodded. Stewart felt ridiculous. What on earth had he just said? It wasn't coherent English.

'Right then, I'll just...'

He motioned with a gesture that he hoped would convey, *I'll just get my laptop from the table and then get out of your way.* He came across as a mediocre mime artist, attempting to entertain by the idea his hand was a snake with a mind of its own. Stewart felt stupid for the fiftieth time in the interaction. He would have to email the agency and have them send someone else. This couldn't happen again.

Safely back in the confines of his bedroom he got down to the pretence of working. Now that he'd told her that was what he was doing, he might as well check his emails and use the time wisely. He bolstered up the pillows behind his back and balanced the laptop across his legs. It was time to pretend to be busy. He did exactly the same when Rosie watched him in the office. Faking a work ethic and blagging productivity could become a skillset all of its own.

He saw it immediately. Nestled amongst shaving subscription offers, flight deals and Rosie's lengthy updates, there was a message that stood out. It wasn't just the title, although that piqued interest with its mystery. It was unmissable due to its extensive use of Caps Lock.

RE: TILDA WILLOUGHBY – EXCITING PLANS AFOOT.

He opened it straight away. A split second too late, he considered that this was probably a scam. Using a contact's name was standard dodgy behaviour and he should have known better. Besides the use of Tilda's name, the title was pure clickbait. It opened and he grimaced at the untold viruses he was installing, before reading the contents.

Hi Stewart,
You don't know me but I'm Bea Charleston and I'm a friend of Tilda's. I'm currently organising a college re-union for Tilda and some of her old friends, and I wanted to include you too. She told me that you'd asked if she were free to meet. She has a lot on right now, but wants to see you too. Are you available on...

Stewart stopped his quick scan of the screen. Who was this? He paused where he was up to and reread it from the start. Did he have this right? It didn't take him more than a second or two to realise he had.

He had heard nothing from Tilda for two months and now she had palmed this off onto someone in the office. That this was exactly the kind of thing Stewart had done to Rosie countless times, was an irony lost on him in the moment. Tears prickled his eyes. It was like being dumped by the popular girl's ugly mate. He sniffed, whilst deep down allowing his hurt feelings to morph into anger.

He carried on reading.

So, check your diary and let me know if that weekend works for you. It might be an idea to come down on

*the Friday night when it'll just be you, me, and Tilda.
Then, by all means stay for the more social event of
the reunion the following night. It'll be fun! Tilda
wants to see you, but I'm sure you appreciate how
busy things have been after her relocation. Here are
some links to hotels close by. I look forward to meeting you then...*

Who the fuck was this Bea woman? Why would
she be there when he saw Tilda? Why was he being
invited to someone else's college reunion and why was
she telling him that Tilda wanted to see him? Why
wasn't Tilda saying that herself? What was going on?
And where the fuck was Aberystwyth?

All his hang-ups about the woman cleaning his
bathroom, disappeared. Angry mutterings and the odd
sniffle peppered the air as he banged the keyboard. He
didn't care if he sounded deranged. He wanted Tilda,
or this Bea woman, to realise he didn't appreciate being messed about. His sarcastic reply would show
them how he felt. He fumed and typed, as he got it off
his chest.

*Well hello Bea,
Thank you so much for your kind invitation on behalf
of Tilda. It is so incredibly benevolent of you to invite
me. How lucky I am! I'd love nothing more than to attend a reunion of Tilda's college pals, as well as arrive
a day earlier to meet you and catch up with Tilda.
Thank you for being so bloody kind to organize all
this. How does Tilda manage without you? I will of
course, stay in a hotel for not one but two nights and
look forward to the long drive to Aberystwyth where I*

will meet a crowd of strangers who have known each other for years.
Stewart

What a waste of time Tilda had turned out to be. As if he were able to ask her advice now. She wouldn't be able to help him with any big decisions if she couldn't find the time for a cup of coffee. It was best to steer clear of her. Clear of her and her lackey, Bea. What a piece of work.

The beep from his inbox alerted him. Bea's reply was instant.

Yay! Nice one, Stewart. Looking forward to meeting you. Tilda will be pleased. Here's my number if you need it. Speak very soon, I hope.
Bea xxx

Stewart groaned. His sarcasm had been more than obvious. How could his email be interpreted any other way? He shook his head. Time to nip this in the bud. Somewhere under his dirty laundry was his phone. And once he found it, he was going to give Bea Charleston a call and a piece of his mind.

CHAPTER TWENTY-ONE

Bea looked through the blinds as her team worked. It was still a regular source of amusement that she had the boss' office. A couple of years ago, she had sat out there with everyone else. *A cog in a wheel, a minion, a slave to the Man.* Her desk had been the one in front of the printer with Tilda sitting opposite. They had faced each other, as colleagues around them had come and gone.

Then it was all change. Tilda left. Then Tan Tights called it a day. Bea had nothing to lose when she had been asked to apply for the promotion. Work had lost its spark when she had no one with whom she could share a laugh. There was no one to laugh *at*, either. Tan Tights was out and Si and Alex stopped being funny and became simply ridiculous the second Bea was on her own. Applying for the Team Leader's job seemed like a logical move. She had needed the change, even if she spent the majority of her time pretending to care about things to which she were completely indifferent. If work had stopped being fun, it could at least pay more. That was the way she had chosen to view the situation.

There were other perks too. With no one breathing down her neck, Bea had researched and booked Tilda's reunion without a second of her own time being taken up. The fact that she had wanted a project to fill the empty hours at home, had been forgotten as soon as she'd done her first hotel search. During working hours, as her team were busy updating polices and providing her with consultation documents, she was knee-deep in Trip Advisor reviews, ringing bars for quotes, and dragging the yellow map man all over the place before making any decisions.

It hadn't taken very long. Just a couple of weeks to send some emails and make the reservations. She had debated whether to get it sorted before she told Tilda. She didn't want to add to her stress. But she reasoned that not knowing what was happening might cause more stress in the long run. She had kept Tilda in the loop on a basic level. Before she made the final bookings, she had checked if the venues sounded all right. After all, this was happening in her town. She might have an opinion on where they held their get-together. It turned out that Tilda knew one of the suggested hotels and had seen the bar that Bea had picked, from the outside. Beyond that she had little opinion. She had given Bea the go ahead to book whatever she saw fit and Bea had done just that.

The morning was dragging. She straightened the zebra throw that covered the armchair and sat down. A few months ago, she had moved it to her office to free up space in the flat. As chairs go, she quite liked it, but Mal was right. It didn't really fit. She curled her legs underneath her and read through the list of tasks still to do.

The emails to invited guests had been sent yesterday. Stewart's, which had been written separately, was sent this morning. She had already had his reply, which seemed enthusiastic, and there had been an out of office reply from Sam. There wasn't much left to do now and Bea was wondering what else she could find to fill her time. Last night, after watching *Something's*

Gotta Give – she had no idea if her choice of film had informed her mood or if it was a simple coincidence - she found herself composing a long email to Mal. If she were being honest, it was more a rambling stream of consciousness, than a coherent email. She had talked about how she missed him and that distance wasn't what she'd signed up for. She had been honest, and explained that she could do with knowing where she stood. Was Poppy the Dog's death still causing a need for family togetherness, or was Mal using that as an excuse to keep her at arm's length? As of this morning, she hadn't received a reply. Her coping strategy so far had been to ignore all thoughts of him whilst planning heartfelt words for the next time she saw him. Whenever that would be. She just needed to keep busy.

Perhaps she should read a book. Or maybe learn a language? After bingeing *Borgen* a few years back, she'd fancied giving Danish a bash. She doubted it would be useful in her day-to-day life, but it would be marvellous not to have to hunt down her rarely-worn glasses before watching her favourite Scandi-dramas. As thoughts of a subtitle-less Kasper Juul and Birgitte Nyborg sprang to mind, Bea's mobile rang. It was a number she didn't recognise.

'Hello, Bea Charleston speaking.'

'Hello Bea? My name's Jonathan and I received an email from you yesterday. About a reunion?'

'You did! Hello Jonathan, how are you? I'm glad you rang. Are you game? Will you come?'

'Bea, you sound utterly delightful. How's Tilda? I haven't seen her in years. I'm ringing for more info. I have to check you aren't a scammer, luring me into a trap with nostalgia, before burgling my house and emptying my bank account. Tell me I'm wrong.'

'Jonathan, you are hugely wrong. Massively wrong.' Bea laughed. 'I'm merely doing Tilda a favour and helping to arrange practicalities. Actually, I'm doing Freya the favour really. Tell me you're coming. I want to meet you.'

'I suppose I am then. I'll be honest, Bea, even the *idea* of a college reunion fills me with dread. But then I do miss Freya. And as for Tilda? Well she was the sweetest person. I feel terrible that I've been so remiss in keeping in touch. I'm not exactly a big presence on social media.'

'Just like Tilda. She's not even on Facebook.'

'It's good to know I'm not the only old fart around. Dhanesh is staying with me at the moment, and he finds the time to mock me at least twenty times a day. This is what happens when you're a mature student. Your university friends treat you like a Grandad from day one. I'm well over fifty these days.'

'Darling, me too! We'll commiserate in the corner and drink our Horlicks as the youngsters dance to nineties house music.'

'Good Lord, I'll hold you to that. Although if I can substitute the Horlicks for a good Malbec, I'll be much happier.'

'Deal. And I'll crack on with the cocktails. See, we're in the prime of our lives. Will you be bringing a plus one? You're more than welcome.'

'No, it'll just be me. The last boyfriend left some time ago, I'm afraid. Dhanesh will be coming with me, though I hasten to add, he's not coming *with* me. Since his divorce he's attempting to be as actively heterosexual as they come. I imagine he won't want his style cramped by having the world assume he's dating me. We find ourselves in a flat-mate situation these days. Or more specifically, he is my lodger. It appears I have become a modern day Rigsby. Without the sexism and racism of course.'

'Jonathan, darling, you sound an utter dream and I can't wait to meet you. You shall be crossed off the list the second we hang up. Is Dhanesh planning to contact me or are you being the grown up for him?'

'I do like the sound of you, Bea. You've got the measure of us already. By all means cross off Dhanesh. He's definitely coming. We chatted about it when your email came. I'll tell him to contact you himself, though. He seemed - as the youngsters say - *well up for it* when he got the email. I'll admit the hesitancy came from me.'

Bea was charmed by Jonathan's charisma. She liked it when she was attracted to a man she didn't want to shag. It didn't happen often, but when it did, she was enthralled. She could have talked to Jonathan all day. She also wanted to put his mind at ease.

'I totally understand, Jonathan. Reunions can be horrendous, can't they? To be honest, if any of my old school friends tried to rope me into anything like this, I wouldn't be able to say *fuck that* quick enough. But this one is different.'

'Of *course*, it is.' Jonathan laughed. He sounded as if he were equally enamoured with her, which she *loved*. 'Go on then, Bea. Explain how it's different.'

'Forget that it's a reunion. It's the word that puts people off. From what Tilda told me, I understand there was a select group of you that studied together.

You travelled all over the country and spent more time than the average student frequenting country pubs and youth hostels.'

'That all sounds familiar, yes.'

'Well, it'll be just like that. It'll be the small group of you. No randoms you don't remember. Just you, Dhanesh, Sam, Jen, Freya and Tilda. I'll be there too, as well as one other person that's visiting at the same time and will be there from the night before. That's all. It's mainly the hardcore geographers. And the best bit is, you won't have to sit on a hillside and chart rock formations, or whatever geeky tasks you used to do. This time you'll get your own hotel room and all that's required is to share a nice meal with some old friends and prop up the bar with me while the others dance around their handbags. Come on, Jonathan. You know you're excited.'

Bea paused and put herself in Jonathan's position. She would never attend a similar event from her own perspective. No matter how intrigued she might be about old school friends. The snooping possibilities of the Internet had made organised reunions a pointless exercise now. It was entirely possible to see who had aged badly, hear who was in jail, and spot who had morphed into the adult swans their teenage ducklings had never once hinted were a possibility. There was no need to stand about in a hired hall drinking warm wine from a box, when a few clicks from the comfort of the sofa could provide the same information. All without having to get dressed up and fake enthusiasm in front of long-forgotten peers. There was no contest anymore. Reunions were over.

And yet *this* reunion - the one that Bea had lovingly arranged - was going to be epic. There was something innocent and pure about it. Freya was coming home. Tilda was finding her feet in a new place. Stewart was going to be carefully handled whilst the others were there for safety. Mal was getting the space he had asked for, and Bea was keeping busy. The feelings of the actual invited guests were almost irrelevant. It had only been Jonathan's phone call that had made Bea stop and think about how it seemed to others.

'Bea, you've convinced me. I'm practically looking forward to it now. Look how persuasive you are. I shall book the hotel this instant. Before I have second thoughts.'

They chatted for a few more minutes before ending the call. Bea had forgotten how lovely it was to flirt for flirting's sake. When it wasn't about sex but the fun of communication. She enjoyed the back and forth. She buzzed from the tingle of a friendly connection. It had certainly been a while.

Minutes later, a ping alerted her to a new email. It was from Dhanesh.

Bea.
Reunion sounds like a top idea. Count me in.
Dhanesh.
PS. Invite lots of single women. Thanks.

Bea laughed at its brevity. Jonathan was definitely the talker of the two. She wondered what *actively heterosexual* looked like, and whether that had been Jonathan's polite way of saying Dhanesh was a bit of a player. Either way, the message and call had perked up her day. That was never a bad thing.

The distraction over, Bea got up and returned to her office chair, wheeling herself into position at her desk. She should probably do some work at some point. She opened the document she had been reading and started again. The spreadsheet and its data danced before her eyes. She read the same table description several times before stopping. Nothing was going in. Maybe she'd digest it better with a cup of tea. As she summoned up the energy to haul herself back to her feet, the desk phone rang. She was getting nowhere fast today. Bea picked it up and answered.

'Hello, Policy Planning department, Bea Charleston speaking.'

'This is Stewart Grady. I'd like a word with you please. If you've got five minutes.'

Bea heard the tone in the man's voice. It was the complete opposite of the lovely, charming Jonathan. Stewart Grady could have used a bit of his charisma. Bea sat down again, ready to utilise all the people skills she could muster.

'Stewart. Lovely to hear from you. How can I help?'

There was a pause on the line. Stewart had assertively asked to speak to her and now he had gone silent. She heard his hesitation. He was either really grumpy or completely lacking in social skills. The email to Tilda flashed through her mind. There was a chance he was just bad at communicating. He'd had his own share of problems in the last few years. Perhaps it had taken its toll on how he presented himself. She should be kind to him and guide him through this social interaction - the one he had initiated but seemed unable to develop beyond its opening line. She made the decision and took charge.

'Stewart, I'm really glad you called. You must be wondering what on earth's going on here. I guess you got my email and want to know who I am and what I'm doing interfering in your life, am I right?'

There were a few seconds pause before a disarmed Stewart found the words.

'I wouldn't say that exactly. I wanted to make sure there hadn't been any confusion. I don't understand what this reunion has to do with me.'

'I completely understand. And you're quite right. In theory, it isn't anything to do with you. Tilda knows you wanted to catch up without other people around.'

'Yes. I don't need to be shoe-horned into a social event. A coffee would have done.'

'I understand, Stewart.' Bea paused for a second. Some men never realised how aggressive they came across to others. She felt sure that Stewart was one of those people. It would have come as a surprise to hear how high he had registered on the Creepometer. She had met men like that before.

Bea chose her tactic and accepted the challenge. She would win him round *without* resorting to brutal honesty. At least for the time being.

'Let me explain things a little better, Stewart. I get that this must be infuriating for you.'

'I wouldn't say that, exactly.'

'You're very kind but let me fill you in. I'm Tilda's friend from Manchester. I've known her for years. Did you know she's in Wales now?'

'I knew she was travelling. She wasn't far from me for a few weeks last year. I was away but I believe she was in Grimsby.'

'Can you believe she's settled in Aberystwyth? She's in a flat and has got herself a temp job. Isn't she mad?'

'Is that Wales? Is that what she wanted?'

'Well, you know Tilda.'

There was another long pause on the line. Bea heard Stewart take a breath to say something before pausing again. She waited for him to find the words.

'The thing is, I don't know Tilda. Not really. I'm afraid I might have built up an idea of her in my head without knowing whether it's the truth.'

Bea trod carefully. Stewart's grumpy bluster seemed to have calmed. His voice had shrunk to a fraction of its initial impact now that a smidge of self-awareness had crept in.

'I can see how that might happen. I don't know much about you and Tilda, except that she knew your brother. I guess that link alone makes the connection feel strong. Even if it's not.'

'She's the only person left who knew him. And I don't know her at all. Christ, Wales is drastic, isn't it?'

'I'd love to be able to tell you she's happy but I think the jury's still out on that one. She's definitely working towards it, though. She's gone through a lot of changes so I think she's just taking her time and not rushing into anything. It's a slow burn. But look at me. I'm telling you things you already know. You've had your own share of change, of course. She told me you met when your Dad died. I imagine you also know how difficult and slow things can seem, when everything's up in the air.'

There was more silence. Bea couldn't tell whether she was pissing off or comforting the tense man at the end of the phone. She was certainly becoming less creeped out by the real Stewart Grady than his email had implied she would be.

'I think perhaps Tilda has made better decisions than I have. I haven't given myself the time to think about what's gone on.'

'I get it. You've thrown yourself into work.'

'Not work. Holidays.'

Bea laughed. She wasn't sure if he had tried to be funny but it didn't matter. Stewart's voice softened. Not quite a laugh in return, but a palpable calming of temperament as he spoke.

'I mean it. I've been on one holiday after another for months, and then I expect Tilda to drop everything to suit me when I requested it. I can see why that mightn't have been convenient.'

Bea felt a rush of warmth towards the man. He was odd but, she felt sure, non-threatening.

'Look, come to this reunion weekend. It'll be fun. I'm going and I don't know anyone either. I wanted to keep busy because... well let's just say my own life is causing a need to tune out reality at the moment. I promised Tilda I'd organise all this so she wouldn't be stressed. Come down. We'll have a laugh.'

Stewart sighed. Bea could hear him weigh up the dilemma. She imagined he was torn between seeing Tilda albeit with a bunch of strangers, and booking yet another holiday that would provide fleeting escape for a little longer. She hoped he'd make the right choice. After this call, she was intrigued to meet him.

'OK. You've convinced me. Count me in. I'll be there for the Friday night but will probably make a move before the - who are they? The Geography Class of 1999? - turn up. I'm sure they'll be as relieved as me that they don't have to make pointless small talk with a fucked-up, non-friend of their old University mate.'

Bea laughed.

'But you make yourself sound so attractive Stewart. A fucked-up, non-friend. Shit, darling, you're quite the catch.'

She heard Stewart chuckle down the line. Job done. Making people laugh was the best. There was nothing like a mutual feel-good moment of shared humour to set the day on the right tracks. The fact she had broken down Stewart's stuffy exterior made her invincible. She was definitely going to have a good day now.

Minutes later, the call was over. Bea opened her planner and crossed Stewart off the list. He had promised Friday but she knew she would be able to convince him to stay for the Saturday too. He was in need of a carefree night on the town, she was sure of it.

There was a knock on her door.

'Yep?'

Justine, the newest member of the team, poked her head around the door.

'Sorry to disturb. You had a call while you were on the phone. Can you ring Mal back? He said it's urgent.'

'Will do. Thanks.'

Bea looked for her mobile phone. She'd spent the past twenty minutes speaking to Jonathan and then Stewart. What could have happened in that time to cause Mal to call the office and say it was urgent? He must have read her soppy outpouring and knew it needed a proper response. Retracing her steps led her to the zebra couch, and then to her phone siting on the cushion. Upon picking it up, the screen glowed into life. She had several Messenger notifications. *Thank you Mal! You read my email!*

The gist was clear within seconds of opening the app. Funny how things change. Three months ago, photos of a naked Mal, would have livened up a boring morning in the office. She would have felt a thrill. A frisson of excitement. *Something.* And while she wouldn't have necessarily been able to respond in a similar way, she would have enjoyed the messages that would have undoubtedly followed. This morning, however, she was irritated. Mal had ignored her email from last night. Or he had read it and thought the appropriate response was to send multiple photos of his dick.

It was her own fault, Bea reasoned. She had always been a woman who loitered around the *dick pic* end of the spectrum rather than the *soppy email* area. Yet here she was. She wanted more. More than dick pics while she was at work. She wanted connection. She wanted commitment. She wanted love.

Bea typed a supportive yet non-sexual response to Mal's pictures. *Bit busy right now, but thank you for thinking of me.* After the carefree conversation with Jonathan, and the thrill of making stuffy Stewart laugh, Mal and his dick were decidedly lower in the pecking order.

Bea's day continued. After the initial burst of reunion enquiries and Mal's misjudged photo gallery, she was even able to get some work done. But all her earlier optimism about what lay ahead, dwindled as the clock ticked on. It was hard to get into a rhythm. She couldn't focus on anything for long. She flitted between work documents and trips to the kitchen to make drinks. Justine was well trained in bringing her regular cups of tea, but Bea needed the change of scenery.

She was bored. She missed the office banter she used to have. Her daily piss-taking of Si and Alex would throw her into a tribunal now. She was not reckless. She knew she had to behave appropriately. The upside of the extra money and responsibility came with a very evident downside. Work bored her. It used to be entertaining but now it made her feel nothing. It was no wonder she had jumped at the chance to organise Tilda's social life. She wanted to do something, *anything* that made her feel. Dealing with Stewart's grumpiness reminded her that her people skills were fairly robust. She excelled at smoothing ruffled feathers. She could flirt, charm, and carouse, knowing which strategy was the best option in any given situation. These days, the only ruffled feathers she dealt with tended to be the stuffed suits around the table in the endless meetings she attended. Meetings whose purpose was never particularly obvious. She was wasted here. She should be a party planner. An events manager. One that was required to deal with argumentative and damaged people in a tactful and supportive manner.

Her mind was wandering again. *Stop it, Bea.* There was no job she could think of that planned parties for argumentative, damaged people. It was another random train of thought that was taking her away from the task in hand. She needed to focus. She reopened the spreadsheet and tried to digest the data.

Her phone pinged. Another email. Holding out hope it was a long and romantic outpouring from Mal, she opened it quickly. It wasn't. It was Jen.

> *Hi Bea, Tilda, Freya, and everyone else.*
> *I love the idea of this reunion, and I am definitely keen to come. Let me check my work schedule and see what I can do. It would be lovely to catch up with everyone again. I can't believe it's over twenty years since we got together. I'll be in touch when I've sorted time off.*
> *Jen x*

Bea highlighted Jen's name in yellow to indicate her TBC status. This mad plan of hers was all coming together. She had inserted herself into Tilda's private life purely to forget the dissatisfaction of her own. She was lucky Tilda had been amenable to the idea. She couldn't imagine the last few weeks if she hadn't had something interesting to do. It had to go well, that was clear. More than well, in fact. It had to be spectacular. What some might describe as a simple catch-up in a bar was, in Bea's mind at least, a glittering event to celebrate long lost friendship. She owed it to Tilda to make it a fabulous shebang. Aside from her own selfish reasons for getting involved, she knew Tilda needed the push to get back out there. She only hoped it was a supportive, gentle push she was providing, rather than a violent assault with no thought for the ramifications.

Bea went back to her computer screen. She found herself opening up her pension statement. She had far too small a pot to retire, but checked it regardless. Her next search was a jobs site. The quick glance proved fruitless. She was way too old to start anything new. Besides, she had a job. It paid her money. She should recognise how lucky she was and get on with doing it.

These valid sentiments aside, she was still unable to focus. She refilled her stapler and straightened the vase of fake orange gerberas that were once stuck to her dashboard. She recalled the time that Mal said she drove a clown's car. His mockery of her cushions and flowers had been in jest. Probably. It didn't matter. None of this was making the time go faster. She looked at the clock. Two more hours and she could be out of here. Just a hundred and twenty little minutes to go. Hardly anything.

She took a deep breath, stretched her arms, and made a concerted effort. She might feel like she was in a slump now, but it couldn't last forever. One day she would feel like herself again. Without the uncertainty, the anxiety, and the constant brain fog. One day she'd be back in control. She wouldn't care that she had started to rely on Mal at the exact same moment he had retreated from her. None of that would matter. She'd be back. Loving her job, loving Mal and knowing he loved her. One day, at some point soon, it had to feel better than this. Surely?

Bea really hoped so.

PART TWO

CHAPTER TWENTY-THREE

Day two of the reunion

The harsh strip lights did nothing to ease her tension. She knew that perpetual NHS underfunding meant there were greater priorities than mood lighting, but still. A flattering light might have helped. The people around her, the ones that were waiting for their own news, were becoming restless. It would be the same all over the country. Friday night. The end of the week. Accidents, drunken mishaps, and violence were far more likely tonight than on a Monday morning. There would be data on it. She'd look it up. That's what she'd do when her head was less fraught.

She wasn't going to look it up now, though. She wasn't sure of the rule about hospitals and phones. Would one Internet search break the ICU machines? She didn't know and didn't want to ask. Besides, her battery was low. She needed to save that should there be some difficult calls to make later. God, she hoped it wouldn't come to that. That was unthinkable.

The chair was hard and her back ached. As with the lights, it was a shame there was no money for comfort. People would be calmer. *She* would be calmer. There was also the issue of her developing hangover. Her head pounded. You cannot drink wine all night and expect to feel amazing. Not when you're kept from your bed due to unforeseen circumstances. Any other Friday, she'd be sleeping it off by now. What was the time anyway?

The movement of her phone made the screen light

up. 02.34. Not Friday night anymore. Yep, she should be in bed. Instead, she was here. Making sure everything was all right. Forcing away the alternative with all her might. Doing her best, in trying circumstances, to stop from vomiting on her knees.

'Hello, Mrs, Miss... you came in with...'

Her stomach lurched. The nausea intensified. Was this it? Was this how they told you, in front of everyone? Her mouth was dry. She wasn't sure she had the ability to speak. She was surrounded by increasingly rowdy people but was only aware of the thump of her own heart.

'We wanted to let you know...' the doctor monotoned. '...there's no news just yet. Everything's stable. We're still waiting for the results and then we'll know more. Would you be able to give us a better idea of what happened? We can talk over here if you like.'

As the doctor motioned to a more secluded area of the waiting room, away from the general hubbub, her body flooded with relief. Thank God that wasn't it. She wasn't strong enough to cope with that. Not on her own. Not here.

Numbly and, she realised, with tears running down her cheeks, she followed the Doctor across the room. She wiped her eyes and tried to concentrate. There was nothing else she could do.

CHAPTER TWENTY-FOUR

Day one of the reunion

It had seemed such a good idea at the time. After she had returned from Birmingham, refreshed and relaxed from a big night out. *'Let me organise a reunion,'* Bea had said. *'I'll take away the stress from you,'* she had said. *'It'll be fun,'* she had said. That was three months ago. Back then, August had felt such a long way off, there'd been no problem going along with it. Easier to let Bea march on with her plans. It had only been to keep her busy, after all. But now...

Tilda's train of thought was interrupted by her phone. She opened the message as the knots in her stomach twisted some more.

> *Darling. My train arrives in twenty minutes. Don't meet me, I'll Google Map it to yours. Will you be in? Isn't it exciting! We're going to party hard, all weekend long. WHOOP WHOOP!!!!!!!!!!!!!!!!*

Partying hard was something Tilda had never done. Not now, nor as a teenager. And if she were being strictly honest with herself, the reunion idea had not been easy to go along with, even back in May. It had taken mental wrangling and the internal consideration of pros and cons. With Bea happy to take away the hassle, it had been possible to push to the back of her mind. Tilda had done nothing. Apart from a brief email here and there, about whether she had a preference about a particular location, there had been nothing for

Tilda to worry about. That stopped now. Bea was bringing all her diversionary activities to her door. A reunion weekend was starting today, whether she liked it or not. Her gut continued to knot with the weight of it.

A glance at the clock told her it was nearly lunchtime. She hadn't slept well and had been up around dawn. Up with the lark and the bin men. Watching the rubbish be collected along the seafront had been strangely hypnotic. She'd sat at her window and watched the truck amble along as the sky brightened in the background. The sequence was the same each time. A man would jump out, unlock the metal bin that was crammed full of rubbish, and drag the bag out before flinging it into the back of his van. He would replace the bag, drive a few metres along the prom, and repeat the process. She had watched him for as long as she could crane her neck to see. The repetition was therapeutic. She would have liked to have filled her day with the safety of a monotonous task. Something she could control. Something non-scary.

Tilda had tried to go back to bed. Sometime around eight, she realised she would flag later if she didn't catch up on some sleep. It might only be the preamble to tomorrow's main event, but it was an emotionally charged preamble, nonetheless. She had lain there, wide awake and willing herself to doze as she tried to sort out the particular feelings that were keeping her from relaxing.

Firstly Freya. Tilda had smiled involuntarily at the thought of her arrival. A positive sign. Her chaotic but good-natured presence during Tilda's University years had kept things livelier than if she'd been left to her own devices. Without Freya, she wouldn't have made friends with anyone else. She had needed the stronger, more sociable person to open the doors to new people. She might be socially isolated now, but when she was eighteen, she was a million times worse. Thank God she'd chosen the seat next to hers in that first lecture.

Tilda had continued to try and force herself to drop off. She wanted to do that rather than think about Stewart. There was no way Stewart's inclusion in the weekend could ever pan out as a good idea. She should have replied to his email and got it out of the way. This was all too drastic. Even just *thinking* about thinking of him caused a stab inside. She would never sleep if she let her mind go there. As she forced the image of Stewart away, she found it merging into the softer, more welcoming memories of his brother.

She smiled and snuggled into her pillows. Her Grady. There would always be sadness over his loss but the memories of their time together never failed to soothe. She had been loved. She was loveable. That knowledge had provided more comfort in recent years than anything else. She closed her eyes. Her jaw unclenched and her stomach relaxed. Grady by the caves. Grady in the café. Grady's letters arriving on her mat. She had drifted away, carried into sleep by the memories she considered the happiest of her life.

And now it was time. Showered, and waiting for Bea's imminent arrival, the churning returned. She would never have the life she wanted if she gave into fear. A sense of community and a support network would always remain elusive if she forever took the safe option. Nothing would change without risk. Her head knew all that. Of course it did. But it struggled to convey the same message to her gut.

Tea was made. The sofa cushions plumped. The mostly empty binbag taken out to the yard. It was clear Tilda was unable to sit and wait passively. Just when she thought she would explode with nerves, the street door buzzed. Bea had arrived.

'Darling, I made it! Come here, you. Excited?'

Tilda hugged her friend and made the appropriate noises. She could well be excited deep down. Underneath the debilitating anxiety.

'I am Bea. It'll be fun. How was the train?'

'Oh, fine. A month's a long time in pest control, and all that. But I'm here! We're going to have the best weekend of our lives. Say whoop whoop with me.'

Tilda laughed. The pressure easing slightly now Bea was in charge.

'Whoop whoop, Bea.' Tilda deadpanned for comic effect. 'Am I enthusiastic enough?'

'Are you, bollocks. You can definitely do better but it's early days. We've only just begun. The night is young and all that jazz. Can I put the kettle on? I'm gasping.'

Tilda ushered Bea towards the sofa and crossed the room to flick the switch on the kettle. The kitchen-cum-diner-cum-lounge area of her flat was small. Teensy, matchbox-esque or cosy. Several descriptions would do the job. The upside to its lack of space was that Bea could continue to chat from the sofa, taking off her boots as Tilda got the tea bags.

It still jarred to see Bea look so different. Today she

was wearing a flattering black wrap top, fitted charcoal jacket, and stylish slim cut jeans. Tilda silently groaned at herself. Why had she used adjectives like that? She was describing her as if she were captioning a fashion spread in a magazine. Yet that's how it seemed to be. A contrived arrangement of carefully chosen pieces for a glossy photoshoot. Not the real-life force of nature that was Bea Charleston and her old clothing choices. She looked amazing but she looked alien. Chic, neutral, the walking embodiment of a capsule wardrobe. Tilda remembered reading an article about it, during some hair cut back in the day. At the time she decided she must also have a capsule wardrobe because she didn't own many clothes. Bea had gone the more traditional route, with specially selected pieces to cover all bases. It was just a shame she looked so unlike herself.

Tilda caught herself and stopped. *Don't be daft, Willoughby. A person's clothes do not matter.* She was ashamed that the superficial thought had come from her own head. Obviously, Bea could wear what she liked and still be Bea. She was silly to think otherwise. It was simply something she would have to get used to.

She poured the kettle as her friend rummaged. From the depths of her handbag, tissues, tampons, and tickets spilled forth. By their tattered look, they'd been at the bottom of her bag for a while.

'So I guess you'll want to know the plan of action, then? I've printed out an itinerary for you. I know how much you love a timetable.'

Bea shoved detritus back in her bag before holding a sheet out to Tilda. In bold capital letters, the title screamed across the page.

TILDA WILLOUGHBY'S BEST WEEKEND EVER

'Good to see you're not getting carried away, Bea.'
Tilda said. 'No overstatement here. Not one bit.' She
smiled at her friend's hyperbole. *Best Weekend Ever*
was quite a stretch. How could this be the best weekend ever when she wouldn't be watching DVDs in her
pyjamas from the early evening onwards? Then there
was the other fly in the ointment. Strictly speaking,
tonight should have been Chip Shop Night. Tilda had
made the decision to move it a week later, but the
longer wait was definitely rankling. Excessive social
interaction with people from the past should never
have had to take precedence over Chip Shop Night.
But when the rest of the weekend's attendees had
managed to find the one date they could all make, it
seemed churlish to stand her ground. She hadn't been
able to fabricate a previous commitment in time to
avoid it. She knew that saying it was Chip Shop Night
to people who were taking time off work, finding
childcare, and booking hotels, just wouldn't cut it. She
had kept quiet and said she was available. Technically,
she was. She knew that, really. But still. Chip Shop
night was delayed. Not good.

'Thoughts? How's today looking? All timings are
subject to change, naturally.'

Tilda scanned the sheet. She knew from her emails
that Bea was a fan of Caps Lock and exclamation
marks. This was no exception.

'Yeah, all looks fine. Today's a quiet one, isn't it?'

Bea consulted her own sheet. One that she pulled
from a file as Tilda put two mugs on the table.

'Yes, today is Phase One. We've got Freya's train arriving in a couple of hours. I said you'd meet her from the station, if that's all right?'

'That's fine.'

'She's bringing an airbed for the floor. In here? We might need to move the table over.'

'It's OK. My sleeping bag fits when it's rolled out.'

'And then Stewart's arriving sometime around five. If you meet him in his hotel bar, you'll have an hour or so before all four of us meet for dinner. I've booked a table at seven-thirty. At the place you said you'd walked past.'

Tilda sighed. It was too late to do anything now. This was happening. That the awkwardness with Stewart would only be for an hour before the others came, almost reassured her.

'Yes, it looks nice.' Tilda had no more insight into the merits of a restaurant in which she had never been. She changed the subject. 'And tomorrow?'

'Tomorrow the geographers arrive! Tomorrow is Phase Two. Tomorrow we get to relive old times with old friends. Tomorrow will be brilliant.'

'You do know that you weren't in our geography group, don't you? They are all strangers to you. And to me, these days. You're getting carried away.'

Bea was quick to respond.

'Darling, since I've been emailing these people, I've had the loveliest of chats with them. Jonathan is a hands down absolute sweetie. And Dhanesh is funny as frig. Constantly on the pull but Jonathan says it's a blatant act because he's bruised from his divorce. And Jen is ridiculously accomplished. She makes organic ready meals and they're in the shops. You can actually buy them! I don't know much about Sam yet, except she's coming and said it would be great to escape her moody teen, but they are all so nice Tilda. It must be lovely to have a group of connected friends like that.'

'You've got friends too. What about your gang?'

'But we weren't at college or school together. We were a mish-mash. It was easier for the group to lose each other once life got in the way.'

'Well, you're more than welcome to be part of the geographers, as you seem to be calling them.' Tilda laughed. 'I think you fit in better than I do. Although it's only Stewart that will really stick out. Like a sore thumb.' Tilda laughed again but with a little more force. She was doing her best to keep things upbeat.

'You know what? I think you might be wrong about him. We've had a few emails and a phone chat too. He's tightly wound, no question, but he's OK you know. I think he just needs a break. Or to be with friendly people for a bit. Or to chat about Grady. He needs something. I'm not sure what but I think he'll benefit from being with us.'

Tilda took in Bea's words. She wasn't necessarily discounting what she heard but she wasn't reassured either. It would all become clear in time.

'Right then, I've had enough swigs of tea. We've got an hour before Freya gets here. How about you give me a tour of the town. I want to see tomorrow's bar, the hotel, tonight's restaurant... I want to see it all. Do we have time?'

Tilda stood up and drained her tea.

'Bea, it's all just minutes away. Let's go.'

CHAPTER TWENTY-FIVE

The tour of the town was nowhere as brief as Tilda had assumed. When she put her mind to it, there were plenty of sights she could share, all giving a flavour of her new life. They just hadn't been the ones her friend cared about. Bea seemed to focus on places of which Tilda had no clue whatsoever. There had been several times that the conversation had been repetitive. Every time they passed a bar, the same exchange took place.

'That looks cool, doesn't it?'

'Yes. I walk past most days.'

'What's it like inside?'

'I don't know.'

She had been inside none of them. Zero. Tilda's tour focused, instead, on the more day-to-day aspects of Aberystwyth life. She included the little Tesco, the big Tesco, then she pointed out the cliff top railway, and finally the Spanish deli on Pier Street. The latter was the most exciting Aberystwyth business she had frequented, and the place she had bought a bottle of posh wine and some marinated olives when she sold the campervan. The expense had felt decadent and celebratory at the time.

An hour later and the tour was over. Despite it drawing sharp focus to her limited experiences, it also provided the smell of the ozone and the truly relaxing experience of watching holidaymakers by the sea. People-watching was at its most therapeutic when the people being watched were chilled out and happy. Bea and Tilda had chattered away, never rushing, and making the most of the weather and alone time before - as

Bea had described the evening - shit got real.

Tilda worked the route so it ended at the station, in time for Freya and her train. Bea, with sensitivity to the rising nerves in her friend, said she was shattered and would meet them back at the flat. Tilda handed over her keys, pointed her in the right direction, and found a bench on the platform. Freya was imminent and she was left to welcome her alone. The ache in her gut returned.

Perhaps now was the time to do some deep breathing. She had once downloaded an app that had taught her how to do it. With her sensible head engaged, it had felt counter-intuitive to pay a small fee for such a service. Breathing had been instinctive since birth. Someone somewhere was making a load of money off the back of people's anxiety. It didn't feel right. But sitting here now, her stomach churning, the clock ticking down until Freya's train, she found herself remembering it. *Breathe in through the nose, hold for five seconds, exhale through the mouth. Breathe in through the nose, hold for five seconds, exhale through the mouth.* She closed her eyes, repeating the routine. Whether it worked, or merely provided a distraction from the particular anxiety the breather was hoping to combat, Tilda didn't know. She focused on being present; of being mindful. Whatever that meant. Of being in the moment and aware of herself? Was she doing it? Had she cracked it? As obvious as she had assumed breathing was, she wasn't convinced she'd made it to expert level just yet.

She felt a little calmer. At least she thought she did. Perhaps it was the power of suggestion; the placebo effect. Was she still stressed but the focus on her mouth and nose had kept her distracted? She couldn't tell anymore. She looked at the clock. Six more minutes till the train. She breathed, held for five, and exhaled some more.

As Tilda was forcing herself out of butterflies, there was a small amount of bustle around her. She was not alone on the station platform. A smattering of people waited alongside her. Now that her breathing had de-escalated from almost asthmatic to mildly excited, she could continue to people-watch as she waited.

There was a middle-age woman standing by the ticket machine. With no bags and her car keys in hand, she was clearly picking someone up rather than waiting to depart. Then there was a group of girls. Perhaps they were young women. They also appeared to be waiting for someone. They were at the age where half fare travel was still possible before going to the pub and getting served. Tilda remembered the rowdy protestations that nineteen-year-old Freya would make on the Merseybus.

I swear on my mother's life I'm fifteen. Honest to God, I was at school today. I've just failed my mocks. Someone nicked my locker key. I knackered my ankle in PE.

And then there was the man. Only his left side was visible. About her age, and sitting on the adjacent bench. He was wearing a faded grey T-shirt, stretched against the muscle in his upper arm. Tilda smiled to herself. She had never known a man to have a visible bicep. Between her dad, her ex-husband, and the male colleagues she had worked with over the years, their unstinting devotion to minimal exercise meant they maintained a distinctly untoned upper arm area. She tried to remember Grady's arms. She had felt them around her, but had she seen them? Whenever she pictured him, he was wearing bulky layers. That's what came of finding the love of her life on a field trip in March. When they met, he told her he liked nothing more than reading books and drinking tea. His arms had never seen a weight or a cross trainer, she was sure of that. She remembered how they felt, though. The memory of his arm draped over her waist as they spooned in her single bed, proved far more effective at calming Tilda's nerves than any meditation technique.

An announcement jerked Tilda back to the present.

The train arriving at platform 1 is the 1519 service from Shrewsbury. This service terminates here.

Bang on time, the carriages slowed to a stop. Tilda's app and Grady's arms had done the trick. The last few moments had been relatively calm. Now the train was here, she was thrown back into angst once more. *Come on Tilda, get it together. Freya is the easy part of today.*

The doors opened. People spilled out. Two young women joined their waiting posse of friends. A cyclist dragged his bike from the carriage, wheeling it onto the platform before jumping on as he hit the exit ramp. A teenager with a blatant laundry binbag was met by the woman next to the ticket machine. Her eyes rolled at the incoming chore despite ruffling his hair with maternal pride. The man with the muscle appeared to have gone. *Probably on the way to the gym or to drink something green,* Tilda mused. Now she had identified him as someone that worked out, she had a specific mental category in which to file him. That done, she scanned the platform. Would she even recognise Freya these days? It had been a ridiculously long time since she had seen her in the flesh. The odd photo sent with her emails meant nothing. She changed her hair colour like most people changed socks.

In the end, it didn't matter. She heard her before she saw her.

'WILLLLLOUGHBBBBBYYY.'

An ice-blonde woman with a massive suitcase, half tottered, half sprinted towards her from a distance. Tilda knew instantly it was Freya. From her body language, her unwalkable footwear, and the chaotic aura that surrounded her.

'Freya, you made it!'

Tilda met her friend halfway, saving her the energy it would have taken to totter towards her in those spiky heeled boots.

'Willoughby! Let me look at you, you absolute beauty. Can you believe it? I'm here!'

Freya flung her arms around Tilda as they both struggled to catch their breath. Nothing had changed beyond the superficial. The tour de force of her old mate had not been dimmed by age. Tilda disentangled herself and managed to find some words.

'Freya, you have not changed one bit. How was your journey? Are you tired? How are you?'

'I am absolutely cracking, mate. I had a good hour's kip after setting off, so I'm perky! Tilds, you big ledge. How are you? What's going on? Where the fuck are we?'

What could have been awkward small talk turned

out to be happy free flowing conversation. Tilda's nerves were at bay once again. Whether this was due to being truly at ease or because she was distracted by Freya and her personality, was debatable. Either way, Tilda and Freya were back together. The reunion weekend had begun.

CHAPTER TWENTY-SIX

The word was incredulous. That's what she was going with. Incredulous or amazed. Or perhaps gobsmacked. Or maybe disbelieving? Definitely in that area. Any one of those words was how Bea had felt since Tilda and Freya had returned to the flat. Because from out of nowhere, Tilda had become an absolute chatterbox.

'...and remember when Kenny was sick on Jen's back, but she was wearing a corset top so we had to sponge off the laces in the toilets? It was so funny! And remember when Jonathan was going out with that girl before he was properly out, and to avoid sleeping with her he said he had diarrhoea every time they had a date? That was a nightmare. And remember when Dhanesh broke his thumb doing the macarena when he slipped on Jen's Tia Maria and coke? All those hours at the hospital. And remember...'

It had been like this for the past hour. Freya jumped in at times but Tilda was certainly holding her own. Bea found the chatty Tilda dynamic hilarious. It was also useful to be brought bang up to speed with the anecdotes that would likely be repeated tomorrow. She was experiencing an intensive course of catch-up and would be an authentic member of the Geography Gang when the others arrived.

She continued her jobs as she listened in. Freya had pulled a bulging plastic wallet from her case as soon as the introductions had been made. Bea was adding Blu Tac to all the photos that it contained, as she listened to their whistle-stop gossip. She was definitely getting a good picture of the student comings and goings of her mate's mates. This was better than the telly. Now she knew how Kit felt when it came to her own messy love life. Real life beat fiction, every time.

The thought of her elderly neighbour made Bea pause. She stopped Blu Tac-ing for a moment, picked up her phone, and sent a quick text. She tended to worry when she was away, even if it were only a weekend. Straight away there was a reply. She must have caught Kit primed with her phone in her hand. Her replies usually took ages.

Don't you worry about me. I'm up to my ears. Jamie drove me to the good butchers. Now I'm making my Mama's jerk chicken and everything smells like home. He's here for the night, bless him. Have a gin for me, dear. Make sure you have lots of fun. Xx

Bea was relieved. Kit's grandson was a nice boy. Knowing he was there meant Bea could relax. Not that keeping an eye on Kit was a chore. It was definitely not that. Yet coming away for two nights had made her conscious about her widowed friend in the next flat. She was getting unsteadier on her feet, and that was before she had a weekend tipple. Good for Jamie, giving Bea the chance to be irresponsible. She resumed her sticking and her earwigging. Freya had got a word in edgeways.

'...all those bunk beds. Jeez, Tilds. We really roughed it, didn't we. Except that one place in the Lakes. The place with Grady. That was the best one, wasn't it?'

'Obviously *I* think it was. Best week ever. But twin

rooms were also a bonus.' Tilda laughed although Bea felt the pinprick of sadness puncture the mood. There were a few seconds of respectful silence before Freya spoke up.

'I am sorry, Tilda. I know it was years ago, but even so. He was a really nice bloke.'

'Yeah. He was, wasn't he.'

All three women kept their thoughts to themselves for a moment. Bea watched the shadow on Tilda's face land, pause, and be dismissed as she took control of the room.

'Right you two. It feels like we're ready for wine. Shall I open a bottle?'

Freya spoke for the room.

'YES mate. Do it, I can't believe we're still sober.'

Tilda busied herself with the task as Bea continued to sort the photos. Freya had obviously been chief snapper on their nights out. There were loads of Tilda and hardly any of her.

'That's Grady, there.' Freya stood over Bea's shoulder and pointed to a man on the photo she was holding.

'That was the week she met him. A beauty, wasn't he?'

Bea looked at the picture. Less posed than the one on the mantlepiece but unmistakably the same person. A sweet looking face, his smile was open and kind. His messy curls gave him a boyish look and his face was carefree and happy.

'He looks lovely.'

A moment later, Tilda was handing out drinks. The sombre tone lifted with the clinking of glasses. Freya made the toast.

'To new friends, old friends, absent friends - not Kenny obviously, probably best we didn't rekindle that relationship - and still-to-be-met friends. Let's have an absolute blast!'

The hour that followed was more of the same. Tilda and Freya didn't stop for breath while Bea finished preparing the decorations for the following day. She was also fielding constant enquiries. Gethin, the owner of the bar, had been in touch. He was confirming the final food details that Bea had emailed the day before. Then Jonathan had messaged to check arrival times. She had typed a quick reply back, picked up the Blu Tac and was rolling a new ball when her phone pinged again. This time it was Dhanesh. He had forwarded a meme showing drunk residents of an old folks' home causing havoc with their walkers. Bea assumed he was drawing a parallel and smiled. Whenever Jonathan messaged with a legitimate enquiry, Dhanesh would follow-up with something daft. She pictured them chatting about the weekend at home, with Jonathan being Dad and taking charge of the details whilst his lodger provided the LOLs and performed the role of child. A moment later when another text came through, she almost ignored it. It would only be banter. Banter with a capital B.

Except it wasn't. This time it was Mal. She found herself opening the message with the same energy as working through her in-tray. Whilst she was having a weekend break, this felt like another piece of admin to box off.

Bea, I've been stupid. Forgive me. I shouldn't have asked for space like I did. You've been so busy recently and I miss you too much. It's all over at home. Finally. We had a long talk and agreed it was best. I'm staying at my brother's tonight. Everything feels numb. We're telling the kids tomorrow. Wish you were here by my side. I'm lost without you x

Bea breathed sharply as her blood ran cold. *He's done it. He's finally made the leap.* She suddenly felt a million miles away from her breezy seaside location. Her head was firmly back up North. This was what Mal had wanted for years. He must be feeling huge relief.

Her head continued to process the message as her arms pricked with goosebumps. This was good news. Her heart pounded and her stomach flipped. *Wasn't it?* As hard as it must have been, his family needed clarity. So did Mal. This could be the making of him.

Bea continued to roll a piece of Blu Tack, with no plan what to do with it. Her mind stayed on Mal. She had given him space to sort out his life and now he had. It was impressive, really. She found her thoughts repeating themselves as the phrase *he's done it* popped up once more. That was all she could think. Beyond that, she was numb. Like him, apparently. She was glad his brother was there for him. She couldn't be. Not at first. Not until he worked through the grief that would come from moving out of the home he shared with his kids. That was a journey he needed to make himself.

'You all right, mate?'

Freya had spotted the change in Bea from the sofa. She realised she'd been staring at her phone without moving for several minutes.

'Yes. Yeah, I'm fine thanks. Just trying to work out when's best to take these decorations to the bar.'

'Tell you what, I need a breather. Why don't me and Tilds go to the bar and see what they say. To be honest, I could do with a heads up to what the vibe's like. I've several outfits with differing levels of drama. I wouldn't want to misjudge what people can handle.'

'Excellent idea. And no matter what the bar's like, I think we need the most dramatic outfit you have. It IS the Geographers of '99 Reunion Weekend, after all.' Bea found the presence of mind to snap back into her personality. 'Check it out and report back. It might be Gethin or it might be one of the staff. Judge the mood and guide us all.'

Freya and Tilda spent ten minutes downing wine, finding shoes, and laughing at everything and nothing, all at once. Bea stayed seated, feeling detached. Once she was alone, she poured herself another glass. She was pretty sure this was what a headfuck felt like. She reread the message, felt sick, and decided to put down her phone. This was not part of her itinerary.

Her phone pinged once more. The gut reaction of putting a cushion over the screen only lasted a few seconds. She needed to face whatever came next. The relief when she opened the message was immense. It wasn't Mal. It was Stewart.

Hi Bea. Just to let you know, I'm here a little earlier than expected. Shall I come to Tilda's address? It's pretty close to where I'm staying. It might be good to say hello now I'm here.

Bea exhaled. The fact it wasn't Mal made even the irritation of Stewart rewriting her timetable, pale into insignificance. She messaged back.

Sure. Come round. I'm in, and Tilda and her mate will be back soon. Come and have a glass of wine with me.

There were a few seconds pause while her phone told her that *Stewart is replying.* She waited. When it came, his message was brief.

OK. I'm outside.

Bea pulled the voile curtain aside and looked down at the doorstep. He wasn't lying. Stewart *was* outside. She buzzed open the street door and unlocked the door to the flat. Then she waited.

CHAPTER TWENTY-SEVEN

He had mulled it over for the past hour. Should he stay sitting in his hotel room, wondering how long to wait before making contact, or turn up early and force the issue? The map on his phone showed Tilda lived a couple of minutes' walk from where he was staying. It was stupid to stay put. The hotel was nice enough but there was no minibar. He could see little point in hanging around without alcoholic refreshment, so the decision was made for him. A moment later he found himself walking to the address he had been sent. By the time he was outside her door, he had second thoughts. He still hadn't spoken to Tilda properly. Bea had been the regular go-between, for reasons that continued to be unclear. The whole weekend felt increasingly overwhelming. As all areas of his life made him feel out of his depth, he wished he had stayed at home. At least he could be overwhelmed near the comfort of his drinks cabinet.

It was too late to back out now. He'd sent the text. The door had opened, he'd climbed the stairs, and here he was. Standing in the tiny flat and wishing he was anywhere other than here. Bea's chatter alerted him to the fact he needed to act normally. As much as he could, anyway.

'How was the journey down? It's a bit of a trek. Did you get the train or did you drive? I got the train but I bet the drive is stunning.'

Stewart struggled to find words. Not only was the situation more than he could cope with. So was Bea.

'Anyway, enough small talk. Let's get you a drink.

I've got wine open. How's that? Or there's beer in the fridge. I don't think there's anything stronger but we can go out and get something if you want.'

Stewart continued to look blankly. He knew he needed to respond. If he didn't, the questions and babbling would carry on.

'Wine is fine. Thank you.'

He watched Bea get a glass from a cupboard and fill it. She motioned at him to sit down so he did, all the while struggling. Struggling with being told what to do by a stranger, in an almost-stranger's flat. Struggling being in a part of the world about which he knew nothing, when all he wanted was to get the almost stranger's opinion about what was best to do with his inheritance. It had seemed much easier on the phone. When he was safely miles away.

He took a sip of wine and found some words.

'Bea. What am I doing here?'

With his awkwardness fully exposed, the tension seemed to break. They both knew this was a weird scenario. Bea had powered through with incessant chatter whereas Stewart had struggled to be anything but mute. Now they were sitting in a minuscule room, in full acknowledgement that the weirdness needed to be addressed. Bea took charge.

'I am sorry, darling. I realise this must seem like the oddest weekend. Believe me, I'm having a small out of body experience myself right now, but back to you. It's my fault, really. Or Tilda's. She let me get carried away. I just like planning parties. It's what I should have done, career wise. Too late now, of course. I'm stuck forever in local council red tape and procedure. In a parallel universe I could be Pippa Middleton.'

Stewart had no immediate response to this. He stayed silent, although the idea of this demonstrative and forthright woman meekly attending to a royal bride, did strike him as absurd. His mind began to wander before her phone's alert snapped him back in to focus.

'Sorry, one sec. I'll just get this message and then I'll...'

He watched Bea open, read, and dismiss something within a three second turnaround.

'Right, darling, let's forget that so I can give you my full attention. I'll explain everything. First of all, you're wondering why I'm here and Tilda isn't. Yes?'

'Yes.'

'Right then, let me put it all out there. Blame the wine, even though I've only had a couple of glasses, but I think you deserve honesty.'

'OK.'

'The email you sent Tilda came across a little strong. I mean, darling. I doubt you meant it, but you scared her.'

Stewart froze. He couldn't remember the exact words he had used. He had only asked to meet, hadn't he?

'I scared her?'

'Well, maybe *I* scared her when she showed it to me. She was only vaguely unnerved at that point. I read it and felt concerned. I'm sorry. I hadn't chatted to you at that point. I hadn't realised you were still in the depths of grief. My bad.'

'I scared her?' Stewart couldn't get beyond that basic statement.

'You sounded needy and slightly desperate. I think she felt she wouldn't be able to help even if you did meet. So she ignored you for a bit, and then I stepped in. The idea was that if you were here this weekend, there would be support around. Support for both of you.'

'So she *is* here?'

'Of course she's here. She's just nipped out for half an hour. She was going to meet you in your hotel later but now you're here instead. It's fine. You'll be able to chat when she gets back. Me and Freya will give you space. But just... you know... think about how you might come across. Put yourself in her shoes. That's all.'

Stewart nodded, not knowing what else to do. He had another swig of wine. He stared ahead, spotting the photo on the mantelpiece for the first time.

'Fuck. That's John. In the frame.' He felt a lump in his throat so drank some more.

Bea looked over to the fireplace.

'Yes. Tilda said you called him John. Wasn't he beautiful? Or is that a weird thing to ask someone about their brother. I certainly couldn't bring myself to say it about mine. Although mine's also an arse. That doesn't help.'

Stewart looked ahead at the picture. A smiling twenty-year old John looked back. Somehow, despite the strangeness of the situation, he found himself opening up.

'He was a happy person. All he wanted to do was be an artist. He would sketch bits of leaves or a raindrop on a blade of grass. He would spend hours looking at the tiniest of details. Nothing like me. He did what he wanted and never compromised. It didn't help him in the end but he would always stand up for himself. I don't think I've stood up for anything in my life.'

Bea moved next to Stewart on the sofa.

'I've found whenever I compare myself to other people, I only ever come in second. Look at Pippa Middleton. I'd never have pulled off that bridesmaid dress. I think it's better to aim for the best version of you, instead of measuring yourself against others.'

Stewart shifted uncomfortably. He never sat this close to anyone. He had his well-embedded defence mechanisms to stop people several metres away. Bea had broken through them without any hassle. He was either extremely vulnerable or she was an excellent reader of people. Maybe both. It was time to regain some composure. He needed to control something, anything, for a bit.

'It sounds like you're as messed up as me. You seem to know exactly how I'm feeling. What is it that made you think you should interfere in Tilda's life and make decisions about who she should meet? That sounds pretty controlling to me.'

He watched Bea sit back as he felt a stab of shame. She had been the only person in months that hadn't spoken to him with disdain. Bea and Richard. That was it. Although the fact he was paying Richard for every phone call and email took the shine off that particular relationship somewhat. Bea, on the other hand, had been kind for nothing in return. He started to think how to backtrack from what he'd just said but she'd already started to speak.

'You know what? You're right. Helping Tilda was selfish of me. I needed a distraction. This weekend was a good way of keeping busy and having some fun. I'm as much of an outsider as you are, darling. I only know Tilda too. Although having said that, Freya's lovely. I met her for the first time an hour ago. You'll like her.'

Stewart had no interest in Freya or anyone else there. He was here to work out what he should do with the money his father's house sale had provided. He had wanted someone - anyone, he didn't care who anymore - to be a representative of John's, who could guide him. To give him consent with whatever he chose. Explaining that out loud sounded ridiculous. It had made perfect sense during his drunken logistical wranglings. When he sent the email to Tilda, he was convinced she would be the one to give him a fresh perspective. Now? In front of Bea? It sounded pathetic.

'I'm not sure this was a good idea. Even if Tilda isn't scared of me, I've still gate-crashed her weekend. The conversations I wanted to have aren't going to happen with all this going on. I think it's best I leave you to it and go back to the hotel.'

Bea sat up straight. She was firm in her response.

'That's a categorical NO from me, Stewart. Just no. You're not going to leave me on my own with two friends who have decades to catch up on. You can zone out and be here in body only, but you're sitting with me at dinner tonight, whether you like it or not. You're my plus one. I'm not being Tilda and Freya's gooseberry. You can frig right off if you think that's happening.'

Stewart sat back in his seat. He drained his wine glass and mulled it over. It might be the longest night of his life but it would all be over tomorrow. He could make excuses for the second night and head back first thing in the morning. In twenty-four hours' time, he would be back in York, in his own flat, with no one telling him what to do.

He opened his mouth, about to respond, when he heard a noise. A key in the lock. Tilda was back.

CHAPTER TWENTY-EIGHT

He had been as surprised as she was. After weeks of being ignored and then palmed off onto her friend, her reaction when she saw him had been unexpected. A long look, a choked sob, and then a spontaneous hug. He had stood for what felt like forever, stiffly at first before allowing his arms to relax and reach around her back. Her tears fell silently onto his chest. He didn't know what to say. He kept on holding.

When she eventually composed herself, she was embarrassed.

'I *am* sorry Stewart. I don't know what happened. I think I forgot how much you look like him.' Tilda wiped her eyes, first with her fingers and then after a brief search, a tissue from her pocket. She blushed. 'I feel silly.'

'I wish I did look like him.' He motioned to the photo on the fireplace. 'He hasn't got my wrinkles.' He attempted a smile. So did she, but with more success. She was back in control and Stewart was relieved. He had expected animosity if anything. Not tears.

'Has Bea got you a drink? Good. Where is she? Where's Freya?' Stewart looked around. A moment ago, Bea and the other woman had been standing in the lounge area with them. He guessed that at the sight of their emotional embrace, they had scarpered and left them to it. Confirmation came via a shout from behind the closed door.

'Darlings, we're doing our hair. Have a lovely chat. We'll be busy for ages.'

Tilda gestured to him so he sat on the sofa next to

her. His hands needed something to do so he straightened the wine glasses on the coffee table. She paused a
second before jumping back up.

'Good idea. I think I need a drink too. Sorry. I know
I'm being rubbish. This should be going far more
smoothly. I didn't mean to cry.' She picked up her
glass from earlier. Her trembling hand caused a small
spillage as she refilled his and then her own.

'I'm not sure it is a smooth situation though.'

'It's my fault. I should have been in touch properly.
You're Grady's brother, for God's sake. If things had
been different, you could have been my brother-in-
law. I don't know why I'm so nervous.'

Stewart took a breath. He was nervous too, but
why? Tilda was being kind. There was nothing to be
worried about. Bea, despite her tendency to dominate
the room, had been perfectly decent to him as well.
The worst-case scenario for the evening was that it
would be dull and uneventful. He could handle that,
yet irritations still niggled.

Tilda sat back down. She seemed determined to
make this easy for him.

'I'm glad you're here, Stewart. I know this isn't
what you wanted. I'm sure a bunch of randoms you've
never met before weren't part of your plan.'

Stewart made an effort to put her mind at ease, in
spite of his misgivings.

'It's probably a good idea, getting all your friends
together. I believe you haven't seen them for some
years?'

'That's right. Since graduation. To be honest, it
makes sense you being here. Other than Bea, everyone

coming this weekend was there when I met Grady. They'll all remember him.'

Stewart swallowed another mouthful of his wine. He hadn't realised that. He tried to play it down.

'It's a long time ago. I doubt they'll recall him.'

She was quick to reply.

'No, honestly, he stood out. Not because he was so wonderful, although of course there was that. But mostly because I was this shy, terminally embarrassed twenty-year old, and the fact I'd managed to pull someone - anyone - was the biggest news of the year. Grady saw in me what nobody else did. He brought out all my confidence. The others will remember him for that.'

Stewart smiled sadly. He understood what Tilda meant. Grady had brought out the best in everyone, even Stewart. But by the time they were teenagers, their chalk and cheese personalities had forced them into opposing factions instead of the strong team of their childhood. The guilt of that was never far away. He cleared his throat and tried to move back to more practical matters.

'Do you think there'll be time to talk over some things privately, before I go back. I was hoping to get your opinion on a couple of matters.'

'How about now?'

Tilda sat up straight, as if ready to listen. Stewart was thrown. He wasn't sure what he had envisaged, but this wasn't it. In the background he could hear muted laughter from Bea and the other woman coming from the bedroom. He had no papers with him. All the brochures from Richard were in his hotel room. He assumed at some point they would be alone, facing each other across a coffee shop table, or in a quiet bar in the middle of the day. Here, on the tiny sofa with their knees almost touching, in the miniscule flat with her friends only metres away, he felt exposed. This was not how financial plans were discussed. He was annoyed but knew he had to hide it. He did his best.

'OK. But how about we go somewhere quieter? Is there a Starbucks somewhere? Or a pub? Somewhere with a table?' He knew he sounded stupid. The table was irrelevant. But sitting opposite something formal made him feel more control. He saw concern flash across her face as she spoke.

'I think it's probably best we stay here. Or we could do that tomorrow maybe? I think I need to be here while Bea and Freya are my guests.'

'They'll be fine. Let's go to my hotel. I think there was a bar next door.' He needed to be in charge of the situation. What didn't she understand?

'I need to stay here. I'm sorry.'

He stopped trying. He didn't understand what the problem was. Bea and the Freya woman didn't need her here. Tilda must have a weird protective streak about her friends. She appeared to treat them like children, assuming they couldn't function without her. The thought brewed for a few seconds until he stopped. In a moment of clarity, he realised the real reason for Tilda's reticence. Bea's words from earlier rang through his mind. *You scared her.* She didn't want to be alone with him because she was frightened of him. He still couldn't believe that was really the case. He was too pathetic to be scary. Stewart looked at her and decided to double check. Bea might have got it wrong.

'Did my email make you feel uncomfortable? I don't exactly remember what I wrote.'

Tilda looked down at her hands. She took her time before answering.

'A little bit, yes. It was overwhelming. Almost creepy.'

Stewart was taken aback by her honesty.

'Oh. You don't mince your words, do you?' He forced a laugh that emerged more of a snarl. Tilda didn't laugh back. She was silent for a few more seconds, apparently looking for the right way to phrase what she wanted to say.

'You seemed to be ranting. You seemed to think I owed you something. I wanted to help because you were in a bad place and you're Grady's brother. I didn't want you to feel pain. But behind your words there was so much anger. That's how it came across. And I didn't know what you were angry at. Was it me? Was it because I hadn't been in touch for a while? I felt like you expected too much from me. But because of Grady, on some level I felt like I owed you something back. What that something was, though, I had no idea. I still don't.'

Stewart's feelings were a jumbled mixture. A swirl of shame and embarrassment, hurt pride laced with frustration. He had never intended to frighten anyone. Aside from his once intimidating court persona, he considered himself to be at the more pathetic end of the spectrum. Pressuring Tilda was not something of which he were capable. Yet the anger that Tilda had identified was there.

Like the damaged person he was, he mentally

turned that anger on to her. How dare Tilda misunderstand him in such a grotesque way. He had been nothing but polite. His email may have been confused but it wasn't threatening. Not one bit. Everything felt blurry and distorted. He wished he could take back the bloody thing and start again. He needed control. He needed clarity.

As his anger reached a peak, he noticed her leg. In the confinement of their shared sofa, her bent knees were adjacent to his. Unlike him, however, the corner of the coffee table was nudging her shin. He pondered again the poky dimensions of the living space, before realising Tilda was pressing her leg into the corner on purpose. There was a deepening visible indent, marking a triangle of skin underneath her knee.

'Ouch, that must hurt. Can't you feel that?'

Tilda appeared to snap into action.

'God, yes, I wondered what that was. Sorry. There's no room to swing a cat in here.' She sat back, rubbing her leg absentmindedly.

Stewart didn't know what to say next. The table corner had distracted him from indignation. He was struggling to pick up the pieces of the conversation. Tilda, on the other hand, seemed to be clear on how she saw things.

'I'm glad you've come, Stewart. Really, I am. And I want to talk to you properly. I just think we should get tonight over with first. Let's have a nice meal with Freya and Bea. We can eat, drink, and share small talk. By the time tomorrow's here, we'll be more relaxed, and be able to talk about whatever it is you want to share.'

Stewart nodded against his will.

'Sure, let's do that,' he heard himself say. Inside, he was fully committed to his plan. He would set off first thing tomorrow. Perhaps it was the distance, but he felt a pang of longing for the safety of the business. He would turn up on Monday morning and tell Rosie he was there to work. It was familiar. It was all he had. This misguided weekend had forced him to see that Rosie and the firm needed his attention. Not Tilda and whatever insights he thought she could provide.

An hour later he was back in his hotel room. They had agreed to meet at the restaurant for seven. It seemed the women required several hours to prepare for this, whereas he only needed to pick up his jacket. He spent the time half-heartedly watching the motor racing as he sprawled on the bed. This hadn't turned out the way he hoped. He wasn't even sure *what* he had hoped for when he agreed to come. Tilda would never be able to help. He had overestimated her. He should have bundled the money into an ISA. The investment options from Richard were intriguing but as he didn't care one bit about anything his father had bequeathed, this quest for clarity had been a waste of time. Monday morning's return to the people and places he knew, couldn't come soon enough.

At twenty to seven he picked up his jacket from the back of the chair. In this weather, he probably didn't need it, but habit made him take it anyway. He pulled the key card out of the slot, checked he had his wallet, and threw his jacket over his arm. He heard a rustle.

Standing in the doorway, he felt the side pockets. Empty. Perhaps a five-pound note had worked its way through a gap in the lining. He felt the hem but there was nothing. He checked the collar and cuffs. No label or ticket stuck there either. Finally, assuming it would be empty as usual, he patted the inside pocket. He heard the rustle again.

He let the door slam and sat on the end of the bed, pulling out a slim envelope. Addressed to Stewart, it didn't take him long to read its brief contents.

Dear Stewart Grady,

Please accept my resignation as Office Manager at Grady and Son Solicitors. I would like to thank you for your support over the years and I am happy to assist in any transition process for my replacement.

Yours Sincerely
Rosie Laithwaite

The letter was screwed up and thrown in the bin. The jacket got left on the bed. Stewart walked out of the hotel and towards the restaurant without the first clue of how he arrived there.

CHAPTER TWENTY-NINE

Once Stewart returned to his hotel, there had been a brief lull in proceedings. Tilda boiled the kettle, telling Freya they couldn't open more wine until at least six o'clock or the evening would be ruined. She made fresh tea for the room as Bea sat back and watched the re-establishing of the double act that was Tilda and Freya. Years might have passed but the friendship had not dimmed.

'So, mate, tell me everything. What do you get up to? What's a Friday night like in Wales?'

'It's like a Friday night everywhere. It's fine.'

'Tilds, mate. No town wants the sentence, *'Friday Night? It's Fine!'* as their marketing slogan. What's it really like? Who do you go out with? Who are your friends?'

Bea watched Tilda skilfully answer the question without appearing as pathetic as she knew she felt deep down.

'You're my friend, Freya. Just you. Who else do I need when I've got the official Queen of the Southern Hemisphere in my flat?'

Freya laughed and rolled her eyes. Tilda sipped her tea and changed the subject. Bea took it all in. It was interesting to see how even in Tilda's longest friendship, she was the same. Slightly uptight, slightly lonely, and adept at deflecting attention from herself. Bea wanted to protect her from real life forever, whilst desperately wanting her to feel whole in her new home. She wanted her to make friends with people who were nearer than a cross-country train ride, or an international plane journey away. She just didn't know how to achieve that. Besides, she had other problems right now.

With a couple of hours to kill before the restaurant, each woman was busy with jobs. The tasks that each felt were of priority, now the buzz of reconnection had calmed down.

For Freya, this meant unpacking the items she needed for the evening. She shook out a selection of glittery numbers, hanging them on the backs of doors to straighten out. Her make-up bag was emptied and the contents dotted across the shelf in the bathroom. Tilda's neat arrangement of toothbrush, toothpaste, and hand soap made way for the shimmering on-slaught with little resistance.

Meanwhile in the kitchen area, Tilda tidied. She gathered the glasses and mugs and washed them at the sink. She re-plumped the cushions, straightened Bea's pile of papers, and moved the table further towards the window so that Freya's parent's airbed would have room to inflate. Then, with the mugs still drying on the drainer, she asked who wanted another cup of tea. It seemed with some empty space to fill, she was at a loose end.

Perhaps it was the offer of another drink that prompted it. Or maybe it was the knowledge that Tilda and Freya were able to occupy themselves perfectly well without her presence. Either way, Bea took the opportunity to escape. She needed to get out. The last couple of hours had given her a headache. She could pretend it was the large glass of wine. She could tell that lie before the honesty of her inner voice pushed through the crap. She knew what was really going on. Her head ached from the forced smile she had kept plastered on her face since Mal's text.

Under the pretext of getting some cash, Bea left the flat, walked down the stairs, and out of the door. Tilda had described in detail the route to the nearest bank machine, which Bea had pretended to absorb before closing the door behind her. She did not need cash. She needed to think.

She should be happy. She knew that. Mal, a man she had known for several months, had lived unhappily at home for years. He had planned to leave that home many times before he met Bea, and now he had. This was good news. She wanted him to be happy and she knew that if what he said about his marriage were true, he'd have the chance to be just that. Happy. Once the initial upset died down, which it would in time. It was exactly what he wanted and now he'd made a start at getting it. It was a good thing. She was sure it must be a good thing.

Bea walked towards the pier and took a left. It was a warm day and she the felt sweat break on her forehead. The sunny afternoon, a hot flush, or her body telling her something wasn't right? She walked up the road, pretending to look in shop windows, hoping to lose herself within the clusters of tourists. Narrow pavements forced her to move aside as she walked. Families with children in shorts and flip flops ambled past. At times she stepped into the road to allow a pushchair and its entourage the space to pass safely. There were children everywhere. Some carrying buckets and spades, some too young to do much but toddle, and some almost teenagers, walking away from parental control, their ears stuffed with earphones.

It was the way he had worded it. *Wish you were here by my side.* That was what was causing her pause. That was the root of the anxiety she was feeling. Her plastered on smile was hiding the fact that Mal seemed to be going about this all wrong.

'Scuse.' A girl of about eight, faced her. Bea was blocking her path. She stepped aside.

'Sorry.' She kept walking but paid more attention. She needed to get to the point where she could put all this out of her mind. She needed her weekend to be her own again.

At the top of the road, she saw the clock tower. Tilda had distinctly told her to take a left when she saw it. Bea turned right. She didn't want to complete her fake task so soon that she'd be back at the flat and be fake smiling again. Not yet. She needed to work things out first.

The right turn took her down a narrow road. It led to another. She walked and walked, circling back on herself down narrow streets, until finding somewhere to aim for. After reaching the end of another road, the ruins of a castle faced her. She climbed the sloping walkways until she was at the top of its small hill. Open space. It was what she needed. Picnic tables were dotted around. A few people were sprawled on the grassy area, relaxing on blankets. Families soaking up the sun. Bea walked around until she found a more secluded spot. Flanked by a chunk of castle ruins, she sank to the ground with her legs out in front of her. She could look down at the sea to the left, and at the streets she had paced, to the right. She leaned her head back on the concrete and slowly exhaled. Time to think.

Mindful of the people around her, possibly having their own moments of private contemplation, Bea took out her phone with the intention of putting it on silent. It sprang to life with the movement, the screen lighting up unnecessarily in the glare of sunlight. The usual raft of notifications was there. Someone had surpassed her ranking on Candy Crush. A BBC News alert told of another set of failed trade talks. A new episode of her favourite podcast had been dropped. Standard stuff. And then there were sixteen messages from Mal. All in her inbox, all waiting for her to read.

She scanned the first one.

Hope your catch-up is going well but I can't wait for you to come home. We never need have a weekend apart again. I hope you're missing me too. We're such a great team. xxx

She opened the next.

I love you so much, Bea. Everything is dire without you. You've kept me sane for months. Ring me when you can. I can't wait to see your beautiful face. xxxxx

And the next.

My children are going to love you. How could they not? You make their dad so happy. xxxxxxxxxxxx

Bea swiped the rest of the notifications away and looked out to sea. She watched the tide swell and counted the seconds between each surge of water. She watched the families - families she probably walked past in town - set up camp on the beach. She saw one dad spend far too long erecting a windbreaker as the rest of his group huddled around.

Would Mal do that with his kids? Would he put up a windbreaker easily or would his wife need to hold one end as he struggled with the other? Would his children roll their eyes and say, 'Daa-aad,' with amused embarrassment as he grappled with something relatively simple? Would his kids ever speak to him again now he was uprooting their entire lives? And in all that mess, what on earth would they think about the fact that in this dark time for their family, their Dad had wanted her to be there with him. What would they think about any of it? She'd bet money they would not love her. Not this way.

Without any conscious thought, she found herself tapping out a text message.

Darling. I've got myself into a right mess, man-wise. The entire sitch has been ramped up to a million. How did I end up like this? Shit has got real on the married man front. Should I be pleased that things have moved up a gazillion notches? It doesn't help that I've got peak brain-fog today. What shall I do? Sorry for banging on. Say hi to Jamie. x

The second she pressed send, she regretted it. Kit did not need to be burdened with her problems. Not without the cushion of gin and wisecracks to lighten the mood, at the very least. She thought about it for a few seconds before opening the app. She would delete the message before Kit read it.

Too late. The dancing dots on screen informed her that not only had it been opened but a reply was being written. Bea leaned back and felt sick. She had no right to bring such a downer to her neighbour's weekend. Kit didn't need that.

Another minute passed. Bea's nausea turned to amusement when she pictured how much Kit would enjoy the drama. Then she felt guilt about interrupting her day with Jamie and the sick feeling returned. The emotional carousel continued until her phone buzzed. Kit's reply was in.

I'm in the kitchen with wet hands. Will call you now.

The phone rang and Bea answered. It only took a *hello*, but Kit's tone was instantly soothing.

'Now dear, listen to me. I've got a pan boiling so I'm going to make this quick. You are a marvel. You hear me? I want you to look in the mirror and say that to yourself out loud. Say, *I am a marvel,* right to your own face.'

'Well I'm outside at the moment so I...'

'Make it the first thing you do when you get back. Because I want no more of this moping. Do you hear? Remember when you rolled up at mine, heartbroken that he'd lied? Hang on, I'm putting you down for a moment.'

Bea heard a loud whoosh as a pan was presumably drained of its liquid. She thought back to the time in question. The night she had drunk herself silly because of the breaking news about Poppy the dog.

'I'm back. Now dear, remember what I said to you then?'

Bea almost laughed. She couldn't even remember being there.

'Remind me. It's hazy.'

'I'm sure it is, dear. I passed on my Mama's advice. When my darling Clive proposed, she told me to think of the places I felt happiness. If it wasn't my head, my heart, my gut, and my *you know where*, he wasn't good enough and I should say no.'

'Kit! You never told me that.'

'I *did*. And it's excellent advice. My mother was very open-minded for her generation. Luckily for me, Clive made me feel happy everywhere...'

'I bet he did!'

'...but if it had only been my... *you know where*, it wouldn't have been enough. Count the places. That's what you must do. You deserve the whole package, dear. Not something simply disguised as it. Now, hang on, I need to get the oven on.'

Bea thought of the photo on Kit's wall. A young couple in the sunshine of their wedding day. A year later, they left the warmth of the Caribbean, spent twenty-two days on a boat, and arrived in England for a new life. Kit talked about it often. A couple of gins into the evening and she'd become misty eyed and nostalgic. Clive's death, a decade earlier, had done nothing to diminish her love. Bea was always moved by her tales. To feel such certainty that you'd move continents with someone, was quite the affirmation. Clive must have been a legend.

Could Bea imagine doing the same with Mal?

Would she speak so lovingly, if they were starting from scratch in a far-flung corner of the planet? She stopped that train of thought in its tracks. She knew the answer. It was hard enough in Stockport. No point adding imaginary problems to the mix. Besides, it would never be just them. Mal had commitments.

'I'm back again. Now where were we?'

'Kit, did you ever regret marrying Clive?'

'Oh my goodness. Not for a single solitary second.'

'OK, not regret exactly. But there must have been times that were hard. When you first arrived here. Did you *never* have doubts? Surely at some point the pair of you had to power through a tough time?'

'My sweet girl. Of *course* there were tough times. But they were made easier *because* of Clive, not in spite of him. What's the point of a partner that makes life harder for you? You're a marvel on your own. Your man should add to that, not take it away.'

Kit hung up to marinate more chicken. Bea texted her a flurry of Xs and sank back against the wall. She let her mind relive the conversation and did her best to let the words sink in. *You are a marvel.* Kit was almost convincing. Just not enough. Bea was a mess. How she wished she knew what to do.

She should be happy. She should feel huge love for Mal and his decision. She should be looking forward to going home and giving him her unwavering support. She should feel a lot of things, but she did not. Every so often, when a shard of emotion poked through the numb, all she felt was *irked*. She hadn't worked out why yet, but irked was the feeling. It was too much to say she was angry and she couldn't really summon up enough negativity to say she was pissed off. She was just irked. Irked but with no real understanding why. Everything had been thrown up in the air and was now falling down around her. And for once, it hadn't been her that had done the throwing. Perhaps that was why she was irked. Perhaps that was why she was feeling everything and nothing all at once.

There was another hour before Bea had to be back. She closed her eyes and tuned out all of life around her. It was all she could control now.

CHAPTER THIRTY

They had been seated by the window overlooking the beach. All of life was on the other side of the glass; an eclectic mix of summer action. Sand-coated families ambling back from the water, romantic couples arm in arm, tourists heading out for holiday drinks. There was even a concert on at the bandstand. An audience had been arriving as the newly-formed friendship group walked past earlier.

Tilda looked at the view. It was still daylight but she knew the sky would be spectacular later. It always was. It was nice to feel a flutter of pride about showing it off to her visitors. Aber sunsets were legendary. She looked forward to sharing it with Bea, Freya, and Stewart. Not that she would say the world *Aber* of course. That was only ever in her head.

She poured herself another glass of water.

'Anyone else?'

She was met with shaken heads and an outright snort from Bea as she tried to offer the jug around. *That's a unanimous no then.* She would be the smug one tomorrow when she awoke fully hydrated and ready for *Geography Reunion: Day Two*.

Initially, there had been a few awkward lulls in conversation. Polite, forced small talk had taken place as wine was quickly ordered. Now the four of them had been seated for nearly an hour. Starters had been eaten and the plates cleared away. They were onto their second bottle of wine and the chatter had been continually bubbling for a while. They had just taken time to warm up.

Tilda breathed a sigh of relief. This could have been a disaster. Between the overwhelming personalities of Bea and Freya, to her earlier chat with Stewart, it had all been a gamble. There had been several ways the evening could have gone pear shaped, but so far everything was fine. Then there had been the last-minute worry that Freya and Bea were too similar and would instinctively hate each other. Tilda could not have handled that but it had been OK. They had bonded over the fact that they'd both been her bad influence at different times in her life. *She always needed a bloody big shove to do anything interesting* is how Freya had phrased it. Bea agreed and they had high-fived in such an energetic way, that they'd both shaken their hand afterwards with the sting of the impact.

Tilda looked around the table. Bea was sitting diagonally opposite her and talking to Stewart. If you didn't know, it would appear everything was fine. But there was a tightness to her smile. The one she would display in meetings when she was barely tolerating the pointlessness of the agenda. Bea was putting on an act. Was it because of Stewart? Was Tilda being a terrible friend because she had lumped them together whilst she caught up with Freya? Her guilt levels rose. Maybe things would get better as the evening wore on. Maybe Bea needed more wine.

Then there was Stewart.

He was seated next to her and opposite Bea. They had not said much to each other since the apartment. That was all right because Bea was occupying him. He was listening and taking the occasional sip of his drink. It was fine. She needed to stop worrying. Of course, telling herself to stop worrying didn't mean she could automatically manage to do so.

She shouldn't have been so brutally honest. There was just something about him that made her need to keep him at arm's length. Perhaps it was the unnerving similarity he had to Grady, even in this older, self-destructive state. Grady would never have pressured her to do anything she didn't want to do. He would have backed off the minute she said no. Stewart had struggled with that.

Tilda's face clouded over. Stewart was a mess. He needed help and he needed someone to help him. She had no idea what or who that was. Maybe Bea would have more luck working it out. It was too much for Tilda, that was clear. She rubbed her leg where the bruise was, and tried to push everything out of her mind. The sky was orange and the wine was flowing. Everything would be better soon. It had to be.

CHAPTER THIRTY-ONE

He'd had worse nights. He was sure of it. Once Tilda dropped the bombshell of him being a *creepy weirdo*, there was only one way the evening could go. It had to get better. And by relocating to a busy restaurant away from the claustrophobia of the world's smallest flat, he could breathe a little easier. It wasn't as if he had much to do. Bea was talking enough for both of them. He could sit back and let her do all the work, while he made an occasional grunt between drinks. Yes, he was sure he'd had worse nights. If he cast his mind back far enough, he might even recall some of them.

'Scuse me, can we have another?' Freya waggled an empty Prosecco bottle at a passing waiter.

'Certainly. Everyone else all right for drinks?'

After a small amount of deliberation, another bottle of red was ordered. Bea resumed her chatter and did not stop. There had been many women over the years that had accused him of being a terrible listener. *If they could see me now,* he thought. He had never listened this hard in his life. It had nothing to do with being a friendly ear to someone sharing themselves. A much likelier reason for his silent attention was it stopped all thoughts of the unintentional character assassination that Bea and Tilda had handed him earlier. If he was listening, or at least if he *looked* like he was, then he wasn't stewing on how maligned he had been, how wrong they had got him, or how hurt he felt.

'The steak?' Out of nowhere a waiter appeared, plates balancing on both arms.

'That's me.' Stewart took his meal as the remaining

dishes were distributed amongst the others.

'Oooh, that looks nice. I wish I'd ordered that now.' Freya eyed up Tilda's duck salad as she pronged a chip onto her fork. 'Of course, these are really *hot* chips, not chips. Or at least they used to be when I first moved over. These days, anything goes. I'll teach you all Australian before the night's out.'

Stewart had no doubt she would try, and made a mental note to return to his hotel before that ever happened. He had no interest in Freya. He was here to see Tilda and was being handled by Bea. Anyone else was irrelevant.

The phone on the table lit up again. It had done that every few minutes since they sat down. Messages. Lots of them. Bea had managed to ignore them during the starters. He had watched her turn her phone face-down and push it to the edge of the table as she ate. She checked it briefly as the plates were collected, and again when the drinks were refilled. The rest of the time she was busy talking. About work, or Tilda, or anything else that came into her head. But the phone was still on her mind. He recognised the action of avoiding repeated contact from someone. Perhaps he had finally tired of being the world's best listener, or maybe he felt he should take a more active part in their conversation. Either way, he found himself getting involved.

'You're ignoring someone.' There was no point framing it as a question. It was obvious.

Bea looked at him for a moment. She was probably wondering what the fuck her life had to do with him. That would have been his response, the other way around.

'Pretty much, darling. Yes.'

'A man?'

'Top marks. You're good at this.'

'I'm no stranger to an onslaught of texts about why I'm not replying. You have to ride it out. He'll get the message eventually.'

'I just needed a break. This is supposed to be my holiday. He knows that. He's trying to insert himself into my *me time*. And I know that sounds like a funny euphemism but for once I don't mean it that way at all.'

Bea sighed deeply and covered her face with her hands as Stewart watched. He had been mistaken. He had assumed it was a clingy one-night stand that wouldn't get the message. Now it seemed it was a partner. He watched her wrestle with keeping her feelings to herself. It was as if she were deciding how much she was comfortable sharing with him. He hoped, very little. He was ill-equipped to deal with his own problems, let alone those of a woman he barely knew. Too late to change the subject, he saw Bea reach a decision. She was going to talk.

'You're a man of the world, Stewart.'

It was a statement not a question. He answered it as such.

'OK.'

'What sort of man promises undying love and makes the claim that they've never felt like this before, when only minutes later they leave your bed to sneak back to their spouse? Who does that? What kind of person decides that it's OK to treat anyone as second best?'

So it wasn't a partner, but an affair? Much more his area of expertise. Stewart was suddenly intrigued.

'Who's second best? You or the wife?'

'Both. But as of today, I'm in pole position.' He watched Bea shudder at the implied ranking system. Regardless of her persona as a free spirit, this wasn't sitting well. He recognised that. He also recognised Mal and his behaviour.

'You believe him?'

'I think so. I did.'

'Right.'

'It's been bugging me all afternoon. Months of giving him space at his own request and now he's demanding attention again. Not only do I have to wait for my slot in his specific schedule to be considered The One, but even when I'm away for the weekend, he takes over and gets in my head. This was two days with my friends. Well, my friend. Hang on, are we friends, Stewart?'

There was no point in worrying about the answer. He would never see her again after tomorrow.

'Sure, why not?'

'Well then, I was right first time. Friends. Plural.'

Bea paused for breath and looked out to the beach. He should leave it there. He didn't care either way so he should stay silent. But a thought was rising. His mind flashed back over recent weekends. When he had tried to make plans but got rejections instead. When anonymous chats with online strangers made him feel emptier and more alone than if he had not bothered. He couldn't stop himself from speaking. He didn't mean to share something so raw but the words tumbled out, unfiltered.

'It must be nice to be loved. Even part time.'

Bea was quick to respond.

'I don't think it is, on reflection. I want it all, or don't waste my time.' She stopped and sighed. 'At least I think that's what I think.'

She hadn't convinced him. Not that he cared one way or the other about Bea's situation, but she was luckier than she realised. Even someone who was full of shit was better than nothing. He still didn't care but he found himself telling her this regardless. What was wrong with him?

'But isn't it a good feeling to hear the sentiment? Even if it's not true but they care enough to make you think it is? No one's ever said they love *me*. That's probably nice to hear even if it's just talk.'

Bea's eyes widened.

'No one?'

'Maybe my mother did. Before I can remember.'

They sat in silence for a moment. There didn't seem much to say in response. Somewhere inside, he felt an empty ache. *Christ. He'd gone too far. He'd shared way too much.* He topped up the wine glasses to force it away and drank some more. Then he spoke again. It was time to turn this harshest of spotlights back on Bea.

'What does he want that's so urgent? He knows you're away.'

Bea rolled her eyes and took a breath.

'Oh yes, he *does* know that. It seems the minute I left the area, he decided it was the best time to tell his wife he was leaving her. Now I'm getting a running commentary about how difficult this has been for him, how he needs me there as soon as possible, and how he wants me to meet his kids. I swear to God, this started as a lovely sex thing that grew a bit, but it's suddenly got *very* real.'

'Sounds like he's chosen you. He's put you first. That's good?'

'Hmmm. I think I'm a touch sceptical about the timing. Funny it's this weekend, isn't it? The first one I've not prioritised him since we got together. Almost as if he were trying to emotionally blackmail me into going home early, don't you think?'

Bea stopped talking. Maybe it was her turn to feel she had gone too far. But Stewart wasn't sure she had. He recognised the behaviour. There was nothing new or unique about this man. And seeing as it had come up, he thought he might as well share his insights with Bea. Otherwise there was a danger she'd change the subject back to how she was wasted in her current job, and how work had been no fun since Tilda left. He had exhausted all of his polite listening faces as far as those topics went. He would do anything to avoid that.

'He's just making a point. He's annoyed you've got plans that don't include him.'

Bea shook her head as if brushing his comment away.

'No, ignore me. I'm being grumpy. I'm sure that's not it. He's been building to this for months. Years, probably. I'm just annoyed the timing was off.'

'It's a bit odd he chooses the time you're away to create a drama. If he'd really wanted you there, he could have waited until Monday. Or next weekend. Literally any other time apart from now.'

'Mmm. I don't think he planned it. It must have got

too much at home. At some point I'm going to have to call him to find out. Maybe I'll do it after the main course.'

It was strange. He found himself feeling sorry for Bea but without being sure why he cared. He could see what was happening. He'd done it countless times himself. Not that he had a wife and kids in the picture but the emotional blackmail part was recognisable. When a girlfriend announced plans that didn't involve him, there were a few options. If he were healthy and stable, he would obviously sit back and let her get on without comment. But he had never been fully healthy nor stable. Not really. Instead of offering encouraging support he would pile on the pressure. He would pick the moment the girlfriend left for her sister's hen do, or her friends' holiday, or her mother's operation, and start sending the messages. He knew Mal was doing exactly the same thing. Once again, he found himself oversharing, even though he was determined not to be interested.

'Let me guess. He keeps texting to say how much he's missing you. He adds sad faced emojis and lots of kisses. He's being demonstrably more affectionate than normal?'

Bea didn't answer but kept listening. He could tell he wasn't far off the mark.

'There will have been some comment about you being away, along the lines of, *but we have so little time together, it's just so hard when you aren't here.*' He makes you feel like you *should* ring him. You feel bad that you're here and not there. You know when you get home, you'll need to make it up to him. It'll feel like you've done something bad and you'll apologise. And he'll say that it's fine and he forgives you. But by the time you *are* home and ready to give him your full attention, he won't care. He won't suggest booking your own weekend away. There'll be no big romantic gestures. No exciting plans to make. It'll be sex. Sex and blow jobs. An hour of that and the soppy messages will be forgotten. Things will be back to how they were before you had your weekend away. Trust me, I know all the mind games going.'

Bea listened to his words of wisdom in silence. She picked at her fish as her gaze moved between her plate and his face. Once he had finished, she took a sip of wine before responding.

'So what's your advice then? Ignore him? Switch my phone off? Send him an upskirt photo to shut him up and let me enjoy my evening? What did women do for you when you played them like this?'

Stewart detected a chill to Bea's tone that hadn't been there previously. He didn't want to cause any trouble. He just knew he could enlighten her. Except this was slightly different from his own experiences. He thought about his answer carefully.

'I never dated anyone like you.'

'What does that mean? Not posh enough? Too old?'

Stewart shook his head.

'I wouldn't have tried this on you. You'd see through it. It wouldn't work.'

'But Mal seems to think it might.'

'Maybe Mal doesn't know the real you.'

'And you do?' Bea was scornful.

'Christ, no. But I've met lots of women and they've not been like you. You're in charge of yourself. The women I tend to date, are not. I don't mean I'm bossy and controlling. I don't think I mean that. But they tend to be more people-pleasing than you seem to be. I don't imagine *you* usually settle for something less than you want. That's why this is new territory for you. I find that women with the lowest self-esteem are the ones that prefer to spend time with me.'

Bea looked at him.

'Are you trying to make a joke?'

Stewart looked back blankly.

'Sadly, I don't think I am.'

Bea left the thought in the air and grabbed his hand across the table. He had really done it now. Lowered the barriers slightly, trying to offer his insights, and now he was getting swamped with pity.

'The thing is...' Bea said, as she leaned back in her seat, '...all that's happened is he's pushing me away. I want him to be happy and I assumed that leaving his wife would be part of that. But this was never about *us* becoming a serious item. Certainly not at this point. He's got a fifteen-year marriage to disentangle himself from. The fact he thinks that it's a good idea for me to share the moment with him, highlights how stupid he is. It's short-sighted, isn't it? No good can come of it, if I'm here for all the mess. He needs to build himself back into a single, whole person before he can offer me anything. I don't get why he doesn't see that. It's such a juvenile view of the world. He's such a fucking *child*.'

Stewart stayed silent. It seemed Bea had let some suppressed undercurrents erupt into their evening. Her face was shocked at the new thoughts she was having. He watched her visibly back-peddle from her outburst before she spoke.

'Is that a terrible thing to say about someone? God, I'm a cow. I'm sure he's winging it and trying his best. It's just a shame that his best is so at odds with what I want. At odds with how I feel. I should never have let this become what it did.'

There was a brief silence. Bea had a final mouthful of her meal as Stewart finished his steak. Despite his best efforts, he couldn't leave it alone. What was wrong with him? It wasn't as if he cared.

'I still think he's more controlling than misguided. He wants things his way. There must have been alarm bells before this weekend?'

Bea sat back and sipped her drink. She didn't seem to be searching her mind for evidence. He could tell. She knew what he was getting at, and was simply choosing whether or not to confirm he was right. A few more seconds passed while she deliberated, before she carried on.

'The warning signs were there, I suppose.' Her eyes focused on the view from the window as she gathered her thoughts. She bit her lip and her face flushed. Whatever was going through her mind was causing some angst. He gave her time. He still didn't care, but he was in the conversation now. It was happening whether he wanted it to or not. Might as well try to be nice.

When she spoke, her tone was more sheepish than before.

'He took me clothes shopping for my birthday. Posh, expensive stuff. I've never owned anything classy and I was utterly spoilt. Lots of designer shops.

Like the *Pretty Woman* scene. Except it was Cheshire Oaks, not Rodeo Drive.'

'But?'

'But they just weren't me. Not in any discernible way. I'm much more of a charity-shop kind of woman. My top search on eBay is 'animal print'. Poshing around in pencil skirts and silk blouses was fun for a day. Like role play. After that, it was silly.'

'He dressed you?'

'No. Not really. I think he just wanted to treat me.' Bea paused. It seemed as if she were reassessing her past few months with a new perspective. 'It was weird though. After a few dates of wearing the stuff, I went back to my old favourite date night outfit. I won't bore you with the fashion details but when I walked into the bar and he saw me in my leopard print faux fur coat, he looked pissed off. And then he remembered to smile and I forgot about it. And later on, he mentioned that I wasn't wearing any of his clothes, which was odd.'

'Are you wearing his clothes now?'

'Mostly, yeah.'

'You look nice.'

'Not the point though, is it?'

'No.'

'It's just occurred to me that the two options I've packed for tomorrow are my old 'me' clothes. It's like I've made the mental distinction to split my wardrobe into 'things for home' and 'things for when I'm away from him.' Bea looked down at a spot on her plate. 'Fuck, I've been stupid.'

Her face froze. Her smile had gone. The woman

who had exuded upbeat positivity all night, had cracked.

'I'm sure he was only trying to be nice.' Stewart felt a twinge of guilt that his willingness to share his knowledge of men behaving badly, had forced Bea into accepting some dark facts. It was probably good in the long term, although not necessarily the right time and place. There was a whole evening to get through. Bea lifted her head and looked Stewart straight in the eye.

'Why did I listen? I loved the way I dressed. It was my thing. Who was he to tell me to change?'

'I'm sure he meant well.'

Bea didn't seem to hear. He watched her eyes glaze over as she shared in real time, the realisations she was having.

'It was all about control, wasn't it? And I didn't even realise. God, talk about being stupid. I let this happen. I let a self-centred and controlling man dictate my behaviour. Well I might be stupid, but he's nothing more than an emotional bully. An emotional bully and a selfish shit.'

Stewart grimaced to hear Mal described so bluntly. In the face of Bea's fresh assessment of her lover, he was thrown into his own thoughts. He saw himself in every one of Mal's behaviours. If Mal was a bully, so was he. If Mal was controlling and selfish, so was he. If Mal was a shit, then so was he. And Bea knew it.

She looked straight at him. He felt her gaze.

'You know what, darling? I think I've sussed you out. You're used to getting what you want too, aren't you? A powerful job, lots of money, people doing what you tell them. You feel some sort of solidarity with Mal, don't you?'

He steeled himself. Trying to be nonchalant, when his insides felt anything but.

'Maybe. Or maybe he really *is* just missing you.'

Bea snorted.

'Thank you for helping me see something I should have realised a long time ago. You've opened my eyes, Stewart.'

She seemed relieved. Her face smiled naturally for a second. She squeezed his hand before letting go and leaning back in her seat. Something had changed for Bea. He found himself feeling glad for her.

Something had changed for him too. Somewhere in his chest his heart pounded. He knew that feeling. The one that used to leave him struggling to breathe as his mind raced in court. The one that had made Rosie force him to see a doctor. The panic attacks were real but at least these days he saw them coming. He rooted in his trouser pocket to see if his tablets were there. Grasping the foil strip, he applauded his foresight. He took two, washed down with a mouthful of Rioja. All of his energy was drained. He felt empty. There was nothing left.

CHAPTER THIRTY-TWO

On the same table, but worlds away from the depths of Bea and Stewart's conversation, Tilda and Freya were discussing the issues that really mattered.

'Right, try this one. Chris Hemsworth or Luke Hemsworth?'

'Freya, once again, I've no idea who either of them are.'

'Yes, you do. It's Thor and his brother. You know, the one *not* in *The Hunger Games*.'

'I'm going to take it as a compliment that you think I'm down enough with the kids to know what you're on about,' Tilda said. Freya was speaking the foreign language that came from living with teenagers. It opened up a whole world of films, music, YouTube videos, and vocabulary.

'Tilds, you're hopeless. You don't know anyone. OK, I've got another. You *have* to know these two. Hugh Jackman or Hugh Grant?'

'Ah, now then. I *have* heard of Hugh Jackman and I definitely know Hugh Grant.'

'Finally. So who's it to be?'

'No question. Hugh Grant. I think he's ageing very well. He was also excellent on *Question Time* a few years ago.'

Freya groaned, clearly exasperated with every one of Tilda's responses.

'For fuck's sake, mate. Feeling a scrap of lust for someone because of their performance on a politics show isn't really in the spirit of the game.'

Tilda giggled.

'Sorry.'

'Playing *Who Would You Rather* should not feel like getting blood out of a stone. We'll have to move away from celebrity crushes. You're depressing me too much.'

Tilda tried to take her seriously but it was proving a challenge. She cleared her throat to straighten her face, as Freya began to speak.

'So, tell me this...'

She rested her chin on her fingers, as though a deep philosophical question was about to be uttered.'

'...are you happier since you left Mike? I know you got to find yourself, but do you ever want to go back home? I don't mean back to Mike; I mean back up North. Back to what you knew. If I didn't have Aiden and the kids, I can't imagine I'd stay in Australia.'

Tilda laughed.

'Course you would, Freya. You're fully immersed in Aussie life. As if you'd come back here. Honestly, this country is a different place from the one you left.'

'Yeah, I don't know why I said that. Obviously, I'd stay.' She laughed at herself as she topped up her glass. Tilda placed a hand over her own to stop Freya doing the same for her. 'I suppose what I mean is, who are your friends? Have you joined any clubs? When you have a week off from the Uni, what do you do?'

Tilda sipped her water. She knew her friend well, even if their time together had totalled one evening in fifteen years. Freya was a natural socialiser. If she'd moved to a new town, she'd have found herself a whirl of social plans in the first five minutes. She'd had the guts to move to a different hemisphere. There was no playing it safe for Freya. Not for a second. It was clear her friend couldn't imagine the limitations that Tilda's own personality placed on her. She had to soften the reality for Freya. She had to make it clear that there was no cause for concern, before her mate staged an intervention.

'If I tell you for real what it's like, it's going to sound pathetic, and you'll feel sorry for me. And that would be a waste of your time. I don't feel pathetic. Not most of the time anyway.'

'So, try me. Tell me what it's like.'

Tilda fiddled with her water glass as she gave the question some thought.

'I can't say I have any specific friends here. Not yet. I've met friendly people at work, and there's a group of us that began temping at the same time.'

'That sounds promising.'

'Well, yes and no. They're very nice but they're half my age. A bit of chat during the day is one thing, but they wouldn't dream of inviting me to one of their nights out. And let's face it, I'd hate every second.'

'Your clubbing days are over?' said Freya.

'I don't think my clubbing days ever began.'

Freya had been no stranger to dancing 'til dawn back in the day. The concept was as alien to Tilda then as it was now.

Freya was not about to give up.

'What about when you're not at work?'

'I tend to keep myself to myself. You know me. I wasn't blessed with the extrovert gene.'

She took the opportunity to fill Freya's wine glass, even though it was almost full. She needed to appear less pathetic. Her friend meant well, she knew that. It just sounded worse that it was, when she said it out loud.

'Right then. We've got the rest of the evening to sort this out. By the end of tonight, we will find you a friend. A partner in crime, a bezzie mate. But you have to do what I say, Tilds. You've got to trust me on this.'

As Freya warmed to her theme, the more animated of her hand gestures sent the bottle of wine wobbling. Tilda managed to grab hold, before it toppled over, averting the small drama that a sodden table would bring.

'I'm not sure you're in any fit state to start giving me instructions,' Tilda said.

'Nonsense. I'm just excited that we have a mission. Tilds, are you ready for instruction number one?'

Tilda sighed but found herself nodding. Freya's misplaced concern was endearing. There was something nostalgic to it. It had been a long time since anyone had worried about her. Her dad had, a lot. And... well that was it. Just her dad. Back then, his worries had been about completing her homework and being careful when she walked home from her weekend job. Freya's focus was in a whole other area.

'OK. Instruction Number One. When the waiter comes back, you have to say something to him.'

'Like what?'

'Like anything. Say whatever you like.'

'What? No. I'll look stupid.'

'You won't. It's what normal people do all the time.'

'It'll sound false. Like I'm trying to be funny when I'm not.'

Freya sighed.

'Now is not the time to be stubborn, mate. Just say something nice about the meal. I'm not making you shoehorn in a code word like 'aspidistra' or 'testicle.' You'll just say an appropriate sentence to a waiter who's working in the restaurant where you're eating. Now look lively because he's almost here.'

She caught the attention of the approaching man whilst audibly whispering to Tilda.

'I'll start off, and then you go.'

A second later he was at the table. Freya cleared her throat.

'Is it all right if you take the plates now? That was delicious, thank you.'

The man smiled and piled up the empty plates. Freya stared at Tilda, who summoned up her best *this is the stupidest idea ever* look. But then she spoke.

'The duck and mango salad was lovely. Maybe, er... maybe I'll try and make it at home.'

The waiter smiled again and nodded. He walked around the table to get Bea and Stewart's plates and was in the kitchen a few seconds later. Tilda blushed.

'Well thanks for that, Freya. I can cross off 'make a show of myself' from the *To Do* list. That box is well and truly ticked, thanks a lot.' She groaned and put her head in her hands. Freya laughed at the drama of it all.

'Right, I can see we've got some way to go. And I'm happy to agree that the dude you just spoke to, is probably not about to be your best mate anytime soon. But we've made a start. We are on the way. *Operation Tilda's Bestie* has officially been launched.'

That only makes me feel anxious, not excited about future friendships, Freya. Is that your plan?' Tilda said.

Ignoring her misgivings, Freya ploughed on.

'Before anyone orders desserts, are you ready for Instruction Two? We're on a roll now, we've got to keep up momentum.'

'This is a bad idea. I'm incapable of change.'

'Nope. I'm not having that one bit. So, Instruction Two. Go the bar and get another bottle of wine. Or whatever any of us wants, that's not the point.'

'Fine. I can do that.'

'I'm not finished. Go to the bar, order something, and then start a bit of small talk with any of the people sitting on the stools.'

'Freya, don't be daft. It'll sound ridiculous.'

'It won't. Pick any of them - the guy in the jumper, that woman with the shoes, or the lad at the end with the pint. Although he looks twelve so maybe not him. Just go over and as you wait to be served, strike up a conversation. Come on, this is easy. You've had a drink, you're relaxed, and they all look friendly.'

Tilda threw her napkin at her, in what she hoped came off as a small act of rebellion. Freya seemed to think she needed pushing. This was not the case. Not like this anyway. But this was Freya. She had made the 20-hour flight to be here. As long as she was visiting, it was best to humour her. She only had good intentions.

Tilda slid off her seat and faced the bar. She took a second to gather herself as Freya egged her on from her seat.

'This is tough love, mate, but it's definitely love. I'm your Fairy Godmother, making all your dreams come true. Now, my sweet, innocent, naïve Tilda... *go get 'em.*'

CHAPTER THIRTY-THREE

Bea made a decision. With the considered opinion that none of the Geography Gang were likely to message over the next couple of hours, she switched off her phone. Nothing Mal could say tonight was going to make a difference to how angry she had begun to feel. The anger that had bubbled away in her subconscious for some time was now making itself known. It was time to salvage the evening. She turned her attention to Stewart, now she was able to give it to him in full. He had been quiet for a while, but with her phone off, it was time to change that.

'Darling, what would you be doing in York if you weren't here? Is it a good place to live? I was there on a hen do, about twenty years ago. There was a stripper dressed as a Viking. Not that it matters. The couple split up in the late-noughties.'

Stewart had been miles away. She watched him jerk back into life and focus on her just as she finished speaking. His breathing was heavier than before.

'Who split up?'

'No one. I was asking about York. What would you be doing if you weren't here?'

Stewart drained his glass and poured another one.

'Oh, the usual. Drinks with the staff after work. A dinner date or dinner party. The normal things.'

'Do you cook?'

'Sometimes.'

'And who do you date? Anyone right now?'

Stewart chose that moment to pick up his glass and sip his wine. Was it a delaying tactic, as he weighed up whether he wanted to share his private life with her? She wasn't sure. Then he answered.

'Yeah. There's a casual person in the background. No one important.'

'Stewart, you big player! Tell me all about her. I get that I'm making an assumption it's a *her*, but my gaydar's usually spot on.'

Stewart took another drink, and with it added on another ten seconds before answering. Was he shy or just annoyed by her inquisitiveness? She ploughed on.

'Go on, who are you seeing? Is she lovely?'

'She's... um... she's called Rosie. I've been seeing her on and off for a while now. Known her for years.'

'And what's she like? Is she a solicitor too?'

'She's from the office.'

'That must be nice. Or is it claustrophobic working in the same place as your girlfriend?'

This time there was no delay. Stewart replied as soon as she asked the question.

'She's planning to leave actually. She handed in her notice yesterday. I've no idea what's going to happen now.'

Stewart's voice trailed off as he zoned out again. Whatever was going on in his head, Bea reasoned, was far more compelling than she was managing to be. Clearly her game face wasn't working as well as she hoped.

To her side, Freya was giggling as Tilda walked to the bar, casting a look back as she did. Whatever was going on with them was causing much hilarity. *Fair play, Tilda darling. You deserve to laugh.* She turned back to Stewart. His face was grey. He looked terrible.

'Are you all right? Do you want some water?'

He stared at her, as if it were taking all his efforts to comprehend what she was saying. He responded with a shake of his head.

'No. I'm fine... well, I'm just... no.'

He pushed his chair from the table as his napkin fell to the floor.

'I'll just go to the...'

He motioned to the toilets and began to walk away. Staggered was more accurate. Whatever was going on in his head was certainly preoccupying him. *What a strange man*, she thought. She couldn't reach him, no matter what she said. One minute he seemed to let go and allow himself to be vulnerable, the next, he was closed off and hidden. In another life, he might have been someone she would find attractive, but in his current state he seemed to be hell-bent on repelling anyone who veered too close.

Bea turned to look at Freya. She was laughing at Tilda, who was talking to a woman at the bar. Bea had no clue what was happening but the lack of tension in their faces was in stark contrast to what was going on at her end of the table. Between Mal's messages and Stewart's intensity, a little less tension would be more than welcome.

CHAPTER THIRTY-FOUR

Tilda leaned on the bar, waited her turn, and inwardly groaned at the ludicrous task. Freya's concern was very sweet, but it seemed that her friend considered her biggest problem a lack of practice at polite interaction. She had been charged with striking up conversation with a stranger. This wasn't hard. It was odd, but it wasn't hard. Tilda had the power of speech, and conversed on a daily basis. A comment about the weather at the Tesco till, a raised eye and a mutual moan with a fellow temp, a *'Sorry, my fault'* if she bumped into someone on one of her daily walks. She could politely speak to people with ease. Her problem was the lack of something beyond basic small talk. Freya's worry that she wasn't trying hard enough, wasn't solved by forcing a stranger in a queue to speak with her about a fabricated matter. And yet here she was. Humouring her friend, and finding it endearing that she cared so much.

'Are you being served?'

'No. Thanks. Can I get a bottle of Prosecco?'

'Sure, do you need glasses?'

Tilda confirmed she did not, before the man turned away. She looked to her left. A woman of a similar age was in the process of buying a tray of colourful drinks. Not being an expert in much beyond wine, beer and the occasional gin, Tilda stared with fascination at the variety of glasses and their contents. The woman saw Tilda looking.

'Bloody kids. It feels five minutes since they'd have been happy with a Fruit Shoot. Now it's all, *Mum, let's go for cocktails.* I'm not daft. It's because they know I'll pay.' She beamed, showing Tilda that the reality was that she loved going out drinking with her children. 'You know what it's like, right. We'd be rich if we hadn't had them but we wouldn't change a thing, would we?'

'How old are they?' Tilda felt the need to distract the woman from making all sorts of assumptions.

'Carly, my eldest, is twenty. She's studying here and working all summer. I've come down for a few days with her sister. Lauren's eighteen. Honestly, they know how to play me. I've forked out more money over the past two days than I would in a month for myself. They'll be the ruin of me.'

Tilda smiled. She could see the woman was living her best life.

'How old are yours?' the woman asked.

'Oh. You know, erm...' Tilda floundered. Whilst not feeling the need to correct the presumption, it felt a bit much to conjure up fictional children to make the conversation less weird. As she dithered, the final drink was added to the woman's tray. Distracted, she pulled her card from her purse and paid the bill. The topic was forgotten in the exchange.

'Enjoy your evening,' she said as she tottered away with the tray in both hands.

'You too.' Tilda watched her go. From across the room, her eye was caught by a grinning Freya, giving an exaggerated thumbs-up. She mentally thanked the random woman with the daughters, if it meant she could return to her seat now the task was over.

'Excuse me?' The bartender had returned.

'I'll be a few minutes, is that OK? We've run out up

here so I need to go to the cellar.'

'Yes, no problem.' Tilda didn't mind. Now she had completed her mission - although it was more accurate to say that her mission had completed her - she was happy to have a few minutes to catch her breath and assess.

Her evening was going better than she thought. With Bea keeping Stewart occupied at one end of the table, she was able to have a proper catch up with Freya. She was glad about that. Stewart would be around long after Freya had left the country. She was comfortable with her priorities this evening. Mostly comfortable. There was still guilt that she had given Stewart so little attention. There was always guilt. But putting that to one side, she felt all right. Her mind flashed briefly to the moment earlier when he had spotted the table corner in her leg. *Damn.* It made her look mad. At the time, it has been a way of dealing with him being so persistent. She forced the memory away, hoping he had forgotten it too.

The sense of shame that threatened to rise, didn't get a chance. She was distracted by an announcement.

'I LOVE this song.'

The guy with the jumper, previously signposted by Freya, pointed to an indiscriminate spot in the air and spoke again.

'I haven't heard this for ages. It's amazing.'

He had a friendly face. His jumper was more the tight fit, contemporary variety than the fisherman or vicar look. On top of that, he had dimples when he smiled. Perhaps she was going to be able to fulfil Freya's mission with her own assertiveness, rather than rely on being led into conversation by the happy but destitute Cocktail Mum. She strained to listen to the speakers, struggling to be heard over the hubbub of customers. It was faint but she recognised it.

'Oh yes, me too. I love Bob Dylan. This one doesn't get played enough.'

The man looked confused before shaking his head.

'No. No. This is Leonard Cohen. I love this song. Listen.'

'It's Dylan, honestly. I've got everything he ever recorded. This is from *Nashville Skyline*.'

The man listened again.

'Sorry, but it's Leonard Cohen for sure.'

Tilda smiled at him. His dimples may have been cute, but they weren't enough. He was wrong. Rather than reassessing his mistake, he was doubling down and sticking with his first guess. Shame.

The man behind the bar returned from the cellar and proceeded to open the bottle. Tilda put the matter to bed.

'I can categorically state this is not Leonard Cohen. It's Bob Dylan. It *is* a good song though, you're right about that.'

She handed over thirty pounds and waved away the change as she left with the bottle. A five-pound tip was excessive but she needed the casual indifference to add to her confident about-turn as she walked back. Five pounds was worth not having to continue being with someone who had a nice face but talked rubbish. At least in that moment it was. Tomorrow morning, she would feel differently. A five-pound tip. Who was she? The Queen?

'Tilds, mate, you smashed it!' Freya approved.

Loudly. 'And good on ya with the jumper guy. He's hot.'

'Yeah. Hot but wrong. I had to walk away,' Tilda said. 'It shouldn't matter that someone misidentifies a song, but really. Don't try and out-Dylan me. I'm not having it.'

'So let's assess what we've learnt, Tilds. Has this helped you in future situations? Any takeaway points? Where are we AT?' Once again, Freya rested her chin on her hands and awaited Tilda's insights.

'Well fresh from the coalface of chat, I can tell you that a woman assumed I had kids and involved me in laughing at how our children spend all our money...'

'OK. Not promising, but go on.'

'...and then I spoke to a vaguely attractive man who became unattractive before my very eyes when he said something inaccurate. And I found great comfort in walking away from him and coming back here. How's that for insights?' Tilda laughed as she summarised her last few minutes. 'Shall I just give up and join the WI? Or the Women's Guild? Is it time to learn to knit so I can join a group? I think Jumper Guy might have been the last straw.'

Tilda topped up their glasses and sat back in her seat. Settling for someone that annoyed her, just so she could have a partner, was never going to happen. She could have stayed unhappily married in Stockport for that. But the insights she had drawn from Freya's little experiment were clear. Never make assumptions about people's family situations - surely that was a no brainer - and never settle for anyone that might be nice in all sorts of ways but thinks they know best. The only person who knew best for Tilda was Tilda. If that was the takeaway insight from the entire evening, then it was damn good one.

She sat back, drank her Prosecco, and felt good. She was doing her best. It would all fall into place at some point so there was no use trying to force it. A feeling of serenity enveloped her. It was alcohol-induced but it was welcome. She was having a lovely evening with friends in her local restaurant that she had wanted to visit for as long as she'd lived here. This was as good as it got. She should savour this feeling of inner peace and remember to do things that brought it about more often.

At that moment, Bea slid out from her side of the table and walked around to the back of Tilda's seat. She bent down and whispered in her ear.

'I don't want to worry you, but Stewart's been gone ages. Do you think we need to do something?'

CHAPTER THIRTY-FIVE

He did not know how long he had been sitting there. Time was something of which he was unaware. He had stumbled his way to the toilets, sat on the closed seat of a cubicle and locked the door. He needed to be alone. In hindsight, the men's loos weren't the best choice. People kept coming in. The regulated flush of the urinal and the occasional blast of the hand dryer provided a gritty background score to his unravelling.

He took a breath as best he could. It was a struggle. His chest continued to feel as if it were squeezed in a vice. He took another couple of tablets. Dry swallowed and forced down by sheer will, he was desperate for his brain to stay away from its old double act. The one where the more panic his head felt, the more panic his body would exhibit physically. The longer he could keep his head and body apart, the better.

His phone was in his hands. He couldn't remember getting it from his pocket. The world around him was in slow motion one minute, then being fast-forwarded the next. Now he was typing. His mind couldn't keep up. The increased activity in his chest led the way. He managed to type a message.

Rosie. Don't leave. I'm sorry.

It took several attempts. He retyped the word *sorry* repeatedly until the predictive text gave up and let him win. Once it was done, he tried to send it but the effort was too much. His attempts at breathing were all consuming. It had been a long time since he had been hit this hard by an attack. He let his head fall forward towards his knees. Nothing helped. He knew that. In the cold light of day, he knew he had to let it happen. He had to ride it out. That knowledge was of little help now. He couldn't think, he couldn't breathe. His hands shook as he swallowed another tablet.

More time passed. How long was unclear. He found he was able to sit up with more ease. He leaned back on the cistern and continued to focus. His breath was shallow. He was sweating and felt terrible. It became of the utmost importance that he leave the toilets. He needed air. He needed to breathe lungs full of oxygen, not air-freshener-laced toilet stink. With an almighty effort, he pulled himself to his feet. His shaking hands unlocked the door. He opened it and took a second to lean on the sink. Then he was opening the main door. He was taking steps. Small ones, but still steps. His feet walked his body past the bar, away from the diners, and out of the exit that faced the sea.

He could see people mingling on the prom. There were children splashing in the water. He stumbled across the road, towards the beach, and made it to the other side. Taking a giant step over the small wall separating the pavement from the sand, he climbed over and slumped down. Perhaps one more tablet would do the trick.

Stewart took the foil from his pocket. There were two left. Raising his palm to his mouth he swallowed them both. It didn't matter. It wasn't as if they were working.

CHAPTER THIRTY-SIX

Bea and Tilda were deep in conversation, oblivious to anyone leaving the restaurant in the moments before.

'He might have gone back to his hotel. Maybe he's had enough of me banging on. I bored him into leaving with all my tales of Mal. I should have noticed when he was silent for most of the last half hour.'

'I can't see it, Bea. Whenever I've looked over, he seemed to be listening. Or talking. It's my fault. I've barely spoken to him tonight. I think I'd been planning to do it later, when we were more chilled.'

'You mean bladdered?' Bea said. 'Yeah, I thought he might need lubricating before you tackled any heavy convos. But it looks like he's chickened out.'

They considered this for a moment. Something didn't feel right.

'Sod it. I'm going to ring him. Even if it makes me sound like his Mum checking up on him. I'll just see if he's back at the hotel or not. He might have gone to the loo and we're all getting carried away.'

'If he's been there all this time, he's got problems,' Freya jumped in. 'Ring him. Do it. Just ask if he wants a drink.'

Bea picked up her phone and scrolled down to his number.

'It's ringing.'

The women paused their discussion of *How D'you Solve a Problem Like Stewart Grady*, as Freya asked a question.

'I'm not being funny, but who *is* Stewart anyway? I meant to ask you Bea, when we were getting ready, but then we got side tracked with your glitter spray. I feel like I've met him before but I can't place him. I thought he was your bloke at first.'

Bea saw Tilda look shocked. Had she forgotten to fill Freya in on the most important of details. She spluttered slightly as she spoke.

'You don't recognise him?'

'No. Not really. He isn't one of the gang but it feels like he's from back then.'

Bea walked away from the table just as Tilda started to explain. She let them have their space. Leaning against the bar, she looked back as Freya's hands were at her face, mouth open wide. Gobsmacked was the word.

'What can I get you?'

'Tequila. Thanks.'

A moment later, with the shot done, Bea walked back to the table. Freya was still shocked.

'I mean now you say it, obviously they look alike. But Christ, mate. He's nothing like Grady. A proper grumpy bastard. I cannot believe they're related.'

Bea let the chatter carry on around her as she tried ringing again. It continued to ring out. By the time she had counted fifty rings, Freya had a suggestion.

'Guys, I need to pee. I'll have a squizz in the gents before I come back. He's probably there. I'll check it out and put your minds at rest.' She left the table and walked to the toilets as the other women watched her go. Tilda looked at Bea, the phone still to her ear.

'Anything?'

Bea shook her head.

'Do you think he's ignoring us? It feels like we've done something wrong. Inviting him to something we didn't really want him at, and then sidelining him when he got here. I don't know. It's a big mess'.

Tilda spoke quickly. Bea could see her guilt rising. She needed to put her friend's mind at rest.

'Darling, he's not your responsibility and yet you very kindly invited him here for the weekend. You couldn't predict how he would behave while he was here. He's probably taking some time out in the loo because I've rambled on about Mal and he can't take anymore. I basically took the opportunity to overshare because I barely knew him. Now all my stress has been passed onto someone who definitely didn't need more of it. This is my doing.'

Tilda listened as she shook her head.

'You're being kind. It's on me too but, you're right. He's a grown man. We should stop worrying.'

'Definitely. Look here's Freya. She'll tell us.'

The women looked up as their friend strode back across the bar.

'Sorry, but he's defo not there. Cubicle doors were wide open and not a peep of anyone having a shit. Thank Christ. I can definitely live without an eyeful of that.'

Bea watched Tilda's face darken again. This was not the way the evening was supposed to go. Her genius idea of streamlining Tilda's mates into one easy-to-manage event, was crumbling in front of them. She had pushed Tilda into this for her own selfish reasons so it was her responsibility to salvage it. She took a deep breath, determined to get a grip, and control events once more.

'Right ladies, here's the plan. You're going to sit

here and enjoy your evening. There's loads of wine left and you're in the same hemisphere for the first time in over a decade. This is your night. I am full to bursting with food and drink so I'm happy to go and check on Stewart. I'll go to his hotel and make sure he's there. Or I'll keep ringing till I get an answer.'

'Bea, let me come with you, I can...' Tilda began to protest but Bea cut her short.

'Sit down, darling. Drink, chat, laugh. I'll ring you when I've spoken to him.'

Bea didn't stick around for further debate. She'd caused this with her selfishness so it was up to her to fix it. Gently yet firmly, pushing Tilda back into her seat, she headed out of the door. She kept her phone to her ear and walked out into the evening. He had to be somewhere. He couldn't vanish.

That thought, rational as it was, did nothing to rid her of worry. Stewart was in trouble. She knew it in the pit of her stomach. And it was all her fault.

PART THREE

CHAPTER THIRTY-SEVEN

Day two of the reunion

The good news was that Freya had not been sick. Not last night, nor this morning either. Tilda was relieved. They had returned to the flat not long after Bea had left them. Some memories were hazy although she wished she could erase the image of Freya accosting the blue-lit ambulance by the bandstand. It was parked up as they left the restaurant, presumably dealing with an emergency they couldn't see. *'Everyone is fine! No one needs you! Unless you want to be Tilda's new friend? Will you be Tilda's friend?'* Freya had crossed the road to find a paramedic she could enlist in her plan. Luckily the siren sounded and the ambulance was away before her task was complete. Another cause for relief.

None of this changed the fact that she felt rough this morning. Despite remaining smugly hydrated, it was still too early to be facing the day. She couldn't understand how Freya was managing to be this perky. It had taken huge amounts of energy to drag herself out of bed and she'd only done that because she was desperate for a cup of tea.

In scenes reminiscent of their University years, the reunited friends were recuperating on the sofa, both huddled under the open sleeping bag. The day may have reached post meridiem status, but they were still wearing pyjamas and biding their time before tackling basic cleanliness. It didn't matter. They were having fun, regardless of their tender heads and parched mouths. Concentrating on a film however, was more of a challenge.

'Now what's happened? Rewind it again, Freya, I can't remember if that guy's a baddie or not.' Tilda was confused. Despite the 12A certificate, it was taking all her over-eighteen intellect to follow the plot. Her fuzzy-head was not helping her concentration skills.

Freya did as she was told and the scene replayed. Within minutes, Tilda's focus had gone again and she got out from under the covers.

'Another tea?'

'Defo. I'm parched.'

Tilda filled the kettle. As she waited, she checked her phone. Five messages since the last time she looked. All in the WhatsApp group that Bea had set up for the weekend. Her phone must be baffled at this new level of activity.

Jonathan

Greatly looking forward to later, my pretties. I shall watch you dance till dawn from a comfortable seat and support from the sidelines. Woooo - as the youths say - hoooo.   *12.09*

Dhanesh

Bring it on! I'll ask them if they do cocoa. Don't forget your pipe and slippers, Grandad.   *1213*

Jen

I've missed this loads! Can't wait to see everyone later. Don't want to jinx the traffic but I'm aiming to arrive by 4.   *12.17*

Jonathan
Dhanesh, so much cheek for one over forty. Jen, it will
be a joy to see you again. If you're in our hotel, let's
have a reunion aperitif at 4.01.   12.18

Jen
Deal. I'll message when I arrive.   12.20

'Have you seen WhatsApp? It's all kicking off.' She held her phone up to Freya, who began searching down the sofa cushions for her own. She found it, read the conversation with a smile on her face, then began frantically typing her own contribution. Tilda carried on making the tea. Seconds later her screen flashed with a message.

Freya
Guys. Aberystwyth is brilliant. I got here yesterday
and I'm having a great time. Bring your drinking
heads. Also, here's our Tilds looking gorge for so early
in the day...   12.45

Tilda read it again, momentarily confused until it became clear. A photo popped up. It was of now. Of Tilda, standing at the sink, pyjama-clad, with hair scraped into a messy pile on the top of her head. Not a photo she would have preferred to share. Not the first picture she would have chosen for her old friends to see. Freya laughed from the couch.

'Sorry mate, but that was funny. Anyway, you look great. I, on the other hand, look like the mother of teenaged boys. Rough as.'

'You've only said that so I'll jump in and say, *No*

Freya, you're stunning. There's no way you've given birth to teenagers, you look so youthful. But you just shared that photo, so you can stay uncomplimented.'

Tilda fished out the teabags, smiling regardless. Bloody technology. It seemed only five minutes since photos involved a week-long wait at the high street chemists. For the gazillionth time that week, Tilda decided today's kids didn't know they were born.

Back on the sofa, she settled under the sleeping bag, and opened the other conversation she'd had. The one with Bea that started last night. The one that sounded normal and plausible.

Bea
Stewart's fine. He went to get some air. Have a lovely evening.   21.34

Tilda
Are you coming back? Is Stewart? Do you want me to get the bill?   21.37

Bea
Stewart's gone back to the hotel and I'm done for the night too. I'll have a drink with him and then head back. Not as young as I was, darling. Yes, please get the bill and I'll settle up tomorrow. I'll get Stewart's share too. You'll be back before me.   21.39

Tilda
No problem. Do you still have the spare key in case I'm not?   21.40

Bea
Yes, all good. See you in the morning!   *21.40*

Tilda
Night x   *21.41*

Bea
Night xx   *21.41*

Tilda
Where are you?   *06.34*

Bea
Early morning walk. Sorting my wine head out.   *06.40*

Tilda
OK. I'm going back to sleep.   *06.41*

Bea
Night night x   *06.41*

Bea
I've gone to the bar to sort out tonight. Shall I bring in some lunch?   *10.01*

Tilda
Yes! Anything you like. We've just woken up. Freya says she'd eat a scabby dog she's that hungry.   *10.58*

Bea
See you in a bit. With food. No scabby dogs, don't worry.   *11.05*

Normal and plausible. Everyday chat between two people who had not clapped eyes on each other since the night before, despite the fact they were sharing a bed. Tilda knew the amount of wine she put away meant she'd have been in a heavy sleep. There was no denying that. But she was also sure that no one had got into, nor out of her bed. Especially not in the early hours of the morning. She'd been alone all night. Yet Bea had answered her messages and was bringing back food. She was out there somewhere, alive and able to communicate. The logic of that didn't do much to stop unease creeping in. It was all very odd.

'Any news from Bea?' Freya piped up as if she were telepathic. 'I'm starved. Tell her to get a move on, will you.'

Tilda forced a smile. She had no intention of saying that to Bea. She didn't want to be pushy. She didn't want to give the impression she was worried. Except she was. The unidentified concern was now conscious and thriving. It had been nearly two hours since Bea was supposedly arriving with food. This was not like her. Give her a job and she did it. And what could she possibly have to do at the bar? Other than paying a bill or dropping off more banners, there was nothing else to take up her time. Maybe it was Mal. Perhaps he had turned up in the early hours. Tilda knew they were still going through their tricky patch. He could have left after work and made it here last night. Perhaps they were in a hotel somewhere, reaffirming their feelings for each other, wife or no wife. Or maybe he'd kidnapped her?

Just as Tilda's imagination reached peak ridiculous,

she heard the sound of a key in the lock. The door opened and with it the waft of chips.

'Bloody get in!' Freya leapt to her feet and met Bea at the door. 'Hot chips! There's nothing better than hot chips. They're just not the same at home. Bea, you absolute legend!'

Freya got Bea a drink as Tilda grabbed plates and buttered bread as if she were being timed for a challenge. Minutes later, all three were on the sofa, half watching the film that refused to give up, and stuffing their hungover faces with a carb overload.

Wearing last night's clothes, Bea curled her feet underneath her and settled into the squash of the cushions. Then, thinking better of it, she turned to face the others.

'While I remember, I think we might be down an honorary geographer tonight. Last time I spoke to him, Stewart was planning an early dart today. I'm not sure we'll see him later.'

Tilda's response was automatic.

'Oh. That's a shame.'

It was an instinctive thing to say, emerging with an autoplay quality she didn't know she possessed. Was it a shame? She had no idea.

'Yeah. I know. I tried to convince him but he said he might have to get back.'

With the information shared, Bea made herself comfortable again. She stared at the television and ate her food. The room soon fell into silence, apart from the film that no one was watching.

Tilda's mind raced. Facing Bea in the office for twenty years meant she had a particular insight into Bea's moods. She had seen her endure hangovers, breakups, and aggressive residents' committees, hell-bent on having their say at the council representative. She remembered the month of the late period when Bea had gone to the doctors for a termination before she had confirmed whether or not she was actually pregnant. She knew what Bea looked like pissed, stoned, and sick. Tilda had seen it all. She had seen Bea see it all. Yet in all those years, she had never once seen Bea look as ashen and exhausted as she did at this moment. Something had gone on. Tilda knew it, and she knew that Bea knew she knew it. That's why Bea was staring straight ahead and pretending to watch a film, the first hour of which she had missed.

Tilda ate her chip butty and gave her friend space. If she wanted to tell her, she would. There was nothing else Tilda could do.

CHAPTER THIRTY-EIGHT

Messages continued to arrive throughout the day. Very few members of the WhatsApp group had real queries requiring an answer. Other than Sam checking the time they were planning to meet, practicalities were not the focus. Instead, their communications veered towards re-establishing the close-knit group they had once been. Jokes were fired off, gentle piss-taking became the norm, the *crying laughing* emoji was used a lot.

As she read her phone, and found herself typing back *'Easy for you to say, it wasn't you that fell down that hill!'* Tilda marvelled at how easy it felt to sink back into these friendships. She had assumed it would be awkward. Not seeing people for decades must impact the ease of picking up where you left off, surely? But then their University experience was fairly robust, what with all the field trips, youth hostels, and country pubs. When she looked back, opting for geography had given her a social life that wouldn't have existed if she had chosen something else. Did sociologists and mathematicians ever leave the lecture theatre? Maybe not. Lucky for her it had worked out that way. She wouldn't have had half as many positive student memories without it.

Tilda put down her phone and went to check on the others. In the hours since she had got up that morning, her bedroom had transformed into a salon. As she entered, the back of Freya's head sported over-sized rollers, and Bea was in the process of blow-drying her hair upside down. There were clothes all over the place.

'How're we getting on? Is the bathroom free if I go for a shower?'

Bea threw back her head and with it, her voluminous mane.

'No problem, darling. We're both done. How's my hair?'

'Huge.'

'Excellent. That's the plan.'

'Like it used to be.'

'That's even more the plan. Thank you, darling.'

Bea continued to enlarge and embolden, using the can of hairspray as if it were a weapon.

'All right?' Tilda asked tentatively. This morning's weirdness was one thing, but Bea throwing herself back into her old look, was setting off alarm bells. Would the chic and stylish neutrals be her outfit of choice later, or would she revert to something a little more kaleidoscopic? She needed to know.

'Everything's fine, Tilds. I think there may be a slight change in my personal circumstances at some point, but I'll sleep on it tonight and see how I feel.'

'You mean Mal?'

'I do.'

'I'm happy to delay my shower if you want to talk. I'm struggling to find the energy for much else at the moment.'

Bea said she was happy to share, so Tilda crawled under the duvet. The shower could wait. She watched Bea open her mouth a couple of times before making a start as Freya applied false eyelashes in the background.

'I've come to the realisation that Mal might be a bit of an arse.'

'Ah. Right then.'

'It's not just the married thing. Even though it's that too. That was never cool. It was also never as over as he made out. Back at the start, anyway. I realise that now.'

'No.'

'But it's more than that. Now I've had a bit of space to consider things, I've realised...' it came out of her mouth in a rush '...he's a big controlling knobhead.'

'I see.'

'And I never thought I could be controlled. Not for a second.'

Tilda stopped responding, letting Bea have the space to express her feelings, but Freya had thoughts from the mirror.

'How did he control you? I can't imagine anyone telling you what to do, mate. You're so strong.'

Bea agreed with her.

'I know, right? I'm full of my own plans and thoughts and opinions. It wasn't like he came along and point blank told me what to do. It was more subtle than that.'

'How then?'

Bea shrugged her shoulders.

'He'd suggest something. Something irrelevant and silly, and then go on about it until I agreed with him. Even when it wasn't important.'

'Like what?'

Bea gave it some thought before coming up with the best example she could find.

'Like a few months ago, he said it made sense to

move my kettle. I had it near the cupboard with the teabags and he said it would be better nearer the tap. Just saying this out loud makes me see how ridiculous it was. Anyway, it *literally* didn't matter to me. Who cares about something like that, right? So I ignored him. Then the next time he came around, he told me again how it made sense to move it. And even though I didn't agree *or* disagree with him, I also didn't feel the need to move my kettle when it was perfectly fine where it was. So, I told him that, and he went quiet. And then he... *sulked*.'

'He sulked? Because you wouldn't move your own kettle to a place you didn't want it in the first place?' Freya was confused.

'Yeah. I know it sounds stupid. And it wasn't a big sulk. Just half an hour of him being a bit funny. When he bought it up for a third time, it just seemed easier to do it. I couldn't be arsed with the pained look when I didn't take his advice.'

Tilda had been listening from the bed.

'Is that what happened with your hair? Is that what he did to make you change it?'

Bea looked sheepish. Tilda could see she had been wrestling with this herself. Maybe this was what had kept her out all night.

'It was a mix of things. I didn't lie when I said my hair wasn't as thick as it used to be. Jeez, let me tell you, the menopause is such a bastard. You don't know which way's up, you're in a fog all the time, and things you used to be clear about, suddenly seem muddled.' Bea paused and breathed. Tilda and Freya were all ears. She smiled at them. 'Thank you for listening to my TED talk.'

'You're welcome.' Tilda smiled back. She'd find out about all that soon enough.

'Anyway, my hair was taking a bit more oomph and spray to get the usual effect. You know, this stunning look?'

She signalled her own head and then curtsied to the room. Tilda laughed out loud this time.

'So, I happened to say it was taking more effort. Just in conversation. Then a week later, he suggested - that word again, *suggested* - that I should rethink it. He banged on about how easier it would be in a different style. I told him that I knew that. I mean, of course I know that. Day-to-day life would be loads easier if I didn't have a hair-do that takes half an hour of styling to look how I want. Life would be easier if I didn't shave my legs or have to remember to take HRT and vitamins, or walk ten thousand steps every day, just so I can drink wine at the weekend. I accept all that, but he seemed to think his words of wisdom were helpful. And then for my birthday, he gave me vouchers to a salon near his work. I turned up, they de-matted and tamed my wig, and that was that. I looked age-appropriate.'

'You looked great. Just not you.'

'Yeah, I know. That was the problem. There was nothing wrong with the new hair. It looked amazing. It just wasn't something I'd have chosen myself. *He'd* chosen it. Same with the clothes he bought me. All beautiful clothes. Just not *my* clothes. Not my style.'

Tilda watched Bea fluff up her hair again. Like she used to, a million times a day in the office. A quick plump before a meeting, before a coffee break, before a phone call. Real Bea was in the room.

'But something must have been nice about him. Back at the start. You were really into him. He was the first person you wanted to commit to. Did he suggest that as well?'

Bea put down the blusher brush and sighed. It seemed the answer to this question dug a little deeper. She walked over to the bed and lay back on the pillow next to Tilda. Freya perched herself on the end.

'I've been thinking about that.'

'Go on, mate. Fill us in.' Freya was intrigued.

Bea got herself comfy. As if she needed cushioning to soften the inner turmoil she was about to share.

'I dated this guy once. Jonesy. A hundred years ago. And he had a smell. I can't describe it. It wasn't a bad smell but it wasn't good either. It just *was*. Washing powder or hair product or something. I don't know. But now, nearly forty years later, I'll be walking down the road and I'll get a whiff of it. Someone will walk past with the same deodorant or soap, and just like that, I'm back.' Bea clicked her fingers for emphasis. 'I'm sixteen, lying on Jonesy's single bed with his grey striped duvet, watching *Fright Night* or *Ghostbusters* and feeling his hard on as he leans across for a cuddle. I mean, he wasn't that important to me at the time but it's such a lovely memory.'

'His hard on?' Freya was direct.

'We never got further than it being nudged up against me behind drainpipe denim. No, I mean the memory of being young. Of spending a teenaged evening in teenaged arms. Pretending to watch a film when you're really trying to inch your mouth nearer and nearer to someone else's without looking like you're making the first move. Don't you miss that sometimes?'

There was a brief silence before Tilda spoke.

'It won't come as a surprise that my teenage years were kiss-free.' Tilda knew Bea never understood how it had been for her. Their youthful experiences were binary opposites. 'But what's Jonesy's deodorant got to do with anything now?'

Bea spoke quickly now the penny had dropped.

'Mal has the same smell. It's the reason why I felt comfortable from the start. I upturned my whole value system the second I met him, because of nostalgia and memories.'

'You mean you never loved him?'

Bea shrugged.

'I loved what he reminded me of. Being young. Having my whole life ahead of me. The *anticipation* of something, rather than the *actual* something. Everything being up for grabs and having all the time in the world to experience it. His smell made all that come back. I felt young again. And as much as I'm OK being my actual age, it's fair to say I'm not sixteen. I don't have unlimited years ahead. I don't have time to waste. And yet for the best part of this year, that's exactly what I've been doing. Wasting time. It's been a bit of a cock up, really. I got so knocked off balance by getting older, I made stupid decisions.'

Bea exhaled loudly. She got out from the bed and moved back to the mirror, assessing her half-completed makeup.

'Even mid-glam, I'm a marvel. Did you know that? *I* am a marvel.'

Tilda smiled.

'I did know that. Always have been, always will be.'

'Damn right, mate. Marvel-frigging-licious.' Freya said. 'What are you going to do now?'

Bea rooted through her makeup bag.

'I'm going to enjoy the rest of this weekend. I am going to meet Jonathan and Dhanesh, and Sam and Jen. Tonight, I'll be wearing a dress with an actual spangly fringe across the shoulders, and then once I'm home, I think I'm going to end it.'

'You think, or you know?'

'I think I know.'

Bea picked up a brush and began to apply bronzer. It seemed that now she was coming back to herself, there was no point in being a pale imitation. Tilda wondered if there was enough golden shimmer in all the world to make up for the past few months. She continued to gently probe.

'Will he handle it well?'

'Not sure. I don't think he'll kick off or anything. It'll be sulks and sadness. Probably pleading with me to see things in a different way. Like it would have been with the kettle if I hadn't moved it. He's used to getting what he wants when he behaves like that. We'll have to wait and see. I imagine it'll descend quite quickly once he realises I'm taking control of things. My things anyway. He can do what he likes with his own shit.'

Tilda lay back in the bed as Bea continued to groom. If Mal was the reason that Bea had been AWOL all night then it had certainly given her strength of mind. Fair play to her. He sounded hard work. Tilda's experience with men was miniscule in comparison with Bea. She had no idea what to say. Even so, it felt like Mal was someone to swerve.

'Can I have a time check, ladies? How long before the rollers come out?' Freya had moved on and was back to practicalities. Bea looked around for her phone as they discussed the rest of the afternoon.

From the bed, Tilda kept her eyes on Bea. Hair in place, eyelid glitter applied, perfume sprayed. Bea was laughing at something Freya had just said. All was normal. Everything was fine. It was going to be OK. It was just odd that it felt anything but.

Half an hour later and Tilda had made it to the shower. She turned the water on to its full power and stood under the cascade. There was no rush. She had time to enjoy the silence. Silence to a point. She could hear muffled chat and occasional laughter through the walls. Bea's distinctive cackle was easily identifiable. Seconds later, the hum of the hairdryer was audible. Freya's rollers were out.

Tilda stayed where she was, and relished the break. Spending time with her friends was wonderful. That didn't mean she wasn't appreciating this particular breather. She rolled her neck, stretching and relaxing the muscles that she knew were prone to tension.

She milked it as long as she could. Aware that she was hogging the only room with a toilet, she couldn't stay there all day. Once her hair was washed and she'd enjoyed the final few minutes of steamy warmth, she switched off the water and found a towel. It was as she twisted it around her head, the street buzzer sounded. *Damn.* She wasn't dressed for guests.

'I'll get it.' Bea shouted from the other side of the door. Tilda was glad of her offer although she couldn't imagine who it would be. She shook out another towel to wrap around herself. If she ran out of the bathroom now, she could be back in her room before anyone made it up the stairs. She had at least thirty seconds. Tilda continued the mental maths from behind the closed door before deciding to make a run for it. It would only be someone for another flat.

A peep around the door revealed a clear coast. Freya was still in the bedroom, albeit with full makeup, as Tilda grabbed her robe, wrapping herself in it as she looked for her slippers in the hall. As she did, the flat door opened. Bea held it for someone to follow.

'Look who I found.'

Tilda watched as a dishevelled and broken man walked in.

'Stewart! I thought you'd gone.'

His voice was quiet. Still audible but with none of the power it had held yesterday.

'I was thinking I might stay for tonight. If that's still OK.'

Tilda was overcome with relief. Relief about a fear she hadn't consciously identified.

'Course it's OK. The more the merrier.'

Bea ushered Stewart through the door and took his coat. Tilda hovered in the hallway, not sure what else to say. She was glad he had come back. She hadn't wanted to leave things in a weird place. The question remained however, what on earth had happened since the restaurant, to cause him to look so ghostly.

CHAPTER THIRTY-NINE

Tilda might have chosen *ghostly* but Bea's assessment was less poetic. *Fucking shocking*. That's how she'd have described Stewart's appearance. She hung his coat as she thought what to do. A flicker needed to be extinguished. Snuffed out before it took over. *Putting out fires is your forte* she reminded herself, assuming control of the situation. *Time to act*.

'Right Tilds, you finish getting ready. Freya, I'll leave you doing your hair. Me and Stewart will put the kettle on. We've only got a few hours before we meet the others. Let's get moving, people.'

She pushed Stewart into the lounge as Tilda and Freya did as they were told. Time was tight after their morning of chip butties and couch-potatoing. As Tilda turned on the hairdryer in the bedroom, Bea closed the door and turned to face Stewart. Before she could open her mouth, he jumped in.

'You left without saying goodbye. I thought I'd dreamt everything.'

Bea led him to the sofa.

'You needed your sleep. Get comfy and I'll brew up.' She took a long look at him as he sat down. A lump rose in her throat and her eyes prickled. 'I'm glad you haven't gone home.'

She swallowed hard and turned away. He wouldn't talk if she was too pushy. This had to be causal. She let the tap run longer than necessary. The noise forced a pause in the need to converse. He needed the pause. When she turned off the tap, he was ready to speak.

'I said I was leaving this morning.'

'I know. But I knew you wouldn't. Not if I wasn't around to say goodbye.'

'Sneaky.'

'Yeah. Soz about that.'

She hadn't deliberately manipulated the situation but it was best he stayed. She watched him. Looking out of the window, he sat bolt upright in the centre of the sofa. He was miles away.

'How do you feel?'

Stewart looked at her.

'Tired.'

'Well you and me both, darling. That's what being up all night will do.'

'Tired and stupid.'

'That's allowed.'

'What do the others know?'

'I told them you went back to your hotel and I stayed for a drink.'

'Did they believe you?'

'I think so. Tilda messaged a couple of times this morning before I was back, but I fobbed her off.'

A thought occurred to him.

'Do they think we fucked?'

Bea shrugged.

'Not sure. Maybe. I found myself telling them about Mal. It took the attention away from you.'

'Thanks. Sorry.'

'No need to apologise. It was helpful. They got both barrels this morning like you got last night. Thanks for listening, by the way. I appreciate it.'

Stewart almost laughed. He didn't appear to be convinced of Bea's sincerity.

'If anyone was there for someone last night, it wasn't me. It was you.'

'Nonsense.' Bea said. 'Your insights gave me stuff to ponder in the small hours.' She tried to smile but struggled. Her eyes brimmed. It was the shock she couldn't shake. Pushing her way through the crowd and finding him. His body slumped against the sea wall with his head lolling on his chest. His open arms as if welcoming a hug, resting limply by his side. In that moment, she thought he was dead.

The gathering tears fell. She couldn't help it. The gut-deep worry that had arrived last night was still present and refusing to leave. *'Hello, Mrs, Miss... you came in with Stewart Grady? There's no news just yet.'* She wiped her eyes on her sleeve and shook her head to shift the memory. It was over now. It had to go.

'Bea, I'm Sorry. Again.'

'Stop.'

'OK. Sorry.'

Stewart's eyes were managing to crinkle even when his mouth was firm. He had never looked so human, resembling the photo on the mantlepiece more than ever. She took his crinkly eyes as a positive sign and attempted to be more upbeat. She had to shake this off.

'So what's your plan today? I realise a night out with Tilda's friends might not be the best option. How do you feel?'

'Apart from tired, I feel... all right. Nothing that won't be helped by a decent night's sleep.'

'Good.'

'I think, if it's all right with you, I'll still come later. Drink water or something, and then leave at a sensible time. I think being around people will be a good idea. I've got lots to think about, but being alone in the hotel might be a bit...'

'Depressing? Claustrophobic? Cause you to do something stupid again?' She couldn't stop herself.

'Something like that. Yeah.'

Bea sorted the mugs and teabags. Minutes later she had taken drinks to the women in the bedroom and returned to the lounge. She carried a mug over to Stewart, her shaking hand spilling only a little, before sitting down on the chair. He sipped his drink. So did she. There wasn't much to say now. Last night had been terrifying. They both knew it, even if they had experienced it differently.

Eventually Stewart spoke up. He had something on his mind.

'I just wanted to say, I know I was stupid last night, but I wasn't *totally* stupid.'

'You were a baby amount stupid?'

'That's one way of putting it.'

'OK darling. Whatever you say.'

He shifted in his seat. Finding the words seemed to be a struggle. His mouth opened once or twice, as if about to start, but he ended up taking a drink instead. Bea waited. She certainly wasn't going to force the conversation. She still wasn't sure she could handle it.

He tried again.

'I know what they thought.'

'What who thought?'

'All of them. It was obvious. But they were wrong.'

She nodded slowly. Showing support rather than agreement. There was more silence. Could she ask?

Did she dare?

'So what really happened?'

She dared. Stewart looked straight at her.

'I didn't stop taking the tablets.'

'I know darling. You took them all.'

His face fell.

'It wasn't like that. It was...'

The right words continued to elude him but he was determined. He pushed on, despite the struggle.

'I need you to understand. I wanted to feel better. But I didn't want to stop *feeling*.'

Bea stayed silent.

'I didn't mean to cause all this hassle. Last night... well, it was the weird situation. Or the booze. They thought I'd done it on purpose.'

'You're saying you didn't?'

He leaned back in his seat. Resting the mug on his thigh, he took a deep breath.

'No. Not consciously, anyway. I wanted the panic to stop. I felt sick at the things you were telling me about your chap. You were right when you said I must identify with him.'

'Oh Christ, I didn't mean anything bad by it. I just meant...'

'But I *did* identify with him. And I felt pissed off that I hadn't chatted to Tilda. Not her fault. I realise how I must have seemed.'

'No, that was *my* fault. I put that in her head.'

'It doesn't matter. This weekend is not why I'm having panic attacks. And it's not why I'm unhappy either. It's more complicated than that.'

Bea wasn't sure if she believed him or not, although the churning had eased a little. Perhaps it was time to tell him everything.

'Remember when we were waiting?'

'Not really. It's blurry.'

You talked. Mostly bollocks. Random words, bits of sentences. I stopped listening after a while because you were sleepy and making no sense.'

'Sorry again. Really.'

'Stop that.'

'Sorry.' This time Stewart's smile reached his mouth. Bea instinctively laughed.

'No, really stop it, I'm trying to make a point.'

'Sorry. No really, I am. But go on. Please.' He mimed a zip across his mouth before she continued.

'There were a few times, several times in fact, where you mentioned your brother. I wasn't paying attention at first because you called him John. I had no idea who you were on about. But then I remembered. Out of all the gibberish that came from your mouth, *Sorry John* were the only coherent words I could hear.'

Stewart put his mug on the table. Leaning forward, he rubbed both hands over his face, stifling a groan.

'Sounds like I made a right tit of myself.' He looked embarrassed. Bea spoke but chose her words carefully. Now was not the time to cause him to shut down.

'I just wonder, and it's only an idea, you don't have to, but maybe talking to someone regularly might help? It sounds like there's lots of stuff going on for you, that you usually keep inside.' She held her mug to her mouth, pretending to drink as she assessed how he was taking it. 'It might be time to let it out? Find someone who could listen. Someone who could help.'

'A shrink?'

'A counsellor.'

'What's the difference?'

'Do you know, I've no idea. Although I always think *shrink* sounds American, don't you? Either way, it might be something to consider. They gave you those leaflets for a reason. Might be worth looking for someone in York. Even if you were, as you say, only a tiny bit stupid and not the full whack.'

Stewart was quiet. He was probably trying to stop himself telling her to *fuck off.* He looked out of the window as she waited. He drank his tea. A minute passed, maybe more. Then he spoke.

'I'm not saying you don't have a point, Bea. You do. I've got the bumph they gave me at the hospital and I *will* read it.'

Her raised eyebrow forced him to commit a little further.

'OK. I promise I'll consider it. I will. But it's also true, I'd prefer to talk with *you* rather than a stranger.'

'Oh darling!' Bea was surprised. She had worried he'd be angry with her for butting in, not asking for more input. 'As touching as that is, I'm definitely not qualified. You'd benefit more with a professional.'

Stewart shook his head.

'No I wouldn't. Not for ages anyway. Look what happened after we chatted over one dinner. All of a sudden I was telling you about the lack of affection in my life. I even mentioned my mother. I don't think I've referred to her out loud in decades. It's like you unlocked something in me. I think I did in you too. Otherwise you wouldn't have opened up about your own dodgy relationship. We shouldn't ignore that.'

Bea was moved. She thought back to their early

conversation. It had been full of oversharing. Full of honesty.

'Maybe we only felt comfortable because we thought we'd never see each other again. Maybe that's why it was easy to be so frank. I don't think I'd have told you about my dissatisfaction with Mal if I knew I'd be seeing you in a few weeks and have you wonder why I was still with him.'

'*Will* you still be with him in a few weeks?'

She knew the answer to his question without any thought.

'No. I won't.'

Stewart nodded.

'Look, all I'm saying is, I really needed last night. You talked to me, I talked to you. You listened to me, you trusted me with your own shit, you...'

'I depressed you with my problems so much, you stormed off and took too many tablets. Yeah, I'm a great influence.'

Stewart's eyes smiled again.

'Can we keep in touch?'

'What does that mean?'

'I don't know. This is new. All I know is I don't want to fuck you. And please take that for the genuine compliment that it is. I don't want an arrangement where if we're in the same place at the same time, we sleep together. I don't want that at all. I just want to be able to talk now and then. Like, if we're passing by, we meet for conversation. Or food. Or a drink or two.'

Something inside Bea finally relaxed.

'Stewart. You're saying you want us to be friends.'

His face broke into a full grin, mouth and all.

'No shit. I knew there was a name for it. Friends! Bea, let's be friends. Great friends. It's a whole new world but I'll give it a go if you will.'

Bea didn't stop to think. She moved to the couch and squeezed in the gap beside him. Her arms opened and she hugged him. Hard. He responded, pulling her in to his chest, and resting his chin on her head. Before last night, this would have been unthinkable but things had changed. The lump in her throat returned and her eyes began to refill. They were both still here. Tired, emotional but still here. Everything was going to be OK. For the pair of them.

A moment later, she disentangled herself.

'Are you all right?'

His concern touched her.

'I'm fine, darling. Thanks for asking.' She moved back to the chair, feeling more weight lift as she did. There was just one last thing to discuss.

'OK, Stewart. I'll be friends, but only if you promise to find someone with actual qualifications, to talk to as well. I can't be solely responsible for your sanity.'

He smiled, appearing touched at her emotion.

'After your help last night, that's not a request I can refuse. It's a deal.'

'Deal.'

She curled up her legs and rooted in her pockets for the tissue she was sure was there. Her tea was cold but she was warmed regardless. Stewart was going to be her friend. It was about time she had a platonic male friend. This could be the making of both of them.

CHAPTER FORTY

The rest of the afternoon was a frenzy of activity. Whilst Stewart went back to his hotel for a sleep, WhatsApps pinged through the air. Dhanesh, who had gone exploring upon arrival, sent photos of as many different seagulls as possible. He managed thirty-seven before realising he was running out of time to get showered. Jonathan sent updates about his panicked rush, with great amusement.

Back in the flat, the women had sped up their own physical transformations so much, they ended up with hours to kill. Rather than clock-watch in Tilda's lounge, they decided to gatecrash the hotel bar where the others were staying. Whilst the official evening started at seven, pre-lash could begin at any point. It was nearly five when Tilda, Freya, and Bea walked down the prom to find the friends that awaited them.

Jen had screamed and Sam had cried. Dhanesh had hugged everyone and Jonathan had beamed. Drinks were ordered, and multiple conversations flowed. The Liverpool Geographers of 1999 were reunited.

Once seven o'clock arrived, the gang moved to the bar on the prom. The one with the Welsh name that Tilda avoided uttering. One day she would make an effort to learn some words. If she was staying here for good it was only right. If this was to be her home, she should embrace it wholeheartedly.

The dancing had started immediately. Not that there was an official dance floor as such. The side of the bar that Bea had reserved had an area of floor space between the tables. Dhanesh proved to be a true party animal when he convinced everyone to dance to *Saturday Night,* that was playing as they arrived. A couple of hours earlier they had toasted their reunion with shots of tequila, which went some way to explain their willingness to embrace public dancing so early in the evening. It had been quite the sight. All the traits that adulthood carefully suppressed, were brought screaming into the open. Jen's swivelly hips, Tilda's lack of coordination, Sam's dramatic lip syncing, Dhanesh's childlike exuberance, and Jonathan's paternal humouring. He had remained on the dance floor for the shortest time, eventually decamping to the bar to enquire about a wine list. Soon after, Tilda followed. Dancing was embarrassing enough. She didn't need a coordinated routine thrown in. Happy to leave it to the others, she pulled up a bar stool next to Jonathan.

'Tilda my dear. You look radiant. But I'd forgotten your inability to control both your arms and legs when you attempt to move to music. The traumatic memories have come flooding back.'

Tilda laughed. She had never been able to dance.

'Oh shut up, you. Luckily my gifts lie elsewhere.'

'Quite right, mine too. Now tell me. What's your preferred grape variety?'

'White.'

Jonathan sighed.

'As usual I'm dealing with absolute Philistines. Dhanesh is just as bad. Last week I took him to a wine tasting, and he told me he liked them all because they were wine and he likes wine. Honestly.'

From the depths of the dance floor, Sam's cry of, *'My son would be mortified if he could see me now. Good!'* made all who heard it giggle. She continued to give her one-woman tribute to every singer blasting from the speakers. From Whigfield, to Aerosmith to Gwen Stefani. She lip synced them all, along with an almost-offensive attempt at Irish dancing when B*Witched came on. It was clearly some time since Sam had been out.

Over on his bar stool, Jonathan was discussing wine options with the man serving the drinks. A bottle was opened, poured and tasted. It got the go ahead and the glass was filled. The man saw Tilda watching.

'A glass for you?'

'Oh. No thank you. I'm fine for now.' She gestured towards her Prosecco. Bea had arranged fizz on arrival and she was happy to sip hers slowly. Her head was only just clear from last night. 'Actually, can I have a glass of water?'

'Of course. Tap, still, or sparking?'

'Tap would be perfect.'

'No problem. Great dancing, by the way.'

The man walked away with a brief flash of a smile. Tilda's face burned. That's what comes of ignoring her natural inhibition. Well, sod him. She didn't care. She would dance badly if she wanted and no one could stop her. Not even the bar guy. There was something familiar about him, though. Not that seeing him before was unusual. She didn't live in a metropolis. She'd probably walked past him in Tesco or strolled by him on one of her walks. There were a few regular faces she recognised from being out and about.

'There you go.' He placed a glass on top of the bar.

'Thanks. And thanks for the compliment. I know I've got rhythm. I know I've got moves. It can be a curse but it's my cross and I have to bear it bravely.'

His reply was just as deadpan.

'Not all heroes wear capes.'

Tilda's mind searched for a witty response but she was distracted. From the dance floor, Dhanesh's voice could be heard above the buzz of everyone else.

'I LOVE this one. Come on everyone. It's Lowestoft '98 all over again!'

A boyband, whose name she had long forgotten, was singing *Everyone Get Up* which Dhanesh was taking as a personal instruction and an evangelical message to spread far and wide. It was of the utmost importance to him that everyone did indeed get up, and get up as soon as possible.

She dragged herself off the bar stool, as the man behind the bar looked on. It was only half seven but the dancing hadn't let up since they'd walked through the door. Perhaps he was amused. Perhaps he was worried they would be rowdy. Perhaps he didn't care either way if he was simply waiting for his shift to end. She stopped imagining his internal monologue and joined her friends in the middle of the space. She knew she was about to look ridiculous but it didn't matter. Tilda was having more fun than she could remember. She placed her water and her Prosecco carefully on a table before shuffling into the middle of the bodies. Flailing arms, jerky legs, who cared? Her solitary life would be back in full swing tomorrow afternoon. For now, she had people. She had friends. She had the worst dancing skills in the world. She couldn't care less.

CHAPTER FORTY-ONE

It soon transpired that Tilda had limited energy for dance. After three songs, only one of which she knew, she found herself slinking away to Bea and Stewart. They had been watching from the safety of a booth, somewhat open mouthed.

'Budge up, I'm shattered.'

They dutifully shuffled along, allowing Tilda some space. She clambered in and sunk into the seat. Bea was amazed.

'Tilds, I never knew you had it in you. All those Christmas dos we had, yet the office never once saw you throw shapes like that.'

Tilda laughed and downed her water, then repeated the action with her Prosecco.

'I don't think they were the right kind of shapes. They were irregular ones. Wait. Do I mean irregular? Is that when the angles are different? I can't remember. School was a long time ago.'

'Darling. Are you pissed? First the dancing, now the geometry chat. This is hysterical.'

Tilda shook her head.

'Not even a tiny bit. I'm just happy. This is the best night ever, Bea. Thank you.'

'Nonsense. It's nothing to do with me. It's about the people, not the planning. Anyway, it was Freya's idea. She's not as daft as she looks.'

They looked across at Freya. She was, at that exact moment, attempting the Dirty Dancing lift with Dhanesh. It didn't go well. Seconds later he was lying in a heap on top of her, having made the gender-blind decision of performing the role of Baby. Happily, their inability to stand up was due to uncontrollable giggles rather than debilitating injury. Tilda watched on, laughing despite her concerns.

'We're going to get thrown out if we're not careful. The man behind the bar keeps looking over.'

Bea looked to see who she meant.

'Gethin? Don't worry about him, he's an absolute sweetheart. Now, I'd get up but I'm wedged. Will you get the drinks in, Tilds. I'm on gin and slim. Stewart?'

At the mention of his name, Stewart's attention moved from the dance floor and towards Bea's empty glass mime. Looking very different from the previous evening, he had finally shaved his bedraggled face. Now he looked just as he had when Tilda first met him. It had been quite a surprise when he had arrived earlier.

'I'm on this lager. The blue one.'

He held up an almost empty bottle. Tilda clocked it was the alcohol-free kind but made no comment. Last night had been a heavy one. She should probably take it easy herself.

Bea continued to chat about the man behind the bar, now that the drinks order had been conveyed.

'Gethin spent all afternoon sticking the photos around the walls. And the banners. Isn't he fab? I've hounded him with emails for weeks.'

Tilda looked around.

'Why do they say *Congratulations*?'

'It was the nearest I could find to *Happy Reunion Night*. If it had been a multiple of ten years since you'd seen each other, I'd have gone for the birthday ones.'

'Well done, Bea.' Stewart raised his bottle before

seeing off the last mouthful. Tilda continued to be perplexed at the decoration.

'The banners are fine but did the world really need to see the photo of nineteen-year-old me in a face pack?'

'Yes it did! I would have never had you down as a face pack kind of gal. This has been an eye-opening education.'

'That's because I'm *not* a face pack kind of *gal*. That was the only time it happened, and I was allergic. Freya took the photo because my face was stinging and she thought it was funny.'

'Tilds, get over it. We have a fundamental right to see terrible pictures of your past. Don't we, Stewart?'

At a second mention of his name, Stewart turned his head. Bea was looking at him, expecting a response.

'I'm sure you're right. Bea. Although I am relieved there are none of *me* displayed in public.' He smiled. Tilda realised this was the first time she had seen him do that since he'd arrived. She felt a sudden warmth towards him. A warmth and a need to apologise.

'Stewart, I'm sorry. I've treated you very badly since you've been here. We never did get a chance to sit and chat. Is it too late now?'

Stewart smiled again. It was reassuring to see him more relaxed. His demeanour yesterday had been nothing like this.

'You don't have anything to apologise for. I thought, mistakenly it turns out, that I needed you to tell me what to do. It turns out I don't. Coming here has given me lots of time to think for myself.'

Tilda was relieved.

'I'm not very good at telling people what to do. I wouldn't have been any help if you needed me to be bossy.'

'Perhaps not. It turns out I didn't need bossy in the end. I needed space. I needed some clarity and I've had a bit of that now.'

'I'm glad,' Tilda said. And she was. This calmer, gentler Stewart made him far easier to like.

'Speaking of bossy, Tilds, where are the drinks? I'm gasping.' She gestured to the empty glasses as Tilda remembered her mission.

'Ah, sorry. Back in a sec.

Jonathan was still settled at the bar. His wide grin indicated he was having as much fun watching from his seat as the rest of the gang were having on the dance floor. Tilda sat back in the stool she had not long vacated.

'How's the wine?'

'Going down nicely. They have a perfectly curated list. Ticks all my boxes.'

Tilda nodded. She had no real response beyond general positivity.

'That's nice.'

'It is. Thank you for humouring me.'

Sweating from excessive dance floor activity, Jen chose that moment to approach the bar.

'Tia Maria and coke, please. I'm spitting feathers.'

'Still with the Tia Maria, my dear?'

'Till the day I die, Jonathan.'

'How marvellously retro. Never change.'

'Couldn't if I tried.'

Within seconds, the man Tilda now knew to be

Gethin, handed Jen her drink. Then he turned to her.

'And what can I get you?'

'Right. A gin and slimline tonic, a bottle of non-alcoholic lager, and...' she realised she hadn't a clue what she wanted... 'erm, I don't know. Let me decide what I feel like.'

Jonathan leaned over.

'I can recommend a variety of wines if you need. Use me, use my expertise.'

'I'm not sure I'm in the mood. I had too much wine last night. I don't want to be a party pooper, but I'm not sure what else to go for.'

Unable to miss out on anymore dancing, Jen raised her glass, saluted Tilda and Jonathan, then strutted back to the dance floor. Tilda watched in awe. She had never strutted anywhere in her life. She had no idea how to even attempt it.

'What flavours do you like?'

'Excuse me?'

'In your drinks. What flavours do you like to drink?'

It seemed Gethin was getting involved.

'Flavours. Tastes? In drinks.'

Tilda panicked. How was she supposed to know that? What flavours were there other than alcohol?

Gethin put Bea and Stewart's drinks down before continuing.

'Some people like sour, zingy tastes. Others prefer sweet, fruity, drinks. Some like a particular spirit as the base, others want the mixer to dominate. What do *you* like?'

Jonathan, who had been watching the exchange in

silence, decided to interject.

'Tilda, this is Gethin. Gethin is a mixologist. Gethin can make you any drink you like. You just have to tell Gethin your requirements. Gethin is here to help. Gethin is your friend.' Jonathan leaned back to his wine bottle, amused at how hard she was finding a basic question. Tilda stumbled over her thoughts.

'I have no idea. I like wine. Just not tonight. I like beer but again, not tonight. I don't drink that much usually.'

'Forget drinks, what's your favourite food?'

Gethin was on a mission. A mission, Tilda worried, she was incapable of aiding. All her answers seemed to be wrong.

'You mean to eat?'

'Yes.'

Tilda closed her eyes and did her best.

'Chip shop chips, Marmite on toast, smoked salmon and scrambled eggs, chorizo...'

'How about desserts? Puddings. Afters. Whatever you call the sweet course after a meal.'

'Ah. Right. Well, cherry Bakewell and custard would be my first choice. Not that I usually bother.'

'Perfect. I can work with that. How's your day been?'

The casual question threw Tilda off guard. She stammered a reply back, fully aware her cheeks were crimson. What was wrong with her? It was only small talk. There was nothing to worry about.

'It was fine. It was good. Yeah. Thanks.'

He accepted her answer and nodded as he opened bottles and poured measures. He was just being polite, but now she felt rude if she didn't ask about his day too. She rushed out her own question in response.

'And how was yours? Have you been here all day?'

He looked at her for a second, straight in the eye. Perhaps he was assessing what level of blagging she needed. Whether it was simply polite back and forth, or if he was expected to be truthful. Once again, she felt out of her depth. Last night she had breezed Freya's small talk test. Tonight, she was struggling.

'I'll be honest, Tilda? Is that your name? I heard Bea say it before. I'll be honest, Tilda, today has been hard work. I've had two staff ring in sick and my crisp supplier's having delivery issues. I've been on hold most of this afternoon and I'm counting down until my day off in the week. But you know what? Forget about that. The bar is full, my customers are happy, and isn't this your big night? Bea told me all about it.'

'You know Bea?'

'Everyone knows Bea.'

Gethin turned away, continuing his mission to make the perfect drink. Jonathan laughed at her.

'I can't believe you suggested a chips and Marmite cocktail.'

At the back of the bar, Gethin grinned to himself as Tilda defended her lack of mixology nouse.

'I wasn't suggesting anything. I just didn't know what I was being asked.' She shook her head. 'I've led a sheltered life.'

Jonathan sipped his wine before placing it on the bar.

'Not that sheltered, my dear. I believe you had a mid-life gap year recently. I did the same thing when I sold the shop. Toured the Australian vineyards for months.'

'I remember Freya saying. I think Australian vine-yards sound a bit more adventurous than Filey and East Anglia, though.'

'It doesn't matter *where* you went. The important thing is you went. You did something. On your own too. When Freya told me about it, I felt so proud of you.'

'Oh, as if! You sound like a Dad.'

Jonathan laughed and put on a tone of gravitas.

'Well, I speak as the father of the group. The elder, the experienced leader...' He paused to chuckle at his own joke. 'Seriously, though. I know I don't *get* to be proud of you as I had no hand in your achievements, but I still feel hugely impressed. It takes self-belief to start again. I've had Dhanesh live with me since his separation and he's finding it tough.'

At that moment, Dhanesh's voice could be heard over all others, belting out the lyrics to the Chumbawamba song that everyone had forgotten until it started three minutes ago. They looked over at the boundlessly energetic, recently divorced, forty-three-year-old.

'Is this *his* midlife crisis? You went to Australia, I pottered around coastal Britain, and Dhanesh sings, dances, and is the life and soul of the party?'

Jonathan looked at their friend on the dance floor and shook his head.

'I don't think so. You tell me. Has Dhanesh changed in any way since you last saw him?'

Tilda was clear.

'Nope. He was an overgrown kid then, and he still is now. I liked him a lot even if I was exhausted by him.'

As if sensing their conversation, Dhanesh looked over, paused his exertions and gave an exaggerated double thumbs up to his friends at the bar, before resuming his dancing.

'You see,' Jonathan said, 'this is the first time in months I've seen him be *Dhanesh*. Until tonight there's been a lot of quiet, contemplative brooding going on.'

'Oh.' Tilda was at a loss.

'Yes. *Oh* indeed. Freya's get-together came at the right time. I think he's remembered who he used to be. I think that's what happens when a relationship ends. It's remembering who you were before, and marrying that with the wiser, slightly damaged version of who you are now. It's how I've always found it, anyway.'

'Maybe that's my problem. I'm still trying to bring my old self together with the new and damaged one. That's why I'm struggling. That's why I'm on my own all the time.'

There was a small silence. She wasn't sure what else to say. But she didn't have to worry. Gethin was back.

'Right then. Tell me what you think about that.' He placed a goldfish bowl of a glass in front of her. 'It's not very strong, I took it easy with the spirits. But the flavours should be right up your street.'

Tilda picked up the glass and put the straw to her mouth. Seconds later she was in heaven. The taste of almonds, cherries and vanilla overwhelmed her. She had been secretly sceptical but was very happy to be proven wrong. Gethin was a genius.

'I'm in awe. Are you sure you didn't just blend up a

Mr. Kipling back there?'

'Promise. I'm glad you like it.' Gethin moved away, smiling to himself. Tilda took another sip and swooned. Jonathan picked up his wine glass and cleared his throat.

'To us. To being exceptionally damaged, ancient and battered, but doing our best regardless.'

Tilda raised her drink in front of her.

'To us. To our well-earned wisdom.'

'Quite right, Tilda. A much better framing.'

They clinked glasses.

She sipped again. It was the most delicious thing she had ever tasted. She savoured the moment and closed her eyes. *Exceptionally damaged and doing her best.* Yep, that felt about right.

The moment's reflection was broken by a loud voice.

'If you want a job done, do it yourself, darling. Is that the lesson you're teaching here?' Bea had arrived for the drinks that Tilda had failed to deliver.

'God, sorry. I was having the best time. Gethin is a genius, taste that.'

'I won't if you don't mind. I don't do egg white but I'm glad you're enjoying it. Stewart's going now. He's knackered.'

Tilda turned to see Stewart behind her.

'I'm off now but will I see you tomorrow?'

Whether it was the thrill of the liquid Mr Kipling, or the fun evening she'd been having, she felt only positivity towards him. He was just like the rest of them. Exceptionally damaged but doing his best. She nodded.

'Of course. We'll do something. Definitely. Lunch,

brunch, whatever. I'll text you.'

He hugged Bea. A long hug, that whilst not seeming romantic, was definitely intimate. Then he kissed Tilda on the cheek.

'Till tomorrow then. Have a great night. I expect to hear all your drunken tales in the morning.'

Stewart walked away as Bea watched him go. There was a definite tinge to the atmosphere.

'What am I missing, Bea? Have you and him *done it*?' Tilda couldn't stop herself.

Bea picked up her gin and smiled over the rim. She did not have a discrete or coy bone in her body and she always shared the details. But Tilda wasn't sure whether she wanted to hear them if they involved Stewart. A bit too close to home for comfort. Bea put her mind at rest.

'No. We haven't. And to be honest, I don't think we ever will. Instead, we're going to be friends. Now don't look at me like that, I'm as surprised as you are. But that's the plan. Stewart is going to be my friend.'

Ever ready for an impromptu toast, Jonathan leaned over with his glass, almost falling off his stool in the process.

'To friends! To us! To damage!'

They clinked. They drank. They laughed. When the opening bars of *Tragedy* filled the room, there was no debate. All three made their way to the dance floor, where despite the amused eyes of Gethin looking on from the bar, they danced like no one was watching.

CHAPTER FORTY-TWO

Back at his hotel, Stewart was experiencing a new phenomenon. Saturday night sobriety. A whole new world. He had left a party early and was now sitting in bed contemplating putting the kettle on. Not ground breaking and revolutionary to some, but for him, a stark change. Perhaps it was the exhaustion from the previous night's drama, but he felt pathetically grateful to be where he was. In bed, a little less fragile than the day before, and able to see through the increasingly clearing fog.

Feelings surfaced that were new to him. It would be too much to say he was happy or at peace. He knew those were sensations way off into the future. But there was something less *desperate* about how he felt. The constant anxiety had been turned down from a raging bubble to a simmer. He felt all the better for talking to Bea. Now he had a couple of hours before sleep, and was determined to make some proper plans.

A film was on the television. *Hot Fuzz*. The one that was broadcast regularly on late night ITV. He had let its sound fill the room as he brushed his teeth and swapped his shirt for a T-shirt. As the tiny kettle boiled, he had given the TV his full attention, aware that even though it was always on, he had never seen the end. Now that he was settled in bed, he lowered the sound. He had research to do. If he got on with his task, he could put the laptop away before he got to the part by when he had usually zonked out.

Stewart began to search. Although not entirely sure what he was looking for, he tried all sorts of key words. *Wealth Management, Charitable Funding Plans, Bursaries.* A range of open tabs filled the width of his browser. He opened more, shrinking the size of each with every added page. He sent an email to Richard for any insights he could offer, and he opened a blank document to make notes as he went. Learning a new discipline at his age wasn't impossible, but he realised it was going to take effort. He also knew he wasn't the most capable person when it came to detail. He had the ideas but he would need help with their execution.

He looked at the television. Nick Frost was falling through a hedge. He had seen this part before. He had time. Even if he missed the end of the film again, it didn't matter. This was more important.

Opening a new email, he began to type.

Dear Rosie,
There's so much I have to say but first of all, I'm sorry...

Stewart knew she was likely to tell him where to go. Or ignore him altogether. Her resignation letter, where she made her feelings more than clear, was still in the bin by the door. He had to try though. He had to give it one last shot. Stewart kept typing. He owed her more than he was capable of repaying but he had to try.

...I've got an idea. A good one I think, but I'll need your help...

His fingers paused as he read back the opening line.

No. Not again. Not like that. He remembered Tilda's response to the last demanding email he had sent. He tried again.

> *...I've got an idea. A good one I think, but I'll need some help. I was hoping you might hear me out. Only if you want to, you don't owe me anything...*

Stewart typed away. It came out as a garbled mess but it was heartfelt. It was tentative. No assumptions were made this time around. It took him ages but he had to get it right. He reread and edited, making sure to avoid the demanding tone he knew had a tendency to present. He expected nothing from her; he only hoped she could see he'd given this some thought.

By the time he pressed *send*, *Hot Fuzz* had been over for an hour. He had missed the evening news, a weather report, and was now in the middle of a *Family Guy* double bill. He peed, turned off the TV, then spent too much time working out which light switch did what. Time for bed.

His head felt clear. His anxiety simmered rather than raged. He saw the leaflets from the hospital on the side and remembered he was going to read them soon. Then he got under the covers. Not a Saturday night with which he was familiar, but one that he would at least remember.

CHAPTER FORTY-THREE

Music from 1996 to 1999 had been the remit. It wasn't the widest timescale she could have requested, nor would it have been her personal choice, but those were the geographers' university years so Bea had duly stipulated the era in an email to Gethin. She offered to provide a playlist but he said there was no need. One of his staff would do it when it was quiet. He had made the joke that they would enjoy compiling music from before they were born.

That comment alone wasn't making Bea feel her age. Even if the late nineties felt half a minute ago, and her own punk and new romantic preferences weren't much earlier, that wasn't enough to dull her energy. Nor was it the physical strain on her knees from jumping up and down to the Venga Boys. Not with her vitamin D supplements keeping her mostly ache free. In fact, for much of the evening she had felt carefree and alive. But that was before she'd read the message from Mal.

Since her realisations the previous night, Bea hadn't given him much thought. The hours spent dealing with Stewart, would do that to the most ardent of girlfriends. Even if her romantic feelings hadn't waned, they could not compete with all the stress. But now Stewart had left and she was free to think. When the message came, she had opened it without fear of its contents. There was nothing he could say now. She hoped he wasn't going to be too lovely and kind. She didn't want him to be making assumptions about their future, now she knew there wouldn't be one.

Taking herself and her phone, she left the bar and stood outside. The August air was nowhere near chilly but still came as a welcome relief from the inside. She took a breath and opened the message.

Bea, I hope you're having fun without me. Things are awful here. I'm still at my brother's and will be for a few days. Today we chatted while the kids were out. She wants to do couples' counselling. I had to agree even though it's pointless. I'll go along with it and then move out properly when the time is better. The kids think I'm away for work. We didn't end up telling them. She wants us to try and work at it first. I still want to leave. I still want to be with you. It'll just take a little more time...

She stopped reading. She was too old for this shit. Quite literally. It appeared Mal was backtracking on his big stand. Marriage guidance? Well good luck to the pair of them. She was well rid.

'Do you want a cig?'

She had been joined by Dhanesh. Bea put her phone away and smiled.

'I don't smoke thanks. Actually, you know what? On second thoughts, fuck that. I'd love one.' She had been an intermittent smoker in the years when less people cared. Now she was feeling reckless. The fact Mal hated it was an added bonus.

'Here, let me.' Dhanesh placed his bottle by his feet, then dragged on his own cigarette igniting the end of hers. 'I've got to say Bea, fair play to you. I'm having a great time. I hadn't realised how much I needed to see everyone again. I feel eighteen.'

Bea looked at him. His brown puppy-dog eyes only exacerbated his youthful face. With the dark of the evening, and from a distance, he could easily pass for eighteen, no worries.

'Dhanesh, my darling, you're like an excitable child. I've seen you on the dance floor. I think it's only a matter of time before you ask for jelly and ice cream, then run into a kneeling skid.'

'What? You mean there's no jelly?' Dhanesh grinned as he smoked.

Bea returned the smile.

'Sorry. You're going to have be a big brave boy.'

They fell into silence. The thud of the beat and the squawks of the gulls, filled the gaps. Just before the quiet fell into awkwardness, Bea filled it.

'So what's it like living with Jonathan? I've had a few chats with him over the months. I reckon he's a smoking jacket and evening sherry kind of guy. Come on, spill the beans. Do you play bridge and retire by nine?'

'Bang on,' Dhanesh replied. 'He wears a monocle, his man servant serves his meals under a silver dome, and he wears those... damn, what do you call them? Those knee socks and baggy pant things.'

'Knickerbockers?'

Dhanesh threw his head back and laughed.

'I couldn't even finish my joke because I forgot the words. Imagine if he were really like that. Sorry, that's made me laugh.'

Bea looked at him. He was creased with laughter. It was endearing.

'It's *not* like living with Hercule Poirot, then? I'm

disappointed.'

Dhanesh rubbed his eyes and took a slow drag of his cigarette. He composed himself before answering.

'No, it's not. Sorry about that. To be honest, he's been great. I moved in temporarily at first. Just till I found something else. But it works quite well.'

Bea revelled in the soothe of her illicit cig as Dhanesh flicked ash onto the pavement.

'Doesn't it cramp your style? I know the pair of you are single but I assume neither of you are celibate.'

Dhanesh shook his head.

'Not really. I guess I'm not looking for anything more than fun at the moment. The idea of jumping head first into a relationship when my divorce only came through a few months ago? Well, it's way too soon. I've got to mend myself before that, you know?'

'I do. Really.'

'Instead, I like having friendly conversations and the occasional snog after a Tinder date. I mean, I've had my moments of being more of a player, but I think I'm getting too old for walks of shame now. And as for Jonathan? He split up with a serious boyfriend a few years ago. I don't think he's seen anyone since. No idea if he was all over Grindr before I moved in, but he doesn't seem to be now.'

Bea took it in. It seemed Dhanesh was handling his split with more sense than Mal. Not that Mal had split up with anyone if counselling was on the cards. She steered herself away from that train of thought. She didn't want to spoil her evening.

'Do you have kids? Have you had to sort out access and custody stuff?' She wasn't intending to pry but it was interesting to see how other people did things.

'No. I think that's been the best thing about it. We never wanted kids. I can't imagine how difficult it must be when your priority is not fucking up the lives of others. Just your own. What about you?'

'Kids?'

'Yeah.'

'Never had any.' Bea paused. 'I nearly had some step-kids once.'

'You dated a single dad.' Dhanesh nodded, grasping the situation immediately.

'Partly. Nearly single. Not single anymore.'

'I see.'

'So are you with anyone? I feel slightly ashamed that you've organised this night for us, and we don't know much about you.'

Bea was touched. The evening wasn't about her.

'I am newly single. Almost hot off the press single. So hot, in fact, that I still need to make it clear to the man involved.'

'Ouch. That must be a bit raw.'

'No, darling. It's a big relief to be honest. I think I decided last night, but my mind was made up just as you came out. I'll message him before I go to bed.'

'What will you say?'

'I am going to firmly and kindly explain to him that we want different things from life, but I am very proud to have been able to help him reach some decisions through this tricky part of his journey.'

'Wow. Nicely done. Hard to argue with.'

'Yeah. I'm sure he'll try. Or sulk. It doesn't matter now.'

Bea looked straight ahead of her. Saying it out loud

made her resolve strengthen. Dhanesh let her have the moment before resuming the chat.

'What is it that *you* want from life? You said it was different from the almost-ex.'

'Do you know, darling, I think you nailed it before. How did you put it? Friendly conversations and the occasional snog after a Tinder date. That sounds spot on. I'm confident that relationships and myself, do not mix. I thought I wanted love, but all I wanted was to love *myself*. Because falling in love can't possibly work if it's at the expense of loving yourself. I hadn't worked that out until recently.'

'That's deep.'

'Perhaps. Who knows? But ramped up, drunken kissing is completely my thing. No question. Quite a niche fetish, probably.'

'There'll be an app for that somewhere.'

'Bound to be. I'll have to download it and crack on.'

'Or...' Dhanesh paused for a second, '...you could skip the app and kiss like-minded people when you happen to bump into them. You know, when you're out and about, in the street, at a reunion...'

Bea smiled.

'That's a thought. I *could* do that. The hard part is finding them in the first place. I mean, I'm in the street and at a reunion right now. Have you seen any like-minded people I could meaninglessly kiss?'

Bea grinned at Dhanesh, exaggeratedly batting her eye lashes as she looked up at him. He returned her faux-innocence with a slow nod and knowing smile.

'Bea. I think we owe it to ourselves. We need to Get. It. On.'

She shrieked with laughter.

'Dhanesh, you sweetie. Why the hell not?'

They giggled their way through the stubbing out of cigarettes and ensuring Dhanesh's bottle was placed against the wall. Seconds later, and with much less care now, they were wrapped around each other like hungry teens. A no-strings-attached, meaningless, but utterly memorable kiss. God, she had missed this. She had missed this more than anything.

CHAPTER FORTY-FOUR

The clock on her phone said it was nearly midnight but she was having none of it. It felt as though only an hour or two had passed since they arrived. Tilda hauled herself up on her regular barstool, noting that the extra effort it had taken might indicate she had been here longer than she thought. She looked around. No one was officially flagging, but the dancing had calmed down. Jonathan was seated to her left. Bea, Dhanesh, Jen and Sam were sitting in a booth on her right. They had commandeered a huge platter of hummus and pitta from the food table, which was now sitting in the middle of them. Their animated four-way conversation would pause now and then as one of them piled up a chunk of bread and guided it towards their mouth. Then they would carry on.

Tilda hadn't realised she needed food until the bar snacks had arrived. Suddenly she was starving and the plate of hot sausages and mustard dip hadn't stood a chance. It had been a long time since the chip butties.

'Have you had fun, Tilda? I do hope so.'

Jonathan leaned across from his barstool. He had remained in position most of the evening as people gathered around him. His regal air of holding court was accepted without argument.

'I have. More than I thought was possible. It's been brilliant seeing everyone again. I'm going to be much better at staying in touch from now on.'

'Quite right. Me too. We can't let each other drift off again.'

The evening might have flown by, but Tilda had

consumed three of Gethin's cherry Bakewell master-pieces. Her defences were as low as her sugar levels were high. She found herself sharing far more than she would have done in the cold light of day.

'I CANNOT drift off again. No really, I mean it. Never again. It's not like I was a big social animal when I was married, but we still *did* stuff. We'd go for the odd meal. For the odd drink.' Her voice dropped to an exaggerated whisper. 'It was *all* a bit odd to be honest because I didn't love my husband.' She resumed her usual volume. 'That's a joke by the way. I know. Ha ha. But back to my point. At least I was out of the house sometimes. At least I had a life. Now and then. But you know what? I've not been inside a pub since I moved here. Not in Wales. I'm too shy to do that on my own, and I know NOBODY. Nobody real. I've missed feeling carefree for an hour or two. I've missed saying, *'It's Friday. Let's go for a glass of wine before getting back for Graham Norton'*. I've missed it a lot. Don't let me drift off again. I need a social life, even a teeny tiny one, every few years.'

Jonathan bowed his head.

'Tilda, even though we are miles apart, we're only a message away. And we will definitely do this again. As the wise ancient elder, or whatever we decided I am, I assure you we'll get together much more regularly from now on.'

Tilda felt the warmth of his promise, even if it was drunken talk. It felt real in the moment which was what counted. She smiled to herself as she looked for her glass of water. It was either hiding in front of her very eyes or she'd left it on another table.

'You're always welcome to come here, you know.'

Tilda looked up. Gethin was talking.

'Pardon?'

'You're always welcome to come here. You said you didn't know anyone but you do. You know me. I certainly feel like I know you.'

Tilda smiled.

'Because I told you my favourite foods and you created liquid magic for me? Does that mean you know me?'

Tilda wasn't sure but she might have just flirted. She looked to Jonathan for approval, which he gave by raising his glass. Gethin carried on emptying the washer as he stretched to put glasses on the shelf above the bar. He smiled.

'No, although the Marmite info was fascinating. Thank you for that.' He kept stretching. Tilda noticed his upper arm, tight against his T-shirt sleeve.

'It's more likely because for the past six months, every single evening, I've seen you walking past the window. The glass isn't just for the sea view. I get to people-watch too.'

'Oh, I see.' Tilda wasn't sure what else to say.

'You aren't as anonymous as you think you are, you know.'

'Well then. Thanks. Wait, were you complimenting me?'

'I don't think so.' Gethin laughed. 'But I'm sure I can find something nice to say if you want.'

Jonathan, who had been listening to the exchange with amusement, took the opportunity to jump in.

'Yes Gethin, say something nice to Tilda. We all want to hear it. What charming sentiments can you offer her? We're on the edge of our seats.'

Gethin laughed as he slid the empty tray back into the washer.

'I don't know if it can be classed as a compliment but this is certainly true. Whenever I see you walk past in the evenings, I always hope you're going to walk in here. You never do, but I still hope, every time. You look like someone I'd like to know better.'

Tilda's face broke into a smile. She knew she must be drunk because she'd never accept a compliment so easily under normal circumstances.

'Thank you. I like that I give off an air of mystery. Will she walk through the door or not? What'll happen this time? Will Tilda break the habit of a lifetime and enter a bar on her own?'

'Well, next time you're passing, just do it. You wouldn't be on your own. I'd be here. You could have your glass of wine and be back for Graham Norton, any Friday you liked.'

'Right then. Well maybe I will.'

Tilda blushed. She hoped her rosy cheeks could be passed off as heat from dancing. That was the least embarrassing explanation, rather than someone quite attractive saying something nice.

If Gethin had noticed her cheeks, he didn't feel the need to comment. There were practical matters to deal with.

'Right guys, it's going to be last orders soon. What can I get you?'

'Just water, please. Sorry, I've lost my glass somewhere.'

'Luckily for you, I have another one.' He reached

up to get one of the newly-cleaned glasses and fill it with ice. Tilda watched him. His arm flexed as he got a bottle from the fridge. She was becoming obsessed with his bicep. That's when she remembered.

'Oh, God. I've been stupid.'

'What about?'

'I recognise your bicep.'

'Sorry?'

'No, *I'm* sorry. I'm not being clear. I saw your arm yesterday. From the side. I didn't realise it was you.'

Gethin looked amused as he took in the latest turn of conversation.

'Which arm was it?'

Tilda pointed as he placed the water in front of her.

'That one. You were sitting this way round.' Tilda swivelled on her seat to re-enact her memory.

'Do you need to see the other one or are we OK as we are?'

'SHE NEEDS TO SEE THE OTHER ONE.'

Jonathan was unable to stop himself. It seemed he wasn't immune to the charms of Gethin's upper arms either.

'Ignore him. And me. But I only just worked it out. I was waiting for the train and I saw your arm. It... well it... stood out.'

'Why?'

Faced with the arm in question, she was reminded of the nostalgic rabbit hole it had sent her down, at the station. From her Dad, to her ex-colleagues, to Grady, to being in the Lakes with Grady, to being spooned by Grady, to eventually feeling calm. It was strange, but having been surrounded by people and conversation for the last twenty-four hours, she had thought less about Grady than usual. She hadn't had the time.

She snapped out of her daydream as Gethin waited for an answer to his question. Why had his arm stood out to her? She didn't bother filtering the answer. She was long past being capable.

'I don't know anyone with muscles. It's like you're from a film.'

Gethin took this information in his stride.

'Yes. It's exactly like I'm in a film. That'll be it. Or, more likely, it's because I shift crates of beer for more hours than is sensible every day. That might be the reason for any unintentional upper body strength.'

Tilda's assumptions of steroids and fitness shakes were a little off the mark. She looked at his face properly now. His eyes were too soulful to be gym-obsessed. No way had he ever felt the burn or worn Lycra. Her distrust of sculpted bodies melted away now she knew it was accidental. And now they had bonded over her evening walks and his strong arms, Tilda felt the need to apologise.

'Look, I don't know much about the last few months, but I get the impression Bea's been in your ear quite a bit. I just wanted to say I hope you've not been run ragged. She was only doing it to help me out. And to forget about a bloke. I hope she's been OK.'

Gethin smiled and shook his head.

'No, don't worry about me. Thanks for saying that but Bea's been fine. I mean, she's got her own folder in my email account, but she's been no problem.'

'She does love a project.'

'I'd noticed. Has everything gone well? I know it's been a long time since you saw your friends. Since you... what was it?... drifted off?'

'It's been perfect, thank you. I can't tell you what a great evening we've had.'

Gethin looked around. By the till was a spiral pad and biro. He scribbled something down, then ripped off the page.

'Tomorrow, if there's any feedback you want to pass on, or something's been left behind, or anything at all, here's my number.' He gave the paper to Tilda. 'It's my private number. You don't need to stick to opening hours.'

She took the paper and folded it over. She was probably drunk, definitely tipsy. She'd had more sugar in one evening than she had consumed in the previous week and she had almost single-handedly polished off a platter of mini sausages. She was aware her judgment may be impaired and her grip on events might be skewed. But she could have sworn that an increasingly attractive man with friendly eyes and toned upper arms had just given her his number?

'Congratulations, my dear. Nicely done.' Jonathan raised his glass her way. 'It's always the quiet ones you have to watch. Without fail.'

'Stop it, you.' She rolled her eyes and laughed at him. It was all in her head. And all in Jonathan's too. There was no reason to think Gethin had passed on his number for any reason other than feedback. But there was a tiny chance that it might mean something else. And if so, it was an unexpected turn of events. But a most welcome one, that was for sure.

CHAPTER FORTY-FIVE

Day three of the reunion

There were dirty glasses all over the place. An empty bottle of red wine had been left on the side, its drips forming a stained ring that would undoubtedly drive Tilda mad in the ensuing clean-up operation. A semi-deflated air bed lay in the space between the table and sofa. Both side panels of the bay window had been flung open to get air moving, although the stagnant oxygen of the morning-after was winning the battle so far. In scenes remarkably similar to the previous morning, the flat had become a refuge for the hungover and bewildered. Bea, Tilda, and Freya were awake but not ready to face the day. Not yet.

It had been the pings of WhatsApp group activity that woke them first. From nine o'clock, the messages had started. First from Jonathan saying he was going to sue Bea for causing his headache, and then a steady stream of jokes and photos highlighting that they were all in the same boat. Everyone was still in bed, feeling delicate, but full of the joys of the previous night. There had been a tentative suggestion from Sam about breakfast but she'd been shot down. No one was ready to make a move. Eventually, after heated discussion, the plan was made for an eleven-thirty meet-up at the flat. They could decide where to go after that.

Bea lay next to Tilda. The party had carried on until the early hours and she could taste the red wine in her throat. Ideally she'd need an entire day on the couch but she didn't have that luxury. There were important things to do. Check on Stewart and then reaffirm her decision about Mal.

She picked up her phone and reread the message she'd sent. As rough as she might feel now, she'd been clear-headed when she wrote it. It was worded exactly as she'd told Dhanesh. Full of fondness and gratitude. *I'm proud to have been able to help you reach some decisions.* It was true. She meant it. He had let her into his life and shared as much of it as he could spare. It was simply not what she wanted. She knew that now.

She had spent some time composing it, staying outside after Dhanesh and his lovely mouth had gone back in. It was important to get right. Then, once she pressed send, she turned off her phone. There was nothing more to say, and she had an evening with friends to enjoy. When she switched it back on this morning, however, a stream of messages pinged to life. All timestamped from the previous evening, they gave a good indication of where she stood. A quick scan through and she had got the gist.

I beg you, give me some time. I can't lose you. Not now.   *10.04*

You're making a mistake. You need me. We are perfect together.   *10.09*

This isn't you speaking. I know you. Someone's putting ideas into your head. Don't listen to Tilda, she doesn't know you like I do.   *10.17*

I almost feel sorry for you. You can't see a good thing when you've got it.   *10.27*

This is over. Fuck you.   *10.39*

It made things easier, that was for sure. There was no doubt in her mind she was doing the right thing, but the swift descent into abuse sealed it. Maybe he was trying to make her feel better. If he acted like an arse, maybe she wouldn't wonder if she were making the right decision. Bea considered the possibility for the briefest of seconds before dismissing it. No. He *was* an arse. He had said sweet things to her once, but his actions had always been suspect. Good luck to the marriage counsellor unpacking all of that.

Bea typed a new message.

Kit, your Mum would be proud of me. I counted the places! Turns out, my head, heart, and gut stopped feeling happiness ages ago. One out of four ain't enough so I've binned the lover. Can't stomach gin for a few days but would be free for cake tomorrow night Are you busy? Shall I bring over some calories? I can fill you in on the grislies.

Ten minutes later, Kit replied.

A perfect excuse to bake! I'll do a rum gingerbread. Very glad you got rid of that fool. You weren't yourself when he was around. Welcome back, dear. We'll eat and I'll drink. Safe journey home now. xxx

Bea glowed. Kit's approval meant the world. She settled back under the covers, disturbing a semi-conscious Tilda as she did.

'What time is it? Do I have to get up yet?'

Bea looked at the time.

'We've got an hour before the others come around.'

'I have to get up then.'

Tilda pushed herself into a sitting position and leaned back on the headboard.

'I'm going to have another five minutes. No, make that ten.'

She closed her eyes and stayed there for twenty.

Dry-shampooed and swamped in a baggy T-shirt, Tilda opened her door to Jonathan and Dhanesh. Jonathan may have had a sore head but his voice boomed as loudly as ever.

'Tilda, my dear. You look dreadful.'

'Morning to you too, Jonathan. Not so fresh-faced yourself.' It seemed she didn't have the energy to take offence. Besides, she had spent the minutes before their arrival telling Bea how rough she looked. She couldn't disagree with Jonathan's assessment at all. Likewise, he took her own observations on the chin.

'I've come to realise, my days of drinking till dawn are over. It was a delight to watch the sunrise over the cliffs, but I'll be fast asleep this afternoon. Luckily Dhanesh is responsible for transporting me home. It'd be too much for me today.'

'Make yourself at home while you're still awake. Anyone want tea or coffee? Sam and Jen are running late so we've time. And we're still waiting to hear if Stewart's coming.'

Tilda switched on the kettle as Bea got up from the sofa to say hello to her new friends.

'Morning Bea,' Dhanesh grinned. 'Are you full of regret and shame? Are you having horrific flashbacks? Can you even look at me?'

She threw her head back and snorted.

'It's me who should be worried. In less than five minutes I went from teasing you about being a child, to sucking face. They'll put me on a register.'

It was Dhanesh's turn to laugh.

'I knew it. You groomed me!'

'That can be the only explanation.' Bea laughed and they hugged. It was as platonic as it was possible to be. Their moment had been just that. A moment. And now a comfortable ease was in its place and they could laugh. Compared to the headfuck she had been dealing with regarding Mal, her lovely entanglement with Dhanesh was the perfect antidote.

As if psychic, he remembered what their kiss had interrupted.

'Did you manage to send your message? When I went back inside you were working out what to say.'

'I did, thanks. I spent twenty minutes composing the perfect sentiments to let him down gently.'

'And?'

'His replies show I'm missing nothing by letting him go.'

'And is that OK? Are you OK?'

'It is and I am. Thank you for asking.'

'You're welcome. I'm glad my exceptional skills made everything clear. It must have been so confusing until I turned up.'

Their giggles continued. Tilda handed out drinks as everyone squished onto the available seats. Jonathan settled back on the sofa, mug in hand, and faced the fireplace. His eyes settled on the framed photo.

'I meant to say something last night, I'm so sorry Tilda. Tragically young. Freya filled me in. One of her emails from a while back. I remember him well from the week in the Lakes.'

Dhanesh squinted at the frame.

'I've got a vague memory but it's hazy. All those trips have merged in my head. I remember you being loved up, just not who it was with.'

Tilda looked at the photo.

'Sometimes I think it's silly to have him there in a frame. It was such a short time, so long ago. But then I think that if it wasn't for his memory, I'd be living a far unhappier life. Knowing he couldn't do all the things he planned, kickstarted me into doing them for him.'

Jonathan sipped his coffee and thought about what she had said.

'There's a danger, though, isn't there. You might have swapped one life of putting yourself second, for another. You have to do what you want, too.'

Bea watched Tilda swing her legs underneath her as she balanced her tea on the arm of the chair. She knew Tilda was making the right choices these days. She wasn't worried that the ghost of Grady was calling the shots but she could see Jonathan's point.

'I know what you mean, but I think I'm doing OK. During my mid-life gap-year, I did lots of grieving and lots of thinking. By the time I emerged here, I was ready to live a new life. I think the picture of Grady is a handy reminder to keep on living. Not only living, but enjoying too.'

'And are you enjoying living now?' The question

was lightly asked, but crammed full of concern. Tilda paused before answering.

'I have been this weekend.'

Jonathan seemed satisfied with her answer. He turned his attentions to Bea.

'As we're doing a full post-mortem of the evening, I have to say I was barking up the wrong tree with you and Stewart. I thought you were an item until you came under our Dhanesh's spell.'

'Ah yes. His spell.' Bea nodded with mock sincerity as Dhanesh burst out laughing.

'I am wizard-like in my wily ways. All the women are charmed by my magic.'

Jonathan wouldn't let himself be derailed.

'Quite. But Stewart? What's his deal? The fact he looks like Grady after being put through an ageing app is disconcerting. Must play havoc with your emotions, Tilda.'

'Do you know what,' Tilda replied, 'I've got used to it. I think I see Stewart as his own person now. For a long time, he was Grady's brother, but now he's just Stewart. It makes it easier because they're so different. It's just the features that are similar.'

'He's definitely hot.'

'Is he?' Tilda seemed surprised.

'Oh totally. Grady, back in the day, was a beautiful innocent. Not my type at all. I'd have only broken him. But Stewart has the same good looks but is already damaged. He's been put through the ringer. As we all have, let's face it. I wouldn't add anything negative to him as it's already built in. That makes him desirable.'

Tilda looked baffled and shrugged just as Bea's

phone pinged, interrupting the moment. Along with Dhanesh, it seemed as if Stewart were psychic as well.

Morning. What time are you around till today? I might not make brunch (don't worry, everything is good) but will still be here this afternoon. Or this evening. I've decided to stay another night. Can we catch up before you go? And Tilda?

She replied immediately. Weeks ago, realising that the weekend would be exhausting, she had booked the Monday off work. She let him know that they would both be around later on.

Tilda drained her mug and placed it on the coffee table. The conversation about Stewart's hotness was still in full flow.

'You've really given this some thought.'

'Not really', Jonathan smiled. 'I was musing over it at the bar last night. When I was trying to decide whether Gethin was asking about you in order to chat to me, or because he was interested in you. I wasn't sure until you joined us. That's when it was clear I was unlikely to be the future Mr Gethin any time soon. I do hope you're going to ring him.'

Bea looked up. This was news to her.

'Tilds, did you pull? What did I miss? Damn Mal, that frigger. I spent so long breaking up with him, I missed massive gossip like this. Spill the beans, Tilda. What's gone on?' She clapped her hands in excitement as Tilda instinctively crossed her arms and set her body language to defensive.

'I didn't pull. Honestly.'

Jonathan wasn't going to let this lie.

'Oh yes she did! I sat at the bar all night. He was friendly to everyone, but much more friendly to Tilda. He gave her his personal number and told her to ring him, day or night, about anything. It was quite the moment.'

'Jonathan, that's a big overstatement and you know it.' Tilda laughed. 'He'll only be wanting a good Trip Advisor review. He'll be doing follow up marketing so we praise his bar to everyone. Let's not get carried away.'

Bea knew what Tilda was doing. The fact that Gethin might have given her his number because he liked her, was a lovely feeling. She had a potential friend down the road. One that, if she let herself be open to the chance, could be someone to share a drink or a meal with one day. But if she rang him for real, the feeling of possibility would vanish. If he answered the phone in any way other than ecstatic to hear from her, she would feel flat. It would kill the excitement that the scribbled number was giving her. Bea could tell what was going on in Tilda's head. She was enjoying the thrill of possibility instead of the crashing reality of rejection. Like Mal's smell had done for her before she let herself get sucked into the headfuck.

Jonathan wouldn't let it go.

'You should definitely pop in for a drink just as soon as you can stomach more alcohol. Tomorrow. Or Friday, like he said.'

The doorbell rang. Tilda got up to buzz in Sam and Jen, as she shut down the conversation topic once and for all.

'Then that will be a long time from now as I am

never drinking again. Looks like the lovely Gethin will remain unbothered by me and my cherry Bakewell needs. I'm sure he will manage.'

She opened the door and welcomed in the rest of the gang. Bea watched her control the conversation so all talk of Gethin was over, and the options for lunch became the focus. Bea didn't mind. She was happy to let her friend feel in control. The topic of Gethin could wait for another day. Because Bea was in no doubt, she'd be bringing it back up as soon as she could. Tilda and Gethin, kissing in a tree. K.I.S.S.I.N.G. Yep, that sounded absolutely perfect.

CHAPTER FORTY-SIX

The goodbyes had taken time. Long hugs, promises of not leaving it so long next time, and a few moist eyes. Sam and Jen had left the café first, after refuelling with bacon sandwiches. Email addresses were exchanged, hypothetical future plans suggested, and then just like that, they were gone. Another round of tea and coffee was consumed before Jonathan and Dhanesh made a move. They had a long drive back to London and wanted to make a start. There were more hugs and more declarations of intent for future plans. A date was even mooted for a get-together in Bermondsey. Jonathan was keen to host an evening and didn't want to leave without a plan in place.

Finally, after more tea and more putting off the inevitable, it was time for Freya to go. Bea tactfully left them to it as Tilda helped get the bags to the station. A sinking feeling had settled in the pit of her stomach as they waited for the train. The feeling of dread that comes from knowing something bad is about to take place and there's nothing to be done but ride it out. Tilda recognised it, she felt its ache, and tried to smile through the discomfort. It was a struggle. Freya took charge of the moment.

'Now listen, you. This is going to happen again. I promise. One way or another. You have an open invite to Chez Freya anytime you like. And I'm not going to leave it so long next time. We'll party again soon enough, don't you worry.'

Tilda had nodded, unable to say anything due to the lump in her throat. Then the train arrived. Their goodbye had been more painful than Tilda could have imagined. A fierce hug later and Freya and her luggage found their way to the carriage. The final minutes ticked by before a whistle blew and Tilda waved off her oldest friend into the distance.

The tension in her stomach eased as the tears came. She had known all morning she was close to sobbing. The comedown of adrenaline, the fact that everything was back to how it used to be, and saying goodbye to people who really knew her - it was all too much. She sat on a bench on the empty platform and let the tears fall. *Better out than in,* her dad would have said. Not that she ever saw him follow his own advice. Perhaps he had also pushed coffee tables into his flesh and made fists of his hands whenever he felt a negative emotion. She would never know. For now though, something inside had changed. She had no desire to control herself anymore. Not in the way she had been recently. She needed a good cry and she was going to have one. It was OK to feel sad, especially when something sad was happening. She looked down the track, where Freya's train was shrinking rapidly. This was simply the downside of having wingpeople. The highs were high but the lows felt awful.

The rest of the day had ticked by slowly. She returned to find Bea cleaning away last night's debris. Some half-hearted helping later, and they both gave up. It would give her something to do the following evening when she was back from work. Back on her own. They messaged Stewart, who had replied immediately. He explained he had a bit of work to do but he'd be free this evening and did they want to meet for food? They did, and so made a plan. For the rest of the afternoon, they slumped on the couch, taking turns to watch TV and snooze. The restorative qualities of both activities made them feel all the better for their lazy afternoon.

At five o'clock Tilda stretched her arms, hoping to force some energy back into her body. Bea was still slumped on the sofa.

'Is it time to go yet?'

'No. We've still got an hour. I'm getting antsy now. I've been sitting down too long. I might nip to Tesco.'

'Tilda, darling, there's no such thing as sitting down for too long on a Sunday. It's the day for sitting down. Sitting down, sleeping, and eating stodge.'

'It's been a highly productive day if that's the way we view it.'

Bea smiled and snuggled against the sofa's arm. She wasn't getting antsy in the slightest. Tilda stood up to move her legs. She had a question.

'Why do you think Stewart stayed for another night? He wasn't even planning to stay for Saturday. I never thought he'd hang around a moment longer than he said.'

'I don't know. Perhaps he realised he needed a break.'

Bea's eyes stayed focused on the television. Tilda let it lie. She wasn't daft. She knew Bea wasn't telling her everything. But she also believed her when she said they hadn't got up to anything. With a complete change of heart, she found herself looking forward to seeing him again. He had been different last night. Thoughtful and considered. She'd warmed to him more than ever. The fact he was still in the area and wanted to meet, made her happy. He was becoming the brother-in-law he had never had the chance to be. She could imagine a future where they sent each other birthday cards. He might message her about a film he recommended and she would tell him whether to bother with the latest drama on the iPlayer.

'Tilds, you've drifted off.' She snapped out of her daydream. 'Come back and tell me what we're doing tonight. What did you say to Stewart?'

Tilda perched on the arm of the chair. She was still restless but was fighting a losing battle in attempting to energise Bea.

'I told him to come here for six and we'd get some food. He wants to talk to us both before he leaves.'

'Where are we going to eat? Will we need to book somewhere?'

Tilda stood up and stretched her arms. She felt the bones crack with satisfaction.

'No need to book. I've got a plan. When six o'clock comes, you'll be in awe of my brilliance. I'm going to give you an Aberystwyth experience to remember.'

CHAPTER FORTY-SEVEN

The cliff railway had seen better days. Tilda knew that in her head. In her heart, however, she was living the dream. The rickety carriages might have trundled slowly up the hill, but Tilda's spirits were soaring.

This was her third trip up Constitution Hill since she had moved here. Initially dismissing it as a tourist attraction, she had given it a wide berth for months. But there had been too many times when she had watched in the distance as the lumbering train at the end of the prom made its way up the hill. She had been curious. She wanted to see for herself.

The first time she had journeyed to the top, she had marvelled at the scenery en route, but then returned to the bottom immediately. She didn't know what else to do. The second time she had ridden up, she had watched families disembark and wander out through the station building. She followed them, reasoning if harassed parents with toddlers, buggies, and nappy bags could step out into the unknown of a cliff top, so could she. That's when she found the camera obscura and café. A drink and ice cream seemed a reasonable way to spend the half hour until the train's departure. Besides, the panoramic views of the sweeping bay were wonderful. She had made the decision there and then that this was an experience she would repeat.

The opportunity to show the town to her friends from a height, had been too good to resist. She also knew the breeze at the top would provide escape from the heat. What Tilda hadn't counted on, however, was Bea's immediate scepticism of historic mechanical transport.

'And you're absolutely sure it's safe? It's making some strange noises.'

Bea's health and safety hat had been firmly in place since they boarded the train

'It's perfectly safe. It goes up and down all day. Has done for years. Beautiful scenery for just a few quid. It's amazing.'

Tilda's enthusiasm was not going to wane. She knew they would love it if only they gave it a chance. Stewart confirmed her optimism with some positivity of his own.

'This is exactly the kind of thing I never got to do as a kid. I love it.' He beamed as he clicked shut the wooden door and sat down. Bea watched with horror.

'How does that stop any of us falling out? That lock is *flimsy*. There's no way I'm sitting near the windows. Both of you, get either side of me, now. I'm not being thrown out. I will not roll down the hill like a tumbleweed.'

Stewart shook his head as he laughed and moved to the end of the bench seat.

'It's seems we've found your Achilles heel, Bea. You might a be a local council mastermind and an events-planner extraordinaire, but you're really weird about choo-choo trains.'

Tilda laughed out loud. Who knew Stewart could be funny? She joined in the teasing, happy to find there was more and more she liked about him.

'Be a scaredy cat all you want, Bea, but remember that in the daytime there's usually a bunch of kids at the front, waving their hearts out. Standing up, not holding on to a thing. They would be laughing at the old lady in the zebra stripes, if they could see you now.'

Bea shut up but was clearly unconvinced. The train began its ascent with both her hands gripping the seat beneath her. She may have been silent but her body language was screaming.

On her right was Stewart. Not riddled with a fear of choo-choo trains himself, he was leaning on the ledge, his chin resting on his forearm. As the train rose above the station, and over the roofs of the houses on the prom, he gasped. The sea had come into view. The sudden appearance of the curve of the bay still caused Tilda goosebumps, so for the first-time viewer like him, it was magical.

An hour earlier, he had arrived at Tilda's, bang on time. Full of friendly good nature, he'd enquired about the evening's plans but Tilda would not be drawn. He also said he wanted to talk about something important. Stewart refused to give anything away, although made it clear they had nothing to worry about. It was agreed he would share his news once they were in place and eating. With food in mind, she left him with Bea as she made the final arrangements, before returning with a full rucksack. She planned on a cliff-top ta-da moment so kept its contents to herself. They left the flat and made the short walk to the bottom of the hill.

Tilda looked at him now. Full of enthusiasm for basic geographical features like a bit of coast and an incline. Once again, the thought presented itself that he really did resemble Grady. His older, lined eyes gave reasonable hints as to how her perfect love might have aged if he'd been given the chance. Would he have grown grumpy and bitter? Would his twinkle have deserted him somewhere in his thirties? She would never know and it was time to stop speculating. Grady was in the past. Stewart was here in the present. In his own right, and not merely a representative of his little brother. It both warmed and amused her that he found her local funicular railway as charming as she did.

'Are we nearly there yet?' Bea piped up, snapping Tilda out of her musing.

'The entire journey takes five minutes. We were nearly there before we'd set off.' Tilda smiled through her exasperation.

'I'm desperate for dry land.'

'Bea, you are ridiculous.' Stewart voiced what Tilda was thinking. 'How will you be at the top? Is it heights or trains you don't like?'

'It's the steepness of the cliff and that I don't for one minute believe this train is capable of making it.'

'And yet here we are!' Tilda exclaimed. As Bea was speaking, the train had braked to a stop. The sides of the carriage were now level with concrete steps, and the passengers onboard were disembarking from their own carriages. Stewart unlatched the door and stepped outside. He offered Bea his hand, who grabbed it as if it were all that kept her from certain death. Tilda stepped past and led the way. The three of them climbed the steps, walked through the station, and emerged onto the café's picnic area beyond.

'Woah. That's beautiful.' Stewart had gone straight to the edge. It was not strictly a direct drop. Bushy crags provided a placebo of safety around the cliff top. But the view, as it stretched into the distance, was stunning. The whole town was laid out below. The pier resembled match sticks in the water while the rows of houses were like toddlers' blocks. The sea shimmered. The sun sat low in the sky. It was mesmerising.

Bea, who appeared to be over her train-related wobbles, was as enamoured as Stewart.

'Fuck. That's beautiful. Look how tiny everyone looks.'

'It certainly puts things into perspective. All the dramas going on in people's heads and yet they're dots.' Stewart stood beside her, looking on. 'Makes you think.'

Tilda would have been with them, re-enacting the *Last of the Mohicans* poster with all her energy, had she not been busy. As Bea and Stewart philosophised about tiny people and their little worries, she opened her rucksack. Three boxes, insulated with tea towels, were spaced out on the picnic table. She rooted further and unearthed three forks, a bottle of ketchup, and some cling-filmed bread and butter.

'Food's up!' She took a seat and felt smug.

Bea clocked it first. She had the memories of the previous day's lunch to guide her.

'No way. The chippy near yours? I knew I could smell them, I just thought they were in the air.'

Tilda nodded. She was as happy about that fact as Bea seemed to be.

'Stewart, get these down you. They are the most beautiful chips you will ever taste. I'll have put on three stone by the time I leave tomorrow.'

Bea and Stewart squeezed their legs through the gap of the bench's seat and got comfy. Tilda poured water into paper cups from a large bottle in her bag.

'We can mix and match if you like. One box is fish, one's sausage, and the other's meat pie. There's chips in all. I don't care what I have as long as I get a bit of sausage.'

'I bet you don't Tilda, you dirty cow.'

Bea made the joke that Stewart was clearly thinking but had chosen not to say. Tilda rolled her eyes. She could feel the blush coming so changed the subject.

'What did you want to chat about, Stewart. I feel like you've got a rapt audience as long as we're eating.'

Bea nodded in agreement, as she forked a piece of pie into her mouth.

Stewart smiled and ate a chip of his own. He looked thoughtful, like he was choosing the words carefully. Tilda wanted to encourage him.

'We won't bite. Whatever it is you want to say, we'll be kind. Is it something about Friday night?'

Stewart was surprised.

'No. Well, not really. Although I suppose it's all linked in the end. What do you know about Friday?'

Tilda breathed sharply.

'Nothing. But something was wrong, wasn't it?'

Stewart ate another chip and nodded.

'Right then, let's start at the beginning. The real thing I need to talk about will make more sense if I do.'

Tilda bit into the sausage. She sipped the water. She prepared herself mentally. And then Stewart started to talk.

CHAPTER FORTY-EIGHT

Stewart smiled, looking directly at Tilda.

'First of all, everything's all right. *I'm* all right. So don't worry.'

'And now I'm worried.' She wasn't trying to be funny. She meant it. Her insides churned, wondering where this was going.

'On Friday, there were a few things going on in my head. Lots of heavy stuff I hadn't dealt with.'

'Your dad?'

'Not specifically him. But his legacy, yes. He's been gone over two years now. That should have made my life easier.'

'But it didn't?'

'No. Not really. At first everything seemed great. I took some time off; the first chunk of real downtime in my life. And once I knew no one expected anything from me, I kept kicking back. The office ticked over, mostly. When I did turn up, I could see I was being managed. I'd taken my eye of the ball and wasn't up to it anymore. I used to be excellent at my work. It was the only thing I had going for me. Once that was gone, I had nothing else.'

'Not nothing else. You had friends, you had a home, you had girlfriends...'

The words were barely out of her mouth before Tilda realised her instinct of trying to boost Stewart's morale was inappropriate. He was being honest with her. She needed to shut up and let him carry on. The least she could do was accept his reality as accurate.

'Sorry, ignore me. I was just trying to be upbeat.'

He smiled.

'It's fine. And you're right, I know in my head I'm lucky. What do they say these days? I have privilege? Well yeah, I know I do. I've got a nice apartment and I can afford to make choices about my life. I'm fine. The *friends* thing is a different point. There's not many of those anymore.'

Upon hearing this, Bea, who had been respectfully silent throughout, felt the need to jump in.

'Nope Stewart. I'm not having that. No way. It's been less than thirty-six hours since we decided we were BFFs forever. Even though saying BFFs forever is like saying PIN number when the N is already *number*. I know the last F in BFFs, is *forever,* but I'm saying it again. BFFs forever. Now give me a high five.'

Bea held her hand in the air as Stewart reached up and clapped it. He smiled despite the painful feelings he was sharing. Tilda ate another mouthful of chips as she waited for him to continue. It wasn't long before he'd gathered himself.

'Of course, Bea. Remiss of me. But before you, things weren't that great. I'd let every other part of my life wither away when I was working so much. Once that was no longer my motivation, there was nothing else there. I spiralled into a slump.'

'So Friday?' Tilda asked tentatively. She didn't want to rush him. 'I feel like you were in that slump when you arrived?'

'So Friday. I was in a bad way in general. And I know now, I went about contacting you all wrong. I think if I'd had friends around at home, I wouldn't have felt the need to depend on you. I saw you as John's representative. Someone to sound out about what I should do. That's not fair on you at all.'

'Maybe not but I get it. I think I've felt the same way about you. You aren't Grady, and it's not fair of me to assume you'll behave in the same way.'

She paused for a moment before returning to her theme. She was gentle in her reutterance. The knot in her stomach needed undoing. She wanted him to keep going.

'So Friday?'

Stewart took a swig of his water and looked straight at her.

'I think it's fair to say the paramedics assumed I'd taken an overdose.'

Tilda felt sick. She knew it was something bad.

'Oh God. Paramedics?' Freya's voice from Friday evening echoed around her head. From when they were on their way home and had seen the ambulance. *Everyone is fine! No one needs you!* At the time she must have realised that couldn't possibly be true. But it had never occurred to her it was for someone she knew.

'What happened?'

'I was really stupid but not like that. I'm all right, really.'

Tilda wasn't convinced in the slightest. Bea looked on as Stewart found the best way to explain.

'I have tablets. Whenever I feel a panic attack coming, I take them. They regulate my heart. Even when my head's kicking up a fuss, my body can't react. It keeps me physically calm until the attack passes.'

'OK?'

'On Friday, the panicky feelings kept coming, so I kept taking the tablets. Quite a few. It didn't help that I was drowning my sorrows in wine. The doctor said I'd regulated my heart so much, it had slowed me into a faint. I passed out on the beach. I was out for a while.'

'Where was I?'

Bea took over.

'Stewart, eat some chips. I'll fill in this part. Tilds, I walked out of the restaurant and found him. There was a crowd of gawpers, huddled around. Luckily one of them had called 999. When the ambulance turned up, I messaged you and said we'd gone back to the hotel. We were in the hospital for a few hours.'

'I knew you hadn't come back that night. You should have told me.'

Stewart, having refuelled with some fish, carried on his story.

'Don't blame Bea. I told her not to say anything. I needed to get my head around what had happened. Once it was clear I didn't need my stomach pumped, everyone calmed down the concern. I had to wait for my heart rate to get back up to normal, but then I was free to leave.'

'So that's it? Everything's fine?'

Stewart considered his response.

'Fine in the short term. No long-term damage done and no one worrying about leaving me with sharp knives or shoe laces.'

'And in the long term?'

'The panic attacks are still an issue. The hospital gave me some info about talking to someone. I imagine I'll think seriously about that sooner rather than later.'

Bea jumped in again.

'Yes, you frigging will. You promised.'

'I did. And I will. I think there's a few things I could

do with unpacking that go back some years, starting with cutting down the booze. On Friday I realised I had been an arsehole for far too long. It's time to be better than that now. Despite outward appearances to the contrary, I'm not my father. I can and *will* be better than that.'

Tilda sipped her water. She speared a few more chips onto her fork but her appetite was satiated. Stewart still had most of his left. He had talked that much it would have gone cold by now. Bea topped up the glasses from the water bottle and glugged down her own. Below them, the sea continued to shimmer, and the tiny people with little worries went about their business.

Tilda realised something.

'When we got up here, you said you hadn't planned to talk about Friday night. What *was* it you wanted to say?'

Stewart closed his half-eaten chip box shut. He placed his fork on top and picked up his water glass. It didn't seem to be a delaying tactic, but more the need to refresh before another huge bombshell. Tilda's knotted stomach returned.

'Right then. Suddenly I'm a bit nervous. Let me think how to start.'

'And yet you weren't nervous with *the other night I made my heart stop because I went pill happy by the sea?*' Bea no longer felt the need to sugar-coat her words. Stewart laughed.

'No, that part was a breeze. This bit's much more important. I just need to frame it right.'

Tilda was getting impatient. There wasn't a great

deal of time left before the last train of the evening would make its descent to - as Bea had called it - dry land. She didn't fancy scaling the sheer drop without it.

'Stewart, we're all ears. Talk to us. We do not, nor will not bite. Promise.'

He nodded. He leaned both elbows on the table in front of him and made a start.

'Ladies. I have a plan. A proposition. I'm hoping to make you an offer you cannot refuse.'

CHAPTER FORTY-NINE

Stewart coughed. He took a swig of water. Then he cleared his throat. This had to go well from the start. He couldn't balls it up by being too pushy or too ill-informed. Or even too prepared. He needed to finely-tune his presentation even though he didn't have all the answers yet. He took a deep breath then began the pitch.

'It all goes back to my Dad's death, really. Like I said, I was completely aimless once I knew no one cared what I did. The business didn't, and still doesn't need me. It's also a constant reminder of him. It will always be William Grady's firm, no matter what. I've been managing it for years, and officially owning it for two, but it'll never be anything to do with me.'

Tilda interjected gently.

'Isn't that because you're still grieving? It's early days. Give it another couple of years and things might seem different?'

Stewart heard the common sense in her question but knew it wasn't valid here.

'I don't think so. If I'd loved my job before, then I expect this indifference would pass in time. But I've never loved my job. Ever. I did it because I gave no thought about what I wanted myself. Once my father died, so did the fear of not doing as I was told. As did the motivation to get up in the morning. I think this is a long-overdue searching of the soul.'

Bea cut to the chase.

'So it's no great leap to say you need a new job. Or could you retire? You said you had the finances to make choices.'

Stewart smiled. She had inadvertently helped him back on track.

'Exactly so. I could and should do something else. More than that, I *have* to do something else. But park that thought for a moment. There's the other part of all this that I need to explain.'

He gulped down more water before continuing.

'One of the things I've found most difficult, is that I'm the last Grady left standing. And I don't mean simply because the name will die out. This isn't about a desire to see a new generation of baby Gradys.'

He saw Tilda swallow and realised his insensitivity. She blinked a couple of times but kept listening. He groaned inwardly before carrying on. Of course, she would have wanted that, back in the day. He thought more carefully about the way he phrased his words.

'If it were just me and my father, that wouldn't trouble me. People who knew us both, would silently think that I was less trouble and easier to deal with than him. In the two-horse race between the pair of us, I just about have the edge. The slightly more tolerable family member is left.'

'But there wasn't just the two of you.' Tilda spoke quietly.

'No. There wasn't.'

He paused. Not quite an official minute's silence for his little brother, but a few seconds' gap for the image of boyish John to flit through his mind. He looked at Tilda and could see she was doing the same. Her eyes were glistening. He waited a few more seconds, giving her the space to remember before continuing.

'I should have felt this a long time ago. I should

have felt John's influence a lot sooner than I did. He just embodied goodness. It sounds overblown but it's true. He was a good person and he wanted to make a difference.'

Now Stewart could feel his own eyes prickling. He didn't want to break down and derail his pitch. He would do that later when he was alone. He swallowed away the lump and carried on.

'Whatever new venture I do now, I want to make things better for people. I've spent my career evicting tenants. I've wound up businesses and made a shit-load of money for dubious landlords, all whilst causing vulnerable people more hassle. I'm generalising but that's basically it. It was a job and it was legal, but it never made me feel anything positive. I can't do that anymore.'

'So what are your plans? Are you going to retrain as something? Sit on the board of a charity? Do you have any ideas, or is it all vague thoughts right now?'

Bea had lots of questions. He liked that. It meant she was intrigued and might give what he had to say next, proper consideration.

'One of the reasons I wanted to see you, Tilda, was to ask your advice. I inherited a lot of money from my father. His house sale has only added to that. I wanted to know what you thought I should do with it.'

Tilda laughed out loud. He had surprised her.

'As if I'd have any ideas about that.' She shook her head. 'Sorry, I'd be useless. Look, I love that you value my opinion, but I don't think I can help with financial planning. You need an expert for that.'

Stewart was happy to put her mind at rest.

'It's OK. Sometime during my night in A and E, I realised it wasn't fair to expect you to be involved like that. But that was my original plan.'

'And what's your plan now?' Bea guided him back to his point once more.

'The details are still sketchy, but here goes. And I know it sounds like I'm plucking ideas out of the air, but I've thought about this a lot. I want to...' Stewart coughed as he stumbled over the words, '... I want to start an art foundation in John's name.'

'Oh'. Bea answered straight away. 'Well then. That sounds interesting. Carry on.'

Stewart exhaled with audible relief. He had piqued her curiosity. That was the main thing. Now he had to keep going.

'I want to provide funding for art students without the finances to develop their craft. I want to hold art exhibitions in the John Grady gallery every year, by the students that have benefited from the money. I want to make sure that anyone that wants to study art can do so, regardless of family support or lack of funds. I want to do something good for people without the means to be artists, to be, you know... artists.'

He stopped talking. Rambling was more like it. His emails with Richard over the previous evening had given him some rough facts and figures. He knew it was possible. He wasn't sure he'd managed to convey that adequately to Tilda and Bea, but the logistics were sound.

Tilda's face gave nothing away. He felt nervous of her response as she opened her mouth to reply.

'That sounds...' Tilda leaned forward on the bench, '...like a love-letter to Grady. It's his legacy, not your

Dad's. Is that the idea?'

Stewart smiled. He couldn't lie.

'I'm not going to say that the thought of his money being used in a way he would hate, doesn't give me a thrill. But it's definitely more than that. If John - if Grady - were here now, half the money would be his. I have no doubt he'd have done something worthwhile with it. I have to honour that somehow.'

'And you definitely don't need it for when you're old? Bea was rooted in reality once again and he was glad of it. 'You won't regret giving away a fortune to a good cause, if it means you have to sell your flat to pay nurses to wipe your arse? I'm just saying.'

Stewart smiled.

'No. My finances are secure. Besides, I still have the firm. I have some ideas about changing the direction of that, but for now it's extra income.'

'What direction do you want to go in?' Tilda asked.

'Not sure yet. I'll talk to Rosie. It'd be her heading it up. At least it will be if I can convince her things will be different from now on. She's my Office Manager and much more besides.'

He realised that statement might add to the misleading impression he had given Bea during the Friday night meal.

'Rosie is not, as I may have implied to you the other night, my girlfriend. Never has been, never will be. She'd rather cut off her arm than touch me like that. She is, however, the most capable person I know and deserves much better treatment from her employer. A pay rise, a significant change of role, and less of me getting in the way would all be part of the plan. Then perhaps as a firm, we could look at more charitable work. Maybe change the focus to something a little more useful in this political climate. There's been so many injustices in landlord and employment practice in the last few years. Immigration law, EU settled-status rights, anything that makes a difference. Again, these are all areas my father wouldn't be interested in. Not that that's my motivation. It's just gratifying to feel I can shift the balance of what I put out into the world.'

Tilda had listened carefully. He appreciated that. He wanted to know her thoughts but didn't want to press any further. She'd said she liked the idea but he needed more reassurance. If she thought he was being ridiculous, it would be devastating. It was essential that she be on board. He took a deep breath and bit the bullet.

'What do you think then? Am I crazy or does it sound reasonable?'

She rested her chin on her hand as she squinted in to the sun behind him.

'I think...' Tilda paused for a second before giving him her answer, '...that it sounds absolutely spot on. Grady would applaud your wholehearted appreciation of what made him tick.'

He sighed with relief and let out a giggle. He had been worried he would come across as delusional. He felt his eyes welling up again and the lump in his throat return. This weekend really had been a roller coaster of emotion.

Tilda looked at her phone and shifted visibly on the bench.

'Right you two, we've got ten minutes before the

last train down. I reckon we pack up and make a move.'

She picked up the rucksack by her feet and started to shove boxes and ketchup into it. Bea stacked the cups and screwed the lid on the bottle. He saw her stop and have a thought.

'You said you had a proposition for us. Did I miss that bit?'

Stewart gulped.

'Shit, no. I hadn't even got to the important part.'

They stood up. Tilda put the rubbish into the bin, as Bea scrambled for her bag under the picnic bench. The train wouldn't wait. He needed to get it out and make his proposal, quickly.

'The proposition is about the actual art foundation, whatever form it might take.'

'OK,' Tilda said as she led them towards the station. 'Go on then.'

'Well isn't it obvious?' He paused. Judging by their blank faces, it clearly wasn't. His pitch went out of the window. Time to stop buttering them up and give it to them straight.

'The art foundation? I want you both to run it for me.'

CHAPTER FIFTY

The excess of the weekend had finally caught up with her. Not long after Stewart had left for the hotel her yawning had become uncontrollable. She noticed Bea was also struggling to keep her eyes open. They made it to nine o'clock before accepting defeat.

Make-up was removed, teeth were brushed, and alarms set. They lay side by side under the duvet, as the ill-fitting closed curtains failed to combat the sun streaming through the sides. Now she was finally in bed, Tilda could collapse. In theory, that was the plan. In practice, she was finding sleep elusive.

'It's a stupid idea, of course.'

She spoke mostly to herself. They had said the same thing to each other the moment Stewart had left. 'It's nice to be thought of, but it's stupid.'

Bea, who was positioned in the role of Baby Spoon should they choose to cuddle, hmmm-ed quietly. She wasn't asleep yet, but judging from the lack of fully-formed words coming from her mouth, she was close.

Tilda turned over. She needed to drop off. The weekend had left her shattered. Stewart throwing out his random ideas and then leaving them to it, shouldn't stop her from giving in to her exhaustion. Yet here she was, wide awake with a racing mind.

'I suppose it's a good idea on paper. Not the *you and me* part, but the art charity side of it. I think that should definitely happen. Grady would've loved it.'

Bea nodded silently. Tilda could feel the movement from the pillow next to her.

'I wonder where it would be based. He didn't seem

bothered about details like that.' Tilda thought back to the polite questions they had asked on the train down the cliff. Even though they thought he was mad, they chatted about his idea without dismissing it outright. That could come later. At that point they were both flattered he had asked them to help with his fantasy.

'He said anywhere.' Bea had found words. 'Here, or online, or anywhere. He needs to do more research.'

She shifted in the bed. Tilda rolled over again and continued to think aloud.

'It might be worth talking to someone at the University. I could find out the best person to contact. Let him know a name. That's the least I can do.'

Tilda clung to a plan that meant she could help Stewart with his proposal, but only on a level that she was comfortable with. Passing on details of a contact was much more her style than running a charity or foundation. Whatever terminology it was that he had used.

'He's thinking too big. He needs to start smaller. Then build up to what he said.' Bea's words were being formed more easily. Polysyllabic and at an audible volume, she was becoming involved in Tilda's sleeplessness.

Tilda gave in and sat up, squishing half her pillow between the headboard and mattress.

'What do you think he should do?'

Bea rolled over to face her in the semi-dark.

'He needs to start with a simple art scholarship. Provide a bursary for a couple of students a year. Pick a University or college that he likes and talk directly to them. The rest of the plans can follow once the basics are established.'

Tilda thought back to their conversation on the train down the cliff. Part business-outline, part-therapy. Bea had nailed it when she asked about his motivation. '*Isn't this another version of not doing what you want? It's not your Dad calling the shots now, but the guilt and weight of Grady's memory?*'

Tilda had been impressed. At that point, her mind had been bogged down with more practical matters, such as *what a ridiculous idea to ask me to get involved with that* instead of trying to ensure Stewart was of sound mind in his offer.

Tilda leaned back on the headboard.

'He just wants to do something good.'

'That's not a bad thing.' Bea replied.

'It's reassuring he wants to do this for himself. He's committed to leaving his own mark, just as much as it's about Grady. I like that part of it.'

Bea, who was now a fully conscious part of the conversation, propped herself up. She was thinking. Tilda could tell from the silence.

'I suppose if he's been evicting and bankrupting people for years, this would feel a million times nicer than that. He'd be doing something positive. You must remember from the office, how many meetings felt absolutely pointless.'

Tilda did.

'I know. And we weren't doing bad things. Just dull ones.'

'What's work like now? Bea asked. 'Any better?'

Tilda sighed.

'It's got sea views.'

'But do you enjoy it? Does it fulfil you?'

Tilda managed to stop herself snorting. It would have sounded far too aggressive a response in the darkness.

'Bea, I'm a temp. I file, I photocopy, I shred and I label. I do it for the money and the money alone. You know that.'

'So what's stopping you taking up his offer?'

Tilda hadn't realised she needed to put it into words. It seemed obvious.

'Everything is stopping me. It's out of the blue. There are no details or business plans. He was sitting in A and E two nights ago with a suspected overdose and now he wants to do something big in the art world, even though he has zero experience of it. It's a mid-life crisis. A completely understandable one, I'll grant you, but a mid-life crisis all the same. It'll blow over soon enough. I'm fully supportive of him wanting to be a force for good in the world, but for me to get involved, I'd need to see small print and planning. And lots of it.'

Tilda hadn't intended to give a speech. She thought the polite *thanks but no thanks* response she would give Stewart in a day or two, was never in doubt. It seemed Bea wasn't so sure.

'What do *you* think then? You're not considering it, surely?'

Tilda wished she could see Bea's face. She couldn't read her tone without seeing her eyes either roll or sparkle about an idea. It didn't matter. Her reply was clear enough.

'I'm so fucking bored, Tilds.'

'With work?'

'Yeah. But with other stuff too. I was bored when I got together with Mal. I must have known deep down he was wrong for me but I didn't care because I liked being *seen* again. Sorry to hark back to my menopausal TED talk, but feeling invisible is rubbish. Life carries on *around* you rather than with you. I'm on the side-lines all the time. It's so boring and it's the same with work. One day's routine after another. No fun. No laughs.'

'You have an office now.'

'When I walk out of it, the chatter stops. They're either talking about me, or they're doing bugger all and think I'll kick off. I remember what we were like. We didn't give a shit about Susan. She was just the old cow who moaned about getting things on her desk by five. Now *I'm* the old cow. It's the circle of life.'

'Oh Bea, you're nothing like Susan. Or the *Lion King*.'

Bea giggled and sat up against her pillow.

'Yeah, yeah, I know. And now I've seen the light with Mal, I need to put myself first and not try to force a bad fit into my lovely life. It's just sometimes, I wish I was more than I am.'

'You don't think you're enough?'

'In my head I know I'm doing my best. But inside, it feels there are better uses of a life than policy admin and getting pissed with my neighbour. Actually, forget the last bit. Kit's awesome. She's my actual role-model. But still, I understand where Stewart's coming from with his sudden rush of philanthropy.'

Tilda was struggling to argue with Bea's logic.

'I understand that bit too. I just don't want to get involved in something that might never pan out. It's got to be realistic and planned. We can't ditch the day jobs and run away with his big altruistic dream if it all comes crashing down in a few months. What if the money runs out? We'd be left high and dry.'

Bea was nodding her head. It didn't mean she was in full agreement with her, but that she was accepting the points raised as valid. Tilda knew all Bea's nods.

'Are you a definite *no* then? Will you be telling him you're not interested?'

Tilda exhaled. That had been her plan half an hour ago. Bea's question of '*Does it fulfil you?* regarding her short-term, dull-as-ditch-water temp job for which she was overqualified, had left her with doubts.

'Maybe I won't shoot him down immediately. I can say I'm open to hearing the details. But I need *excessive* details for it to change whether I want to hear more. What about you?'

Bea nestled into the foetal position and snuggled her pillow.

'I can't lie, darling. I'm interested.'

'Really?'

'It's probably stupid and reckless, and he might be a liability to get mixed-up with when a salary's involved, but I'm up for hearing more. Come on. Stay on the fence for a little while longer. More info can't hurt.'

Tilda smiled.

'Sounds like a vague and cautious plan. What will we tell him?'

Bea rubbed her eye with the heel of her palm.

'I reckon we say just that. We haven't made any decisions, but a five-year business plan and an outline of the long-term plans are essential. There's no rush but that would be the minimum we'd need before we could consider it further.'

'Bea, you already sound like an entrepreneur. Are you secretly Deborah Meadon?' Tilda chuckled in the dark.

'Yes darling. That's exactly who I am. I'm Deborah Meadon. And now, do you think we've reached the point where we might have another bash at sleep? I've got a mofo journey in the morning. I could do with cracking on.'

Tilda agreed and plumped up her pillow. She shimmied back to horizontal and got comfortable.

Bea's breathing was heavier immediately. Minutes later and she had gone. Tilda lay there, dropping off slower, but definitely getting there. She thought about her life. The life she had rebooted when she moved to the coast. She thought about how boring her days were, how exciting this weekend had been, by having the purpose of hosting friends. She thought about Stewart and his newfound sense of charity. She thought about Gethin and how he had flattered her without using naff chat up lines. She thought about Jonathan and Dhanesh, and Jen and Sam. She thought about Grady.

She was almost there. She let herself drift into sleep, happy in the knowledge she had an exciting and potentially life-changing decision to make. She might end up rejecting Stewart's kind offer. But there was also the chance she might not. And that was thrilling.

Tilda sat on the bench and ran through the lie in her mind. When she left the flat, she had told herself it was for her evening stroll and now she was simply having a breather. She forced herself to believe these statements as she rolled up her earphones. Neither were true. She had quite deliberately walked to this bench and sat down. There had been no evening stroll and she did not need a breather.

She put the earphones in her pocket. A couple of days before, she had heard a song on the radio that she liked. Using the magic of technology, she identified the song and singer, and had spent the last fifteen minutes listening to the album. She never remembered musicians' names when anyone asked what stuff she liked, but now she had an answer. She liked Lizzo. She had no idea who Lizzo was, but it didn't matter. She was living in the present for once. As she enjoyed the fake breather she didn't need, she continued to think about newly-discovered music instead of clinging to her past repetitions. That way she could forget why she had left the flat in the first place.

Her mind continued to wander. She opened the calendar on her phone. Assuming her day to be blank, it was a surprise to see a notification. She clicked on the date and saw the event she had forgotten. Chip Shop Night. The rescheduled entry forced by last week's reunion, had now arrived. Tilda marvelled at the change in her. The thought of chips hadn't crossed her mind once. Instead of counting down the days and filling her fantasy world with images of wooden forks and salt shakers, she'd had other things to daydream about.

Bea's call earlier had been instrumental in that. As she thought back to it, the memory triggered some butterflies. The good kind. The ones that anticipate something exhilarating.

'Darling he's come up with some figures. Proper ones. Not just the back-of-a-fag-packet stuff he had last week. I told him you'd need nothing less if he wanted you to go any further.'

'You're still interested?'

'Even more so. I know, I know. I'm still not getting carried away, but he's definitely working through the details. It's hard not to feel the buzz. He sent through a spreadsheet this morning and it was properly horny. Just imagining being part of something new and noble felt fab. I know I'm not making sense.'

'Course you are, Bea. A perfectly normal response to a spreadsheet.'

'Darling, you know what I mean. Ring him. Get the gist yourself.'

'I will. Tomorrow.'

'Also, breaking news. He's spoken to Rosie. He'd just finished meeting her when I called.'

'What happened? Was she willing to stick around?'

'Apparently she was thrilled. Knowing she can now be in charge with the job title and the authority was exactly what she needed. Stewart says she's well up for changing the direction of things. *Discrimination Rights R Us* is what he called it. Right up her street, apparently. That ball has definitely started rolling.'

The good kind of butterflies were still fluttering, reminding Tilda that it had been far too long since she had felt excitement instead of fear. It had been seven days since the reunion weekend. Seven days since her life had become more complicated and seven days since she realised her greatest fear was of never again feeling the joy of connection. She stretched out her legs in the evening sun and pondered that thought. Nothing Stewart had suggested was scary. Not when compared to that.

She knew what she was going to do. At least she thought she did. That would come in a phone call in the morning, just like she had told Bea. Here on the bench in the warmth of the evening, everything felt manageable. Even easy if she were being honest. It was when she got up that the nerves would return. Tilda decided to have another few minutes before jumping off the cliff edge.

That image jarred her fully into the present. She was not going to jump off a cliff. She looked up to her right and saw the train slowly ascend in the distance. The literal cliff at the end of the prom stopped that metaphor in its tracks. Nothing bad would happen, no matter how much her stomach flipped now.

Tilda stretched her arms across the back of bench. Seagulls strutted nearby. She was convinced the bird by her foot was the one that used to stalk her. Over time, he had moved on. Perhaps he had tired of her. Maybe he no longer saw her as a stranger. She was part of the furniture now. He must have decided to direct his attention to another perceived interloper. Tilda was now an established resident of the area. Within the seagull community, at least.

Her mind was wandering. Back to business. She would make the call to Stewart. She would tell him she needed more information but was willing to listen. She would explain that her fears lay in needing a reliable income. If he could deal with that, then she was willing to take a risk with anything else. The call was the easy bit. She had nothing to lose and everything to gain. And if she lost nothing and gained nothing then it was still worth it. Tomorrow was when she would enact the second part of the Brave Tilda plan. Tomorrow was for Stewart.

For now, she had to deal with Part One. It had started a few days ago, during her weekly flat clean. She had paused, mid-dust, as the thought crept upon her. She didn't dwell for long but made the decision with a clear head. Later, she had pulled down the chest from the top of her wardrobe, and carefully rehoused Grady's photo. It didn't matter where it was. He would always be a part of her; a part of who she had become. Tilda had spent the rest of the evening going through the WhatsApp photos from the weekend. There were plenty of suitable options to enlarge in the frame on the mantlepiece. It was time to celebrate her living friends for a change. Her wingpeople.

So Part One had begun but was not yet complete. It's not that she was putting it off. Not really. It just seemed a shame to hurry the evening when she could enjoy a few snatched moments in the sun. Her mind continued to jump from one random thought to the next. She moved away from a working future with Stewart and Bea, and found herself flashing through scenes from the past. Her mum smiling though her illness, as she played with eight-year old Tilda. Her dad, alone and lonely, trying his best at the most basic of parenting skills. Mike being unable to hear anything she said, even when he was listening. Jonathan telling her he was proud of her. Freya's hug at the station. Grady waving goodbye from a distance, becoming smaller and smaller but still smiling with love...

She swallowed the lump away. That wasn't how the evening was going to pan out. She was ready for new adventures now. Happy ones. One more minute and she'd make a move. She watched the paddlers and the parents. She saw the lifeguard station and the ice cream kiosk. She wasn't putting it off. Just gathering herself. Ten more seconds.

Her phone vibrated. An email from Mike. She opened it immediately, although she couldn't imagine what there was to say.

Hi Tilda, hope you're well. Just wanted to let you know that I've been seeing someone for a while. A woman from work. Anyway, we got engaged last week. I know I don't need to, but I wanted to let you know.

Speak soon,
Mike.

Tilda read it twice. She checked herself and read it again. Did she feel anything? Yes. She had a definite sense of something. She looked at the water and watched the spray. *There's no rush. Take your time.* She read the message once more. What was the feeling? *Just let it surface. It'll come.* Tilda inhaled fresh air and closed her eyes. She heard the water lap over shingle as the gulls cawed above. She felt the warmth of the sun and smelt the ozone in the air. All the while, she waited for the emotion to reveal itself.

And then it came. There it was. She'd identified the feeling. Relief. Relief with a side order of contentment. The guilt she'd carried for having left the marriage had gone. Mike had moved on and met someone else. She was happy for him.

Her jaw ached and she realised she was smiling. Widely. Then a giggle or two emerged from her mouth. Everything felt lighter. Breathing was easier. All of her lungs were now in on the act. She knew her life with Mike had been clenched but she hadn't fully relaxed like she thought she had. Until now. Now he was marrying someone else, and his happiness was no longer her responsibility. Tilda hadn't realised how much she had needed to hear he'd moved on. The thought of having to count cutlery seemed suddenly ludicrous.

Tilda gave her ex-husband and his new fiancé a moment more of her time. She hoped the woman was nice. Mike didn't deserve a terrible future just because she had changed from the person she had once been. Just as he had. She made a last effort to check there were no deep-seated, hidden resentments, but there were none. It was momentous news for a person she used to know and now no longer did. For her, nothing had changed. And now she was ready. Ready to be brave. She cleared her throat and made sure her urge to giggle was under control. What a wonderful feeling to feel so free. There was nothing stopping her now. It was time to make the next move. Time to embark on her plan.

Tilda stood up from the bench. She ruffled up the back of her hair, as she'd seen Bea do countless times. Then she had second thoughts. She was not Bea. She patted it down and tucked the sides behind her ears. She didn't need big hair. She needed her own hair. She needed to be herself or not bother. Being herself was enough.

With her back to the sea, she faced the road. Cars looking for an elusive Aber parking space, crawled along. She waited for a particularly slow driver to pass before she crossed over. She could see her destination the entire time. The words she was still unsure how to pronounce looked back at her from the sign. She would ask in a moment. That could be her opening line. Not wanting to rush for fear of being out of breath, she slowed her pace. It made no difference. She had arrived. She was here.

Tilda opened the door and stepped inside. Straight ahead of her was Gethin. He held a bottle of spray in one hand and was wiping a table with the other. He heard the door and looked up. A smile spread across his face.

'You came.'

Tilda looked at him.

'I did', she said.

ACKNOWLEDGEMENTS

The writing and publishing of *Assembling the Wingpeople* took place from 2019-2021. Eagle-eyed readers will notice that period coincides with the Coronavirus pandemic, which certainly added extra challenges to a process that is already riddled with them. But here we are. The book is finally complete and I couldn't be happier or grateful to those that helped along the way.

In the pre-virus early days, I was able to chat to a variety of people, all in the name of research. Thank you to Claire Mullen, Stephen Rew, and Phil Tyman for their many insights into all sorts of things. From online dating apps, to medication and side-effects, from depression to grief. They kindly shared their experiences and expertise, which I squished to fit my story. All inaccuracies are on me. More hands-on research took place when I was befriended by Kirsten, Alana, and Ruairigh, during an evening of solo drinking in Aberystwyth. They bought me shots, answered my questions, and gave me lots to think about amidst the natter. Legends. Likewise, thank you to Charlie the bar man. He kept the Prosecco flowing as I scribbled notes, ultimately becoming the inspo for Gethin. All from one night in Aber. Wild.

From the beginning, early chapters were shared with the *Poised Pen* writing group in Liverpool. Their feedback was essential, as were the benefits I received as they read their work to me. The pandemic kicked in just after I had shared what became Chapter 14. I hope they will be intrigued as to how the story pans out.

Once again, the editing work of Claire Dyer at *Fresh Eyes* was invaluable. Her nurturing support and enthusiastic encouragement kept me going, whilst her critical eye enabled me to tackle the gaps and weaknesses littered throughout. The end result is all the better for her input. Another bundle of thanks must go to Gary from *Portal – Design and Illustration*. He never fails to turn my garbled ramblings about plot and theme, into a truly beautiful front cover. His artistic talent, as well as his technical know-how, gave me the peace of mind that the finished cover would be marvellous. And it is. Thank you.

I was lucky enough to pass on the (almost) final draft to a discerning group of critics. My beta-reader family members. Thank you to Mary Bond, Frank Bond, Dom Bond, Monica Bartley Bond, Beth Bond, Lucy Keavy and Ashley Preston. They gave up their time to humour me, despite having lives of their own. Their feedback was essential.

A massive thank you must also go to the staff of *Stephens Pharmacy*, Liverpool. When I wasn't locked down, I used their upstairs office, shutting myself in for whole days at a time. No one batted an eyelid as they carried on around me, letting me crack on with my nonsense. I can't adequately convey how useful that was. Thanks for putting up with me.

A final thank you has to go to Emma Thompson. Yes, THE Emma Thompson. If you listened to her guest appearance on *My Dad Wrote a Porno* in 2018, you may recognise the advice that Kit gives Bea over her love-life. Emma Thompson kindly gave me permission to use her sentiments in this way, and I'm very grateful. It's definitely the best relationship advice I have ever heard and should be used in schools ASAP. So there.

ABOUT THE AUTHOR

Nicky Bond worked in Education for twelve years before discovering her inner-Jessica Fletcher and writing a book in her kitchen. *Carry the Beautiful* was published in 2017, followed by *Leeza McAuliffe Has Something To Say* in 2019 – a novel for pre-teens and those that care about them.

Nicky fills her time with top bantz from her nieces and nephews, writing a weekly blog – *Nicky Bond and Writer's Ramblings* - and drinking more tea than is sensible. She lives in Merseyside.

Lightning Source UK Ltd.
Milton Keynes UK
UKHW011041150821
388855UK00001B/132

9 780995 657434